THE DOOMSDAY REPORT

THE DOOMSDAY REPORT

A NOVEL BY **ROCK BRYNNER**

WILLIAM MORROW AND COMPANY, INC. NEW YORK

Grateful acknowledgment is made for permission to quote from the following:

Antonin Artaud, *The Theater and Its Double* (copyright © 1958), reprinted with permission from Grove Press.

Ross Gelbspan, *The Heat Is On: The High Stakes Battle over Earth's Threatened Climate* (copyright © 1996), reprinted with permission from the author.

Paul Kennedy, *Preparing for the Twenty-first Century* (copyright © 1993), reprinted with permission from Random House.

Richard Leakey and Roger Lewin, *The Sixth Extinction: Patterns of Life and the Future of Humankind* (copyright © 1995), reprinted with permission from Doubleday Books.

Scott J. Lehman and Lloyd D. Keigwin, "Sudden Changes in North Atlantic Circulation During the Last Deglaciation," *Nature* magazine, April 30, 1992, reprinted with permission from Macmillan Books.

Van Morrison, "Astral Weeks" (copyright © 1969), reprinted with permission from Warner/Chappell Music.

Norman Myers, "Mass Extinction and Evolution," *Science Magazine*, October 24, 1997 (copyright © 1997), reprinted with permission from The American Association for the Advancement of Science.

Ezra Pound, "They will come no more, The old men with beautiful manners." From "Moeurs Contemporaines" (copyright © 1915), in *Personae*, reprinted with permission from New Directions Books.

Dylan Thomas, "The Force That Through the Green Fuse Drives the Flower" (copyright © 1933), reprinted with permission from New Directions Books.

Edward O. Wilson, *Biodiversity* (copyright © 1989), reprinted with permission from the National Academy Press.

Edward O. Wilson, *In Search of Nature* (copyright © 1996), reprinted with permission from Island Press.

It is the policy of William Morrow and Company, Inc., and its imprints and affiliates, recognizing the importance of preserving what has been written, to print the books we publish on acid-free paper, and we exert our best efforts to that end.

Library of Congress Cataloging-in-Publication Data
Brynner, Rock, 1946–
The doomsday report : a novel / by Rock Brynner.—1st ed.
p.   cm.
ISBN 0-688-15919-2
I. Title.
PR9160.9.B78D66   1998
813—dc21   97-36568
CIP

Printed in the United States of America

First Edition

1 2 3 4 5 6 7 8 9 10

BOOK DESIGN BY BERNARD KLEIN

www.williammorrow.com

to Isaac Tigrett
gentleman, visionary, and beloved friend

ACKNOWLEDGMENTS

I wish to thank Mr. Alvaro de Soto, United Nations Assistant Secretary General for Political Affairs, and Dr. Angela Kane, Director of the UN Library, for providing me with access to the global demographics referred to throughout the novel, and to the latest finding of the 2,500 scientists who make up the UN's Intergovernmental Panel on Climate Change (IPCC), undoubtedly the greatest exercise of peer review in scientific history. It is largely upon those findings, presented in *The Second Assessment Report of the IPCC* (1995), that the science of *The Doomsday Report* is based.

Heartfelt thanks also to my sage editor, Betty Kelly, at William Morrow, and her assistant, Maria Antifonario, for their enthusiasm and encouragement; and to Janis Donnaud, who brought me to them.

CONTENTS

Things fall apart; the center cannot hold;
Mere anarchy is loosed upon the world;
The blood-dimmed tide is loosed, and everywhere
The ceremony of innocence is drowned;
The best lack all conviction, while the worst
Are full of passionate intensity.

—W. B. YEATS, "The Second Coming" (1919)

THE DOOMSDAY REPORT

PART ONE

MERE ANARCHY

Homo sapiens is poised to become the greatest catastrophic agent since a giant asteroid collided with the Earth sixty-five million years ago, wiping out half the world's species in a geological instant. . . . Dominant as no other species has been in the history of life on Earth, *Homo sapiens* is in the throes of causing a major biological crisis, a mass extinction, the sixth such event to have occurred in the past half billion years. And we, *Homo sapiens,* may also be among the living dead . . . not only the agent of the sixth extinction, but also one of its victims.

—RICHARD LEAKEY and ROGER LEWIN, *The Sixth Extinction:*
Patterns of Life and the Future of Humankind (1995)

Our species retains hereditary traits that add greatly to our destructive impact. We are tribal and aggressively territorial, intent on private space beyond minimal requirements, and oriented by selfish sexual and reproductive drives. . . . In the relentless search for more food we have reduced animal life in lakes, rivers, and now, increasingly, the open ocean. And everywhere we pollute the air and water, lower water tables, and extinguish species. The human species is, in a word, an environmental hazard. It is possible that intelligence in the wrong kind of species was foreordained to be a fatal combination for the biosphere. Perhaps a law of evolution is that intelligence usually extinguishes itself.

—EDWARD O. WILSON, "Is Humanity Suicidal?"
from *In Search of Nature* (1996)

THE UNSOLICITED
MANUSCRIPT

Human beings and the natural world are on a collision course . . . that may so alter the living world that it will be unable to sustain life in the manner that we know. . . . We, the undersigned senior members of the world's scientific community, hereby warn all humanity of what lies ahead. A great change in our stewardship of the earth and the life on it is required if vast human misery is to be avoided and our global home on this planet is not to be irretrievably mutilated. . . . No more than one or a few decades remain before the chance to avert the threats we now confront will be lost.

—World Scientists' "Warning to Humanity" (1992),
from 1,600 scientists, including the majority of
living Nobel laureates in the sciences

Terry Bancroft arrived at her office above Fifth Avenue early on the Monday following New Year's Day, and even before removing her rain-soaked jacket, she signaled the start of 1998 by logging on to her computer. She replaced her Doc Martens with conventional flats and combed back her short, dark hair, which still showed streaks of purple when it was this wet. After filling the coffeepot, she settled behind her desk, smoothed her skirt, and braced herself for whatever the publishing industry might hurl her way. She had spent Sunday evening marshaling her enthusiasm for the job and trying to rekindle the businesslike fervor she admired in others—that calm brand of zeal which actually gets things done.

This was her favorite time of the day: she had at least an hour before her boss, Danvers Creal, would arrive. In the afternoon the cramped little antechamber—her "veal-fattening pen"—often seemed hostile and unhealthy; by then she was aware of a chemical odor that she associated with the fluorescent lights but that probably came from the recycled air. In the morning, though, before everyone arrived, the little office leading to Danvers's corner suite seemed friendly and comfortable. The Monday editorial meeting she usually attended with her boss had been canceled because of the holidays, so she filled her coffee cup in the hall and then, at her screen, pulled up Danvers's appointments: nothing for two hours. Perfect.

Terry ramped up to her chores by scanning the e-mail. There were two messages from Danvers, which she took in with a critical eye: "Terry, call Joni regarding possible penalties for further delay in delivery of Muller book." Overwritten, she thought. The second said, "Find manuscript of *Belacqua Report*." Never heard of it. Then she confronted the huge pile of snail mail that had collected since the Christmas party. First she separated the letters from the fresh stack of unsolicited manuscripts on her corner table, sorted through the envelopes, and studied the disappointing harvest. Only two letters were addressed to her, both from authors; Danvers's mail didn't look any better. Setting the envelopes in a tidy stack near the corner of her desk, she knocked her cup to the floor.

"Damn," she said aloud, and then added, under her breath, "Darn, I said 'damn.' " This year she'd made a heartfelt New Year's resolution to cleanse her speech of curses and vulgarities, as one of the last elements in her deliberate two-year makeover from puckish Smith girl in boxer shorts and high-top sneakers to assistant to the executive editor of Commonweal Books, mature and urbane. This was also her fifth day without a cigarette. So far it had been easier than she'd expected. Terry had already made more substantial changes than renouncing her purple do and removing her eyebrow ring, and by now her occasional profanities sounded like the last vestiges of a previous self, which in fact they were. She wasn't being prudish or hypocritical; she was simply sick to death of angry words, hateful, ugly, and dirty words. Two years at one of the largest publishing houses in New York had sensitized her to the abuse of language, and by now some conversations could give her a rash. So without another word she mopped up the spilled coffee with a cocktail napkin from Danvers's office.

Then she settled down to proofread the galleys of *Football and Freud* by Dr. Timothy Dewey, which was listed in Commonweal's fall catalog. The manuscript had been acquired by the former executive editor, Joe Goodstein; when he moved to Humanities Press in '97, he had been replaced by Danvers and the Dewey book had been orphaned. Terry had taken pity and copyedited the manuscript, shepherding it through to galleys. She did not like the book, or football, or Freud, but it was either Dewey or the first draft of *Chained to the Wheel: The Vanna White Memoirs*. There was also *The Flame of Barungia*, the new Laura Goldman title for Commonweal's romance/thriller imprint, Guilty Pleasures. But apart from the erotic scenes, she found Goldman's novels profoundly boring. Predictable in plot and packed with excruciating detail and décor, Goldman's books were nonetheless written in a voice that was clear as a bell, and each had sold hundreds of thousands of copies since 1995. Still, except for the lovemaking, Terry could not stomach them, and she did not care to start this workday aroused and atingle, thank you. She had just spent much of the holiday in bed with Bobby, exhausting both their capacities. So Terry picked up *Football and Freud*.

Dewey's thesis went something like this: in every human society, sports serve to exorcise the fear of war (Dewey cited several social anthropologists), while providing bonding rituals that unify the players and prepare them for actual battle. In modern America, he went on, football provides the country with a powerful subconscious consensus. This national cohesion derives from the experience shared by the spectators as players act out the great subconscious fear that haunts modern society, according to Dewey: the dread of a head-on automobile collision.

"Suppose you wanted to dress up a man to resemble an automobile," wrote Dewey in Chapter 3. "You would broaden his shoulders to look like fenders and put a hood ornament on his head, with a bumper, or chin guard, in front. Then you would paint a license number on him, add socks like whitewall tires, and make him hunch forward on all fours." By lining up a half-dozen of these "auto-men," football unwittingly simulates the lanes of a broad freeway. Therefore, by placing two teams in this position, opposing each other face to face, you could, with the appropriate "traffic signal," replicate a massive multivehicle head-on collision. And since players hardly ever died from these furious smash-ups, "the spectators' collective psyche is progressively freed from the subconscious terror of the highway."

"Brother," she muttered, dropping the galley pages back in her drawer. This was decidedly not what she'd expected to do after studying American Lit at Smith. She would rather return unsolicited manuscripts than proofread such psycho-fluff. When she felt mascara dried on her cheek, from the rain, she did a quick repair job right there at her desk. Except for the huge brown eyes, her own face always seemed unfamiliar in the mirror, especially when she leaned in close to do the eyeliner. She had high cheekbones, and when she was just a little too thin, her cheeks were beautifully hollowed. She liked the arch of her upper lip; she did not like the veins in her temples.

The first call of the day came from her hungover boss. "Morning, Terry," he croaked.

"Good morning, Danvers. Happy New Year. How are you?"

"Sitting up and taking nourishment. What's on for today?"

"You're due at eleven with Elgin, the consultant from the photo department."

"Why?"

"The Redford bio, remember? He's the freelance researcher—"

"Can't make it. Will you let him know?"

"If he's not already on his way here. And a two-o'clock with Reverend Muller."

"That one I'll make, but he'd better have a second draft or he's wasting my time. Listen, Terry, we've got a manuscript there somewhere called. . . ." Danvers paused to clear his sinuses directly into the phone. "I think it's called *The Bellagio Report*. Sent to us in mid-December."

Terry checked the mail log. "Who submitted it?"

"An Air Force general—Shreiver. It's an important scientific thesis, but he's not the author, Bellagio is. The general says FedEx confirmed delivery: apparently you signed for it yourself."

That news made Terry uncomfortable, as intended. "I don't see any title like that."

"Damn. We have to get it back to him right away if no one's going to read it." This was Creal's passive-aggressive style of assigning the job to her. "I got a letter over the holidays from this General Shreiver, who's attached to NASA. Then he called me about an hour ago. I hate to say this, but it could even be among . . ." He felt silent.

Terry shuddered. "The unsolicited manuscripts?"

"Afraid so. If it isn't in your log, you'll have to look."

She winced. This had never happened, but she had always dreaded the day. Why was Danvers suddenly interested in some unsolicited manuscript?

"Be there at two. Give you a hand." Danvers adopted the brusque tone he had picked up from T. Coraghessan Boyle the year before. "Peculiar. This NASA general got my home number and left a message on my machine. He wants to meet Friday evening at O'Donoghue's, so if it's interesting, I'd like to read it."

"I'll find it, Danvers. See ya later." Of course, when he said he wanted to "read" the manuscript, that was a euphemism: what he meant was that he wanted Terry to prepare a reader's report, including brief excerpts. Danvers rarely read an entire manuscript himself; even when bidding a six-figure advance, he relied on Terry's judgment. He had long since lost track of how dependent he was on her; even more so since his divorce.

Unsolicited manuscripts were the bane of her life. Even now her jacket was dripping on the carpet behind the office door because her small closet was filled from floor to ceiling with unsolicited manuscripts, and every editor in the building had a similar slush pile. It was Terry's job to return these to their authors, unopened, with a form letter politely suggesting that Commonweal Books would prefer a hostile takeover by Marvel Comics to considering a submission that didn't come from an established literary agency. Still, every damn day six to ten new boxes of literary aspiration arrived. Every darn day. Once a month Terry would spend an afternoon shipping the parcels back, but at that rate she'd never catch up.

There was a bright flash outside her window, and the dull rum-ble of thunder. Odd—rain in January, especially after such a cold autumn and that heavy snowfall in early October. The storm had begun the night before, just when Bobby was rushing to catch the Washington shuttle. As Terry watched a steady torrent fall upon the Plaza Hotel, she wondered how much rain it would take to wash away all the sight-blinding dirt. More than the skies could summon. At twenty-four, she was not well traveled; the only other cities she'd ever visited were Boston and Washington, and they weren't much better—certainly not as clean as Minneapolis, where she had grown up. But the cleaner cities, she'd heard on the Web, had lost their character. Terry watched the pedestrians scurrying to their appointments while traffic sat motionless, honking helplessly and emitting noxious fumes. What would Dewey make of that? As the gloom of urban isolation crept over her, she gave in and with just a few keystrokes sent off a passionate message to Bobby; after November's phone bill, they'd agreed to stick to e-mail. Then, remembering Elgin, she called down to the photo department just in time to head him off.

Tony, his gurney full of manuscripts, suddenly appeared at her door with a conspiratorial wink. Tony was one of her pet projects. He was a good enough kid from Bensonhurst, but he couldn't even ask a girl out without sounding like one of the Jerky Boys. Because they were the same age, Terry had confided to him a little about her life and times as a rave maven, after she gave up grunge, and how she sometimes felt like a spy sent by the Gen-X troops to report on the activities of the serious, the industrious, and the intellectually committed. Tony hated "humpin' 'scrips"—especially the collating. He was really, he said, a frustrated janitor with a powerful calling to wax floors. Instead he was assigned to the Xerox room, tracking the manuscripts that flowed through in various stages of revision and returning them each morning with copies. Go figure.

Tony was wearing a big grin. "Yo, Terry, check it out, man!"

"No way!"

"Way! I did it!" Leaving his gurney in the hall, Tony slipped into Terry's office and closed the door mysteriously. He pulled up his Giants sweatshirt, which his mother always ironed, and displayed his pierced nipple.

"Way cool!" Terry offered. "I hope you didn't show it to Marissa on your first date." He nodded—she groaned. "Where did you go on her day off?"

Tony pointed out her window across Central Park. "First I took her to see the dinosaurs at the museum, ya know what I'm sayin'?"

"Old bones. Very retro," she deadpanned. "Interesting choice, Mr. Erectus. Then what? Did ya jump *her* bones, or were you nice, like I said?"

"We went downtown and caught Keb' Mo'."

"Tasty."

"Yeah, cool. And she was so beautiful, man." Tony in reverie evoked Saint Theresa with a Vandyke. "I took her home by cab, walked her to the lobby, and planted a big kiss. An' like, she didn't mind—ya know what I'm sayin'? So then I copped a feel."

Terry's eyelids snapped shut. "Tony, man, you're really dragging your knuckles into the next millennium—ya know what I'm sayin'? Get out of here, I gotta work."

It was ten past ten, and the morning parade had begun. There went Judy Corliss, followed by Marshall's assistant, Sebastian: he was so stupid he couldn't count to twenty-one unless he was naked. Terry hadn't seen these faces since the Christmas party, when that weasel from the art department, Fred Reilly ("Please, call me Tristan"), had made a pass at her, and Franco Sherman, president and CEO of Commonweal Books, had not—although, come to think of it, he had smiled at her. But Mr. Sherman, a widower, had never hit on anyone at Commonweal, to the chagrin of some: the single women all agreed that he had it goin' on. Even after dating Bobby for three months, Terry still sometimes daydreamed about Franco and rarely bothered to stop herself, since he was safely inaccessible. His title, his income, and his age (forty-seven) placed him beyond the pale, so she could enjoy any fantasy she liked without risk of disappointment. If that was being unfaithful, well, so be it.

At that moment the object of her daydreams sailed smoothly past her office on his way to Judy Corliss's. Like others who only knew him slightly, Terry thought of Franco as a force of nature. So after she'd fast-forwarded through some imaginary intimacies, refining and embellishing, she returned to the job at hand. She rechecked her log of incoming manuscripts, but there was no *Bellagio Report*—or was it *Belacqua Report*, as Danvers's e-mail had it? She rose stiffly to confront the slush pile and felt the muscles of her inner thighs. Every night of the holidays, sex with Bobby had become more prolonged, if unadventurous.

Terry opened the closet and stared at the gloomy stacks of intellectual ambition and pretension. Amateur authors: the sight of their work made her cringe. Aside from being horrible pests, they were usually endowed with the kind of fanatical persistence one might admire in anyone except an amateur author or a serial killer. They cranked out boxload after boxload of freshly Xeroxed manuscripts and hauled them by the dozen to the post office, smothered in stamps of small denominations. Usually they tried the top ten publishers first, looking up the addresses at their small-town libraries or on the Web, and calling up ahead to learn the name of the executive editor. Then with one last, private ceremony—a pat, a rub, or a kiss—they sent their whelp off to the big city and held their breath. A few months later the parcel arrived back at the author's cottage or condo or garret together with a form letter rejecting the work out of hand. But by then most of those authors had already started on the next volley of *chefs-d'oeuvre,* thinking, This time it will be different.

Terry loved fiction (though not indiscriminately); it was only the self-centeredness of writers she didn't much care for. Literature had always been her guiding passion: she reveled in the language of fine storytelling, and in every other departure from the monosyllabic bluntness and simplistic syntax of the nineties. While she had no ambition to become a writer herself—she could never be that reflective—she made an effort, most of the time, to think and speak like one. Consequently her own *monologue intérieur* was almost bilingual: she tried to cultivate her conversation without sounding snooty, and avoided exclamations like "Way cool!" She hated when she did that.

Amateurs weren't the only writers who were pushy and self-centered, of course: some of the most successful authors she had met were creeps. Not the more enlightened, who were usually quite considerate. Even Norman Mailer. Winston in publicity had told her terrible old war stories about him, but then she'd sat in on several heated meetings between her boss and Mailer (regarding a collaboration with a Commonweal author that fell through), and he'd always been a perfect gentleman with everybody. Same with Philip Roth; now, there was an older man she could . . .

But the majority of writers Terry had dealt with, men and women, fiction and non, acted as though they'd done the world a service and were waiting for their tip. They tended toward intellectual vanity and whined extensively about the shabby car that picked them up on their book tour, blah blah blah. The excessive delight they took from trivial compliments in the press was equaled only by the *Schadenfreude* they exhibited shamelessly at each other's failures. Franco's former assistant Marcia Merton had put a sign up over her desk that read "Save a Forest—Shoot an Author"; and while Terry lacked that citified hostility, she shared the sentiment. The publishing industry was needlessly extravagant in its waste of paper; and with few exceptions, authors gave her the creeps.

As she leaned into the closet, a cramp moved up the back of her calf and her knees buckled slightly. Leaning precariously on a stack of manuscripts, she lost her balance, and the whole pile toppled across her foot.

"Ratfuck!" she shouted, grabbing her toes. To hell with New Year's resolutions.

A green manuscript box on the floor had burst out of its FedEx envelope, which meant she'd have to rewrap it. When her cramp subsided, she reached for the box: it broke, and four hundred pages spilled out. Now the author would think someone had actually read the damn book. She knelt to collect the pages.

There was a beautiful pink stain on page 83 of the manuscript: a graph from some sophisticated plotter. It reminded Terry of a Rorschach test she'd taken in the psych department to earn pocket money. She couldn't make any sense of the graph. Then she glanced at the title page: *The Belacqua Report* by Dr. Roger Belacqua. More than a hundred manuscripts in that closet, and she'd stumbled upon the very one.

As she collated the pages, she glanced through them, and then opened the manuscript on her desk. Obviously, if it had come in over the transom, it couldn't be very important. Still, the graphs and illustrations piqued her curiosity. She peeked at the introduction.

The scientific evidence that follows is the result of scrupulous research carried out by a team of environmental specialists over the past decade, including the latest data (Oct. '97) from NASA's Daedalus satellite.

Our research, presented here for the first time, demonstrates unforeseen interactions at work between the rising temperature of the planet, the ulceration of the ozone layer, and the growing inability of the earth's oceans to dispose of our excess carbon. These interactions signal grave consequences for the earth's future.

The Belacqua Report shows that an irreversible cascade of extinctions has already begun, in which crucial species at the bottom of the food chain, especially marine and insect life, disappear, followed by species that feed upon them, collapsing the diversity critical to sustaining all the higher orders, ourselves included.

In short, we have learned that the earth is dying: the process leading to the mass extinction of *Homo sapiens* over the next forty years, along with most other species, has already begun.

Whew, that's harsh! she thought. She read on.

Even a decade ago we had a window of opportunity for reversing the decay of our ecosystem by restraining population growth. Now that window has shut and cannot be reopened. Decay is not a reversible process. Species cannot be regenerated. Thousands of delicate, irreparable strands in the food chain have been severed.

This will seem unthinkable to most. The notion of mass extinction is counterintuitive and offends our fundamental assumptions about how and why the world exists. As well, the effects of global warming are not widely understood, and may even include colder weather in spots. It is the trend toward unprecedented weather—climate *change*—that is so alarming, including the devastating floods of 1997, from the Pacific Northwest to the Great Plains and North Dakota, that cost hundreds of lives and many billions of dollars. Even the damage caused by El Niño in 1997–1998 owed its severity to the larger pattern of climate change.

What was this, she wondered: science or fiction? Whatever, it outranked *Football and Freud,* big-time. She went on reading.

Four hours later, just as she was finishing the last page, her boss arrived, soaked to the bone. Even through his toxic fog of self-involvement, he noticed something was different about Terry: her eyes were swollen, and mascara ran down the collar of the white blouse he'd always wanted to unbutton. It occurred to him, almost by chance, that Terry had been crying. Observant to a fault, that was Danvers Creal.

"Afternoon, Terry. Sweetheart, what's the matter?" he asked in the solicitous tones of Scott Peck, whom he resembled slightly on a good day. He glanced at the manuscript. "You found it! You know, you are the finest editorial assistant a man could have. Remind me to have you cloned." With Danvers, political correctness wasn't even skin-deep. After an excessive show of relief, he started for his office.

Terry wiped her face and tried to sound persuasive. "Danvers, remember you once told me that if I ever insisted on a really important manuscript, you'd publish it sight unseen?" Danvers nodded. But they both knew that that had been back when he was still trying to talk her into bed; he'd stopped after seeing her at the Temple Bar late one night, smooching with Bobby.

She stood up to him, teary eye to bleary eye, and pointed at the manuscript. "Well, this is the one. Commonweal has to publish this book." It sounded like a threat.

"Or else?"

"Well—" Obviously, she hadn't thought this through. "If you won't champion it with the editorial board, I'll find someone in the building who will."

"My my my." Pushy broad, said his eyes. "Bring me a cup of coffee, Terry."

That's when she remembered about Danvers and environmental issues: this was the guy who thought *Exxon Valdez* was a Spanish explorer. Staring at her, he strode slowly into his office with his hands behind his back, just like George Bernard Shaw.

At forty-two, Danvers Creal had a whole panoply of personalities sticking out of his psyche like fish fins. He housed a menagerieful of pet mannerisms too studied to be shed, all congregating beneath a shock of unruly hair. In profile he resembled a Chia Pet; in character he resembled many people, himself not included. Within his shell, incongruous shards of identifiable individuals—writers, mostly, and film stars—dwelled side by side in moody dissonance. Lytton Strachey and Gary Cooper, Norman Mailer and W. C. Fields, Balzac, Jeanette Winterson, and Eugene O'Neill: large personalities contending to seize the helm of his "personality." The upshot was a relentless civil war. When Danvers Creal was alone in his head, he was behind enemy lines.

Friends thought it strange that Danvers chose to wear so many masks, until they realized that his condition was involuntary. Besides, Danvers was always too busy winning over new friends to waste time on the ones he'd already used: that was the very mark of his character, or lack of it. Insincerity was his only creed. Once, after Danvers had dined with Donald Trump, he asked Terry to revise his address book, adding new names for which he didn't even have addresses yet and deleting dozens of old friends. As an editor, Danvers Creal could rearrange a Korean technical manual till it sang like the Song of Solomon. Socially, he could barely assemble the facade of a cohesive individual, in a profession where facades are as big as Macy's.

Danvers had earned his position by hard work, shrewd knowledge of the market, and an undeniable talent for pandering. He had created a new imprint for Commonweal's romantic thrillers—the kind of paraliterature that isn't so much written as it is extruded endlessly at factories somewhere in the Midwest. He'd signed a half-dozen former Harlequin writers, paid them like hacks and promoted them like princesses (all were women), and turned a 300 percent profit in less than two years. He'd even chosen the imprint's candid name, Guilty Pleasures; actually, that had been Terry's idea, which he'd appropriated. After his promotion she heard him boast that the name had just "popped into his head." So it goes.

Danvers had been made executive editor following the imprint's stunning success, and had aspired to become the company's next president. Instead Franco Sherman was recruited directly from academia, while Danvers was left poaching in his bitterness toward Bob Milton, chairman of Macro Foods and Enterprises—Commonweal's parent company. Milton's acquisition of a publishing house had been the by-product of a complicated stock swap. Actually, Macro was a leader in the canned goods business, but under Milton the company had become one of those gluttonous conglomerates that enjoy having a little publishing on the side, like horseradish.

Ten minutes after Danvers went into his office, Terry brought him his cup and waited patiently while he left a message with Mort Janklow's secretary. Then he set the phone down and took a sip from the cup.

"This is tea," he complained.

"You forgot to say 'please.' " She knew she'd never get away with this stuff if he weren't so dependent upon her. "Danvers, listen, I'm sorry if I seem out of line, but you *have* to look at *The Belacqua Report.*"

"Isn't it all about how Mother Earth is having a bad hair day?" Terry glanced around for something to throw. But then Danvers dropped his Noël Coward mask along with all the others—which he could do, for minutes at a time. "Do you really think it's big?" he asked, starting to salivate like one of Pavlov's unfortunate dogs.

"The biggest," she replied, "unless it's a very sophisticated hoax. Look, I know you're not into environmental issues, but—"

"That's not true!"

"You're a one-man ecological disaster!" She put her hands on her hips. "You waste reams of paper! I even saw you throw a soda can into the bushes in Central Park."

"But I'm doing something more important for the planet." She looked at him askance. "Well, aren't environmental problems caused by overpopulation? So," he explained patiently, "as long as I don't have children, I'm *entitled* to litter."

Reverend Ben Muller arrived just then. He may have saved Danvers's life.

"Terry, bring me the Stallone contract, *please?*" He used his bitchy tone, borrowed from William Buckley, while covering the phone's mouthpiece. Since chastising the preacher, he'd spent an hour badgering Stallone's literary agent, Burt Logan.

A moment later she arrived with the folder and *The Belacqua Report.* She already had her shoes changed and her jacket on. She had to get out of the office. "I'm taking the rest of the day off," she announced. "Here's my synopsis of *The Belacqua Report.* Read it."

He curled his eyebrow like Clark Gable, but without the effect. He wouldn't stop her while Logan was on the phone, she knew that: he was the only agent in New York who never returned his calls.

"Just a second, Burt." He glanced at her synopsis. "You think—?"

"I think we're all fucked," she answered truthfully.

"But is it a best-seller?"

"That's what I said." Congratulations, Danvers: you just made the cover of *Duh Magazine*. "But it really doesn't matter."

"Doesn't matter?" Danvers's jaw dropped at her sacrilege before remembering the matter at hand. "Sorry, Burt! I have it here—"

Later, on his way out, Danvers picked up the manuscript. His curiosity whetted, he read Terry's four-page summary over dinner; he was so intrigued he even turned off the TV. But ten minutes later he put away the green box. Fascinating stuff, he thought, but not my flavor. He wasn't interested in trying to ram a scientific manuscript past the editorial board. Besides, he'd just spent all his political capital getting *Bloomsbury World* approved. I have other cats to whip, he thought, *à la* Genet. But . . . what if Terry is right? *Sacrebleu!* Despite her edginess, her instincts had proved reliable—especially with the name for the imprint. Maybe he should recommend it to another editor. But his own instincts—bottom-feeders all—suggested that if he shared it, and the book was a success, he would be subject to ridicule. So he decided he would pass on *The Belacqua Report,* and left a message to that effect on Terry's e-mail, asking her to blow off his Friday dinner with General Shreiver and return the manuscript.

Terry walked back to her apartment on East Fifteenth in the cold rain rather than breathe the subway soot. She had a tentative date that night, but by the time she got to Union Square, she just wanted to slip into her jeans and listen to something classical—*Astral Weeks*, maybe.

Unkempt. That was the word for her apartment, the fifth since she'd gotten to New York two years ago. It wasn't actually dirty: she hadn't seen any roaches since October. It was just dusty, in a bohemian sort of way—like *Rent*. Anyway, she was in her kitchenette when she noticed a fluttering on the floor beside her jacket. It was a butterfly, mostly orange and yellow, about twice the size of the little monarch that she'd had tattooed on the inside of her thigh. Terry kneeled beside the flapping insect and wondered how it could be alive in midwinter. Pinned beneath the weight of its ineffectual wings, it was dragging itself torturously toward . . . nothing: it would find no food, no pollen, no mate. This lone individual could do nothing to survive, nor could Terry help. It was just like that damn deer in Massachusetts.

She had been returning to Smith on a beautiful autumn day in '94 with tall, gangling Andrew Dooley, her new boyfriend, a biology major at MIT. She'd caught a ride up to Boston for the weekend and now he was driving her back to Smith. As they turned off the Mass Pike toward Northampton, they hit a deer. Actually the doe hit them, glancing off the fender and flying to the edge of the road. They screeched to a halt and ran back to where the wounded animal lay, all four legs broken at the knees and flapping uselessly. Terry had become hysterical, racing back and forth to the highway, where she tried to flag down a policeman to no avail. The doe pitched and rolled, her breath heaving, screaming voicelessly, torso twisting in agony. Dooley, twenty years old, from Manhattan, was as panicked as Terry: neither of them had any idea how to put the animal to death. They kept hoping a hunter would drive by, but none appeared, and all Dooley had in his Datsun was a small Swiss Army knife. Terry screamed at him to slit the doe's throat, but it was just not something the boy was capable of. So after witnessing the doe's anguished thrashing for more than an hour, they left it there, suffering by the roadside, knowing full well that unless somebody came by with a gun, they were condemning the doe to a terrible, protracted death.

For a long time this mundane tragedy had suffused her life like an awful stench: proof, if it was needed, of nature's vulnerability to man. Now, staring at the butterfly, she felt the same helpless remorse. As the chain of life collapsed, wrote Belacqua, the last hapless survivors, like the butterfly and the deer, would die off in the isolated patches of earth we'd neglected to pave, soon to be swarmed over by the cockroaches that would linger long after all other insects had vanished. Millions of creatures would die like roadkill—displaced victims of a species that did not create them, would not nurture them, and could not save them from suffering and oblivion. "But," Belacqua wrote, "of all the condemned species, only one will await its extinction consciously." That message was threaded throughout the doomsday report.

She decided to register online with the Belacqua Research Center, to "receive further scientific data by e-mail, address questions to Dr. Belacqua himself, and check the schedule of his infrequent speaking engagements." So she went to the website at http://www.belacqua.com. Her screen was immediately taken over by a multimedia extravaganza: slow, sweeping graphics accompanied by choral passages from the *St. Matthew Passion*. From the formation of the solar system to the cooling of the earth and the progressive dissemination of life in all its forms, the video was a hypnotic ten-minute recapitulation of the planet's history. When the time line reached 1998, the word PROJECTED was superimposed beneath the images. The last few minutes showed the progressive degradation of the oceans and the atmosphere, and then the first of Belacqua's depopulation scenarios—detailed endgames for the human race, based on different variables and contingencies. The rest of the scenarios were available for downloading, except Terry didn't have enough RAM, which pissed her off: the graphics were so cool, they'd make a fantastic CD-ROM.

Back on America Online she finished paying her December bills, which left under $300 in her account. Then she talked to her mom, an old-school Rachel Carson environmentalist, who told her Lake Harriet was already starting to melt—in early January!—and after their chat gently reminded Terry of the value of "moral clarity."

That evening Terry stayed in, partly because of the January rain-storm (was that global warming?), but mostly because she knew if she even saw a cigarette she'd break down and smoke. She started making pasta primavera, but while searching her fridge for a red pepper, she opened a Tupperware bowl of something unidenti-fiable (blue gnocchi? green cotton candy?) that totally grossed her out.

After she finished proofing the Goldman galleys, when she pow-ered up to send Bobby a message, her laptop repeatedly failed to reboot. It happened three times, and that really scared her, be-cause she hadn't backed up her files for months. The fourth time she hit F8 at the Windows prompt and went into Safe Mode; after that it started up fine. No big deal, just a visit from Sparky the Clown.

That was when she learned from her e-mail that Danvers had rejected *Belacqua*. Ratfuck. Well, what did she expect? Danvers wasn't a real editor—he was barely even a real person. He was more of a one-man literary vaudeville team, like Boswell and Johnson, Pegler and Broun, Amis and Barnes. She fell asleep mentally scrolling through her options and planning her campaign for *The Belacqua Report*.

The next morning she really really meant to go to work, but, well, between the intention and the act falls the shadow, just like T. S. Eliot said. It just didn't seem to matter. *The Belacqua Report* was still rumbling through her bones like a Marshall amp—an earthquake of undetermined proportions. If Belacqua was right, this was the most awful truth, hideous and inescapable. But the climax of the unstoppable cataclysm was still forty years away, so her gut reaction was strong but confused. Like in the country song, she didn't know whether to kill herself or go bowling.

She slept late and then lay in bed daydreaming—until she started to think level-headedly about her relationship with Bobby, which, despite all the sex and everything, wasn't really working, for reasons she didn't care to dwell on. So she slid into her spandex and old high-tops (rather than ruin her Nikes in the rain), popped Van Morrison into her Walkman, and went for a run up the East River.

By the time she was halfway to the UN she was soaked up to her knees, thinking, Puddle-wonderful, my ass. Then, at Third Avenue and Forty-sixth, as the rain turned to ice, she veered off into a Korean deli and emerged smoking a cigarette. "Fuck it," she said out loud, which sounded better than some lame excuse. Hell, if we're gonna be extinct . . .

With that she turned into O'Donoghue's just as they opened and ordered a draft lager.

She left O'Donoghue's before noon when she realized that Creal might come in for an early lunch, or even Franco Sherman; she couldn't risk her paycheck. But outdoors the two beers hit her: she was really hammered! By now the snow was falling heavily enough to hide traffic thirty feet away. She would have hailed a cab, but all her cash—$12.50—had gone on cigarettes and beer, and she'd forgotten her ATM card.

She tried sprinting, but that was a slippery effort in her red Converse high-tops, and she was weaving a little too. When she stopped, she lit her fourth butt of '98. You've come a long way, baby—yeah, about a block. As the wind picked up she started to run again. So amid the parade of parkas and overcoats, hats and hoods, there was Terry, in spandex, smoking a cigarette as she jogged through a blizzard, half drunk on a workday morning, her icy, bare feet squishing in her sneakers.

Halfway home she noticed a tall man in a green parka with an umbrella who seemed to be following her zigzag path. He even slowed down when she did, and then sped up again. At Union Square she turned and stared—looking, perhaps, just a little crazy—but he hid his face in his umbrella and veered off onto Seventeenth. She almost followed *him* before stopping herself and chiding her overheated imagination.

At home she scraped off the wet spandex and flopped across the bed. She woke up again, sweaty and dehydrated, just in time for Oprah. The butterfly had not died yet. There was *still* nothing in the fridge, but at the back of the cabinet she scored big-time: half a bag of Pepperidge Farm cookies—one of the four basic food groups. Then, after a shower, she headed back out wearing long underwear, ski pants, and Gore-Tex.

It was five-thirty when she hit the street, already dark, and the snow had turned back to icy rain. At The Galaxy, she was about to order dinner when she started talking with a tall, youthful accountant in gold-rimmed glasses who had been born, like herself, in July 1973. His name was, um, Gerald, and since he had already had dinner, Terry just kept emptying the bowl of peanuts, which the bartender refilled. As it turned out Gerald was not a great talker but he was a pretty good kisser. To make a long story short, they went back to his place and got into some serious groping on his couch, which she enjoyed as much as her clothing would allow, and she wasn't about to take any off. Two hours later she left without exchanging phone numbers, much less bodily fluids. Drag and drop; into the remainder bin. She bought groceries at the A&P and finally cooked herself some pasta. She was pissed off with herself: she'd *never* messed around with a total stranger. And for what? Peanuts?

The next morning she was so ashamed she stayed home again: the alarm rang, but she turned it off and slept till eleven. After the anonymous fumblings the night before, she felt hollow as a dry gourd—which might have had more to do with her erratic eating than guilt toward Bobby. By late afternoon it was sixty degrees, but Terry stayed in to do her laundry and finish the Goldman book, while wondering what to do about Danvers: finally she e-mailed him, saying she might be carrying the Hong Kong bird flu.

Then Maurice called to remind her they had tickets to see Prodigy at the Beacon that night. Maurice, her trusty friend from Springfield, Mass., made big bucks cutting hair at the Helmsley Palace, so it was his treat, and he was really psyched. To celebrate the event they agreed to get punked out. For the first time in ages Terry sprayed her hair purple, twisted it in a knot, and applied black eye shadow the way Maurice wore it: more like Gene Simmons than Jean Simmons. She added blue lipstick, a Sex Pistols T-shirt, baggy boxer shorts over torn fishnet stockings, and black high-tops. Waif-wench.

The concert was like all the mad confusion of adolescence, and by the encores, out of nostalgia, Terry even joined in the mosh-pit follies. Afterward they went over to Cybilla's on East Sixtieth, where her friend Teddy tended bar, and drank shooters on the house.

"Worldwide," she mused to Maurice, citing *The Belacqua Report,* "women average five pregnancies in a lifetime. So the population of the earth grows by ten thousand people per hour."

"Wow," Maurice intoned philosophically. "That's like . . . another Lodi, New Jersey, added every day. How long can that go on?"

Later they skipped up Park Avenue, laughing till the mascara ran down their cheeks, playing air guitar and singing, "It's the end of the world as we know it, an' I feel fine." Near Fifty-third, out of breath, Terry realized she was also out of butts, so Maurice waited as she ran to the newsstand.

She asked for Marlboros and reached for the last copy of *Harper's* just as a well-dressed gentleman plucked it from the rack. She knew he was a gentleman by the way he handed it to her with a smile. Only then did she realize it was Franco Sherman.

"Here," she said, handing it back. "You can have it, Mister—" She stopped herself.

"No, that's all right, miss. Please, take it," he replied affably. "I'll find something else." Didn't he recognize her? They'd been introduced at least four times, and she had sat in on every weekly editorial meeting since November as an "observer" (to remember everything Danvers forgot); she usually sat halfway down the big table from Franco. But her punk vamp getup was a pretty effective disguise, especially with mascara that was more de Kooning than Pollock.

Not a flicker of recognition crossed Sherman's eyes: instead, he furrowed his brow in mock counsel and pointed to *The Nation*. "You should read the two together," he said, "to get *both* sides of the story." Talk about your dry humor! His straight-faced tone was conspiratorial, and when he followed it with his boyish smile, it suddenly dawned on Terry that Franco Sherman was coming on to her. She stared at him like the first time she ever saw algebra. Nodding slowly, she smiled back and gave the newsboy a five; he handed her the cigarettes and change.

"Could I just see one thing?" Taking the *Harper's* from her hand, Franco glanced at the solution to December's crossword. Then from under his coat he produced a pen and started to write; but changing his mind, he handed the magazine back to her shyly.

"Thanks," he said, turning toward Park Avenue, just as Maurice rushed over.

"That," she whispered, "was the president of Commonweal. I think he was putting his moves on me."

"No way!" Maurice whistled. "Has he ever done that before?"

"No. But he's never seen me like this."

"See, love?" said Maurice. "I told you you should dress this way at work."

After an encounter of such significance, going in to the office on Thursday was obviously out of the question. What frightened her, when she thought about the Event, was that she might have blown her credibility for pushing *The Belacqua Report*.

That night she went out with Josie and Willow from Smith, who lived together in Boston now, and Mariah, who worked in advertising. They were all in Jenn St. Onge's wedding on Saturday—she was marrying the guy who sang the role of Ron Goldman in the upcoming Broadway production *O.J. and I.* So for a lark they wore their pink bridesmaid's dresses to dinner, complete with the stiletto heels Jenn had chosen. That was her first mistake. A little later Mariah made a pass at her. Now, making love with a woman was one of those things Terry had always meant to do in college but never got around to—like skydiving. But this wasn't the night for it; she was polite but firm. *Then,* when she got home after midnight, she couldn't remember where she'd hidden her house keys. Alzheimer's Lite. So she ended up in Maurice's armchair for the night.

By the time she woke up it was almost noon on payday. What a *loser!* Despite the bridesmaid's outfit, she snuck into the office, remembering that Danvers had an early lunch with Princess Stephanie. She padded through the corridors of the twelfth floor in her pink strapless cocktail dress, carrying the damn heels.

"Yo, Terry, where ya been?" Tony came gamboling down the hall, taking in her morning-after look. "Hey, yer eyes are really red, man."

"So?" she said defensively. "Maybe I'm a white rabbit. Hey, Tony, would you do me a favor?" She led him into Creal's office and handed him Belacqua's green manuscript box from Danvers's table. "I need ten of these: they have to be distributed to all the board editors before two o'clock."

"No problemo. Just do me the paperwork—"

Terry shook her head. "Not this time, okay? No fuss, no muss. I'll send you down a cover note to go out with each one. Okay, amigo?"

"You got it." Tony grinned and raced back toward the Xerox room.

At her desk, Terry composed an anonymous memo:

> Friday, Jan. 9, 1998
>
> Please put the MS of *The Belacqua Report* at the top of your reading schedule for discussion at our meeting on Jan. 19.

How would the editors react? Most of them had their reading slated well into May. She didn't even have a plan—she was making it up as she went along. She sent Tony ten copies of the unsigned memo, which left no way to cover her tracks. Danvers was going to be at the meeting, of course: he'd know damn well how the doomsday report got to the others, and unless they *loved* it, he'd fire her for cause, and that meant no unemployment. So be it. She would look back knowing that she had done the right thing, pulling this manuscript out of the slush pile and bringing it before the Guardians of the Imprimatur.

She thought about Danvers. Even if she could somehow persuade him to stand up for Belacqua, he wouldn't do a good job—and at the editorial meeting, she couldn't jump in. When push came to shove, he'd hoard his political capital for the next Bloomsbury bio. This was the guy who thought the Madonna movie was about Vita.

So who would be the *best* person to bring this manuscript to the table? That was obvious. Fearlessly, she called Franco Sherman's secretary, Millie, and scheduled a few minutes on Tuesday afternoon "for Danvers to pitch a manuscript." No problem.

Okay, that left Danvers. It probably wouldn't help her case if he found her sitting there barefoot in a strapless gown after having disappeared for four days, so while she waited for her paycheck, she left him a message saying she'd drop by his apartment over the weekend "to go over the MS." He'd think she meant the Goldman manuscript.

When the phone beside her rang, she answered it.

"Pentagon calling, General Albert Shreiver for Danvers Creal, just a moment, please." Terry was put on hold, and that gave her time to think. This was almost too perfect.

"Mr. Creal? General Shreiver." The clipped military cadence was unmistakable.

"I'm his assistant, Terry Bancroft," she said. "Mr. Creal isn't in. May I help you?"

The general's voice became more hesitant. "I'm supposed to fly up for dinner with him tonight to discuss *The Belacqua Report.* Just making sure we're good to go."

"Ahh, no. Mr. Creal was called out of town at the last minute." What the hell, she'd already laid it on the line for the damn book. And President Clinton says there's lots of new jobs out there. "But Danvers is *totally* interested in the manuscript and, um, he wanted to know if you could come discuss *The Belacqua Report* with our editors, say in ten days? Monday the nineteenth—come to the twelfth floor at ten: I'll take you in." She was taking him in, all right. Okay, she could cover February's rent by selling her mountain bike. "That way you'll meet Franco Sherman and the other editors: they'll all have read it." *What was she going to do about Danvers?*

"Yes," the general replied slowly, "that's fine. I'll see you then.

Remind Mr. Creal that secrecy is vital. This project has powerful adversaries. Good-bye."

This is crazy, she thought. *Crazy.* Too many Linda Fiorentino movies. She hadn't even gotten his number. Since her paycheck still hadn't been delivered, she sat there motionless, projecting the last three days onto the blank wall in front of her. What a horror show. *Loser!* What ever happened to "moral clarity"? She mouthed the words like the name of a new flavor from Ben & Jerry's.

At two-fifteen, when her paycheck arrived with the office mail, she bolted.

FRANCO SHERMAN

The distance from the surface of the earth to the far edge of the inner atmosphere is only 12 miles; the annual amount of carbon dioxide forced into that limited space is six billion tons; and the five hottest consecutive years on record began in 1991. The hottest year in the world's recorded weather history was 1995. The planet is warming at a faster rate than at any time in the last ten thousand years. . . . The facts beg a question that is as simple to ask as it is hard to answer. What do we do with what we know?

—Ross Gelbspan, *The Heat Is On* (1997)

Franco Sherman was surprised to learn that Danvers was bringing him a manuscript personally; clearly, the executive editor did not want to lose this book to another house. Peculiar as Danvers was, he'd always acquitted himself professionally, though he had gone overboard with that coffee-table book about Bloomsbury, even threatened to resign. Still, most editors had pet titles that would never break even, but whose losses could be made up by a moderate amount of, well, commercial crap. Franco's own hobby horse was American history—it was also his B.A. and M.A. at Columbia, before he turned to English Lit for his doctorate. Franco even had his own imprint with Commonweal Books, named Historical Perspective, intended for academic works that would never find a commercial publisher: its "big" titles sold only a fraction of what Danvers's romance-thrillers did. It was not too much to say, then, that Guilty Pleasures provided for Historical Perspective. And though Danvers's peculiar deportment made Franco uncomfortable, when it came to crap, his taste was right on the money.

Franco was not, on the face of it, likely corporate material: in fact, his journey to the top had been a complete fluke. While lecturing on American literature he had created and published Clio-Wings, a history database that had been marketed by Macro Enterprises before it acquired Commonweal. Then Macro's chief, Bob Milton, had looked around for someone to take the old-school publishing house into the computer age. So in a move that many at Commonweal found astonishing and some, like Danvers, took as a personal slight, Milton had appointed Franco Sherman editor in chief and subsequently, in '96, president and CEO. This came during the four-month leave of absence Franco spent with his children after his wife died.

In the next two years Franco had raised Commonweal Books back to a position of respect, and increased revenues by 14 percent, partly from his hand-picked educational CD-ROMs, partly from Guilty Pleasures; he'd also cut costs without layoffs. So he was something of a hero in the publishing realm—itself an over-populated world, with some 50,000 newborn titles a year, most of which had about the same shelf life as a quart of milk. He'd also prodded his editors to ferret out ground-breaking manuscripts.

So naturally he was open-minded that Tuesday afternoon when Danvers strode into his spare, elegant office with Terry and set a green manuscript box on his desk. Editors were not obliged to make a personal pitch, but if they expected opposition from the board, they sometimes sought Franco's endorsement before the collective decision was made. Franco could override the editors if he so chose, to veto or promote a particular project, but not without undermining the board as an even-handed mechanism for assessing acquisitions. Unlike his predecessor, Franco kept a light hand on the tiller.

"You seem serious about this, Danvers," he said with a smile, reading the title on the box. "What are you so excited about?"

Without looking at Terry, Danvers glanced at the notes she'd prepared after persuading him to pitch the book to Franco. Selecting a persona for the occasion, he settled upon Carl Sagan. "This is a scientific study of the biosphere, written for the layman by a respected scientist. It evaluates the threat to mankind and the geopolitics of prolonging our survival." He paused, recalling what Terry had emphasized.

Terry studied Franco nervously. He was very good-looking: his refined manners and smooth features, together with the hint of a Continental accent, suggested both Mediterranean and Anglo heritage. His dark hair was straight and rather long for an executive his age. In the hallway he had an unusually lithe gait, which, together with his hands, Terry found especially appealing. There was also a melancholy about him that reminded her somehow of bay rum. When she caught herself staring, she shifted her gaze to the large freestanding globe behind his desk and rooted silently for Danvers: he had done his homework and she had done hers. She had spent half of Sunday at Danvers's bachelor studio coaching him in Belacqua's vocabulary and logic. Still, she was poised to leap in just in case Carl Sagan suddenly morphed into Jim Carrey.

"Back in '92," Danvers continued, "a distinguished panel of scientists issued a 'Warning to Humanity,' stressing that there was only a brief window of opportunity to save the planet from the effects of global warming." Franco nodded hesitantly. He tried to stay informed, but his credentials as an environmentalist had long since lapsed. "Then, in '96, the UN scientific panel announced that greenhouse gases would cause the temperature to climb six degrees Fahrenheit in the next century, and that, without a dramatic reversal, the atmosphere might reach a point where the damage would be irreparable." Danvers pointed at the manuscript. "Well, this report shows that both those estimates were wildly *optimistic*. When the global temperature rises just two degrees, that triggers reactions in the oceans that cause the food chain to collapse much faster than anyone had ever guessed. 'Once triggered,' says Belacqua, 'the process becomes *irreversible*.' This deterioration continues until. . . ."

"Until what?" asked Franco, entirely engaged.

Danvers paused dramatically. "Well, he says those climatic triggers have already been tripped and we have passed the point of no return. In about forty years, life will be extinguished from the face of the earth, except for a few bugs. Belacqua says that all we can do by now is delay our extinction by a decade or two."

Franco gazed up Fifth Avenue and spoke slowly. "He says there's no solution? Humanity will disappear in forty years regardless of what we do?"

Danvers nodded. "And it's our own fault. As Pogo said, 'We have met the enemy, and it is us.' " By now Terry had figured out that Pogo was the Bart Simpson of the fifties.

Franco turned, poker-faced, and looked at Terry; his thoughtful gaze fell to her hands, which were gripping a pen. "Well, I don't know who this guy is," he started slowly, "but that's the most far-fetched prediction I've ever heard. Frankly, it's a little silly."

Terry leaped to her feet when Danvers failed to. "That's *so* not true! Even if it turns out he's wrong, it's not farfetched, Mr. Sherman. For starters, look at Belacqua's credentials: he's been a consultant with NASA for a decade. He even helped design the Daedalus satellite—so he's the only ecologist who's ever seen its data on cloud cover."

"Cloud cover?" asked Franco.

Here Danvers jumped back in. "Low, thick clouds reflect heat back out to space; high, thin cirrus clouds trap the heat in the atmosphere. The satellite pictures from last October show these cirrus clouds literally blanketing the earth." Terry almost cracked up, hearing Danvers explain the environment.

Franco looked from Danvers to Terry, perplexed. "From this one book, you both believe we're on the verge of extinction?"

Danvers read from Terry's synopsis. " 'The gradual but inevitable eradication of human civilization has already begun. At this late date the only policies that could even postpone our extinction are too repugnant, ethically and politically, to be options.' "

Franco whistled. "Heavy furniture! But how come no one else has figured this out?"

"Maybe," Terry interjected, "Belacqua's just the first."

When Franco spoke again, his manner suggested that he'd dug in his heels. "Okay, I'll take a look and we can discuss it next Monday. You've given copies to all the editors?" Terry nodded quickly, to Danvers's obvious surprise. "It's hard to buy. How could such a disaster happen so quickly?"

"Ask the dinosaurs." Terry pointed to the green box. "Or think about this: the last ice age was caused by a six-degree cooling that took thousands of years; so just imagine the impact of a six-degree warming in less than a century! How many species can survive that? And when plants and animals disappear, they condemn other species up the food chain: that's called a 'cascade of extinction,' and it doesn't take long at all."

"And nothing can stop the process? There must be measures we could take *today* to maintain the status quo until we find a solution. This has to be a hoax or something."

"This is no hoax," Terry answered. "Anyway, you're missing the point." Her manner was just this side of insubordinate, but it was the kind of defiance Franco encouraged at Commonweal, springing from conviction rather than disrespect. "Once the critical limits have been exceeded, it's too late for solutions. It isn't obvious yet because of lag time in the oceans' absorption of carbon dioxide. It's like we're forty feet away from a head-on collision, thinking we're okay—trouble is, we need fifty feet to stop."

Franco's eyes reluctantly registered interest. Her confidence growing, Terry continued, almost exactly in Belacqua's words, "Primitive life forms evolved into millions of species—that's biodiversity." She leaned forward to seize his attention. "But just in the last fifty years, the rate of extinction has increased a thousandfold."

Danvers shifted restlessly. "Thanks, Terry. That's probably enough."

"I'm just trying to give Mr. Sherman the lay of the land. . . ." She blushed like a teenager at her accidental double-entendre— *What a loser!*—but then recovered, plowing on through her own self-consciousness. "The global environment has been poisoned by the evolutionary success of a single organism—the human animal. That's why Belacqua compares the spread of the human population with the metastasis of cancer cells. I know that's a little, um, harsh. His point is that we evolved as part *of* the ecosystem, but then developed separately, like a hostile parasite. Nature's greatest creation has conquered Nature. Talk about your Pyrrhic victory!"

"What is he, a Luddite? Sounds like the Unabomber." Franco's eyes returned to the young woman who'd taken over the presentation. He liked her heartfelt brashness, but wondered why she was so enthralled with this grim vision. "The atmosphere is vast—"

"The atmosphere," she interrupted, "is just two hundred city blocks thick—the length of Manhattan. I've jogged that far in an afternoon." Well, almost. "Ninety-eight percent of that is water vapor. Belacqua has shown exactly how fiddling with the two percent is like pushing on a long lever: a tiny push can bring huge changes."

Franco recalled the Great Barrier Reef. "The oceans are so immense, so clean—"

"You don't get out much, do you?" was what Terry refrained from saying; he'd probably never seen the Jersey shore. Instead she said, "Most of the carbon ends up in the oceans, and they can no longer absorb the impact of our exploding population: the carbon dioxide, methane, blah blah blah." (God, did she say that out loud?) She pointed at Franco's huge globe. "Most of the earth is blue because of the oceans. When conditions become toxic to plankton and other microorganisms, decay sweeps across them. That has already begun."

Franco answered with a sigh, "It doesn't mean the process is irreversible."

Talk about stubborn! In her impatience, Terry's professional persona blew off like a veil in a gust of wind. "Look, Franco—may I call you Franco?—you've seen food go bad in the refrigerator, right? Well, ever seen it turn around and get better again?"

Franco chuckled, bowing his head in deference to her metaphor.

She pressed her advantage. "Part One of the book is science, Part Two geopolitics. Belacqua explains why international cooperation can't be achieved. Not without enslaving all six billion people by military force."

"Is *that* what he's advocating?"

"He isn't advocating anything: he's proving that the biosphere has reached saturation point with toxic gases."

Franco grew even more skeptical. "I suppose this doomsday report offers a blazing indictment of the greedy *Überklass* since the industrial revolution?"

"What's really chilling," Terry replied, "is that there is no one to blame. He's saying it's because of our brains that the population has outgrown its natural habitat—not because of a few evil corporations."

Danvers jumped up impatiently. "Look, Franco, will you read the manuscript?"

"Sure, but I'm not likely to be persuaded. Maybe the book will attract readers who liked Hal Lindsay, or the Von Daniken books.

Who knows?" Franco grinned. "This could be the pessimists' *Road Less Traveled.*" He looked at Terry. "How about calling it *The Empty Road?*" She didn't laugh. "Anyway, if the science is questionable, it's not worth short-term profits." To their crestfallen stares, he added, "But I'll read it."

"Check out their website, too," said Terry. "The graphics'll make a great CD-ROM—they're way cool." D'oh!

After they left, Franco realized he hadn't asked which agency had submitted the doomsday report, or what kind of advance they were looking for. No doubt it would be steep.

It was five days before he got back to the manuscript: that week the Macro directors were meeting, so Bob Milton was in from Fort Lauderdale, expecting kid-glove attention. This was the part of his job that Franco truly hated. He was not a political animal, and he conducted his business with Milton in blithe ignorance of how he was meant to behave. He was polite, of course, even mildly deferential. But lacking a talent for bowing and scraping, he never tried. Franco wasn't sure if his boss appreciated his directness or resented him for not kowtowing like everyone else.

Finally on Saturday Franco loaded Juliette and Max into a Dave-L limo with Emily, their nanny, to visit the Bronsons in Westport. He spent the morning wading through the flood of news articles about "Fornigate," wondering as he read whether or not Bill Clinton had in fact used the power of the presidency to get laid.

After lunch, when he'd finished his phone calls, Franco prepared for the reading, as he often did with important manuscripts, by showering and shaving. Then he went into his den and, though he was alone in the apartment, shut the soundproofed door with a click. The dark, comfortable room was furnished with a handful of pieces he'd inherited from his mother, and its gentle familiarity evoked a more reflective spirit.

Beside the sofa where he settled with the Belacqua manuscript there was a shelf arrayed with three carved wooden spheres from the seventeenth century, poised upon delicate stems. These exquisitely crafted, Escher-like puzzles were among the finest examples of French woodturning. Each was the size of a softball and had a symmetrical porthole in its surface that revealed other carved figures captured within—spheres within spheres—and each was carved from a single piece of wood. Franco had inherited them from his father, Giorgio Sherman, who had abandoned his son and his wife in 1968 and settled near Rapallo, where he had produced a large second family. In his will, he'd left this collection to his "American son."

Franco picked up the manuscript, and within minutes he was deeply absorbed. He read about flaws in current general circulation models of the atmosphere; how new Daedalus photographs revealed an unusually thick layer of water vapor at the edge of the atmosphere, dubbed the "eggshell effect"; and how, at a critical temperature, phytoplankton sank too deep to resurface, while salps—small, tubular mollusks—became too clogged on carbon to reproduce. It also detailed numerous interactions that had been overlooked: between, for example, increased ultraviolet penetration and zooplankton destroyed by ocean warming.

Belacqua framed his general argument in historical perspective. Since the early 1900s, a global struggle had been waged between mankind's power to despoil the earth and Nature's power to absorb the damage: a battle between entropy and regeneration. The biosphere could withstand a phenomenal number of insults, but somewhere around the ten millionth smoke-spewing factory or the five hundred millionth combustion engine, Nature had lost the battle. Now, between the threats to so many species on the land, in the sea, and in the air—including honeybees (from the Varroa mite) and frogs (the deformed frogs that had appeared all across the northern tier of America, from Washington State to Quebec)—the fragile ecosystem's capacity for self-repair had been overwhelmed.

Franco knew he wasn't qualified to evaluate Belacqua's detailed arguments. An expensive scientific assessment of the manuscript would be needed before Commonweal could possibly commit, even if the editorial board was itching to publish such a work, which he doubted. Still, as he read along, Franco noted the author's subtle talent for addressing objections as soon as they sprang to mind, and his skepticism began to lose its edge.

When he came to the geopolitical analysis, Franco admitted grudging admiration for Belacqua's even-handed arguments. There were no villains here: it was not the rapacity of a few individuals or nations that threatened the world.

It is the success of *Homo sapiens* that has condemned us, not our stupidity, or our greed. The instincts that governed millions of years of natural selection to produce the human animal have brought about our own destruction. Our triumph as a species translates directly into population growth. It took a million years to reach a population of one billion; that was in about 1800. But it only took until 1950 to reach two billion. And in less than fifty years since then, our population has tripled, to six billion. Now, we add a billion more people *every eleven years.*

For millions of years our genes have had to replicate themselves as quickly as possible to assure their survival: until very recently, zero population growth would have been ruinous. But even now that it is obvious that ZPG is the key to our collective survival, our cultures, like our genes, still command us to *go forth and multiply.*

Diplomatic cooperation sufficient to save the planet was not feasible, according to the *Report,* except by a global government with the authority to reduce populations and squelch economic and industrial growth. How can the People's Republic of China, for example, with one-fifth of the human race, be persuaded not to poison the atmosphere with lipnite coal, when it has no other resources? "But," Belacqua asked rhetorically, "would Americans pay higher taxes to provide China with solar energy? This question suggests the difficulty of the issues that must be addressed. To postpone our demise would require immediate, draconian laws enforcing population limits, and an abrupt end to 'the Age of the Individual.' Let me hasten to add that worldwide tyranny is not an acceptable option: absolute power still corrupts absolutely. My point is that not even dictatorship could reverse the decay."

As he turned the pages, a hollowness invaded Franco's torso. These were not abstractions: it was the fate of *this* world the scientist was predicting. "We have contaminated our only sanctuary, and as a result we confront a scenario more horrific than Mutually Assured Destruction; nuclear obliteration, after all, was always preventable. Though it falls to me to announce these facts, they will soon be corroborated by scientists around the world."

When Franco finished the manuscript he powered up his desktop, went to Belacqua's website, and, after registering, sat back to watch the visuals, accompanied by Bach, which recreated the emergence of life and its periodic eclipses, ending with the sixth mass extinction in the mid-twenty-first century. He hyperlinked to a second website and watched the other doomsday scenarios unfold; then, switching off his computer, he poured a glass of wine and sat down to reflect.

Absurd. Intriguing, yes, but unbelievable. The thrust of the manuscript wasn't so different from that of Richard Leakey's book a couple years back, *The Sixth Extinction,* and Doubleday hadn't hesitated to publish that. But alarming as that study had been, *The Belacqua Report* was something else again: a doomsday report that damn near named the day of death's dominion. It was compelling, even persuasive. But without confirmation, it meant little, even to Franco, who was more emotionally disposed to believe that the world was doomed than most people—he knew that much about himself. But until his work had withstood extensive peer review, Belacqua sounded like Nostradamus in a bad mood.

Still, what if his findings were confirmed?

Franco began to pace. Denial collided with an eerie sense of *déjà vu,* as if on some level he had been expecting this terrible news. But how could billions of people suffer mass extinction in two generations? Not to mention the entire animal kingdom. Even if it was true, it was not believable. And broadcasting such news seemed somehow immoral, nihilistic. He doubted that the editorial board would acquire a book like this, and Danvers Creal wasn't likely to change their minds. The young woman, Terry, now she was convincing, because she was so convinced herself; she was also articulate and very appealing, in a waif-like way. But assistants only monitored the weekly meetings, which lasted too long anyway, and her opinions would not be welcome. The upshot was that unless he championed the manuscript himself, this wasn't going to make the list. Good thing, though, that Terry had distributed copies. The collective will would be done, and then maybe some other house would publish it.

He continued pacing, and meandered out onto the terrace into the mild January night, where he gazed down at the wild array of man-made lights reaching to the eastern horizon. Ah, the poor, piss-stained old earth, he thought to himself. People were waiting for cabs in front of the Waldorf. He looked up at the apartment buildings nearby, filled with sleeping families, and imagined all the grief this book might cause. The youngest would suffer the most from the knowledge, including his own kids: Juliette had just turned nine, and Max was seven. If this report was to be believed, they and their children would die along with everyone else, either in an epidemic or a food shortage, when crop failures produced social upheavals, or at the end from asphyxiation, the final upshot of overpopulation. How could he prepare his kids to live out their shortened lives with such fearsome knowledge?

But he had only to look out from his terrace to see that life went on as usual. No green plague oozed from the sky, no fiery finger pointed down in recrimination: there was only a gentle breeze and a placid moon obscured by high cirrus clouds. The warm January night was delightful, even to the bruised sensibilities of a forty-seven-year-old widower for whom nothing remained, it seemed, but a leftover life to kill.

Lillian had died at the age of thirty-six in a head-on collision on the Merritt Parkway as she returned from a wedding near Norwalk, while Franco was on a business trip. Her beige Volvo 850 was crushed when a Chevy pickup driven by John Finley, twenty-three, of nearby Wilton, jumped the divider; he was also killed. That was June 16, 1996. A year and a half later Franco was still in shock, sleep-walking, shell-like, almost transparent, invisible in a crowd.

Lillian's memory was already fading for Max and Juliette, something he had dreaded. She wouldn't have wanted to be a burden, but she'd have wanted to be *remembered*. The truth was, though, she was fading for him too. Except at night, in his dreams, where he lived his real life. Much as he loved his kids, it was only there that he found rapture now. Part of him spent the days resting up for the nights, while his skin and bones went through the motions of being a loving father and CEO of Commonweal. Asleep, he came alive to a world that was always there, awaiting his return, like an endless Russian novel peopled by his own overwrought imagination. And most often at the center of the story was Lillian. Each day began as he tore himself away from his last chapter of dreaming.

In the street below, two taxis discharged a group of revelers whose hollow whistles and hoots echoed between the buildings. Franco watched their carousing departure and wondered if their evening would have been different if they knew that the last forty years of civilization had begun. Perhaps they'd go on about their lives the same old way, slogging to their jobs, driving to the shore on summer weekends, calculating their IRA accounts. Maybe not. Maybe everything would change. Maybe the whole global culture would grow up, get serious, and devote its collective efforts to survival. Or perhaps society would slide toward listless abandon, indolence, and dissolution. "Eat, drink, and be merry . . ."

In *The Belacqua Report,* Franco saw silhouettes of the great ethical dilemmas: Does our existence have a purpose? How much must the individual sacrifice for the welfare of humanity? And does the right to self-government outweigh *all* other considerations—even our collective survival? He wondered how the public would react to all this. There'd be alarm, probably, maybe even panic. Clearly, some sectors of industry and government would not—did not—want this book published. They might try to employ prior restraint, or even violence. If Belacqua's science was impeccable, then it was going to sell many millions of copies worldwide. If not, this would be the biggest farce since *The Hitler Diaries.*

Franco walked back to the living room and settled on the sofa in the dark. This was usually enough for his dreams to swell up from beneath, like a dark and agitated sea, to fetch him down. Recently Juliette had often found him half off the sofa in the morning, an unbound manuscript dribbling down his chest. But now relief was not forthcoming, and though he'd all but dismissed Belacqua's hypothesis, the dread of ecological Armageddon had already sunk in, colored by his own imagination. A vision as old as the Great Flood had come to pass. Man broke the very rules that brought him into being; such hubris had a price, as Bible-thumpers had been saying since Moses.

An hour later he was still staring at the darkness, contemplating images of a silent earth. He moved to his computer to jot down some notes, but when he switched it on, the damn thing wouldn't crank up properly. It took three or four tries, and by the time Windows was running smoothly, he'd forgotten what he was going to write. So he returned to the sofa, where he soon fell asleep. In the morning he could barely remember the erotic dream he'd had about the waif-wench at the newsstand.

Franco tapped his pencil thoughtfully on the legal pad before him while a dozen editors and assistants waited respectfully around the polished rosewood conference table, with boxed copies of the Belacqua manuscript. Franco's first act at the helm of Commonweal was to move the weekly editorial meeting to Monday morning. Since it was at these meetings that editors dueled for their pet projects, they cut their long weekends short—everyone except Danvers, it seemed, who was late today. Franco's executive secretary entered quietly and handed him an agenda.

"Thank you, Millie," he said. "Has Danvers come in yet?"

"No. Terry hasn't heard from him, either. But she'll be here in a minute."

After Millie left, Franco looked up at Judy Corliss, senior vice president, a tough, bitter woman seated across the table from her husband, Joe Mercer, who led the token poetry division. Whenever Franco met with Judy he felt as if she were jabbing him in the chest with her forefinger; for him, Joe's frequent snarls needed no explanation.

"So, Judy, what do you make of *The Belacqua Report?*"

"Tree-hugger mythology posing as science," she answered without hesitation. "Whether or not he's established, Belacqua's a kook. If his conclusions were in line with other scientists', we'd already know about this."

Franco let her opinion sink in around the table, knowing that it carried some weight. Judy Corliss brought a remarkable sales record to the table, as well as nine years' seniority over Franco. In '87 she'd coaxed Laura Goldman to leave Dodd, Mead and bring her upscale bodice-rippers to Commonweal. Judy had "turned" ten other profitable novelists, then bullied Franco into doubling her salary, threatening to take her whole brood to Dell.

"Does anyone here know what other environmentalists think about the imminent threat to our survival? Do you, Judy?" Franco asked.

"She doesn't know what she's talking about," interposed her husband. Their editorial marriage put the fun back in dysfunctional. Judy's eyes flashed double-daggers. "I'm as familiar as most people, I suppose—more so than *him,*" she jabbed. Like other couples, they'd started out politely editing each other's remarks; by now they used the weekly meeting as a domestic weapon, consistently voting down each other's pet projects. Since each of Judy's romance-thrillers generated more sales than Joe's entire poetry division, she acted as if her opinion carried more weight, which it probably did. Like a starving poet at a booksellers' convention, Joe was rarely more than a spectator to the acquisitions process.

"Maybe he *is* a committed eco-freak who believes this stuff," said Judy. "But even if his predictions were partly true, it's such a downer! And it's unverifiable. He says so himself: his research will take ten years for another lab to confirm. I have to vote this one down. I think Belacqua's out for money and ink."

Franco turned to the harried lawyer beside Judy. "Marshall, do you agree?"

"Yeah. He's Chicken Little with an attitude." Marshall Pierson, Commonweal's counsel, also edited legal works. "But this guy doesn't just shout that the sky is falling—he's merchandising the idea. He probably figured, 'Hey, end of the millennium—the perfect marketing tool for Armageddon. *Carpe diem!*'" Marshall, a tall, robust tennis player in his forties, often served as Commonweal's unofficial strategist—Dick Morris without the hooker. (In fact, he dated so many models, Judy said once, he'd probably get turned on by a CARE poster.) He'd been working on a fast-paced courtroom thriller for five years, and his pallor had turned leaden lately: mood swings often left him mute during the meeting, which suited everyone there just fine.

"Any other thoughts?" asked Franco. By now he was expecting a unanimous thumbs down. The dynamics of the meeting were governed by a zero-sum reality: since every editor had projects to push for, and the acquisitions budget was closely scrutinized by Bob Milton over at Macro, everyone there had a vested interest in shooting down *The Belacqua Report*. Without someone to champion the book, it would be off the table in minutes.

"This isn't very different from tabloid headlines," Marshall added. "I suppose it'll be lucrative if it catches on with the trailer-park crowd, like *The Late Great Planet Earth*. How much of an advance does he want?"

Franco shifted in his chair, squeaking against the leather. "Danvers didn't say. I expect it's in the high six figures."

"It's like a cynic's antidote to *The Celestine Prophecy*," chimed in Walter Windom. "But I bet it has legs that'll give Redfield a run for his money."

"You're for it?" Franco asked Windom, whom he'd recruited

himself. Walter had been a protégé of Skip Gates's at the Dubois Institute, and often voted as the conscience of the board, together with Roy Raymond. A thin, handsome African American, Walter knew his way around a bookshelf.

"Well, obviously, if we're interested in this, the science will have to be vetted. If it passes muster, I think Dr. Belacqua will sell more books than Dr. Spock. Your call, Franco: do you want to spend ten, twenty grand to have it evaluated?"

"That's definitely the first question," replied Franco.

"If Danvers had checked him out," said Marshall impatiently, "I'll bet we wouldn't be wasting time on him. And even if his credentials are legit, the conclusions are just *too* implausible. He may be cashing in his career for a one-time killing." Marshall didn't seem to have a problem understanding that choice.

Jamie Quinn cleared her throat. "It's obviously important. Couldn't we publish it without standing behind the details? Like fiction?"

"It isn't plausible enough," said Judy dryly. "I reject novels like this every day."

"As a cautionary tale, then: sort of non-nonfiction?" Everyone smiled warmly and no one bothered to respond. Jamie was adored by all, but while her line of children's books was hugely successful, she wasn't the sharpest knife in the drawer.

Michael Pencak raised his head toward Judy. "Why would someone spend a decade on a hoax when he knows it'll be investigated every which way?"

"So?" Franco asked Michael directly. "What do you think?"

"I think it's *On the Beach* for the nineties." His conviction was unabashed. At the scent of an advocate, alertness spread around the table like hot gossip. It was the first time Michael had stepped up to the plate for a manuscript. This short, intense man—"a dime among nickels," he insisted—had been with Commonweal only a few months. "First, this is *not* out of line with mainstream research," he began. "What's actually been done since the 'Warning to Humanity' six years ago? Populist efforts recycled a few soda cans, and that's about it. Last month, in Kyoto, the world agreed to binding limits on greenhouse gases. Now that treaty goes before the Senate Foreign Relations Committee: so, the world proposes and Jesse Helms disposes. Which leaves Clinton hanging out to dry, like Wilson with the League of Nations. Meanwhile we keep on pumping billions of tons of pollutants into the thin atmosphere, and nobody cares, because there's no drama in it. Nuclear war—kaboom!—now *that's* dramatic. Global warming is not. It's like a frog in a pot over a fire—and that fire is population growth. But economically we all depend on growth, so even if the world suddenly wakes up and smells the smog, we can't reduce pollution without devastating people's lives. And as Belacqua says, there's no playing catch-up with Mother Nature: when something's dead, it's gone, whether it's a single cell or an entire species. Even mandatory conservation can't save the oceans by now."

They all felt Michael's adrenaline kick in and watched his eyes bounce off his legal pad: the guy actually had notes. "Forget Belacqua for a minute and look at the facts. We don't need Stanford's general circulation model to see how a phenomenon like El Niño causes agricultural havoc worldwide: we can't even guess where droughts and deluges will destroy the crops. In Texas lots of people think the drought of '98'll be worse than '96. And the flooding in '97—four and a half million acres from the Northwest to the Midwest: *that* could become an annual event, you know. And for all we know, so could El Niño: it's been around for six of the last seven years already. Look at the speed with which oceans are reclaiming the shores since the Larsen Ice Shelf broke off. You saw that report last month in the Science section of the *Times?* Eight feet of beachfront has vanished along the East Coast in fifty years, and the pace is accelerating."

Franco glanced at Judy: at her insistence, she and Joe had recently bought a shorefront home in Amagansett, instead of renting annually. Radiating her confidence that the Hamptons were exempt, Judy turned to Michael. "Explain the 'scenarios.'"

"Well, Belacqua's also proposing a CD-ROM: he has already produced fantastic graphics for his website. He doesn't pretend to know what the *exact* sequence will be as the ecosystem and human society unravel, so he lays out various doomsday scenarios based on different variables which, with the CD-ROM, you program in. For example, with a six-degree rise in temperature, epidemics like Ebola, dengue fever, and malaria may keep the population from tripling *again* in forty years. So you provide the parameters, and your computer plays out the consequences. It's a hot idea."

Marshall was frowning. "Isn't that like making a board game of the Apocalypse?"

"It raises awareness," Michael answered. "Anyway, Belacqua's only saying that environmental degradation has accelerated faster than expected. That isn't news."

Marshall squinted. "So we should publish this because it doesn't say anything new?"

"No," Michael answered, "what *The Belacqua Report* says is new and urgent, but it is based upon facts established by the two thousand scientists of the Intergovernmental Panel on Climate Change. And yes, it's depressing because they are facts. This is scary and real. But we still have to use what powers of intellect we can muster globally to sustain our habitat for as long as we can. Meanwhile maybe we'll colonize Mars." Now he was overreaching, and modulated his tone. "The self-destruction of intelligent life proves it wasn't so intelligent after all. Because whether the crunch comes in forty years or four hundred, we're still not doing a damn thing about it!" Michael had crossed the line from advocate to eco-freak. When he finally noticed the looks he was getting, he sagged like a ballerina on Valium.

Marshall was bursting his seams. "But the time frame is laughable! After millions of years of evolution, the planet is shutting down in forty years?"

Jamie Quinn cleared her throat again. "If we learned that a comet was going to hit the earth next Wednesday, then forty years might seem like a very long time to solve our problems. Anyway," she lowered her eyes, "that's my candied opinion." It sometimes seemed as if Jamie was deliberately mocking them with her innocence.

Franco proceeded around the table to the Grand Old Man of Commonweal. "Roy?"

"I think it's legit," rumbled Roy Raymond, placing the weight of his whole career behind *The Belacqua Report,* and completely altering the dynamics of the meeting.

Although the editorial board was generally apolitical, undertones divided its members into three camps: aging yuppies (Judy, Marshall, Danvers, and Marlene Conrad); traditional liberals (Joe, Jamie, Windom, Michael, Ben Steiner, and Franco); and then there was Roy Raymond, their sacred relic of the vaunted era when publishing was a noble profession. Roy had grown up in Baltimore, and his very first job had been as an office boy for H. L. Mencken. In 1952 he'd been blacklisted for editing Howard Fast. They were so honored to work with Roy that no one ever mentioned his drinking problem. And when on occasion he stood in the hall swaying to and fro and singing old Wobbly songs like "The Triangle Shirt Factory Massacre," they all did their sorry best to join in, out of respect. Even now his breath smelled of bourbon and toothpaste.

"As Michael said, this report comes after *thousands* of studies of greenhouse gases. The only news here is the timetable." Fingering a strand of his unruly white hair, Roy looked squarely at each editor in turn. They were so damn young, he thought; more likely to have M.B.A.s than M.A.s in Lit. "Of *course* we should publish it," he boomed. "It's the righteous thing to do! Otherwise every other publisher is justified in rejecting it for the same reasons, and that amounts to censorship." Roy squinted at his young boss. *"You* have to agree, Franco, our First Amendment scholar. If this is valid science, the government will try to suppress it, sure as God made green apples."

"I agree, in part." Franco knew that sounded indecisive; he'd been wrestling with the issues for days. "But that's no reason for publishing any book. Look, I ask the same three questions about every manuscript: Does it shed new light on some aspect of human experience? Does it merit Commonweal's imprimatur? And is it a sensible investment in the long or short term? Without a scientific evaluation, I can't answer any of them. I read it through twice, and my gut tells me this is the real McCoy."

"It convinced me," chirped Marlene Conrad, who rarely disagreed with authority figures. Marlene edited self-help books, which, to judge from the histrionics of her personal life, hadn't been very much help.

Franco went on, "I'd like a scientific evaluation: then we can reconsider."

At that moment the door opened and Terry appeared, wearing her most conservative blue-gray tweed and a nervous smile. Behind her stood a solemn figure in uniform.

"Could you wait here?" she said over her shoulder. The officer nodded as Terry stepped into the room, looking anxiously at Franco: arriving late was just not done—especially by an assistant.

Damn, she thought, Danvers isn't here yet; he was supposed to warm them up. "Good morning, everyone. Um, Danvers should be here any second. General Shreiver is just outside: he's the Air Force intelligence officer who submitted *The Belacqua Report* on Dr. Belacqua's behalf." Terry stifled her nerves. "I know it would be highly unusual to invite an outsider to—"

"Ask the general in, Terry," interrupted Franco. She beckoned to the commanding figure. Franco rose to shake his hand and offer a chair, while Terry took a seat nearby.

Tall, but quite gaunt, General Shreiver was in his sixties, with snow-white hair and a trim mustache. Anyone familiar with medals could track a distinguished career across his chest. His manner was uncommonly emotional for a military figure.

"General Shreiver," said Franco, "we're anxious to know if the report is valid."

The general looked around the table slowly at his rapt audience: ordinarily these New York sophisticates would have feigned nonchalance. "Dr. Belacqua's report," answered General Shreiver slowly, "is entirely legitimate. His conclusions, I'm afraid, are irrefutable."

Terry, her scheming vindicated, leaned back. The room was silent.

Marshall sat forward: now his disbelief would have to cede, or harden into denial. "So, General, the human race is doomed to mass extinction in the next fifty years?"

"Along with most life forms." His tone left no doubt: this was a *fait accompli.*

"What can you tell us about Dr. Belacqua?" asked Franco.

"I met Roger a couple years ago, after NASA adopted his proposal for a special camera on Daedalus to examine the 'eggshell effect' in the ionosphere."

Ben Steiner spoke for the first time. "So the administration is aware of all this?" Ben—a childhood survivor of Auschwitz—was Commonweal's political editor. His next book was a devastating biography of Ariel Sharon. Today he was carrying water for an insider's look at the Supreme Court, written by a current clerk.

The general nodded. "Gore took Roger in to brief Clinton over a year ago." With that, Marshall's opposition wilted.

"How did the President react?"

General Shreiver pursed his lips. "I hear he's brought up *The Belacqua Report* in several cabinet meetings. But the administration doesn't seem to care: the spit won't hit the fan on their watch. Many scientists agree with Roger's work."

Just then Danvers entered, waving to the table with insouciance. "Sorry, everyone, I had— General Shreiver? *I'm* Danvers Creal." He reached to shake hands. Late as he was, the expressions around the table suggested Danvers was man of the hour for inviting the general. He adopted his Robert Frost pose as he took his seat. "Please go on."

Joe Mercer piped up as Judy glared at him. "You mean the U.S. is doing nothing?"

"Not yet. But neither have they moved to suppress or refute Belacqua's conclusions, to my knowledge. They monitor his work, and provide him with satellite data and other classified information. Maybe that counts as good news."

"Do many people in government know about *The Belacqua Report?*" Franco asked.

"A dozen. Roger's also shown it to about twenty other scientists. Have you spoken with him?"

"No," Franco replied. "I'll call him today. General, why did Dr. Belacqua ask you to send the manuscript to Commonweal? Has he offered it to other houses as well?"

"Absolutely not. He has kept his work completely under wraps. The oil and coal industries are doing all they can to discredit information like this—especially since the Kyoto conference last month. Discretion is crucial. I came here today to emphasize that point. Last month Roger asked me to call Mr. Creal to present his work, so you'd know he's not just some kook." Judy hid behind her legal pad. As the general rose to his feet, his voice turned gruff. "That's all I came for," he concluded abruptly. "I'd rather you address your questions to Dr. Belacqua personally."

Rising to leave, General Shreiver shook Franco's hand, and Danvers's, before addressing the room with a candor that belied his authoritative mien. "I should warn you, this book's enough to drive you right off the deep end. I've been a soldier most of my life: down-to-earth, practical-minded. But emotionally, this book hit me like a ton of bricks: denial, anger, guilt, despair." The general lowered his eyes. "It may even produce a surge in an individual's sex drive." He cleared his throat. "Anyway, knowing what fate has in store makes day-to-day living seem so futile: for us, our children, and our grandchildren. If we have any grandchildren." He started toward the door. "I must advise you again to keep this secret. There are several unscrupulous organizations that want to keep this research from ever seeing the light of day, even inside the government. Good day." The general left, escorted by Danvers.

Terry watched the editors as they reassessed the situation, and wondered about the sex-drive thing. Was that why she—

Joe aimed a smug grin at his wife. "Just some kook, eh?"

Judy rose abruptly. "Excuse me, I'm having an attack of marital thrombosis."

"What's that?" asked Ben Steiner, alarmed.

"It means I'm married to a clot!" She left, passing Danvers as he returned. She would have to wait to unveil her well-documented exposé by a Washington dominatrix whose clients included a former majority whip.

Franco slipped the general's business card into his pocket and looked up. "It seems so unreal, doesn't it?" he said quietly. He turned to Danvers. "What kind of advance does Belacqua want?"

Danvers shook his head. "There was no cover letter, just a phone number. Terry?"

Franco took her note. "You know, apart from titles for Historical Perspective, I don't meddle with the editing business. But I think this time—*if* we publish it—I'll oversee the process personally, with help from all of you. Given the possible security issues, and the emphasis that the general placed upon confidentiality just now, I think it's better if I take full responsibility for this project."

The table erupted noisily: "We can't publish a . . ." "Bravo, Franco!" "This is ridiculous!" ". . . biggest damn book since the Bible."

"I'm glad you all feel so strongly," he said, cutting them off. "I'm going to hire specialists to evaluate it for us." He glanced at Terry, who was on the edge of her seat, smiling warmly at him. "God knows what Macro will make of it if we sign it." He paused. "Or how the world will react. I've thought about that. Even how I'd tell my kids about it." His voice trailed off; then he returned to business. "Ben, find out what the administration thinks. Not just public posture: I want to know if alarms have gone off in the executive, or at Interior, or State, maybe the NSC." Ben nodded. "Marlene, we need a psychologist or sociologist to predict public reaction to the book. Are people going to jump off buildings? Will the market crash? Someone who can keep quiet."

"How about Jonathan Fischer?" she said.

"Perfect! Bring him in when he's read it. We'll discuss his new book as well."

Martin turned coat. "Shall I see if we'd have any legal exposure? It's arguable that publishing this book is like shouting 'Fire!' in a crowded auditorium—the First Amendment doesn't protect that. If Belacqua's wrong, we could end up like RKO after the Orson Welles broadcast."

"Ask Kaplan if we need a disclaimer," said Franco. "And discuss possible suits from industries Belacqua fingers as culprits: he doesn't name corporations, but even nuisance suits could be gargantuan."

He stood and walked to the corner window that faced south. "I hope you've all been discreet about this?" Everyone nodded as he tapped his pencil a few more times. "Okay, I'll meet with Belacqua as soon as possible. If he wants more than a million, I'll take it up with Bob Milton: he may well worry about the impact on Macro's stock when a subsidiary forecasts the end of life."

"Are they that small-minded?" Michael was appalled. No one bothered to reply. Milton was a cutthroat industrialist, and they all knew it. He had never wanted to own a publishing house: it came with the canned goods business.

"I'd be grateful," Franco continued, "if you'd all take a look at the existing literature on global warming, biodiversity, and the like. Terry, would you compile a list and assign reading to everyone here?" Hushed groans. "Roy, I'd like you to chair the search for three scientists to evaluate Belacqua: experts who aren't likely to agree with him. They also have to be discreet, or someone will bootleg Belacqua's ideas before they're in print. After their evaluation, we'll vote. Please, *do not make copies*. Now, any other business?"

Danvers sat up. "We have to decide if we want that steamy exposé of Goldie Hawn." Franco stared at him for a second before cracking up. Everyone else tittered until the giggles turned to belly laughs. Danvers never got an answer.

"If I call an urgent meeting, please show up," Franco added. "And please, discretion! Clearly, there are people who don't want this book to be published."

With a friendly glance around the table, Franco strode from the room. Terry, her eyes ashine, lingered to overhear the editors' exchanges. Marshall and Walter were surprised General Shreiver had been invited in—Danvers took credit for that—while Joe Mercer and Ben Steiner speculated on the political fallout. When Marshall's gofer, Sebastian, started flirting with her, she left. In the hall she overheard Roy Raymond counseling Joe Mercer, "Don't let her go, Joe. Believe me. For years I've been going to bed alone, waking up alone—"

Joe angrily cut him short. "All that means, Roy, is, *you* don't have to go to the bathroom to jerk off."

Recoiling from that *haiku* by the poetry editor, Terry raced back to her office at max warp, savoring her success, dimmed only by the memory of what it had taken to change Danvers's mind about the manuscript. Then she picked up *Football and Freud.*

In his spacious office Franco Sherman stared at the array of Post-its stuck across the surface of his elegant desk—evidence, he thought, of his personal entropy. Chores, contracts to peruse, invitations to decline—by mid-January his lunch dates were booked through April, and dinnertime always belonged to the kids. For a moment he allowed the shroud of grief he'd lived with since his wife died to settle over him like a familiar comforter.

He was sorry he had no morning appointments; he'd have preferred to think about something other than Belacqua. He half wished they'd never received this manuscript; but that was a cop-out. He'd felt the same angst when they'd published the diary of the midget serial killer Tiny Messingkauf, who had never been apprehended. That was when Franco had started keeping a .38 locked in the drawer beside the bed.

He dialed Belacqua's number: the area code, 802, was unfamiliar. After two rings the phone was answered by a woman with a faint accent who transferred the call.

"This is Roger Belacqua." He sounded sixty, possibly older.

"Dr. Belacqua, this is Franco Sherman at Commonweal Books.

Pleased to speak with you. We've read your manuscript, and our editors met with General Shreiver."

"Did you? Very good, then."

"I'd like to meet with you, at your convenience. Can you come to New York?"

"I have to be there this week. Are you free for dinner on Thursday, just the two of us?" It was as if Belacqua had expected his call.

"That would be fine, Doctor. How about the '21' Club?"

"Of course. At seven? And, Mr. Sherman, let's keep our meeting secret for now. Not to be melodramatic," Belacqua tried to sound offhand, "but there are reasons."

"We're all treating this project with discretion. See you Thursday, then."

"Fine. Good-bye." Franco hung up.

For a time he sifted through the contracts on his desk, but his attention wandered. As General Shreiver had warned, the apocalyptic *Report* reverberated through the minutiae of his day. He didn't know what to believe. It was like grappling in the dark with some huge, undiscovered creature: either a harmless illusion, like a dragon at Chinese New Year, or a monstrous beast poised to destroy everything irreplaceable. He *had* to know which. He wrestled with his conscience for a moment before looking up Connors's private number in Washington. In 1996, at the request of FBI officials, Franco had postponed a book's publication solely because of John Connors's assertion that it would scuttle an ongoing investigation.

Connors answered the phone himself.

"It's Franco Sherman here. How are you?"

"Okay, Franco. What can we do for you?"

"Listen, I hate to ask for a favor, but since you offered—"

"Try me."

"I need deep background on a scientist named Dr. Roger Belacqua. Heard of him?"

"No, but I'll check. B-E-L-A-"

"-C-Q-U-A. Roger Belacqua. Works on environmental issues, mostly, and is well respected. Was a NASA consultant on Daedalus. That's all I know."

"I'll see what we've got. If we have his profile, I'll fax it to you."

"No. If you find anything, leave me a message and put it in the mail."

Connors paused. "Want to tell me what this is about?"

"We're deciding whether or not to publish a book he's written."

"Something hot?" There was a raunchy curiosity to Connors's tone. "Probably isn't a best-seller without a lot of sex, eh?"

Franco resented the notion that it took one-handed readers to make a best-seller. That was less than half the truth. "I'd like your help, Connors."

"Don't worry, I'll take care of this myself. Bye."

"Thanks." Franco hung up, feeling somehow diminished. He wasn't kidding himself: Connors would give him what they wanted him to have.

Franco buzzed Millie. "I'll be out for the rest of the day," he told her. "I want to go over *The Belacqua Report* at home." With that, he picked up his briefcase with one hand and the manuscript with the other and walked out the door.

Terry noticed Danvers was cranky as soon as he returned to the office.

"Get me John Lom," he said bluntly. Terry looked askance. "The agent with the Goldie Hawn book. Damn, he also sent over the poison-as thriller. Did you look through it?"

Terry nodded. "It reads like any old episode of *Mannix.*"

As Danvers loped past, he saw her ashtray full of butts. "Didn't you stop smoking?"

Terry smiled sweetly at her boss. "Fuck it," she replied.

Danvers grunted. "How about that resolution to clean up your language?"

"Fuck it." She changed the subject. "You did good at the meeting. Thanks."

"I think Franco's interested," agreed Danvers. "You were brilliant, Terry."

Nice compliment, Danvers, she thought: one in a row.

Marshall called Sebastian into his office and dictated a memo, giving Franco an overview of Commonweal's potential exposure if they published Belacqua. Then, when he was alone, he pulled a little brown bottle from his fob pocket and poured a tiny hit between his thumb and first finger. He snorted it. Mmm. Like a martini, the blend of a speedball has to be *just* right. He poured another hit and snorted it up the same nostril: his left side had been blocked since Labor Day. Both hits were too small, so he took a third, and that made his eyes well up. Yeah.

He tried Lee Kaplan, who was in a meeting; Marshall hung up, cursing silently. Looking for something to do, he realized he'd left his Hermès agenda at home. So he swiveled toward the window and watched the construction crew on the building across Fifty-fourth Street, marveling at all the work they'd done. Then he took another hit.

Franco got home at six and helped Juliette with algebra. Emily had made spaghetti again: it was all she could cook, but she was such a good housekeeper that he never complained. After dinner, while Juliette finished her homework and Max replayed Kasparov/Karpov Game Eight for maybe the twentieth time, Franco reviewed the copy for the fall catalog: Laura Goldman, *Football and Freud,* a new self-help book from Jonathan Fischer . . . his concentration leached into the void.

How much longer could he go on like this, aloof from life? When Lillian died, he had learned how quickly spring could turn to winter. Surely he'd thaw out again someday. But they say Lazarus never smelled the same again. Maybe he should just . . . go out and get laid. He even considered calling Angela; she had volunteered at two ABA conventions in a row. Then he thought about the waif at the newsstand. Was it, he wondered, the decadent eye shadow that made her so appealing, or just the copy of *Harper's?*

At nine the kids went to bed and Franco stared blankly at the network première of *Birdcage,* remembering the night he and Lillian had seen it at the Coronet; afterward they had eaten sushi and discussed the house they'd looked at near Wilton. Turning off the TV, he mourned quietly for ten minutes, his evening quota, before retiring to the bedroom, leaving his door ajar. There, exhausted, he rolled under the covers.

He awoke sometime later, his sheets wet with chilled sweat. He could just make out the glowing digits: 4:21. The hall floorboards creaked. Probably Juliette coming to— No, the door to the den. Click. Max, using the computer? But he has his own now, with modem. Then Franco saw the beam of a flashlight sweep across the corridor wall. That wasn't one of the kids.

Ping. Every nerve in his spine stood alert, but he stopped his adrenaline from racing off with his judgment. He rose quietly, developing a strategy: if he was quick, he'd trap the intruder in the corridor. He slipped into his robe and had started toward the door before he remembered the handgun. The burglar would be near the kids' rooms, so Franco retrieved the key taped under his nightstand and opened the locked drawer. As he fumbled for bullets on his closet shelf, the beam of light approached his door. He grabbed three bullets and slipped one into the chamber with a loud metallic click. He raced to the door and snapped on the hall light.

The intruder, framed in the doorway of the den, dropped his flashlight. His hat brim was pulled down over dark, heavy-lidded eyes of Mediterranean or perhaps Middle Eastern aspect. The lower half of his face was hidden by the velvet collar of his chesterfield. One gloved hand carried the green manuscript box, and a small silver revolver protruded from the other.

"Drop that," Franco said softly. The man shook his head and cocked the revolver.

Franco lowered his weapon. Unless the kids rushed out of their rooms, they'd be safe; and he wasn't about to risk his life over a robbery.

The intruder picked up the flashlight slowly and took a step sideways toward the kitchen, then another, still aiming at Franco's chest. Two more steps and he was through the swing door. Franco heard the click of the service entrance, but waited before following. Through the little window in the swing door he saw the kitchen was empty, and he ran straight through to the back hall, but the service elevator was already gone.

Franco grabbed the house phone and buzzed Sean, but the doorman didn't answer. He set down the gun and dialed 911 on the kitchen phone. Then he noticed the key on the kitchen table, the one Emily left under the service-door mat on Monday nights for Eddie the cleaner. He hung up and ran to check the kids. Then he went to see what had been stolen. One of the carved French spheres lay on the carpet, but nothing was missing. Three manuscript boxes had been opened, and his computer disks had been rifled.

He again buzzed Sean, who answered this time: he hadn't seen anyone since midnight, but then Franco knew he usually fell asleep in the lobby.

He dialed 911 again, but changed his mind and set the phone down. He just couldn't bear for the kids to wake up to a big scary scene with the police. It would keep them awake for nights to come; Juliette had an especially low anxiety threshold. Nothing but the Belacqua manuscript had been stolen, as far as he could see, and he knew the cops couldn't catch the intruder. What would he tell them, anyway? That the guy wore a chesterfield and a Borsalino? That he smelled like licorice? Franco was embarrassed that they'd left the key right there under the mat. But mostly he was relieved that the intruder wasn't the serial killer Tiny Messingkauf, who had written in the diary Commonweal had published that he used a box-cutting knife "for the pleasure of the thing." Franco would have recognized him: he was four feet tall.

By dawn Franco was asleep on the sofa, and in the morning the ephemeral incident had paled beside his vivid nightmares. A new security system was installed, and Sean was reprimanded for sleeping on the job. Franco said nothing to Emily. Since he had no one with whom to discuss the intruder, the break-in was soon buried under the landslide of daily events, compost for future nightmares.

3

ROGER BELACQUA

> So important are insects and other land-dwelling arthropods that if all were to disappear, humanity probably could not last more than a few months. Most of the amphibians, reptiles, birds and mammals would crash to extinction about the same time. Next would go the bulk of flowering plants and with them the physical structure of most forests and other terrestrial habitats of the world. The land surface would literally rot.
>
> —Edward O. Wilson, *Biodiversity* (1989)

On Thursday evening Franco watched Peter Jennings from an armchair in the "21" Club lounge. Despite protests in the UN, Armenia was putting a damaged nuclear reactor back into service. Negotiations with Syria had broken down. The European Community was on the verge of abandoning the euro, while France was in political turmoil over a new wave of immigrants from North Africa. The latest flooding in Bangladesh had left millions homeless. The UN Population Fund announced new figures confirming that, globally, food supplies were falling behind population growth, The newscaster noted that as of 1998, "the number of human beings alive on the planet has officially reached six billion—three times the population in 1950. And the rate of growth continues to accelerate: we now add a billion more people to the earth each decade." It was as if Peter Jennings were reading from Belacqua's manuscript. In the Southwest, meteorologists were predicting more flooding even as fistfights had erupted in the Nevada state senate over a water diversion project favoring Las Vegas casinos over cattle ranches. Finally, on the American Agenda: the growing movement in favor of a national convention to revise the U.S. Constitution. Its supporters included many who wanted a balanced budget amendment, others who sought a federal law prohibiting abortion, and some who intended to redefine the right to bear arms, one way or the other. Franco was amazed: his Historical Perspective imprint had just reissued a book on the subject of a new Constitutional Convention by Professor Richard Wylie, his old mentor at Columbia, whom he revered and still visited from time to time.

After the news, Franco glanced at the door, wondering if he'd recognize Belacqua from the voice on the phone. He was more confident of his ability to gauge whether or not Belacqua believed his own report. The scientists whom Commonweal was commissioning, a panel of three, would determine if Belacqua was accurate, but Franco had to decide if he was convincing. At ten past seven, as Franco began wondering if he should order another Campari, Walter, longtime maître d' of "21," came to report that a gentleman was waiting for him at a table: apparently they had both made reservations. Franco followed into the crowded dining room, where a slim gentleman with white hair and an amused expression rose to greet him.

"Mr. Sherman, welcome! Sit down, won't you? Prefer to face the room?"

"Hello, Doctor. No, this is fine." Belacqua was older than he'd guessed. But the first thing Franco remarked was his startling resemblance to Jacques Cousteau; then, the unreserved merriness of the fellow. Franco had expected something different from the herald of doomsday: a measure of solemnity perhaps, or the urgent intensity of the crazed street prophet who shouts, "The end is nigh!" Instead he was greeted by a handsome, lighthearted, and urbane older gentleman with a twinkle in his eye so permanent it seemed like a surgical implant, poised over a body too small for his gaunt skull. Belacqua was possessed of a debonair humor and old-school charm, and a hint of rakishness in the length of white hair swept over the slight stoop in his shoulders. His hands, Franco noticed, had an excitability all their own, as if powered by a different source. Franco was quite taken with Belacqua. The scientist called to mind some long-forgotten verse: "They will come no more, the old men with beautiful manners."

"I ate here regularly in the fifties," Belacqua began. "Bill Paley and Walter Cronkite often had lunch at that table."

"Unusual hangout for a young scientist," Franco observed.

"I'd already been very lucky. My first patent was awarded in the fall of '56—a new polymer for filaments. That same day I came here for lunch. So I was delighted that you chose to meet here." Belacqua's twinkling eyes focused with pleasure on that distant time. "The fifties were wonderful for scientists, you know." He puffed out his chest. "We were the pioneers of Tomorrowland, gladiators of the Sputnik era. *We* had crushed Japan with our atomic savvy, and *we* would put men on the moon—real, John Wayne men." Leaning forward, he confided in a mock whisper: "Best of all, no one dreamed our work could ever have undesirable consequences or noxious aftereffects. Tanker trucks cruised the suburbs spraying tons of DDT across whole neighborhoods, and kids played hopscotch in the puddles after they passed. Shoe stores had X-ray machines you could stick your feet in, to watch your bones move: boys and girls spent hours pressing their little groins up against those X-ray emitters, wiggling their toes. Obviously, if it were harmful, scientists wouldn't produce it and government wouldn't allow it! Oh yes, that was a glorious era for scientists. We had a grand old time."

Quick out of the gate, thought Franco.

"Anyway, my polymers were snapped up by a chemicals giant, so I ended up eating here quite often. Ever since, industrial work has freed me financially to conduct environmental research without intrusion." He sipped his wine. "I didn't intend to offer my résumé, but since I have, may I ask how you came to be where you are now?"

Franco looked around the room. "I grew up here in New York, an only child, and a bookworm. When I was fourteen my parents moved to Paris, and I was sent to the International School in Geneva, Switzerland. They divorced just as I started at Columbia, where I completed my Ph.D. and lectured for a couple of years." Franco was bored with his own story. "By the eighties we had kids, so to make some money I produced a CD-ROM from a database I'd worked up for American Studies. That led to the job at Commonweal."

"We've both been lucky, then," said Belacqua gently. "Shrewd, too. I keep my gratitude alive, along with my sense of wonder." A waiter hovered nearby. Belacqua chose the *salade niçoise* and Franco the filet of sole.

"So," Belacqua asked coolly, "you'd like to publish *The Belacqua Report?*"

"In principle, yes," Franco replied, "but a number of important questions have to be resolved first."

Belacqua ordered from the *sommelier,* and then said, "Ask your questions."

"Your book is well written and very convincing. I had the curious feeling you were reading my mind: each time I doubted an assertion, you took up my objections in the very next paragraph. Now, your arguments are both scientific and geopolitical. With the first, I'm at a decided disadvantage. We'd need scientific corroboration—"

Belacqua broke in. "Let me make this easy. I'll open my lab to any scientists you choose, to examine the data and interview my assistants. If you're still uncomfortable, you can print a disclaimer in the book. Does that address all your qualms?"

Franco looked surprised. "Actually, yes." Those were exactly the conditions he required. The wine steward arrived with the wine, and Franco noted its unusual bottle.

"Saran. It's the wine produced by Dom Pérignon in limited quantities," explained Belacqua. "Same grape, same bottle. I find it . . . quietly celebratory." The *sommelier* filled their glasses. "Excuse me," he added, "I'm famished."

He tucked into his salad with unqualified zest, and spoke between mouthfuls. "Let's proceed, then, as if my scientific conclusions have been confirmed."

"How would you sum up those conclusions?"

"Damage to our ecosystem has passed the point of no return, and we cannot reverse the degeneration. Even under some 'enlightened' global tyranny—which is a delusion, at best—ninety percent of earth's species will be extinct in about forty years, including *Homo sapiens.* Beyond that, scientific analysis must give way to geopolitical evaluation."

"And those arguments must also be thoroughly examined."

"I welcome an editor's hand. Christiane, my wife, has been a great help. Tell me—may I call you Franco?—as an historian, do you find my conclusions compelling?"

"Which conclusion, exactly?"

"That the nations of the world cannot amass the unity of purpose necessary to alter our fate. Sacrifice and cooperation might postpone the outcome a few decades."

Franco raised an eyebrow. "Some readers may find it a tad presumptuous of you to predict the actions of billions of people over the next forty years."

"Takes gall, doesn't it?" He was smiling. "Do you have any idea how many people have lived since hominids built the first campfire, a million years ago?" Franco shook his head. "The figure generally accepted is ninety billion, over about ten thousand generations. So about ten percent of all the humans who *ever* lived have been alive *during my lifetime*. What would the world be like if the same were true of, say, tigers? Or mosquitoes? Or rats?" Belacqua returned to Franco's point.

"Our fate will not be decided by six billion individuals, but by a few governments whose political legitimacy ranges from democracy to thuggery. And that's only one problem."

Franco wanted to hear a sound bite. "Explain your argument for the layman."

Belacqua's spine straightened and he spoke as if to an interviewer. "Despite the technological triumphs, the human species doesn't have the maturity or the commonality of spirit to control its own growth." Every sentence emerged fully formed, as if poised on his lip. "We'd need complex multilateral agreements to enforce draconian laws whereby leaders would effectively determine which of its citizens would live, and which would die for the sake of the next generation. And it's *still* too late. Besides, we have no model for global government. Not even the scaffolding."

"What about the UN?" The International School of Geneva, where Franco had graduated, had been created at the inception of the UN's predecessor, the League of Nations, in 1924.

Belacqua pursed his lips. "Ah yes, the UN. A noble idea in a not-so-noble century. It was inspiring, last summer, to see Clinton, Blair, and Chirac discussing global climate change before the General Assembly. And we shall see if last month's Kyoto Protocol is ever really implemented. But look at the disrespect each of the superpowers has shown the UN at one time or another! And how shamelessly Congress uses the power of the purse to try to control it. No, a new organization would be necessary, one unencumbered by historical baggage, yet powerful enough to take on world governments—and the energy industries."

"What about the scientific naysayers, who insist that global warming is a myth, or that it is caused by sunspots, not greenhouse gases?"

"Solar activity may indeed make the earth even warmer; I say so in the report. But only the shills for oil and coal say greenhouse gases are no problem, and they don't subject their research to peer review. To learn how the 'greenhouse skeptics' are funded—Balling, Michaels, Lindzen, Singer, all those clowns—you should read Ross Gelbspan's book, *The Heat Is On*. But even if fossil fuels were outlawed tomorrow, it wouldn't save us. It might postpone the collapse of social organization, or it might wreak enough economic havoc to hasten it on. Profound changes in our national priorities cannot be achieved hastily—not even by constitutional amendment. Just look at the fate of the ERA, which only aimed to guarantee women the same opportunities as men—and it *failed*. How, then, could laws be passed to reduce the use of fuels? Americans won't accept a government designed to *limit* life, liberty, and the pursuit of happiness."

Franco listened, realizing for the first time how threatening Belacqua's implications would be to existing governments, along with nationalist-minded citizens everywhere. As if reading his mind, Belacqua added, "I've already received personal threats from a group calling themselves the Concord Militia. One in particular was rather graphic."

With another sip of wine, Belacqua, his zeal refreshed, jumped back into his recital. "Understand, I'm not indicting free enterprise. A handful of greedy men could have adapted to solar power sooner, but it wouldn't have changed the outcome much. Which country would shell out trillions extra for cleaner energy if other nations were unwilling or unable to do the same?" Franco shrugged. "Will democracies respect the binding treaties they sign, like the Kyoto agreements? We shall see."

Belacqua emptied his glass. "Suppose all the nations created a global executive, chosen by majority rule. Who would object to that? The answer is: Americans would—they'd object like hell! To start with, the U.S. has just four percent of the world's population, but generates almost twenty-five percent of man-made greenhouse gases. And 'democracy' at the global level would mean that the most overpopulated nations could govern the most advanced nations. If China, India, and Indonesia voted in a bloc, *they* could determine which cars Detroit should produce, or how many residents of Los Angeles could drive to work. They might dictate food distribution, water allocation, and so on. Oh yes, we love the idea of government by the people, unless it puts us in a minority. But sooner or later, ardent nationalists around the world are going to have to recognize a simple nautical truth: you can't sink just one end of a ship."

"What about government by nations with the largest gross domestic product?"

"A global aristocracy?" Belacqua frowned. "The wealthy ruling the poor? Shame!"

Franco wrestled with another idea. "What if nations delegated authority to a panel of disinterested scientists? Like yourself," he added pointedly.

Belacqua grinned mischievously. "Now you're talking! An enlightened oligarchy: a permanent international Council of Geniuses. But who selects this council? Who guarantees that the geniuses don't just protect their own interests? And what happens when these Wise Ones are toppled by mobs, enraged at harsh new restrictions?"

Listening, Franco tried to understand what Belacqua *felt* about his own argument; he sensed in the scientist a wound so old he was inured to further grief, much like himself. But when Belacqua showed enthusiasm for his work, the effect was ghoulish.

Belacqua sat back. "Care to come to my hotel for a nightcap?" Then he beat Franco to the bill; for an author dining with an editor, this was a novelty.

"My apartment's just three blocks," said Franco. Later he realized that, apart from dinner parties, he'd never had an author to his home. But as they departed, a little unsteadily, his relationship with Belacqua already seemed more than professional.

At the penthouse Belacqua admired the décor—Lillian's work—as they settled on the sofas in front of the chimney, and Franco poured snifters of Calvados.

"I understand your wife died in an accident," Belacqua said. Franco returned a slight nod, wondering how he'd heard. "Few people can understand the effect of such loss."

"And you can?" asked Franco.

"Ten years ago," he half-whispered, "my son and daughter died in the crash of a private plane." He knocked back the snifter and reached for the bottle. "By then Christiane and I couldn't have another child." His face was reshaped by melancholy.

"I'm sorry," said Franco.

"It was especially . . . You see, I was the pilot." He affected a wan smile.

Franco wondered if his loss had made the prospect of extinction more acceptable. "How does it feel," he asked slowly, "to be so certain about our fate?"

Belacqua had to reflect. "Much like the loss of my children," he said. "At first I went through shock, denial, anger, and grief. Now it's just a dull ache."

"I have a boy and a girl," Franco said softly. "When Lillian died, my grief for them was even greater than my personal loss. Reading your manuscript only adds to the sorrow."

Belacqua smiled. "So you believe what you've read?"

"I suppose so," Franco sighed. "I saw a Johns Hopkins report saying that the maximum 'carrying capacity' of the earth—eight billion—will be reached within twenty-five years. I can extrapolate from that. The best world I can imagine forty years from now would be a crowded, polluted hell. The picture is quite vivid."

"If you're like me, that's especially true at night," the older man murmured.

Surprised, Franco agreed sadly. "Nighttime used to be my friend."

"Me too. After all this research, it's worse. You wouldn't *believe* the visions . . ."

Franco raised his chin. As Belacqua's eyes grew bleary, he looked less like Jacques Cousteau at St. Tropez and more like Ezra Pound at St. Elizabeths. "Even if your work is corroborated, I'm not ready to write off the problem-solving talents of humanity quite yet. Like most people, I expect, I'll keep on believing a solution is possible to the bitter end, even as I struggle to find some ray of light in my life. I have only my children and their future; that makes your conclusions seem so personal." He thought a moment. "It's almost subversive how your book forces us to reinterpret our metaphysics. Has this always been our destiny? From Mesopotamia to the Empire State Building—is *this* where we were headed all along?" Franco pressed on, his emotions fueled by Calvados, which also made his tongue too thick to curl around every syllable. "Plato's *Republic,* Angkor Wat, the Sistine Chapel, and all the plays of Shakespeare— all this was just . . . written in the sand? It seems absurd that civilization evolved only to choke on its own exhaust. Even the cynics I know believe some underlying logic produced the human spirit, without which we would live, copulate, and die like animals."

"Like the animals we always were. Now the world must face it all."

"Was this *inevitable?*" asked Franco.

"Not at all! As late as the sixties we could have reversed the situation, based only on what we knew then. Remember *The Limits to Growth?* Schumacher's *Small Is Beautiful?* We had the means to find solutions, but culturally we were not equipped to face the music. We lacked the leadership, the political will, and most of all the imagination." Franco had expected "wisdom." Belacqua's voice warmed with the embers of what must once have been a mighty anger. "Had we looked up from our petty passions, we would have seen the looming tidal wave. But it would have taken great imagination to reverse the catastrophe."

Franco clung to his tattered optimism. "Couldn't Mother Nature still intervene?"

Belacqua shook his head. "Nature is utterly indifferent to the fate of her creations: her only job is to try every possible variation on the theme of life, every configuration, from twig-shaped insects to marsupial pouches. But whether or not a given species succeeds or fails is of no concern whatsoever to her, be it the dinosaur, the passenger pigeon, or the human. Our predicament is unique only because intellect allows us to know our fate. Had we used our intelligence to govern reproduction, things might be different. However—and this is hardly an original observation—the intellect of most humans is subservient to the sexual drive that Sophocles described as 'a mad and savage master.' "

They contemplated that truth drunkenly. Then Belacqua chuckled. "New life forms will evolve in the millennia after our demise.

They will probably use our empty concrete shells the way marine life uses sunken ships."

"Your book ends with scenarios for the termination of life. Which is most likely?"

"Truthfully? Those are wild guesses. There are just too many variables." Belacqua replied. "But Christiane says they're perfect for the CD-ROM. This is no single series of events, but separate processes of decay that accelerate each other. That said, some facts are certain, though hard to imagine: catastrophic theories like H. G. Wells's or Velikovsky's seem quaint in light of Darwin's gradualism. We're used to steady-state models of nature—until suddenly a flood kills thousands or an earthquake rearranges California."

"So, the end of history will come suddenly."

"Yes and no. First, economies will be frittered away by relentless catastrophes: hurricanes, droughts, disease. That's the reason insurance companies support emissions reductions. Continuous disasters will produce negative GDPs in some nations, devastating the shakier economies; others may actually benefit from climate change in the short term. In this country, like most, immigration will be cut off abruptly. And civil liberties will be among the very first victims of an ecological emergency." His words had the numbing banality of Eichmann's quotas; he was so damned offhand about it. "As the climate becomes more unstable, the key policy issue will be food production: fishing rights and the like. Epidemics will run rampant with the kind of warming we'll see by 2010: without killing frosts in winter, disease-carrying vermin and insects will thrive." His voice grew softer. "After years of crop failures, global ZPG will be achieved the hard way, not by diminishing numbers of births but by increasing numbers of deaths. Social turmoil will necessitate force to maintain critical industries like public transport. Travel will be limited by the threat of contagious diseases, even after masks have become mandatory in public.

"As society slides into chaos, martial law will be critical. Forced to choose between human rights and human survival, governments will do what they have to do. And as population dwindles, taxation will virtually enslave citizens. Then, after the oceans turn deadly with rot, the atmosphere will snap into a peak temperature regime in a last accelerated phase of decay, until finally, one day, the earth will fall silent." His inexorable logic was chilling.

Franco quickly changed the subject. "Are you still a pilot?"

"Certainly. I flew down from Vermont this morning. I have a twin-engine Baron, mainly for research trips. If you want to bring scientists to see my work, I can fly you up."

"Roger, why did you bring your manuscript to Commonweal?"

"My wife oversees our computer activities—the graphics and website, and she heard about your background with CD-ROMs. So, last month, right after the Kyoto Conference fizzled, we asked General Shreiver to approach Commonweal."

Franco had almost forgotten another important question. 'How much of an advance do you want? Or will you leave that to your agent?"

Belacqua laughed. "I don't have an agent. Seven hundred fifty thousand will do, plus half a million in development money for the multimedia version of the scenarios—with a little additional production, that can be released as an interactive CD-ROM."

It was about as big a financial commitment as Franco could authorize without consulting Macro. He nodded slowly. "If your science checks out, that should be no problem."

"There are some stipulations: guarantees for the advertising budget, and approval over promotion. I don't want to hear some stupid jingle about the end of the world."

"Don't worry. The tabloids will supply the cheap shots for free."

Belacqua turned somber. "Expect some hostile reactions. Many will say I'm out for a buck, others that my agenda is fascist or Marxian. But I have no use for wealth, nor heirs to leave it to. And I'm not interested in world domination. I'm no John Galt."

"Is that a literary allusion?" asked Franco.

"Hardly. It's from Ayn Rand." They shared a chuckle about that; then, when Franco yawned, Roger began rising to his feet. "I must be going. I have to fly to Washington in the morning."

Franco walked him to the elevator, where they shook hands.

"I'll call you in a week or so," the publisher said.

"Good," replied Belacqua. "I've enjoyed our evening. I hope we'll have more."

"So do I," Franco answered truthfully, as he waved toward the elevator. Then, in the den, he settled on the sofa, closing his eyes and allowing the darkness to fetch him down. His doubts about Belacqua's sincerity had evaporated. That didn't mean the conclusions were necessarily accurate, only that he was convinced the old man believed what he was saying.

As Franco slept, a wall of human flesh appeared before him, long as Fifth Avenue and tall as the Empire State Building, carved in *bas-relief*: bodies were stacked like tombstones at the Prague synagogue. Ninety billion pairs of soulless eyes stared out from that wall in disbelief, weeping at the trash heap that remained when the last mortal body joined the wall.

The panorama of human achievement unfolded before Franco's eyes in a vast array that stretched from the Flatiron Building to Central Park. There was Moses, and the Buddha too, and the Four Horsemen of the Apocalypse. Dante and the great Genghis Khan were there beside the poisoned river of Lethe, where Odysseus grieved and Jesus wept. Then, beside the wall, the Procession of the Damned began up Fifth Avenue like a St. Patrick's Day parade at Armageddon. There was James Madison himself, wading through the rising muck of human waste, on his way to the Constitutional Convention in the acid rain. High atop the ash heap of St. Patrick's, where liability lawyers shouted "Hosanna," two children appeared, steeped in chemicals; an armed prowler in a Borsalino and a chesterfield, reeking of licorice, pushed them from the spire. Max vanished immediately; waving to Franco as she wept, his Juliette melted into the human wall like the Wicked Witch of the West, joining all the voices that moaned the same refrain. "Do not forget that I once lived, I beg you," they pleaded into the night, all ninety billion. "From time to time recall that *I was here!*"

The sky was black as bituminous coal when the parade reached its end in front of the Plaza Hotel, beside a golden statue of Lillian driving the car she died in, sighing, "Franco . . . Franco . . . Don't let the rapture pass you by. . . ."

"Burlington Tower, this is Baron three seven six eight Sierra, twenty-five miles south at thirty-five hundred, inbound with information India."

"Baron three seven six eight Sierra, squawk eight niner six niner."

Belacqua dialed in the number. Then, as he throttled back both engines, he dropped the gear, and the small plane settled through plump clouds streaked by late-morning sunlight. Franco watched from the right front seat with ill-disguised apprehension despite Roger's experienced hand.

"The Baron's so slick I drop the gear early to slow it down," Belacqua's voice boomed over the engines. "Come in too fast, and pieces of airplane start falling off."

"I hate it when that happens," replied Franco genially, trying to concentrate on anything else. Amid the snow-covered peaks of northern Vermont, he stared down at a brown hillside to the east. Belacqua noticed, and banked steeply to the right, turning so that the three scientists in the rear could hear him over the engines.

"That hilltop was green with fir trees until ten years ago, when they all died."

William McAdams leaned forward, raising his eyebrows theatrically. "You're not suggesting that's a result of so-called acid rain, are you?" A strikingly handsome fellow in his late forties with fashionably long auburn hair, silver eyes, and a jaw like Dick Tracy, McAdams was as shrewd as he was articulate. He was the country's most highly paid "environmental consultant," corporate America's best-known apologist. *Newsweek* had made him famous as "the businessman's ecologist," and after he testified on behalf of the chemical corporations during the Love Canal debacle, Ralph Nader had dubbed him "the polluters' poster boy." He had even defended Union Carbide after Bhopal, and had recently served as an expert prosecution witness against Green Fist, the eco-terrorist group based in Oregon. McAdams was the first scientist Franco had enlisted to critique *The Belacqua Report,* and he had demanded the highest fee.

"See that, Mr. McAdams?" Belacqua pointed to a well-defined swath in the snow. "How else would you explain that color?" The broad streak was a sort of "Don't-flush-I'll-go-after-you" yellow. But just then the tower okayed a left-downwind landing, ending all conversation until the wheels kissed the runway and they taxied to the General Aviation hangar. With a tailwind, the flight from La Guardia took only an hour and change. As his passengers climbed out on the right wing, McAdams turned back to Belacqua.

"You know, Dr. Belacqua," said McAdams, "a twin-engine plane like this is about as environmentally friendly as an oil spill."

Belacqua laughed mischievously. "I know. I rationalize it by insisting that my work obliges me to fly privately." There was the twinkle in his eye. "The truth is, I love buzzing around up there."

The station wagon that picked them up for the ten-mile trip to Belacqua's home and research center was driven by Jimmy Lundgren, a whiz kid whom Belacqua had lured away from Woods Hole Oceanographic. Nothing about Jimmy's appearance suggested his achievements: slack-jawed and gawky, he wore a faded flannel shirt with overalls that fit right into the countryside like camo. Plain-dressed and plainspoken, Jimmy seemed a very serious young man.

Belacqua's estate, purchased in the early seventies, had formerly been a small ski resort, with a large main house and a dozen other structures, including five log-built chalets from the 1920s; though it now housed research facilities, the place still had the feel of a vacation spot. That, Belacqua explained, was why he renamed it the Last Resort.

Apart from Roger and his wife, only six people currently worked there, including Jimmy and his girlfriend, Suki, who cheerfully shared many of the housekeeping chores. As Roger went off to inspect one of the marine tanks, Suki greeted them in the main house (formerly the lodge) with a hearty luncheon. Suki Herlihy was a marine biologist in her mid-twenties, educated at the University of California at Santa Barbara, who'd done research at the Scripps Institute on the life cycles of krill and other plankton, including the elusive deepwater salp. She was also a drop-dead gorgeous blonde who radiated sensuality. Her left-coast vocabulary seemed at once profound and vacuous, featuring words like "energy" and "aura." Still, she had a genuine talent for setting people at ease, and by the time she took them to their rooms in the chalet named Davos, the mood was noticeably lighter. After dropping off their bags and laptops, they returned to the main house, where Mme. Belacqua was waiting for them beside a stone fireplace the size of a Buick.

Christiane Belacqua could be mistaken for Catherine Deneuve, an impression reinforced by the Gallic diphthongs in her otherwise flawless mid-Atlantic English. Her angular elegance recalled the fragility of a gazelle and belied the strength of a cheetah. Christiane was somewhat younger than Roger, but older than Franco, and had been raised in Paris, on the right bank; her aristocratic bearing seemed bred in the bone, not learned in a school. Her handshake was more like an event than a mere formality.

Franco introduced Christiane to James Bushnell, the avuncular, much-published ecologist from Toronto; to Bob Landry, who specialized in stratospheric studies, and whose new circulation model was widely praised; and finally to William McAdams, who, though polite, seemed much more interested in the young Californian.

"Bet you folk get in some great hunting here," he teased, "when you aren't being so damn politically correct."

"Sure do," replied Suki, smiling. "Just yesterday I tracked down a newt."

"Belacqua must have hired you to charm me," said McAdams confidentially. "He knows I'm here to kick some environmentalist butt."

"Oh please, Mr. McAdams," said Suki coyly. "I hope you won't kick mine." McAdam's eyes stayed fixed on her breasts when he turned his head.

Christiane led them to the buffet. While they ate they listened to Bushnell, a short, balding man with a face as crumpled as his safari jacket, describing the decimation he'd seen recently in the rain forests, "the lungs of the earth." Then, over salad, as Belacqua explained their operations, Franco noted the dynamics between the hosts, who complemented each other—an observation friends had often made about Lillian and himself. When Belacqua's excitable fingers began to flutter in conjunction with his discourse, Christiane reached for his hand. And they shared a commitment to scrupulous methodology. They'd clearly gone to great lengths to achieve unambiguous results, with no concession made to convenience. Roger emphasized the group's efforts and personal sacrifices. "It's a lot quieter now than ten years ago, when all the projects were in full swing. Now, we're wrapping up our work with salps and plankton, and spectographic analysis from Daedalus. You're welcome to examine all our data while you're here."

"I was hoping," McAdams said, "we could take copies with us."

"I'm afraid not," replied Belacqua. "As you're well aware, raw data are subject to misuse. But feel free to take notes."

"Roger," interjected Christiane, "why don't you start the tour without me?" The men seemed collectively entranced by her accent. She settled her hand on McAdams's. "William, would you enjoy watching me put down some rabbits? That would make you happy, *non?*" To her husband she said softly, *"Ça lui fera jouer."*

"Despite what you may have read about me in *The New Republic,*" replied McAdams, "I derive no pleasure from the death of small animals. Not even gerbils."

Belacqua rose. "Gentlemen, come. You won't need coats—the chalets are connected by covered walkways."

He led them down a solar-paneled corridor to the Zoo. That's what the first chalet smelled like, too. Belacqua, who'd ushered many scientists through, sounded like a tour guide. "You've all read our research on stratospheric ozone depletion, and the impact of a melanoma 'epidemic' over generations."

In the cages before them, dozen of white rats, rabbits, and cats, their backs and sides shaved, were in various states of activity and repose. Above them hung calibrated sunlamps. Beyond these cages lived the control groups, in average daylight. "For seven years we've studied the effect of *increasing* UV-B rays over many generations."

"Extrapolating from animals to humans must be a dubious step," observed Landry, a soft-spoken man in his forties.

"Dubious extrapolation is the very stuff of *The Belacqua Report,*" offered McAdams.

"The animals there," Belacqua continued, "have been exposed to UV levels expected through the year 2030 as a result of ozone depletion. Here's the microscopic photography," he said, pointing to albums of photos of the animals' cell structures."

McAdams was unimpressed. "You know perfectly well that since the Montreal accords of 1987, chlorofluorocarbon numbers are dropping."

"And still," Belacqua chided, "Russia alone produces ninety thousand tons a year."

McAdams tacked on his course. "Research by the Frelinghaus Corporation shows the ozone layer is actually repairing itself. UV-B rays could actually diminish."

At this, Alex Jones looked up from his microscope with a wry smile. He was a middle-aged, hippified environmentalist from Texas who had volunteered his assistance to the project. "Sorry for buttin' in," he said. "Here's a critique of Frelinghaus from the Natural Resources Defense Council. Take a good look." McAdams pocketed the newsletter without a word.

Belacqua opened the album. "Those blisters are melanoma. The pathologies appear sixty percent faster each decade. Genetic predisposition seems to arise after ten generations."

There was a long silence before McAdams spoke up. "No rabbit stew tonight, eh?"

Bob Landry ignored him. "What do these results mean for human pathology?"

"*Any* extrapolation from one species to another," McAdams insisted, "is mere soothsaying."

Pointing at a graph on the wall, Belacqua said, "In 2035, a child who spends two hours a day outdoors will have a forty percent chance of developing skin cancer."

"That," said McAdams, "is a parenting issue. With appropriate protection, the risk disappears." The others exchanged glances of disbelief.

"True, but could everyone in the world use sunscreen all his life? Are we prepared for a world in which even Bain de Soleil has political implications?"

Christiane arrived with coffee and served everyone except Landry, who was looking at the rats. "*Mon amour*, why don't you take Professor Bushnell and Mr. McAdams to the Pond Room with Franco? Bob seems interested in the animals."

"Isn't that why we're here?" Landry asked, pleasantly enough.

"Exactly," said Belacqua soothingly. "You all go ahead and we'll catch up."

"Gentlemen, follow me." Mme. Belacqua took Franco's arm and led them through the next covered walkway. Outside it had begun to snow.

"Were you involved in research when you met Roger?" Franco asked Christiane.

"Not at all," she said. "We met in Paris, during the demonstrations of May 1968."

"Paris makes everything romantic," he murmured, recalling his honeymoon.

"Hardly! I met Roger in the back of a paddy wagon, courtesy of the riot cops. And I was eight months pregnant." Her short laugh sounded more like a cough. "The public-spirited Dr. Belacqua was there for a conference, and joined us student protesters. He stayed for a year, till he won me over. *Then* I became involved in research." She turned to the others. "Here, each of you take a jacket—it's chilly in there."

An unpleasant smell wafted their way—something green, thought Franco. Christiane offered them loose lab coats. Entering the Pond Room, they were assaulted by the stench of rotting aquatic matter. There were four huge tanks, covered in temperature monitors, with wave machines that kept their oozy muck undulating.

"The water in these tanks circulates through the large artificial ponds out back," explained Christiane, just as Suki reappeared. "The first experiments began in August '88. Later, thanks to Suki and her salps, this work eclipsed all the rest." She pointed to the fourth tank, in which three tubelike creatures an inch or two long floated near the center of the glass.

"Their population in the South Atlantic has doubled since 1980," said McAdams.

"Explain again the significance of salps," asked Bushnell.

"Must we plod?" McAdams complained. "I hate plodding."

"Two billion tons of carbon generated by humans each year seems to disappear," Suki began. "We used to call this 'the Missing Sink.' We knew plankton absorbed carbon, but in '95 planktologists at the University of Rhodes showed how salps consume the plankton and deposit harmless carbon pellets on the ocean floor. That's called the 'biological pump.' Fact is, the future of our species depends upon the future of this species." The little fellows were barely wriggling.

"And as the ocean's temperature rises," McAdams chimed in, "more salps appear."

"So," Franco interrupted him, "you agree that the planet's temperature is rising?"

"Within a narrow range. The Southern Ocean has risen two point five degrees Fahrenheit—and salps have multiplied fourfold." McAdams knew his stuff. "But the idea that they can become saturated with carbon is bogus. These little suckers can never get too much."

"Oh yes, they do," Suki broke in. "That's what we've shown here.

If the plankton contain too much carbon, the salps' digestive tracts clog up; they starve and die. Those few there are the only survivors out of thousands. The rest died at the carbon-enriched levels predicted for 2020."

For once McAdams was speechless. Just as Belacqua arrived with Landry, the phone rang in the anteroom. Suki answered, and gestured to Franco. It was Millie: she thought he'd want to know right away that a fax from Connors at the FBI said background on Belacqua was in the mail. Franco thanked her, and asked her to delete any mention of *The Belacqua Report* in the in-house bulletin; he'd discuss this with Bob Milton first.

When Franco returned to the noxious Pond Room, Belacqua was summing up, his hands aflutter like a speed freak reciting Leviticus in sign language. "But *below* forty-six inches, sunlight reaching the plankton is insufficient for photosynthesis. Unable to rise from that depth, the plankton die, producing that ugly odor, and their rot gradually kills other marine life, triggering a chain reaction. Gentlemen," he announced, "the odor here is nothing less than the smell of the future!"

In the weighty silence, Franco felt as if he were tasting the fate of the earth.

Then McAdams erupted in forced laughter. "Belacqua, you belong in the movies. You're Oscar material." Christiane cast him a sidelong glance of smoldering contempt.

Roger chuckled cheerfully and defused the tension. "You're right, I *should* have been an actor: joyfully creative and gloriously irresponsible. Then it would have fallen to someone else to reveal these awful facts. Let's move on to the Observatory."

"I'll be outdoors," said Bushnell, his face green, as Belacqua led the others along.

The next chalet was Belacqua's office, furnished in authentic Shaker, with a desk for every project, each stacked precariously with books and papers. On the walls were huge blowups of the earth and spectrographic color analyses. He sat his guests as he turned to Suki's boyfriend, who'd arranged the chairs in an arc. "Do me a favor, Jimmy," he said. "Professor Gilvey at MIT has the infrared prints ready—could you drive down to get them? Safer than courier service. He'll only be there till six; you'll have to leave now."

"Sure," said Jimmy, with a good-natured grin.

"I'll fly our guests home in the morning, so when you get back, leave the prints here."

"Okay, chief." Jimmy bolted out. Roger resumed a pedagogical manner. "Most of the sun's rays are reflected back into space by the outer atmosphere, but greenhouse gases trap sunlight and heat the biosphere. From the Daedalus photos, we see how those gases have compressed the thick layer of water vapor above the stratosphere. *Et voilà.*" As he tugged at the world map, it rolled up like a venetian blind, revealing a photo of a segment of the earth and its thin skin of atmosphere. Two layers of color enveloped the planet, one in pale blue, the outer in amber. "NASA provided me with close-ups that haven't been made public." He passed around photos showing the well-defined phenomenon.

"I call this layer of water vapor 'the eggshell effect.' It's a mile thick, increasing at the rate of sixteen feet a day, and that rate is accelerating. The inner edge is pushed centrifugally outward, forming a gaseous crust beneath the ionosphere that retains heat *far* more effectively. We never knew it was there until we sent up Daedalus six months ago to study El Niño. Questions?"

Everyone glanced toward McAdams, who raised both hands in mock defense.

Landry was staring, wide-eyed, at a photograph on the other side of the room. "That photo, from '91, the band around the center—?"

From beneath Belacqua's layers of maturity one could suddenly glimpse the excitement of the boy who had once dreamed of becoming a scientist. "You know what that is, Dr. Landry? Only a few NASA scientists have seen this. I just received a copy this week, so it wasn't in the manuscript. Guess what caused these rings around the earth? This thermal photograph was taken three months after Saddam Hussein ignited the oil fields of Kuwait. We call those 'the rings of Saddam'—a belt of petroleum. No guessing the long-term impact."

Depicted in dark pastels, the continents stood out boldly from the oceans. The most prominent feature was a thick scarlet ring from which fanciful swirls spiraled upward and downward toward the poles. Franco stared at the global graffiti that one man—one petulant monster—had sprayed over the planet, dwarfing in size all other human achievements: the Great Wall of China, the pyramid of Cheops, the tallest buildings were microscopic beside this. Staring at it, Franco was almost persuaded on the spot to publish *The Belacqua Report*.

McAdams revived when Suki returned with tea and little treats, fixing his eyes on her, with only a disparaging glance at the cucumber sandwiches.

Suki chuckled. "You'd probably prefer beef."

"Now you're talking!" He turned to Belacqua. "Where can I get a cheeseburger?"

"There's a McDonald's in Burlington," she answered.

"Why don't you take Mr. McAdams there, Suki?" offered Belacqua.

McAdams almost leaped from his chair. "Would you?"

"Sure." It was only much later that Franco learned she was a vegetarian. She led McAdams out as the others watched him leave with relief—even Franco, who was paying him to be there.

"Why does the government give you its data?" Bushnell asked Belacqua.

He registered dismay. "The Clinton administration has been ambivalent. Of course, they're wary of the economic implications. And Gore knows he has to tone down his environmentalist image to get elected. Right now, Gephardt is talking like the greenest presidential candidate. Still, the NSC forwards me confidential new data. Maybe they think my worst-case scenario makes their predictions seem less extreme. Now," he added, "I need a nap. I left home at six this morning—I don't want to fall asleep over dinner. I'm sure you'll find Christiane entertaining. Jim, Bob, you have all the data you need?" Both men nodded.

Near the door Franco noticed a faded photograph of the Belacquas, much younger, with their children: Jean-Loup, maybe seven years old, and Cybèle, with dark hair to her waist, perhaps ten; he could make out Sacré-Coeur in the background. Roger had probably been more involved with his children than he himself was with Juliette and Max.

As they returned from the "Davos" chalet, Franco saw Christiane carrying a small, heavy cage into the woods near the main house. Although he was without a coat, he went to help.

She flashed a smile. *"Merci,* Franco. I do this out of earshot of the other rabbits."

"Do they make noise when they die?"

"No, but I am very protective with them. Roger pointed out that my maiden name is Lapine: perhaps that is why."

In jarring contrast to this sensitive consideration was the sang-froid with which she dispatched the three young rabbits with jabs of a syringe. She let Franco carry the carcasses to the bins marked BIOLOGICAL WASTE, where she emptied the cage herself.

"It seems you've given your lives over to this project completely," said Franco. "That must have been difficult?"

"The science, yes. And the bookkeeping: I did not inherit a gift for mathematics, nor did any of my children. Otherwise, the work . . . well, it passes the time," Franco took it that she was acknowledging her endless sorrow. It wasn't, he thought, all that hard for her to condemn the world to death.

"Tell me, madame," he asked abruptly, "why do you suppose someone broke into my apartment to steal the manuscript of *The Belacqua Report?"*

"I have no idea!" She seemed amazed. "Did that really happen? Are you sure that's what the burglar was after?"

He nodded.

"Have you told Roger this?"

He shook his head.

"I will tell him when we are alone. *C'est bien bizarre, ça.* See you at seven, then," she said, as they reached the house.

That evening the party gathered for dinner. At the start of the meal—spinach soufflé followed by trout that Jimmy had caught that morning—Roger made a toast to "the publisher—*spero!*—of *The Belacqua Report,* Franco Sherman." But the evening was curiously dispirited. Before dessert McAdams retired "to copy Belacqua's raw data." Soon after, Franco and Bob Landry also left Roger with Bushnell and returned to the guest chalet, consisting of four small bedrooms, modestly decorated.

Franco took the manuscript to bed, but by ten o'clock he'd dozed off, falling deep into a dream, making love to the punky girl. The sex was urgent, carnal, and anonymous—tainted with a fevered wickedness. For the longest time he could hear her moaning.

But when he awoke the sounds of lovemaking continued. He listened for a time before he realized that the woman's voice was coming from McAdams's room. He was appalled. It was almost an hour before he drifted back to sleep.

In the late morning, as blinding sunlight reflected off the fresh snow into the living room, the group held their last meeting. This time the gregarious showmanship was gone from Roger's delivery. He spoke to them gravely, hands hanging at his sides.

"I want you to be as critical as possible about my work," he said, looking rather pointedly toward McAdams. "I welcome scrutiny. If there's anything you feel doesn't add up, I'd rather explain it to you in person. Has anyone spotted something amiss? Jim?"

Bushnell shook his head. "I'm no expert in all these fields, but your results seem conclusive. Bravo, Dr. Belacqua! You've confirmed our worst nightmare."

"Thank you. And you, Mr. Landry?"

"I was skeptical. I stayed up late cross-checking your data on my laptop. Everything seems to add up. The geopolitics is something else, but there, too, your conclusions are not easily dismissed. I still want to check your sources and talk to some colleagues, but for now, I concur. Something of a more personal nature needs to be said: as an individual, the message to me is that my grandchildren, Wendy and Todd, will die in a mass extinction. Can a global society even function with that kind of knowledge?"

"I don't know, but—does it function now? I heard somewhere recently that every single day, forty thousand infants die of malnutrition: that sounds like mass extinction to me. Perhaps it's only a matter of degree."

"Your point is that it's too late to do anything. Such news may produce a final generation without purpose or faith. Maybe doomsday shouldn't be advertised."

Belacqua sat forward. "We thought about that. But I cannot suppress the truth, and besides, other scientists will announce it soon enough anyway. It wasn't an easy decision to arrive at, yet in the end I believe that if the world were ending next week or next year, I would want to know it, and so would many other folk. But perhaps Mr. McAdams has found an error in humanity's favor?"

Franco turned to McAdams, who appeared to have an unholy

hangover. He squinted at Belacqua as if admitting that his head was not clear.

"I wish I could copy these documents—" He paused. "Frankly, Dr. Belacqua, I think you're driven by the same impulse as Dr. Kevorkian: the urge to control life simply by ending it. And I will show these gentlemen," indicating Landry and Bushnell, "the folly of their ways, as well as Mr. Sherman—and any other publisher you approach. So I'll be in touch in my own sweet time." In the silence, the only sound was Suki sweeping the kitchen floor.

Belacqua rose. "Well, Mr. McAdams, I'm sure you'll be very articulate in your criticism. Now, shall we get an early start back to New York?"

As they gathered their bags and thanked Christiane, not a glance passed between McAdams and Suki, but only Franco noticed that. An hour later they were above the clouds at eight thousand feet. Now Franco felt quite at ease in the copilot's seat.

"What's your top speed?" he asked during a pause in radio communications.

"A hundred eighty knots without a tailwind. With oxygen, in the jet stream, it could go three hundred, ground speed."

"We can't do that now?"

"No, this plane isn't equipped with oxygen. In that thin air we'd start giggling like loons, and then we'd pass out."

"What's the plane's range?"

"With the extra fuel bladders, a thousand miles. We usually fly to Costa Rica in two days."

Radio communications kept Belacqua busy all the way in to La Guardia. They landed amid the commercial traffic and taxied to Butler. Roger shook their hands as a lineman refueled the Baron.

"Hope you come back to town soon," Franco told him. "Depending on these fellows"—meaning McAdams—"I should fax you a deal memo in the next few weeks."

"Grand," replied the scientist, smiling. Then from his jacket pocket he extracted a floppy disk. "This is the text of the whole book. Your copy editor can work from this. But please, no copies."

Franco nodded and put it in his pocket. "*Ciao*, Ruggiero!"

Franco led the scientists to his waiting car. It was three o'clock, and a cutting wind from the northeast blew the stretch limo toward the city.

Franco got home before the kids and laid out a little tea party with Juliette's favorite silver and *petits fours* from Balducci's. When the kids walked in he was in his bathrobe, the way they liked him best, with *Treasure Island,* which they hadn't read in a month. They loved it when he played Long John Silver and rolled one eye like Robert Newton.

After he read for a half hour, they did homework, and Juliette showed Max a trick for simplifying fractions. Then they had TV dinners and, after the kids bathed, they curled up on the sofa to watch the *National Geographic* video, Lillian's favorite. After Max fell asleep, Franco and Juliette watched as if they'd never seen it before, and she even got him to promise they'd go to the opening of Disney's Animal Kingdom in May.

"Dad," started Juliette, pausing the tape, "can dead people see and hear?"

They'd had many metaphysical discussions since Lillian's death. "Of course, sweetheart. When you want to talk to Mom—"

"I don't mean her. She's my guardian angel and all that. I mean, are George Washington and Abe Lincoln watching, wondering why the world went wrong?"

Franco's jaw dropped. "You think the world has gone wrong?"

Juliette put her hands on her hips. "Well, Daddy—duh!" Then the nine-year-old studied her finger. "In Home Room, Mr. Tomkins said George Washington would be ashamed of how the world is now. He said us kids would pay for the mistakes you guys made, polluting the water and the air. Is that true?" Flummoxed, Franco nodded. "But the planet isn't really *poisoned,* is it?" He took too long answering, and when she looked up suddenly, her eyes caught his by surprise. Whatever fib he was cooking up came unglued; she always knew what he was thinking, which usually seemed like a good thing.

"It's a shameful mess. There are many reasons why, but there's no excuse for it."

"And now kids like us have to clean up after you guys, right?" He nodded, stunned by the timeliness of her questions. Was the whole world waking up, twenty years too late?

A broad smile strobed across the nine-year-old's face. "That's okay, Dad—you clean up after me and Max all the time!" With that, his beautiful daughter blessed and forgave him, withholding recriminations that would have echoed in his nightmares. He kissed her head and with one eye closed, accompanied her to her room, limping just like Long John Silver.

Terry had been waiting for word about Franco's trip and the evaluation of *The Belacqua Report,* but none of her friends at Commonweal had any news, and the office e-mail wasn't giving up a thing. Meanwhile, while nursing Danvers along, Terry proofread galleys, coaxed chapters from recalcitrant authors, and solicited blurbs from big-name writers for books in the fall catalog.

But one evening, a few days after Franco's trip, Danvers sent her to Franco's apartment with the final draft of the deal memo for Belacqua. Riding up to his floor, she patted her hair and hoped her breath didn't stink of cigarettes. Then she glanced at the postcard in her pocket, already finger-fretted. "Terry, This makes no sense. I'm moving back to SoHo. I miss you. Bobby." She wasn't sure how she felt about that.

Emily opened the door for her, and she followed the Irish nanny past the children to Franco's den, peeking into the rooms along the way.

"Come in, Terry," he called, in what sounded like his deepest, gentlest voice. She was still flattered that he even remembered her name, and she was glad it was so cold outside: her pink cheeks would hide her blush.

"Hi, Mr. Sherman. Danvers asked me to bring you this." With only the desk light on and all the somber paneling, the den was so dark her eyes took a moment to adjust.

But the room lit up as soon as Franco smiled. "Sorry to take you out of your way after work, especially on such a windy night. Ah, could you wait until I've looked this over? That way you can take it to legal in the morning, already signed. . . ."

"No problem," she said, perching herself on the edge of the leather settee a few feet from his sofa. Terry stared at the three finely crafted spherical wood turnings on the shelf beside them. Then, with the singular intensity of a kitten waiting for dinner, she concentrated on the person of Franco Sherman.

"Uh, Terry," said Franco uncomfortably, "why don't you go ask my daughter, Juliette, to make you a cup of tea? Or perhaps you'd like something to eat?"

Terry rose awkwardly, half bowing before she left the room and half kicking herself after. *Loser!* Twenty-four years old, and I don't know how to wait unobtrusively. She would have loved to sit quietly and watch him studying the draft contract, but her stare was too intrusive to allow him to think. Damn. Now she really wanted a cigarette.

In the living room the kids were playing with scissors and paste, while storms of canned laughter poured out of the TV. This seemed like the place for her, so she sat down with Max and Juliette and chatted about kid things, like skinned knees and *Eloise* and if-Pluto's-a-dog-what's-Goofy?

Franco spent longer on the four-page memo than he intended, trying repeatedly to reach Danvers to discuss the paperback royalties, where the deal became unusually rich for Belacqua. He was still surprised that the scientist wasn't asking for a much larger advance; it almost made him seem too eager. However, Roger *had* demanded a half million up front for developing the CD-ROM, and paperback royalties one point higher than Michael Crichton's. Clearly, the Belacquas were confident about the book's success.

An hour later he found Terry on the living-room floor with the kids, whispering, giggling, and pasting snippets from magazines onto thick paper. It all struck Franco as uncommonly normal for a motherless household. At the same time there was something unusual about the scene.

"Uh, Terry, I'm done with this. Sorry it took so long. Could you join me, please?"

Terry blushed perceptibly and glanced at the kids. "Be right there, Mr. Sherman."

He smiled. "Won't you call me Franco? Everyone at Commonweal does." Then he realized what was unusual: the TV was off. He turned back to his dark lair. A moment later he heard the scampering feet of Max and Juliette, followed by Terry.

Juliette entered the den first, glowing with pride, with Max close behind. "Look what I made for you, Daddy," said his daughter, and handed him a card with a big red heart pasted to it, surrounded by a collage of words and pictures clipped from magazines. "FANTASTIC! . . . GROOVY POP . . . VALENTINE'S DAY SPECIAL . . . DON'T MISS IT!" Beneath, in Juliette's studied script, it read "Happy Valentine's Day, Daddy, I LOVE you." Max's card was a little more abstract, with cutout photos of cars and planes and a tiger. Franco was amazed: the kids usually went to the store with Emily and bought him cards. Not once since Lillian's death had he remembered Valentines. He hugged them, and made a mental note to do something special with them in the coming week. Then he scooted them out of the room and turned to Terry.

"I've tried reaching Danvers to discuss the percentages . . . What is it, Terry?"

Eyes shining, she held out another Valentine, also made from letters and words pasted together. It said, "Happy Valentine, FRanCo, You're THE BEST. Terry."

He was genuinely flustered, to her delight. "That's very sweet. I don't know what to say. Uh, yes, about Danvers . . ."

"He's out to dinner. Trying to lure Ann Beattie away from Knopf."

"I see." It was obvious that she managed most of Danvers's responsibilities. "Here, Terry," he said, handing her the manila envelope. "We both know this deal memo is your accomplishment. What else do you do? Do you copyedit?"

"I sure do. I did the Tiny Messingkauf diary. I just finished the new Goldman novel. And *Football and Freud*. Sophie Sorkin taught me; she's retired, but she'd recommend me if you gave her a call." All Terry could think was: I-am-not-worthy.

Franco considered the attractive young woman in front of him. Despite his misgivings about any appearance of sexual harassment, he wouldn't mind spending hours going over this difficult text with her. He was promptly ashamed of the idea. "Impressive reference. Any background in science?"

"I was studying advanced physics when I went to Smith." Okay, not actually *at* Smith, she failed to add, but in high school just before. Her hopes crashed: she really didn't have the right laminates for this gig.

Franco pursed his lips and thought for a moment. "Would you help me with the editing of *The Belacqua Report?* I haven't done it in a while, and I need to work with someone discreet and professional, to keep as much control over this book as I can and avoid the usual process. If we work on it together, we won't even have to give it to a copy editor. But, well, you know what an enormous job this is: you're already in the loop."

Maintaining her composure, Terry nodded. This was, like, the greatest thing that had ever happened: she was in the loop! "Mmm. Challenging. But it's also the most polished manuscript I've ever seen: meticulous. He's even done the index. And it's the most important book ever." She was perched over his desk and he was leaning back, stunned by her ardor. "Since the day I read it, I went *way* beyond the call of—" That sounded immodest. "I'd love to work on it. I'll do it for free." Then she shook her head. "But Danvers won't let me go for that long."

"He won't object." Franco smiled. "I'm in a position to arrange that, you know."

"He says—" she scrolled down for an appropriate phrase—"that he relies on me."

Franco wasn't concerned. "Why don't you start this week, at home? Do a sample, and I'll look it over. I'm still not sure we're going with this book. I want to see the written opinions before we vote. We'll find Danvers another assistant, and you can coach her—or him. Meanwhile we'll keep you on payroll at the same level, plus a six-thousand-dollar consultant's fee. Is that fair?"

All Terry could do was nod, so she nodded twice.

"Do you have a copy of the manuscript to work from?" She shook her head. "Oh, wait, Belacqua gave me this." Franco dug the floppy disk out of his desk drawer. "So you can work on the text directly."

"Wow," she said, "that's really cool!" God, she sounded dumb. "What's he like, Dr. Belacqua? You think he's for real?"

"He's a dedicated scientist who has invested years in this work. If he's wrong, I'm pretty sure he doesn't know it. So are we clear?" When she nodded, he smiled, and in that smile it seemed to her as if the whole planet had been saved from destruction. "Good. When you've done a couple chapters, call, and we'll go over it. and," he added sheepishly, "you can remind me which little editor's squiggles to use."

"I'd be happy to . . . Franco."

"Well, good night, then."

"Good night, Franco." She said good night to the kids and found her own way out.

Alone, on her way down in the elevator, Terry unconsciously ran her left hand over her breast. By the time the cold wind slapped her cheeks, they were already bright pink.

METZAMOR

The present climate system is very delicately poised.
The system could snap suddenly between very different conditions with an abruptness that is scary. It's a
strongly non-linear response, meaning shifts could happen very rapidly if conditions are right, and we cannot
predict when that will occur. Our studies tell us only
that when a shift occurs, it could be very sudden.

—Scott J. Lehman and Lloyd D. Keigwin,
"Sudden Changes in North Atlantic Circulation During the
Last Deglaciation," *Nature*, April 30, 1992

Terry threw herself into the job like an impatient suicide off a low
bridge. That same night, when she got home, she worked till dawn,
finishing the introduction and much of the first chapter. At that
pace, she'd be done in less than three weeks.

But of course it did not all go smoothly. The next day, when she
came to the scientific analyses that would be debated for years,
her breezy pace bogged down in a thick soup of numbers. Though
Belacqua insisted in his preface that the book had been rigorously
vetted by scientists, she felt that Franco wanted her to take responsibility for its contents as well as its language; that was a huge
stretch, given that she knew little physics, hardly any chemistry,
and no biology. By Chapter Two she knew her edit would have to
be reviewed by a specialist.

When she needed a break, she turned to other chores. She left
a message for Danvers saying she'd call in when she'd made some
headway on her new assignment. And she called her mom in Min-

neapolis, as she did every year on the anniversary of her brother's death. Terry had never even known Jimmy: he'd died at Quang Loc in '72, the year before she was born. She told her mom about the copyediting job, omitting, for the time being, Belacqua's unforgiving conclusions. Her mom asked if she'd seen Bobby since he moved to D.C., and implied that she should be meeting new people.

In the afternoon Terry suited up and went for her usual run along the East River. At the UN she stopped to gasp a few minutes before turning back. But south of Thirty-fourth her ankle turned wonky and she slowed to a half-limp. Along the river a sudsy yellow tide of debris flowed past (was that a syringe?), and her thoughts returned to *The Belacqua Report* and Franco. She wondered if other readers would react to the book by going crazy, and obsessing about sex. That reminded her that she was out of condoms. Which reminded her that Bobby would be back soon in his old apartment near Alphabet City. She didn't know how she felt about that. 1998 sure had started out weird.

That's when she thought a man was following her again. She couldn't be sure it was the same man—the first time, she didn't see his face clearly. He was tall, wore a fedora and gold-rimmed glasses, and carried a laptop case in faux alligator. She'd definitely seen his face before, but where? He was pretending he didn't notice her as they turned west onto Twenty-third, not fifty feet apart. Who was this guy? Someone from work? From Massachusetts? Minneapolis? What did he want with her? Scrolling through scary urban nightmares, she realized she didn't have her pepper spray. Her pulse was racing faster than when she jogged. She reviewed her self-defense techniques and added a confident swagger to her limp. But when she spun around to get a bead on the guy, he was gone. It was only when she got home that she realized why he was familiar: it was the guy she'd smooched with—um, Gerald—after she first read the doomsday report. D'oh!

She showered and ate a bowl of muesli, then popped in the backup copy of Belacqua's disk that she'd made and, her edge rehoned, settled in for a long siege. Errors that slipped past her would cast doubt on the entire book's validity, so with maniacal fastidiousness Terry plowed through the formulae and data that littered the footnotes, checked technical language on the Internet, and tried not to think about sitting beside Franco Sherman, reviewing the hieroglyphics of editing.

When she heard a key in the front door, she freaked and grabbed for the pepper spray in her purse. It was Bobby! She never thought he'd be back this soon. They hugged and rocked back and forth until they tumbled to the floor, giggling. But when he tried to kiss her seriously, she left him panting.

"I gotta eat," he said, while he caught his breath. "I haven't had anything since D.C." Terry pulled her sweatshirt back down over her breasts and bolted to the kitchen. There was nothing in the fridge but an old salad, condiments, and—was that a red pepper? So they raced out to Union Square, chattering about the new Rusted Root album.

Terry had met Bobby Anderson one Friday night at The Galaxy during her first year in New York. He was her height and very scrawny, kind of like Beck, but with thick, wavy hair past his shoulders, which Terry really liked. They were both twenty-two, with a disdain for yuppies and jocks. Terry had had purple hair then and usually reeked of patchouli, after a bottle spilled into her drawer. For Bobby, who studied poli sci at Princeton and worked as an aide to conservative Congressman Borner, Terry was an acquired taste, but in the two years they were "just friends," Terry became more conventional, while Bobby loosened up, especially after working for Nader's campaign in '96. Even while working in D.C., Bobby never cut his ponytail. Though they were mostly happy, they'd been noncommittal about the future after he moved away. Now, she couldn't figure out why he was here.

When they sat down at a small candlelit table, Bobby was gleaming with amazement. "So work's good, huh? Editing the most important book since the Bible."

"Oh, *that.*" Terry waved it off with supreme nonchalance. "It's just . . . the greatest thing!"

"Have you met Belacqua yet?" Terry shook her head. When Bobby turned serious, he looked even more boyish. "And what's it like, working with the CEO?"

"We haven't really started. But I really admire the guy, as you know."

Bobby erupted, "How did you get the job? Did you do him? Did you *do* Franco Sherman?"

There it was. He had come all the way to New York to make that one ugly accusation.

"What?" Her cheeks flushed with rage. "No, I did not!" She might have been angrier if the idea hadn't crossed her mind. She shook her head in disbelief and tried to decide what to do next. She opted for telling the truth. "I did mess around with another guy. I had to get pretty drunk to do it, and I didn't much like it. It was no big deal."

Bobby cocked his head. "Well, actually, I've been seeing a woman in D.C. I thought I should tell you."

Terry's jaw fell. This was like Truth or Dare without the party favors. But to her, the biggest revelation was that she didn't really give a damn. Yes, she was surprised, but if she wanted to break up with him, this would make it easier.

They tucked into their salads while Bobby stewed. "You know what? I think you're planning to sleep with your boss. That's okay. A twenty-year age difference isn't so important, I guess, what with the planet going putrid and all." He was all bruised and over-heated, probably because he was the one who had actually cheated; no wonder he was so quick to suspect her. "Look," he said, adopting a reasonable tone, "I'm only here till Friday. Let's just have this week together, then we'll see."

She stared at him in awe. "You're incredible! First you push me into bed with Franco Sherman, then you reel me back in—and all the while I'm just sitting here!"

"You're right. So, promise me this one week. Then we'll figure it out."

"Sure." Which wasn't how she felt; she just wanted to get back to work.

"Something else." He pulled out a pack of Kents. "I only made it till January 17th."

Terry took a butt and lit it. "I started smoking again after reading Belacqua."

"Even if life on earth *was* gonna end, that's no reason to die young from cancer."

"Guess my e-mail wasn't very convincing about *The Belacqua Report.*"

Bobby looked amazed. "No. Why? You actually believe all that?"

"I've been really confused since I read it," she admitted. "It's hard to believe."

"It sounds like a tabloid headline. Quacks like him piss me off."

Later, after dinner, they returned to the apartment, and while Terry backed up her work on the Belacqua disk, Bobby crashed, which suited her fine. Now everything between them was bad, and like old food in the fridge, it wouldn't get better again. Bobby even looked different to her, almost adolescent. Then she realized she was comparing him to Franco.

She didn't wake Bobby when she went to bed, and left him sleeping in the morning when the phone rang. It was Danvers, or his Captain Bligh incarnation: How dare she not show up for work without telling him? Was she *determined* to make a fool of him? The new girl, Consuelo, couldn't find a thing, and publicity had to have blurbs on *Football and Freud* by noon. Kvetch as he might, he was powerless, and they both knew it. Franco had left explicit instructions that Terry was not to be disturbed, and try as he might, he couldn't disturb her.

After reviewing her work two more times, she took the introduction and the first two chapters in to work and, plucking up her nerve, plowed into Franco's office suite. Millie was deciding whether or not to let her in without an appointment when she got a call from Ben Steiner, and while she was occupied, Terry marched boldly past her.

Franco had begun his day with the delicate chore of informing Bob Milton about *The Belacqua Report.* He was not obliged to do so, but in this case it seemed prudent, according to rules of diplomacy that Franco didn't understand very well. This dimension of his job would be easy for a bootlicker, but groveling wasn't part of his repertory. For this reason and others, Franco didn't expect to keep his job for very long. That was why his humble imprint, Historical Perspective, meant so much: it was the only perk of this position that, contractually, Bob Milton couldn't touch.

"I don't normally disturb you about this or that book, Bob," he began on the phone, "but we're deciding whether or not to publish something really different." He stored up a breath. "A detailed work which proves that the ecology of the earth is doomed to collapse within forty years, causing the mass extinction of all living species, including mankind."

"Swell," said Milton. "Bet you had to go mustache-to-mustache with Korda for that."

Franco's tone betrayed nothing more. "We're thinking of bringing it out as a special, after the fall list. It's certainly a big book, but since the advance isn't enormous"—that might be misleading—"we can afford to promote the book aggressively. And there's a CD-ROM that I think is going to be huge."

"Well, that's your forte. Who's the author?" asked Milton.

"He's a scientist, well respected in government and environmental circles. I have three ecologists evaluating his work, and for now it seems conclusive."

"A scientist? Brilliant! But is he also an established novelist?"

"Novelist? Why, no. Uh—perhaps I wasn't clear. This is a scientific report that proves we've missed our chance to save the planet. Nothing can reverse the situation."

Milton's long silence grew longer. Finally, he laughed. "Okay, you're making me nervous. I missed something, so tell me all over again, okay? What's the gimmick? I'm a dumb guy from the canned goods business." Franco tried again, but Milton refused to countenance the notion of human extinction. "My boy, that isn't just foolish, it's *heresy*. God didn't create the earth just to destroy it."

"It isn't God who's destroying it, Bob. It's man."

Kaboom. "Jesus fucking Christ, Franco, you can't just accuse humanity of pissing all over the planet and then say, 'Too late! Nothing we can do now!' " Milton stopped for a deep breath, recommended for angina. "Look, you're doing a great job. Last month all the directors saluted you. So do what you think's best: I wouldn't want someone else to grab a best-seller. But if my wife reads this book and gives me grief, I'll pass it along. So have a nice day."

"You too, Bob," Franco answered, before sighing with amazement. "You too."

Right then Terry barged into his office wearing a skirt that stopped at mid-thigh, with wool leggings, and Bob Milton vanished from Franco's thoughts. Everything about her entrance took him by surprise: no one had ever made it past Millie.

He greeted her with aplomb. "Good morning, Terry. What do you have?"

"The introduction and two chapters, just as you asked." She was all business. "I also brought you a key explaining the squiggles in the margins. Shall I leave it over here?"

Millie beeped to tell him that Ben Steiner was on the phone.

"Ask him to wait. No, don't, Terry: I won't know what to make of it. We could do it after hours, maybe at my place. Um, we'll probably have to get something to eat."

His invitation was so clumsy that Terry giggled; when Franco realized why she was laughing, he blushed. "Sorry, I've forgotten how to ask a lady out. Will you have an early dinner with me tonight? Afterward we can review your work."

Terry resisted asking what she should wear, or noting that "lady" hadn't been PC since '87. "I'd love to have dinner with you. So, shall I come back at six?"

"Splendid. See you then." He watched her leave, wondering offhandedly if he still had the wherewithal to fall in love with a young lady—or should that be woman? Then Millie put Ben Steiner through to his speaker-phone.

"I've learned," Ben reported, "that the administration is of two minds. Apparently Clinton believes Belacqua's conclusions enough to commission a study, but it's expensive, and bringing it to Congress before the Kyoto Conference was out of the question. The Gore campaign would definitely rather keep this quiet for now."

Franco caught himself thinking about Terry. "Has Belacqua really met Clinton?"

"Yes, over a year ago. A detailed briefing had been scheduled, but the President was late, so it was more of a Kodak moment. Still, Belacqua had his say."

"Anything else?"

"No, I get the feeling there isn't much more to learn."

"Okay. We'll vote after we hear from the scientists. Thanks, Ben."

By the time Franco hung up, it had occurred to him that Terry probably had a boyfriend. And he was also concerned about sexual harassment: not the potential for litigation so much as the effect on morale if he was even accused of hitting on a pretty assistant editor. Obviously, he had to put her out of his mind.

A new archipelago of Post-its was stuck all over his desk—a visual metaphor of his disarray—each calling for a decision. And there was Connors's letter, confirming that Belacqua had top scientific clearance from NASA; but there were also three reports— raw data—which raised other questions. In April 1970, on the first Earth Day, Belacqua had been arrested in a raft on a river outside a chemical company near Nazareth, Pennsylvania: he was installing a pipe from the factory's outflow to its freshwater intake. That gave Franco a laugh. Ten years later, it was reported, Belacqua had chained himself along the Stanislaus River in California as the state began flooding its narrow valley. In both incidents, Roger had received a suspended sentence.

The third charge was more curious. In 1989 Belacqua had been empaneled by the pharmaceuticals giant Gellis Drinnon Gombach to test a new suntan lotion for infants. Two of the five scientists adjudged the formula carcinogenic: Belacqua, the swing vote, insisted the product was "non-nefarious." But the FBI thought that Belacqua had falsified test results, skewing the data to prove the formula's safety. The suggestion was that he'd taken money to do it: no evidence—just speculation. Later, the FDA determined that the product's safety was questionable, and GDG never marketed it. Belacqua was not censured, but he was effectively blacklisted from similar panels.

What to make of this? Was Belacqua framed, or just mistaken? Had he been bribed?

Besides, what would Terry think if he made a pass at her? If she rebuffed him, would she then worry about her job?

Millie beeped him: Roy Raymond, the house patriarch, was calling. Roy, who had little to do but counsel neophytes and listen to all-news radio, had just heard about a major earthquake, 7.2 on the Richter scale, centered in Armenia. There were only a few casualties, but there was grave concern for a nearby Soviet-built nuclear reactor, considered less sound than Chernobyl. Roy thought he would want to know right away.

Maybe Terry would actually be interested in him romantically, even though he was damaged goods with two kids. What about the Valentine she'd made for him that he kept on the dresser? This might even be her dream: his timidity might be the only obstacle to— Hold it. Who was he kidding? This young lady—woman—was twenty-four, same age as Monica Lewinsky. Nonetheless, for the first time since 1981, he removed his wedding ring and put it in his desk drawer.

Roy was mistaken. At that moment, Franco wasn't interested at all.

At six o'clock, Terry waited nervously in Millie's office wearing a deep-blue waisted dress emphasizing her slimness without exactly shouting about it. It was Bobby's favorite, and he'd tried not to act pissed off that Terry was wearing it to dinner with her boss. Terry continued to resent Bobby, and they still hadn't made love. So she was delighted to get away for the evening.

After changing into a dark suit, Franco came into Millie's office. Acknowledging with a polite glance how attractive Terry looked, in a businesslike manner he guided her down to his waiting limo. Shunning anything resembling a quiet, intimate environment, he took her to the Oyster Bar, deep in the bowels of Grand Central Station. A dismal choice, but it was all his.

Over dinner they discussed *The Belacqua Report* and its possible impact on the public, and speculated about when other scientists might reach the same conclusions. They also discussed colleges, Massachusetts writers, and expatriates in Paris. By the time coffee arrived, the gulf between them had shrunk.

"I thought you taught history," she said, impressed at his extensive reading.

"I studied history, but I taught English lit."

"Really?" said Terry, wide-eyed. "My roommate once went to geology stoned."

"No, I meant literature—" But then he got her little joke.

"Just kidding," she said. That was *sooo* dumb! But as she became comfortable enough to tease him, things got easier.

They talked about films and especially music. Franco was proudly describing his record collection when he recalled how young she was. "You probably don't even own an LP."

"Of course I do," she objected (she'd inherited her brother's records), adding boastfully, "I'm older than compact discs, but younger than eight-track." Franco nodded, acutely aware of being older than stereophonic sound.

After dinner they went back to his building, where Franco asked his driver, Giuseppe, to wait to take Terry home. Upstairs, he poured them each a glass of wine, and they parked themselves on the settee in his den. There Terry walked him through the marked-up manuscript, explaining each change she'd made, backing herself up with *The Chicago Manual of Style,* and pointing out small problems she'd found.

By ten they'd finished the introduction, in every sense. They had laughed, and argued, and made up, and laughed again within the microcosm of a few hours. So when they took a break after Chapter One it seemed entirely natural, within their island of dilated time, for Franco to lead Terry by the hand out to the terrace, where he draped his cashmere overcoat around her shoulders. Surely that wasn't sexual harassment.

It was unusually mild for late February, almost springlike. They stood quietly gazing toward the East River, their shoulders touching, which seemed unremarkable by then: simply the next step along a path they'd already tacitly chosen. The airplanes flying from Kennedy and La Guardia looked like toys in the dark, and it made Terry shudder to think how the wealthy and powerful must feel as they looked out over the city with something akin to pride of ownership.

Franco's fingers responded cautiously when Terry slipped her hand into his. Then his fist gripped tightly and they turned toward one another and stood there for the longest time. Finally Terry couldn't keep a straight face anymore and, chuckling, said, "So, Franco—what's it gonna be?"

With that he kissed her. His lips were tentative, but hers were not, and after a moment every distraction faded. Their kiss slowly grew more passionate. Then, as Franco's right hand wandered from her back to her shoulder to her breast, he felt the unambiguous enthusiasm in her breath and in the taste of her mouth, turned sweet with desire. They leaned back and smiled, and took the first steps toward their next way station.

Only when they arrived in the bedroom did Franco think of his wife, which led him to wonder about Terry's past: clearly, she had felt this way before. And that thought loosed a musty collection of unpleasant ideas from the basement of his brain. At the very threshold of his king-size bed—his and Lillian's—he began torturing himself with ignoble thoughts. Who—whom—had Terry slept with before like this, at the first opportunity? How many college boys had scored? How many junior executives had wined and dined her, and been granted a taste of her charms? And had one of them left some viral billet-doux with Franco's name on it? When he realized he didn't own a condom, he seized up like an overheated motor just as they lay down together.

Terry felt him go cold. With her gentlest smile, she said softly, "I bought these this afternoon, in case you . . ." With that bold declaration she produced a condom from God knows where, and they returned to a languorous embrace.

For the longest time their mouths were joined, expressing all their excitement and hunger as, fully dressed, their bodies rubbed slowly together. It was Terry's urgency that moved them along.

Her breathing quickened, and she nibbled on his lower lip and whispered, "Touch me, Franco, please touch me." When she unzipped her dress, his hand moved down from her shoulder. Franco had never known such girlish breasts, with nipples the size of dimes. Responding to his spiraling tongue by arching her back, she felt him throb against her thigh, as hard as Japanese arithmetic. Eager though she was to take him between her lips and between her legs, she loved the pleasure he took from her breasts. So as she unbuttoned his shirt, she leaned over his mouth and grazed his lips with her nipples.

When at last his hand traveled hesitantly beneath her skirt, he found her thighs moist with excitement, and for the first time he groaned. She rolled away just long enough to pull off her dress and stockings, even though he was still fully dressed. Breaking away to remove his own clothes, he found the room filled with the perfumes of her body. Then Franco noticed the tattoo of a butterfly, orange and gold, that seemed to have crawled up the inside of her thigh. He knelt down to study its tiny green eyes before kissing it, licking it, and stretching out beside her again.

Her nakedness against the length of his body excited him more than he could bear, and as her tongue traced his chest and beyond, he stopped her before she reached her goal, slipping his fingers down her flat belly and through the wisps of her hair.

A moment later, without warning, Terry rolled away and stood up beside the bed, crossing her arms over her breasts. She spoke softly. "I think I should go home now."

His engine racing, Franco sat up. "What— Oh God, did I hurt you?"

She shook her head. Reaching for her clothes, she turned her back and began to dress again. "No. I just really have to go."

He stood up and came around the bed. Putting his arms around her, he stopped her fidgety dressing. "I'm getting mixed signals."

"That's because I'm giving mixed signals." She sat down on the bed, and when she had composed her answer, spoke directly. "I'm sorry, Franco. Look, I want to make love with you. But this just isn't me, rushing like this." She ran her hand along his cheek, and spoke with a trace of disappointment. "You're so—I don't know, it's hard to describe." She took his face in her hands and said, in a soft growl, "You have no idea how much I've wanted you. Even before you knew my name. Remember when you were working on the serial killer's diary? Tiny Messingkauf? Did you ever find a Post-it note stuck in the manuscript, with a little heart, 'From a Secret Admirer'?"

Franco thought back through those weeks. "No, I didn't."

That meant her note must have gone to Sebastian in legal. D'oh! "Well," she shrugged, "it doesn't matter. It just doesn't feel like you're all here, with me, right now, tonight."

"Terry . . ." Franco's mouth hung open. "I haven't felt so—"

She continued putting on her pantyhose. "I know you do, physically. But your thoughts are somewhere else, with somebody else. Which is understandable and all. I just don't like the way it makes me feel."

He sat down on the bed and leaned against his pillow, looking away as she stared at him. Then he nodded. "I suppose you're right." He turned toward his nightstand, and with a puzzled air, he said, "That's funny, I was reaching for a cigarette."

"Okay," she said, starting to go for her handbag. "Go right ahead."

"But I haven't smoked since '73." His surprise turned sheepish, and he gazed at her unguardedly as he volunteered a boyish confession. "That was the last time I made love with someone I hardly knew."

"Well," she said philosophically, "that doesn't make you a bad person."

Instead of laughing, he looked at her askance and then continued, "I haven't made love with anyone since my wife. Please, I was just starting to relax. Come back."

After a moment she lay down, and soon they were altogether in the here and now. Franco undressed her again and took command of events, guiding her swiftly to the first crest of her pleasure, where she whimpered with relief.

Now he was completely absorbed in his desire: he wanted everything. After she recovered, he kissed her mouth, parting her lips wider with his fingers. Then his mouth and hands assailed the slim expanse of her body, twitching and trembling. Slowly, his mouth approached the petals and folds and all the complicated beauty at her core, and as he fed upon her new and unfamiliar sweetness, her excitement peaked again.

They'd been making love for ages before Franco felt pressed to reach a conclusion. By then they were so familiar with each other's bodies it did not seem untoward for Terry to roll the condom down over his heated flesh before he sank deep into her wetness and began a pulsing rhythm. This too lasted a long while, until her body kicked into overdrive and she single-mindedly sought her own satisfaction. She became so animated and uninhibited that he could wait no more, and his pleasure flared up within her.

By morning, they were halfway in love.

Franco rose an hour before Emily woke the children. He had dreamed of a tropical grove—papayas, maybe—beside a waterfall that tinkled like a clavichord. He snuggled with Terry to wake her, and before he knew it, he was aroused again. So while she was still in her own dream, he awakened her from within. Not long after, he served breakfast in bed and then called downstairs to learn, with embarrassment, that Giuseppe was still waiting. He saw Terry to the door and promised to call at the end of the day.

Dressing for work, he thought: It's such a simple remedy for misery, lovemaking. He couldn't honestly say what he felt about Terry; nonetheless he walked to work with a spring in his step and half a smile on his face. As he entered the Commonweal building, working up a solemn expression, he felt as if he were wearing a sign on his back: THE PRESIDENT OF COMMONWEAL GOT LAID LAST NIGHT.

But when he passed the newspaper stand in the lobby, he spotted the huge headlines: NUCLEAR DISASTER IN ARMENIA. He bought three papers and, in his office, devoured the reports.

After the earthquake there had indeed been a meltdown at one of the reactors at Metzamor, which provided 30 percent of Armenia's electricity. Built by the Soviets in the seventies, the reactors lacked even a rudimentary containment dome. So a poisonous radioactive cloud had been venting unimpeded for more than twenty-four hours across Yerevan, population two million. This earthquake was five times more powerful than the temblor of '88 that had destroyed fifty-five villages and claimed 25,000 lives; then, all six reactors had had to be shut down. But in late '95, desperate to resuscitate their economy, the Armenian government had fired up the reactors in spite of international protests; the chief engineer had told a *New York Times* reporter at the time that Armenians were "not the kind of people who can set our houses on fire and injure our neighbors."

The invisible radioactive blight was twice the size of Chernobyl's and growing. A freak cycle of southwesterly winds through the spring—a tertiary effect of El Niño—drove the nuclear cloud toward central and western Europe. From Turkey to Ukraine, vast regions were evacuated. In Switzerland citizens were queuing up at the huge fallout shelters that had been carved into the mountains in the 1960s.

As he read, Franco was swept by a familiar queasiness, akin to the restless dread he'd felt when he first read *The Belacqua Report*. Among all the environmental horrors detailed in the book, nuclear contamination was hardly mentioned. Nonetheless this catastrophe also clearly arose from the success of the human species. He wondered how the anxieties raised by this disaster would affect the public's reaction to even more terrible news.

He turned his attention to the two scientific assessments waiting on his desk. James Bushnell had written a succinct analysis of Belacqua's methodology and results, disposing of possible objections, and in the end acceding to all *The Belacqua Report's* conclusions, though he allowed that some geopolitical solutions might still be possible.

Bob Landry had written a nine-page environmental lament, a sort of Requiem for Our Ruination. Less science than sermon, his jeremiad was heartfelt and devastating, and concurred completely with Belacqua's observations. He even upped the ante, citing arguments from cosmology (Big Bang), the Bible (Revelation), and physics (second law of thermodynamics), and remarking, "It is no surprise that 'an eye for an eye' has left civilization blind to its own self-destruction."

McAdams's evaluation, sure to be the most critical, hadn't arrived; Millie had been trying to reach him for three days. Finally, that morning, she had gotten hold of the managing editor at his magazine, *BoB* (*The Business of Business*), and learned that William McAdams had died of a heart attack five days after their trip to Vermont. Apparently, Millie reported to Franco, he hadn't had a medical checkup since 1987. Still, his sudden demise was unsettling.

Franco asked her to send copies of the two assessments to the editors with a note mentioning McAdams's death, and an announcement on the office e-mail that they would vote on *The Belacqua Report* at the Monday meeting.

When Terry emerged from Franco's limo in front of her apartment, she could see Bobby staring down from her bedroom window. The four flights of stairs had never seemed longer.

There were no recriminations at first, but Bobby's laptop and duffel bag were packed and waiting beside the door.

"I'll be in SoHo," he said coldly.

She nodded with exhaustion, relieved that he didn't want to talk. "I'll call you in a few days." Pretty feeble.

As Bobby opened the front door, his well-nursed anger swelled up. "Christ, Terry, why did you have to go do the guy the very first chance you got?"

"You're right, Bobby. I fucked up." She held her breath. "But I plan to see him again, as soon as I can."

Bobby started to cave. "We could still have our week together. You promised." Terry lowered her eyes and shook her head. His hands fell to his sides. "He's twenty years older than you, for chrissakes. Is he really *all that?*"

Terry sighed. "I can't have this conversation now, Bobby. I've got to get to sleep."

"But in bed, it wasn't like us, was it?" Bobby's jealous frustration and bitter desire were all ajumble. He needed details, for the pain, and when they were not forthcoming, he rammed his fist into the wall. He stared at her, then he stomped across the room, threw his apartment key at her feet, and slammed the door behind him.

Alone, Terry felt relief and confusion. Their friendship was what she had loved, and the future was a subject they had always avoided. She was sorry she'd hurt him, very sorry; and she had known that was what she was doing when she had finally decided to spend the night uptown. But she could no more have resisted Franco than the earth could resist the rain.

So without another glance backward, she sat down to *The Belacqua Report* and began unraveling the complexities of Chapter Three, which detailed the miscalculations of naysayers like Richard Lindzen at MIT, William Gray at Colorado State, and Pat Michaels at the University of Virginia. He also explained circulation models and the latest results (October 1997) from the National Oceanic and Atmospheric Administration's Geophysical Fluid Dynamics Laboratory, debunking the "optimistic" view that a reversal was still possible.

In Chapter Four, Terry was stopped cold by a math problem: the projected accumulation of carbon dioxide stubbornly refused to obey the rules of arithmetic. Not for the first time, she regretted taking responsibility for Belacqua's argument as well as his grammar and punctuation. Finally she lay down on her bed and surrendered to wispy memories of the fantasy that had come true.

When she woke up much later that morning, she checked the headlines at nytimes.com and learned about the earthquake. Then she called Franco at work.

"See?" she burst out. "The earth *did* move."

The conversation that followed was a little awkward. That was all the proof she needed that things really had changed, that he wasn't retrenching to the preromantic stage, or pretending nothing had happened. Terry asked for Belacqua's phone number, to straighten out her math problem, and then they hung up. They didn't need to make plans to know they'd see each other soon.

Minutes later Terry was nervously dialing Roger Belacqua. He listened patiently to her problem and promised to call her back after checking his figures. Half an hour later he called and acknowledged a misprint. Belacqua gave her the correct numbers, in gigatonnes of carbon (GtCs), and thanked her for her diligence.

After she'd hung up, Terry erupted with a whoop of glee: she had actually helped Dr. Belacqua! With his math! And he had sounded just as she expected: warm, wise, and precise.

This, thought Terry, was the best week of her life.

Marlene Conrad, the self-help editor, escorted Jonathan Fischer into Franco's office, and the two took seats in front of his desk. Fischer, the renowned psychologist, was hip and cozy, all at once, which meant he was invited back on *Oprah* and *Good Morning America* whenever he had a new book, and that happened about as often as rabbits gestate. A funny little man who looked a little like Martin Short, he was gentler than William Gray and more authoritative than Leo Buscaglia, but when he broke into a smile, even large carnivores could not resist his charm. He'd read the manuscript, and it was clear that he got the picture.

Franco's tone was grave. "I'm hoping you can gauge how the public might react."

"I'm not sure what you mean." Fischer gave him that piercing gaze analysts wear to remind you that they're never really off-duty.

"Could this book promote social disorder?"

"In a society like ours," Fischer asked sadly, "how could we tell?"

Franco wasn't expecting such gloom from the warm and fuzzy shrink. "Well," he answered, "police statistics would show a . . . Look, Jonathan, do you think this book in and of itself constitutes a threat to society?"

"I think the so-called civilized nations will take this news with aplomb," replied the psychologist, with a lilt in his voice. "Throughout this century we've endured a relentless barrage of unthinkable atrocities, from mustard gas to Mutually Assured Destruction. Today they tell us that in Armenia we're facing a nuclear disaster ten times worse than Chernobyl, which released ten times more radioactivity than Hiroshima. Our self-inflicted suffering knows no bounds. So I expect the jejune will take Belacqua's news in stride: 'The end of the world, ho hum.' " Franco was trying to remain emotionally detached from their conversation; then he realized that that was exactly what Fischer meant.

"Our senses have been deadened," continued Fischer. "Sarajevo, Rwanda, Dunblane—television makes these our personal experiences. Gradually the unbearable becomes unexceptional. Last night, after reading the manuscript, I was compiling instances of the brutality we've all been exposed to, not even counting warfare: Sharpeville, Jonestown, Lockerbie—these and many more have shaken whatever faith we had left in human nature after Stalin, Auschwitz, Hiroshima, Pol Pot."

"I've often wondered about the cumulative impact," said Franco softly.

"Accidie," Fischer replied. "An emotional soup of disorientation and exhaustion, torpor and sloth. Rather like the 'donor fatigue' we experience when the twenty-third beggar of the day hits us up for a quarter. For self-preservation, we filter out the ugliest aspects of the world. It's a sort of defensive anesthesia."

"You know," said Marlene, "since reading this, I've felt . . . bleached out."

"A nice simile, Miss Conrad," replied the shrink. "The spiritual rainbow, reflected back through the prism of despair, returns as white light."

Franco had spent his life avoiding the kind of fancy conceits for which Fischer was renowned. "What about suicides?"

"After Belacqua's facts have been corroborated? Many, I'd guess," replied Fischer. "Marlene had asked me to think about that. There's no way of estimating, but it could be as much as a tenth of a percent of the U.S. population."

Franco squinted and calculated. "That's two hundred and fifty thousand, just in the U.S., who might die because of this book?"

"*Globally* I expect the figure would be higher; in some countries, maybe one percent. And many of the suicides might elect to eliminate their families as well, especially their children."

A grim chill ascended Franco's spine. Would *that* fact persuade him not to exercise the First Amendment? Would *any* dire social prediction? His belief, he discovered there and then, remained ardent: the truth must out. "Well," he finally replied, "I hope that psychologists like yourself will do all you can to reduce those numbers, counseling the public in your books, and on the airwaves. What about crime? Would you expect havoc in the streets? Murder, rape, and pillage? Society run amok?"

"Yes, frankly, I would. While a handful of hardy atheists can do without traditional faiths, civilization as a whole cannot; I'm convinced of that. Shared faith is the source of the shared assumptions that provide the only basis for morality. If humankind's highest purpose on this planet was merely to rise to great glory for a few thousand years and then sink back into the soil, then how can we adhere to the beliefs that have sustained us? And one key function of paternalistic religions is to restrain our ugliest tendencies. In *The Brothers Karamazov,* Dostoevsky wrote: 'If there is no God, then everything is permitted.' For atheists, nihilists, and sociopaths, Belacqua is preaching to the choir. As the impact of *The Belacqua Report* sinks in, our flimsy web of shared values may collapse like the biosphere, and with it, our restraints and inhibitions."

Franco fell silent. The editorial board would be responsible for the decision to publish, but Franco knew that he would hold himself accountable. And what if the world ran amok, God forbid, and then Belacqua was proved *wrong?*

A beep from Millie: Franco was due at his meeting with the ABA associates. "Thanks for coming in, Jonathan. Marlene, would you write a summary of this discussion for the other editors?"

"It's admirable that you're considering all the eventualities, Franco." Jonathan turned to Marlene. "Didn't you mention my new contract?"

Franco looked up absentmindedly. "Your books are always valuable assets. Marlene, work it out with his agent, Lynn Nesbit, would you? Good morning, Jonathan."

By the time they left, all Franco could think about was how anxious he was to see Terry again. He called and got her machine. It wasn't easy to admit that he wanted to see her. "Hi, er, it's Franco. I—uh—hope you're feeling the same way I am. Could— uh—we have dinner tonight? I'll call again when I get home. We could go down to Sarafina's—it's small and dark. I hope you'll call." He picked up his attaché case and hastily left the office.

During dinner that evening, side by side in a cramped booth, their conversation was less strained than it had been the night before, but still self-conscious. They were more familiar with each other's bodies than with each other's background. When they ran out of conversation, waiting for their tiramisù, Terry took his hand under the table and pressed it beneath her skirt. That made them conspirators again, setting them at ease even as it keyed them up.

In the cab their heavy petting became so extreme they had to break apart and laugh at themselves.

In the apartment they tiptoed past the kids' rooms. With the bedroom door locked, they tried to linger, to nurture the rising passion. That proved impossible. Instead, he was inside her before they were fully naked. While he was still pulsing, Terry strummed herself urgently, arousing him even more, and they rode their wave together. He was still inside her when they fell asleep.

Franco spent Sunday evening alone, recapping the arguments for and against publishing *The Belacqua Report*. He'd already decided that when the board met the following morning they would cast secret ballots as they had with other controversial submissions, including the Goebbels bio and the firsthand account of Tiny Messingkauf, the serial killer who was still at large. The secret ballot would highlight the stakes involved, along with the potential for recriminations down the road. He'd also discourage any lobbying, though he would answer any questions he could about Roger's career, for example, or the endorsements of Bushnell and Landry.

Franco tallied up his own reasons in favor of publishing the book: a well-established, NASA-authorized scientist was publishing a decade's worth of self-financed research, dedicated to his late children. He glanced at the photo on his desk, which Ben Steiner had gotten from AP: President Clinton greeting Belacqua in the Oval Office. This research was not all that far out of line with a broad spectrum of experts. In fact, eventually Belacqua's doomsday scenario was *inevitable*, most scientists agreed: only the time frame—forty years or four hundred—was in dispute.

Finally, he allowed any lingering doubts to subside: he would vote for publication, but abide by the will of the board. Only then did he admit to himself that, of course, if Commonweal published the book, he could be sure of spending much more time with Terry, at least over the next few months.

The next morning, February 23, after considering Franco's admonitions about how much could be at stake with this manuscript, the editorial board voted by secret ballot, five to four, in favor of publishing *The Belacqua Report*. The pub date was set for Labor Day weekend.

*　　*　　*

At Commonweal Books the fall catalog went out early in April, as usual, to all the chains and bookstores in America. In addition to Dewey's *Football and Freud,* Laura Goldman's *The Flame of Barungia,* and two new titles by Dr. Jonathan Fischer, the list included several authors who sometimes turned a profit.

The '98 fall catalog included a flyer: "An Important Note from Franco Sherman, President of Commonweal Books." It read, "This September we are offering the most important book that Commonweal has published in its illustrious history. In the short time available it has not been possible to prepare a description that can convey the impact that *The Belacqua Report* is certain to have, by virtue of its scientific analysis. Without overstatement, we may say that this book has no precedent: it will dominate international dialogue for decades to come. In fact, by separate mail we will be sending out an advisory about the attention this book is certain to receive."

The flyer was barely even noticed. At one time or another publishers had tried every gimmick imaginable to highlight a star title, and this apparent hyperbole seemed no different. Meanwhile Franco met with the publicity department on a regular basis to devise a sensitive approach to selling *The Belacqua Report.*

A team of marketing wizards spent hundreds of hours brainstorming, trying to come up with an appealing "persona" for the book. That was no easy task. Images of a stinking planet ruled by cockroaches were unlikely to sell books. But there wasn't much to justify happy pictures. The art department struggled, week after week, to come up with something that could be used, not just on the cover of the book and the CD-ROM, but on book displays, print ads, billboards, and even the promotional tie-ins that marketing was pushing for, and that Franco vetoed immediately. "Tasteful" was the guideline in the PR department, where everyone tried to figure out what that meant with *The Belacqua Report.* Especially Berling, the head of publicity.

If Berling had a first name, his own mother had probably never used it. A dark-skinned Caucasian who looked almost Sephardic, Berling had a permanent stubble that made Nixon's jowls seem pubescent. His eyebrows were as black as the long hair he combed straight back, and when he raised them he looked a little like Brezhnev, only thinner. A large man with a cruel temper that sometimes spurred him to the brink of clinical derangement, Berling was a legendary figure throughout the interlaced worlds of publishing and promotion. He was also sociably affable, when it was called for, though no schmoozer. He had achieved his status by virtue of his surprising, imaginative touch, followed by hard work. Most recently, Berling had pushed *The Diary of Ella Fitzgerald* to the top of the list after every other publisher in town had declined the manuscript.

It fell to Berling, of course, to handle the promotion of *The Belacqua Report*—a challenge he accepted with both relish and foreboding. If this unique venture didn't break every sales record, he'd never forgive himself. So from March through May, he whipped his staff into a creative frenzy that left them mute and wilted by the end of each day; still, they failed to devise a campaign that would satisfy him. By mid-April, they still had no idea how *The Belacqua Report* would be presented to the world.

On Tuesday, April 14, as on most mornings since Terry had begun staying with him, Franco awoke at five forty-five and wrapped himself around her. Since mid-March she had more or less settled in, albeit tentatively. Franco had explained to Max and Juliette that Terry would stay in the guest room while they worked on a project together; and, the kids were glad to hear, it would be a long project. Of course she kept her apartment downtown, and an answering machine that relayed her messages forty blocks up to Franco's— mostly from her mom, and from Bobby, who sounded more and more agitated and bitter.

Their third evening together, over sushi, Terry had told Franco nervously about Bobby. She hadn't planned to volunteer so much so soon, but she wanted to be forthright: there was nothing—well, almost nothing—she wanted to keep from him. So rather than appear mysterious, she acknowledged that she'd been romantically involved with Bobby until, um, very shortly before she and Franco first made love. He had accepted this news with a facade of insouciance, and while he didn't feel threatened, neither was he indifferent. Besides, he thought, if this perilous adventure of the heart headed south for some reason, he could always retreat to a familiar vegetative state. But every day he spent with Terry, and every night, he became more aware of a renaissance within himself, as he slowly shed the incubus that had pinned him down for so long.

"I had shut down, emotionally," he told Terry early on. "So if ever I'm not all here, then drag me out of my shell, the way you did the first night." Terry evoked a degree of tenderness he'd never felt toward Lillian, or else couldn't bear to remember, and he spent hours wondering why. Her self-suffficiency—which often prompted her to take the lead, in her work and in their life together—was one of the qualities he admired. There was none of the wounded sparrow about her, as there had been in other women he'd known. Terry's resolute independence of judgment was especially apparent during the last painful weeks of work on *The Belacqua Report*, when problems with the footnotes and last-minute changes in charts and diagrams raised blood pressure to critical levels in the production department. But that wasn't what touched him so.

Neither was it her relationship with Juliette and Max that pulled on his heart like an undertow: he melted at every funny, sweet exchange she had with them. Nor was it her sensitivity to his own needs, so acute she knew that he needed to scratch his ear before he even twitched. It wasn't even her stubborn determination to articulate the ineffable. Terry took it as a personal challenge to find the words for complex situations, though when he pointed this out, she didn't know what he was talking about.

What Franco fell in love with was what he thought of as her abundant presence, her largeness of spirit. Which was coupled with her fearless determination to rise to every occasion. Whether she was pitching him the notion that the earth was doomed or tackling the copyedit of *The Belacqua Report* without a background in science, or taking on a widower nearing middle age, with kids, she was all there, overbrimming her edges and reaching into his own, and the kids', and everyone else's who met her.

All these things passed through Franco's mind in the first few minutes of that April morning. When the alarm rang again at six, Franco fetched coffee—without which Terry could barely sit up, much less rise to any occasions. By eight they'd showered, dressed, and shifted to their platonic mode before breakfast with the kids. Franco had planned to go to his gym, but this had been one of those rare mornings when they made love; their unhurried, intimate hours were at night, sustaining each sensual adventure for as long as possible, playing, exploring, and consuming each other, blurring the boundaries between their bodies. That became much more true once they relied upon the pill instead of condoms.

They adapted to business mode on their way to work each day. By the time they entered the Commonweal building, a gifted savant wouldn't have known they were lovers. As long as no one knew, Terry could continue to work on *The Belacqua Report* without feeling ill at ease. She was also gradually taking responsibility for the CD-ROM. Christiane Belacqua had done a remarkable job overseeing the graphics offered at the Belacqua website, which would also be a major part of the CD-ROM. But much remained to be done. Terry assembled a new team to write, produce, and design the whole package. So even though she remained an assistant, Terry took pride in the knowledge that, because Franco trusted her judgment, she exercised considerable influence over Commonweal's production and publicity, as well as acquisitions.

That April morning Terry left early to meet novelist Laura Goldman, who was arriving at Newark Airport at eight forty-five. At about that moment, Franco was walking through the lobby of the Commonweal building wondering how to promote the book. He did not especially like Berling, or his methods, or his eyebrows, but the man had always gotten results. This time, however, nothing was happening. He had asked repeatedly for preliminary sketches, or layouts, but none were forthcoming. At this point he was—

SCIENTIST PUBLISHES DOOMSDAY REPORT

Franco stared at the headline screaming from the *National Enquirer* at the lobby newsstand. Must be a coincidence. He rushed to buy a copy of the rag and shamelessly read its account on an elevator full of corporate literati who glanced at him with disdain.

The tabloid had the whole story, garbled beyond comprehension. Somehow it had gotten hold of the manuscript and beaten everyone to the draw—even Commonweal. Dizzy with anger, he half-stumbled into his office and shut the door without a word to Millie. For the rest of the day he alternately thrashed about for some appropriate strategy and guessed at the identity of the mole who had leaked *The Belacqua Report* to the tabloid press.

The nuclear plume sweeping westward from Armenia had already contaminated villages, factories, schools, military installations, crops, livestock, vineyards, lakes, rivers, snowpacks, ski resorts, and forests. In less than a month, Venice would be threatened, along with the many unique species in the Adriatic. The reactor's failure was universally declared the greatest catastrophe ever caused by man. No one dared estimate the number of fatalities that would result, even in the short term.

Because this was only the beginning. There was still *no* prospect of containment, as the white-hot core sank like a branding iron deeper and deeper into the skin of the earth, releasing radioactive gases in such volume that, had the core been contained, it would soon have burst its structure. At the behest of the UN Security Council, physicists and engineers from around the world had gathered in Paris to determine exactly what had happened, and what could be done to contain the disaster. The Armenian leadership insisted they could handle the situation themselves, though it was readily apparent that they could not, and they were stingy with critical information about the extent of the catastrophe. Meanwhile, the radioactive fog meandered lazily toward Western Europe.

Franco arrived home that evening with the haunted stare of a destitute diabetic in a strange city at night. He retired immediately to the bedroom. Terry had supper with the children, and after sending Juliette to bed because of her cough, she played a quick game of chess with Max, which she lost, as always. Then she found Franco sprawled on his bed. He hardly acknowledged her presence, so deep was his funk.

He'd barely functioned all day, stuttering through conferences, staring through a luncheon, and canceling his other meetings. The book's credibility had now been compromised, he reckoned, in the eyes of anyone who frequented supermarkets. And since the sleazy *Enquirer* article named Commonweal as publisher, even quoting Franco's own words from the catalog flyer, he knew damn well that soon there'd be a call from Bob Milton about some rumor his wife had heard from her bridge partners.

Terry tried to guess what was wrong. She was pretty sure it had to do with *The Belacqua Report,* since it was Franco's greatest preoccupation. She'd never seen him so upset. After several attempts to arouse him, one way or another, she followed his finger to the attaché case near the door. The headline screamed out at her.

"Ratfuck," she said softly. She read the article through without another word, and then scanned the whole piece again. Then she went to the bed and lay down silently beside her damaged man. After an hour, Terry went to the kitchen to make mint tea. When Franco had had a few sips—his first sustenance all day—he rolled over and stared at the ceiling.

"It could be worse," she said lamely.

With no warning he erupted in a Vesuvian fury. "Worse? A rusty fork with mustard on it up my ass couldn't be worse. What could be worse?"

Man behaving badly. She determined that his question was rhetorical, and without taking offense, she went into the kitchen and poured him another cup of mint tea with a spoonful of sugar and a drop or two of fresh-squeezed lemon. Then she smiled and ran back to the bedroom, spilling some of the tea. She slowed down and by the time she stopped beside him, she seemed as somber as he was. She reached for the legal pad on his side of the bed and started to jot things down.

"You gotta turn it around, Franco," she said firmly. "There's nothing else *to* do." Her resolve sounded so tightly wound that his gloom gave quarter to her determination. After a dramatic pause, she handed him the pad on which she'd written the words "MAKE LEMONADE."

He released a groan, barely mastering his omnidirectional rage. He was grateful now that Terry had kept her own apartment. "Here I am contemplating the end of the world," he said, "and you are thinking about citrus fruit."

"There's no choice, Franco," she repeated. "There's only one way you can play this situation." Then, animated, she poured out her ideas. As she spoke, she rose from the bed and began to pace; after a moment she picked up the yellow pad and began scribbling notes again furiously.

"Look, instinct tells you to ignore this trash. Instead, what you're going to do is raise hell, with lawsuits and an open letter to the *Enquirer.* You accuse them of distorting the most important scientific thesis ever written and warn the world to withhold judgment until they've seen the real McCoy." She planted her feet beside the bed. "At the same time, we're going to speed up publication and give copies of the book to the press by the end of next week."

"Next week?" Franco spluttered. "That's delusional!"

"We can do it! We produce special copies for the press, techno-perfect, by desktop publishing: we use Belacqua's own disk—copyedited—to set the type. That way you can give the first five hundred copies to the media *next week,* with another five thousand available a week later."

"I can?"

Terry nodded. "And get the book directly to the cutting-edge readers you want, so that the word of mouth gets the message out *accurately.*"

"How?" Franco was less enchanted. "Hand out free copies on college campuses?"

"No, we make the first four chapters available through America Online's Book Report: Anyone can download it for free."

His eyebrows rose slowly toward his scalp. "Terry, that's crazy! Those are the people who should be buying copies. This is still a publishing *business,* and I don't own it. The shareholders do, starting with Bob Milton."

Terry settled on the floor beside the bed, resting her forearms on his knees, and spoke with patience and precision. "How big a best-seller does it have to be, Franco? This book's going to be racing out of bookstores for years to come. What did you write in the flyer? 'Not since Gutenberg has there been such a paradigm shift blah blah blah.' As long as Belacqua is right, forty years from now people will crawl into bookstores and"—she made a choking sound —"with their very last breath they'll say, 'I'd like a copy of—' If, however, he's *wrong,* well"—she did Gilda Radner—" 'Ne-ver mind.' So for a few weeks make it available for free to anyone with a modem. It'll help promote the CD-ROM; and they'll *still* buy the dead-tree edition."

She was on a roll, and Franco could only sit back and marvel. "Starting next week, Berling puts Dr. Roger Belacqua on *Nightline,*

Dateline, and *Primetime, Meet the Press,* and *60 Minutes.* Next month he makes the cover of *Time,* and by September he'll be dressed as Ben Franklin on the cover of *George.* The PR department is going to concentrate on *correcting* misinterpretations like this crap. As for the actual copies, they're going to be absolutely *artless:* no fancy cover, no catchy blurbs. Nothing on the cover except the title, in Courier typeface. I'll call production now—if you agree—and tell them we've got to rush this like never before. How does that grab you?"

Franco stared as once again Terry rose to the occasion. She was right and he knew it. A distorted version of the book was already in every supermarket: the real story was being preempted by a knockoff. "Franco, if the book isn't out until Labor Day, it will have been completely discredited with the cognoscenti and the general public."

"So," he said slowly, "what do you suggest we do first?" He wasn't convinced, but after a day spent in a stupor of indecision, he was keen to adopt almost any plan.

"Let's call Dr. Belacqua now and tell him what's going on. Then we finish the edits, reformat, and print copies directly in almost no time. A place in Northampton does bindings for dissertations; anyway, there must be a company here in the city. We should be able to get professional-looking copies in a few days."

"Up to Commonweal's standards?"

"No," Terry answered flatly, "but better than the *Enquirer*'s. And better than the bound galleys we send to reviewers. Don't get too fussy. This is an emergency."

Franco was barely keeping up. "What about the CD-ROM?"

"The development guys are working on the programming for Belacqua's approval: it'd help if you lit a fire under their butts, but it's still gonna take a few months."

She began pacing again, while jotting notes. "We're going to need some trucks at our disposal twenty-four hours a day. And please, would you call Danvers yourself and tell him I'm busy for the next few weeks?" He nodded. "And we need Belacqua to be available soon or this won't work. You're going to make a lot of public appearances yourself, you know. So pull yourself together. You look like a stunned mullet."

He continued staring at her, speechless, as she scratched

around in his attaché case for Belacqua's number and reached for the phone. Franco was still preoccupied with blaming someone for leaking the book to the tabloids, but obviously Terry's strategy was more useful. It was several moments before he finally spoke.

"Could I have," he said, "another cup of tea?"

Terry kissed him on the cheek and set off for the kitchen, but as she passed the kids' rooms, she heard Juliette calling weakly. The little girl was sitting up, eyes wide with panic as she struggled for breath. Terry screamed for Franco.

An hour later Franco and Terry were sipping industrial coffee from a machine on the third floor of Lenox Hill Hospital. Juliette's first asthma attack had ended, and she was resting comfortably in a private room.

PART TWO

THE BLOOD-DIMMED TIDE

Not Chaos, not
The darkest pit of lowest Erebus,
Nor aught of blinder vacancy, scooped out
By help of dreams—can breed such fear and awe
As fall upon us often when we look
Into our Minds, into the Mind of Man.

—WILLIAM WORDSWORTH, "The Prelude" (1850)

5

DETECTIVE JORDAN

Within a generation we may commit the biosphere to a grand-scale depletion that will disrupt evolution for at least 200,000 generations, or twenty times as long as humans have been a species.

—NORMAN MYERS, "Mass Extinctions and Evolution," *Science*, October 24, 1997 [italics added]

"Yo, Tyrone, my main man! How it is?"

"Hey, bro, what's shakin'?"

Professor Richard Wylie was shuffling home slowly when he overheard this exchange between two young men on 125th Street, that frail Maginot Line between Harlem and Columbia University. He listened for them to slap a high five, and then said "Bingo!" aloud, as he often did. Approaching home, he was in high spirits: he'd found a small but valuable trove of anti-Federalist correspondence at the New-York Historical Society dating from 1787. But just then he was recalling the afternoon fifty years before—his freshman year at Columbia—when he heard that Israel had declared independence. It seemed very long ago. But when he recalled the day he'd heard that Gandhi had been assassinated, it seemed like the day before yesterday. Strange, he marveled, how subjectively time dilates and contracts.

There wasn't really much you could point at that had changed since 1948. There had been some impact from the new "conveniences" that Wylie shunned: television, microwave, and the computerized card catalog—fads!—but the drone of city life was much as it had been in the mid-twentieth century. There had of course been a loss of civility: the mangle of modernity had squeezed the juice out of social behavior. In the old days, everybody in midtown dressed up; only delivery men wore dungarees. Now only the old and the wealthy seemed to care how they looked: the rest wore T-shirts to restaurants, jeans to the theater, bathing suits in the street—symptoms, wondered Wylie, of what? The flowering of democracy, or unrelenting dehumanization?

Approaching the corner of Amsterdam and 122nd, Wylie saw a figure waiting in front of his small Columbia-owned building. Wylie couldn't quite put a name to the man: tall, good-looking, in a double-breasted suit, carrying a briefcase. Oh, the fellow who had reissued *Second Republic* last year. Master's thesis on Madison and the Constitution: a talent for synthesis; tended to bite off more than he could chew.

"Professor Wylie . . . Franco Sherman."

"Ah yes, it's been a while! Coming up for coffee?"

Franco nodded, grateful almost to tears that the old man and his rituals endured: like Kant in Königsberg, Wylie returned home each weekday at precisely 5:50 P.M. Franco followed Wylie's dark baggy suit upstairs, and recalled climbing those four flights every Thursday for his seminar. The most exhilarating conversations of his life had all taken place in Wylie's rooms.

The stooped old man showed Franco into his home, one of the smaller two-room apartments the university kept for lecturers. Most tenured professors had posh apartments on Riverside Drive, overlooking the Hudson. But Wylie rarely took the time to look out the window anyway, and he felt that, as a committed bachelor, such luxury would have been largely wasted on him. All the sights he wanted were the forsythia blossoming outside Fayerweather in May, as they were right now, and the occasional glimpse of a pretty girl's ankles. Not a hard man to please, Professor Wylie.

"Historical Perspective—isn't that you? What brings you uptown, Franco? Research? Nostalgia? Or just making sure I haven't moved to the bone orchard yet?"

Franco laughed. "All three, Professor, and something else, too. Before I forget, here's another check." He laid an envelope on Wylie's coffee table.

Wylie smiled. "Strange. The royalty checks are getting *larger.*"

Wylie sometimes suspected Franco of providing a charitable annuity.

"There's been some talk of a new Constitutional Convention, so *Second Republic* is selling more and staying in the stores. Publishing has become so—"

"Profit-oriented?" Wylie offered.

"Bingo!" said Franco, remembering the old man's exclamation.

"I'm flattered to have a president of publishing visit. Don't suppose you have time for other presidents, eh? Like Madison?" With the kettle on, the old man removed his hat, scratching his rubbery scalp and stringy white hair with enviable satisfaction.

"No. My job runs my life," Franco replied. "But today, it brings me here."

Wylie considered whether to sit until the water boiled or wait on his feet, leaning on the counter. He chose to lean: these days, rising from a seat wasn't his forte.

Franco waited until Wylie had propped himself by the stove, taking comfort somehow from the professor's frayed cuffs and hand-sewn elbow patches. "We're publishing a book . . ." And with that, he outlined the findings of *The Belacqua Report.*

"Belacqua," he concluded, "says it's too late to achieve the treaties necessary to lengthen our survival time. So according to him, our species is doomed."

"Well, it's about time someone said so!" said Wylie, not the least bit surprised. "I've been expecting something like this for thirty years. Haven't you? It wasn't hard to predict. You only had to watch the population explosion to know that this was inevitable—the environment had to succumb. Cream and sugar as usual?"

"Yes, please." Franco was astonished. "You saw this coming?"

Wylie enjoyed surprising younger folk. "You're an historian, Franco: you *know* the terrible truths of the past. Of course, the storybooks tell us that human history is a tale of virtue and victory, patriotic lore, and above all *progress.*" He laughed aloud. "But that's not the whole truth, is it? Our triumphs mask our tragedies: domination and genocide do no credit to our genes—the Y chromosomes in particular. This century has achieved new dimensions of barbarity: one hundred seventy million civilians slaughtered by their own governments. Such numbers have no precedent."

Franco remembered how enraged some students had been by Wylie's perspective. "Professor, I wanted to ask your opinion about one aspect of this report. You'd have to read the book, of course, but in a general way, what chance do you think nations have of joining together to save our skins? Could some two hundred nations ever cooperate?"

Now Wylie was thoroughly engaged. "This Belacqua thinks not?"

"He argues that only global dictatorship could limit population and economic expansion, but that such a tyranny is unthinkable."

Wylie poured the boiling water into his Chemex. Along with an occasional ticket to the opera, fresh-ground coffee was his greatest luxury. "I doubt that any effective world government could be formed. And the idea is certainly anathema to ultranationalists everywhere." He paused in reverie. "Interesting: if survival depends on it, could humanity draft a constitution for the world? I can't see it. Of course, I'm better acquainted with the eighteenth century than the twentieth. But it would require a collective rethinking of the nature of states and governments. Is Belacqua somehow connected with this movement toward a Second Constitutional Convention?" Wylie served coffee with the grace and concentration appropriate to a Japanese tea ceremony. He sank gently into his tired old armchair and rubbed his scalp unselfconsciously.

"No, why? Could a Constitutional Convention really produce viable reform? Wouldn't moneyed interests have their way with it?"

"That's the danger," agreed Wylie. "But you know, when the stakes are high enough, all the ol' patriotic blarney can evoke honor from even the most corrupt."

Franco felt as if he could see Wylie's thoughts through the translucent skin of his head. To the old man, this was recreation: a chance to play fast and loose with the grand sweep of history, a kind of global calculus. "American individualism is ill-suited for global cooperation, and harsh limitations on personal freedom run counter to our pioneer traditions, of course. However repugnant, totalitarian tyranny like China's—with one-fifth of the human race on a short leash—might extend our survival better than democracy. Which poses a classic dilemma: is this perhaps the one situation in which the ends *do* justify the means? If only a dictatorship could save the planet, wouldn't *that* warrant abandoning democracy? It would be much like martial law imposed in a national emergency, but worldwide, and lasting until the end of civilization." Wylie's eyes twinkled as they did whenever he posed his riddles.

Franco shook his head. "Is global dictatorship the only solution?" He glanced at Wylie's groaning bookshelves as if looking for another.

"Oh, it's no solution at all. Because power still corrupts, and absolute power corrupts absolutely. Besides, only brute force could suppress well-established democracies. Maybe a grassroots movement—that's where everything always begins here. But the threat would have to be clear: the enormous American effort in World War Two was inconceivable until Pearl Harbor was attacked; but then Americans were ready to go much further for their noble ideals than even FDR had imagined. But such sacrifices can't be forced." Wylie's face turned grave. "The rest of the world . . ."

Franco sipped his coffee. It wasn't very good, but Franco loved its brackish taste. "They *might* follow, if America and China led the way."

Wylie started to soar. "Such enormous sacrifices would require a revolution of the spirit unlike anything history has seen, more profound than the Renaissance or the Age of Enlightenment, shared all around the world. To succeed, that revolution would have to be inherently American in character, to its core. And inherently Welsh in character; and Russian, and French, and Chinese, and Zulu, and Armenian. . . . In short, it must speak to the deepest, most universal precepts of all cultures, and of our selves. And this will have to be achieved with our eyes wide open. We would have to start by recognizing the short, tragic existence of billions of people today; it is certainly not by sacrificing compassion that we will preserve life, nor by abandoning democratic principles, or losing sight of faiths and traditions widely shared across our species. Even then, it would require an unceasing grassroots, global agitation. Direct democracy, local and community oversight, would have to be built into the framework of global government to resist corruption. But—it's beyond me how one could ever forge transgovernmentalism from the grass roots up. The population would have to grasp the threat of extinction in some very personal way: that's difficult, with a gradual, progressive catastrophe."

"Tall order. We're more like a frog in a pot, someone said, coming slowly to a boil."

"The human race would have to act as one. We would have to find a way to communicate globally, contributing individually, almost like neurons in a single great, worldwide brain—the holistic human mind."

He's really wailin' now, thought Franco.

When Professor Wylie spoke again, it was in morose tones. "These are the wild meanderings of an old man, sad to think the world will go on without him, and sadder to think that it won't. You know, Ortega y Gasset once said, 'Yes, it's true: life *is* nasty, brutish, and short; but please don't tell the children.' "

That, thought Franco, was exactly what *The Belacqua Report* did: it told the children. He drowned the last muddy sip of coffee and rose.

"I've already taken up too much of your time. Thank you for the coffee and all that came with it. Perhaps you'd join me in midtown for lunch someday? I'm over on the East Side. You could catch the subway."

Wylie shook his head. "Don't go over there much. Can't stand the elevated trains."

Franco started to tell him that the Third Avenue El was dismantled in the early fifties, but decided Wylie was teasing him. "Well, I'll come back in a few weeks," he said at the door. "Maybe I'll bring my girlfriend. Is your phone number still—"

"University six, four five seven nine."

"Good. Thanks again, Professor. I'll send you *The Belacqua Report.*"

"Oh, I won't get to it. My reading's still bogged down in the eighteenth century, I'm afraid." At the threshold of the apartment Franco shook the old man's hand warmly, and, descending the staircase, he thought to himself again: They will come no more, the old men with beautiful manners.

Terry formally left her job at Commonweal Books on June 1, with Franco's encouragement. This was partly because of Juliette's asthma. The doctors couldn't explain its sudden onset, and Juliette had been so frightened, especially by the emergency room, that she did not want to leave Terry's side, afraid of another attack. Besides, without living as hermits, Franco and Terry couldn't hope to keep their relationship a secret much longer. With the issue of her job out of the way, the only obstacles to their living together were the children and Terry's stubborn determination to maintain financial independence. The kids, of course, were delighted their dad had asked Terry to live with them. Neither was the second problem intractable: working eighteen hours a day on *The Belacqua Report,* she knew she was entitled to a consultant's fee. So reluctantly, she accepted a salary: that way, she could keep her apartment as an office and still live with Franco while remaining independent.

Eight days after the first tabloid article, five hundred copies of *The Belacqua Report* went out; five thousand more were FedExed a week later to major newspapers and national magazines, network bureau chiefs, political periodicals like *Foreign Affairs,* and various UN publications. Franco also sent copies to James Bushnell, Bob Landry, Floyd Henley at the Natural Resources Defense Council, and General Shreiver.

As for the final book, a copy of Terry's revised, edited floppy disk was sent directly to the printer in Pennsylvania, who six days later produced a preliminary softcover edition. Terry ordered a quick run—five thousand copies marked "Uncorrected Proofs"—while the first major run of forty thousand went for binding. The first printing would be shipped June 7, while the standard edition was scheduled to be ready by the Fourth of July—the same week the movie *Armageddon* was going to open. Though hardly a conventional beach book, what with its melanoma studies, it was still expected to fly out of the stores.

For once everything worked like magic, and the only hitches in Terry's plan were quickly overcome. Mostly. Franco had personally drafted a disclaimer, to appear on the copyright page, that he sent to legal for vetting, intended to protect Commonweal's backside against key industries accused of contributing to global warming, as well as nuisance suits from individuals. The draft sat on Marshall Pierson's desk for three weeks. Finally, Marshall's assistant, Sebastian, got it into the book just in time, but without legal review. That was because, at the same time, Marshall was preparing a suite of suits against the *National Enquirer,* seeking an injunction against further misleading stories, damages, and discovery of the *Enquirer's* source for the manuscript. A week later the *Enquirer* filed countersuits regarding the first two issues, but offered to comply with the third.

By early May the nuclear cloud, often referred to as "the blight," had wafted east almost to the Alps, broadcasting its dust more widely. General circulation models that predicted an early dispersal were thoroughly discredited.

A wide belt of famine soon spread along the wake of the blight, and despite unprecedented relief efforts, potable water and untainted grain were completely unavailable to millions of families. Cholera followed, and soon desperate residents throughout the region ignored public warnings: they drank from rivers contaminated by radiation they could not see, instead of waiting for fresh water they could not get. Estimates of radiation poisoning ranged from two to twenty million people, but these were guesses. In the most affected regions (Bosnia, Romania, Bulgaria, Turkey, and Georgia), there was no way to relocate the population living in the radiated swath; families there remained in their homes to face slow, agonizing deaths.

Medical teams from around the world established triage centers and began treating the contaminated. But unless they risked exposing themselves to radiation, they could treat only those who were out of harm's way and least in need of medical attention. The Red Cross, serving as the international clearinghouse for aid and relief, was overwhelmed.

Meanwhile, in Armenia, containment remained a distant prospect. Although new techniques intended to reduce the temperatures underground had been partly successful, no one yet knew where things would lead.

"Millie, get me Belacqua, please." As he waited for Roger to come on the phone, Franco stared at the short, cynical piece in the *Daily News*—one of the few papers to mention Commonweal's lawsuit. "Doomsday Report Rushes to Press" was the headline on page 11. "Commonweal Books registered its displeasure with the *National Enquirer* yesterday by a lawsuit that accused the tabloid of dis-

torting its upcoming nonfiction chiller *The Belacqua Report.*
Franco Sherman, current president of the house, announced an
accelerated production schedule of the work, which, according
to the *Enquirer,* proves that global warming has doomed the
earth to—"

"*Ciao,* Franco!"

"*Ciao!* Roger, we'll need you here this weekend. Has Berling
been in touch yet?"

"Yes, he gave me my schedule for the *Times, Newsweek,
Nightline,* and a few others. Suki's my secretary now: she's coordi-
nating with Berling's assistant." In the back of his mind, Franco
could still hear the sound of Suki's distinctive moans coming from
McAdams's room.

"Good. We need a list of ecologists who'll confirm your
conclusions."

"*Certo.*"

"*Grazie.* Now, when do you and Christiane get in to New York?"

"Monday—we're flying commercial."

"Terry and I would be happy if you stayed at the apartment, but—"

"You don't need the fuss. Berling has us at the Ritz-Carlton."

"Okay, ask Suki to let us know when we can have dinner."

"Will do. See you next week."

Franco stared at his desk, stretching his mind to cover all the
angles. Who else would speak up for *The Belacqua Report?*

"Millie, get me General Shreiver on the phone."

"I'll try, Franco, but. . . ."

"But what?"

"Well, I FedExed the early edition to the address on his business
card, but the package came back marked 'Wrong zip code.' "

"Well, try his number."

A moment later Franco was on the phone with Shreiver. "Good
morning, General. I expect you're aware of everything going on?"

"Well, I just heard you're publishing *The Belacqua Report* in
a hurry."

"That's right. We FedExed you a copy, but the package was
returned."

Shreiver laughed. "Damn, my business cards. It takes six months
when I requisition them, so my secretary went to a civilian outfit,
and they fouled up. That's okay, I'll buy a copy."

"I wondered if you'd help us out by doing a couple of interviews. An officer of your standing would add credibility."

"I'm on my way to Alaska for some fishing. Sorry."

"Even one interview before you—"

"I'm sorry, no." His tone had the finality of a disconnect notice.

"Well, I'm sorry to hear that, General. Good-bye."

Strange. For a moment he wondered if the general had learned something. Franco glanced out the window: another day of record-breaking heat. "Millie, I'm going home. Would you please forward my calls? Not the boring ones."

"Of course, Franco."

Emily was watching a rerun of *Star Trek* in the kitchen while Max played with his chemistry set and Juliette held a toy tea party with Jennifer from 22G. Terry was working the phone in the den, trying to speed up deliveries of the desktop edition—there was a union problem. So as Franco arrived home, he answered the second line.

"Franco, Marshall here. The *Enquirer* just named its source for the manuscript. His name's Bobby Anderson."

"Does he work for us?" The name seemed familiar.

"I don't know. Want me to check?" Marshall sneezed right into the phone.

"Of *course* I do, Marshall," replied Franco, as irritably as his good manners permitted. "Jesus, you've had that head cold for over a year!"

"Yeah, it's a doozy. Okay, I'll check with personnel and get back to you."

Franco hung up and hugged Terry. "What's new?" he finally asked.

"Juliette got an A on her French exam," she answered proudly.

"Amazing! And what was that I heard about shipping?"

"Solved. Without crossing the picket line." She wrinkled her nose mischievously. "But it's gonna cost you." She kissed him. "What's new with you?"

"Oh, just—more."

"Who was that you were being crabby with?"

Franco kicked off his shoes and sprawled on the sofa, where Terry joined him. "Marshall, in legal. I'm not sure his staircase makes it all the way to the top floor."

"Well, it's common knowledge that he has, um, a problem."

"What's that?"

Terry had to decide if this was snitching. "The devil's dandruff," she answered. Franco looked at her askance. "Cocaine."

Wonderment crossed his face. "Of *course*. Well, I will have to fire him immediately."

Terry frowned. "Naah. Get him into a program. There's others, you know. Not to mention the potheads." Franco shook his head in disbelief. "What made you cross?"

"He found out who passed the manuscript to the *Enquirer*, but didn't bother to check if the guy works for us."

"What's his name?" Terry asked.

"Bobby Anderson."

"Oh no! Damn, that's where my backup disk went." Now she couldn't hide the truth if she wanted to. "He's my ex-boyfriend. He must have stolen the disk. He even said something about how this was like a tabloid story."

Franco swallowed. "He made an unauthorized copy?"

Terry shook her head and blushed. "No. I did. When I was working on it." She squinted, angry at herself. "Shouldn't have done that. I fucked up, Franco. Remember the first night we made love? When Giuseppe waited all night to take me home? Well, Bobby was there, pissed as hell, when I got home, and then he stormed out. But he had an extra key. I bet he came back and took the disk I thought I'd lost. I'm sorry."

Franco's lunch was still bouncing. He started to say something too harsh.

"I didn't sleep with him again after you and I—" she volunteered.

Terry sat teary-eyed while everything ganged up in Franco's head. The leak to the *Enquirer* wasn't something he could afford to dwell on. Next week a firestorm was going to hit Commonweal, and he'd need all his wits. So he leaped up energetically, alarming Terry, and hit the speed dialer.

"Millie, call the Vertical Club and schedule a training session every day at four, starting today, okay? Thanks. Any calls?"

"Yes, Bob Milton. His wife heard Commonweal was publishing 'heretical dogma'—call him at home. Then a Detective Bill Jordan called from the NYPD, Midtown North. Want the number?"

"Did he say why he was calling?"

Millie hesitated. That was unlike her. "It's about a homicide investigation."

Well, that capped Franco's day. "You're kidding! Who was murdered?"

"He wouldn't say."

"I'll call." He took down the number. "Better cancel today's training session."

Her poise regained, Terry braced herself for the next shock. "What was that?"

"Something about a murder investigation," Franco replied, dialing.

"Detective Jordan," came a laconic voice packed with street smarts.

"Yes, this is Franco Sherman. You wanted to talk to me?"

"That's right, Mr. Sherman, thanks for calling so quick. I need ta see you, to ask some questions about the death of William McAdams."

Overload. "Uh, he died of a heart attack, didn't he?"

"Well, between you an' me, this new coroner, Hennessy, he's a finicky man with too much time on his hands. Anyway, after a second autopsy at the widow's request, he felt there was . . . problems. If we could just meet for a few minutes in your office, maybe tomorrow. I don't wear a uniform, so no one'll. . . ."

Franco had never known the victim of a murder, if that's what McAdams was. The whole course of *The Belacqua Report* was strewn with unnatural events. He struggled for nonchalance. "Certainly, Detective. How's nine o'clock?"

"Appreciate it, Mr. Sherman. See you tomorrow at nine, at yer office." He made it sound like "orifice."

That night, as Terry lay snoring lightly beside him, Franco dreamed of murder and mayhem, of radiation and pollution, mass suicides, and global extinction. And for every hideous brutality that appeared before his eyes, there was a reporter there, side by side with a policeman and a judge, all accusing him of being personally responsible for the whole damn mess.

Detective Jordan was not a dapper man. He was not a well-spoken man. He was not a happy man. He was a large, blunt, bitter fellow with an eye on his pension, who often took out his frustration on subordinates and witnesses. He entered Franco's office as if, in a just world, it should have been his own. He took a chair in front of the desk, proprietorially, and spoke only after he was seated.

"Hello," he said, and cut to the chase. "Okay, look: William McAdams died of a heart attack—no question—but was it deliberately induced, is what the coroner's askin'. Because there were traces of something suspicious in his system, he's thinking sclerosis was a contributing factor, not the actual cause of death."

"I see," said Franco. "Why are you interviewing me? Am I somehow a suspect?"

Jordan's chuckle sounded like a series of short burps. "Course not, Mr. Sherman. But since Hennessy has this bug up his ass, we hafta waste manpower tracking down everyone who saw him before he croaked. You were with him a few days earlier, so here I am. You were all guests of some Roger Belacqua"—his Brooklyn accent made it sound like "black one"—"in Vermont?" Franco nodded as a fast-breaking wave of anxiety crashed over him. "Didja know McAdams well?"

"I didn't know him at all. We had just hired him as a scientific consultant, to assess a book we're about to publish. A book by Dr. Belacqua."

"And did he finish the job?"

"Not as far as I know. No report was submitted."

"Ah." Jordan sounded as though the trial had just ended in conviction. "He didn't seem unwell, did he? I never met the guy, but he wasn't exactly frail."

"No, he seemed quite hearty. I remember he had a good appetite," Franco added coolly, again hearing in his mind the rising moan from McAdams's room.

"And, ah, was he alone on this business trip?"

"Yes. certainly. We were only there overnight. Dr. Belacqua himself piloted us all up to Vermont and back. I met McAdams for the first time at La Guardia."

"Hmm. So you wouldn't know whether McAdams was getting any, on the side?"

"Getting any what?" Franco felt something like cold sweat on his neck.

Disdainfully, Jordan glanced sideways, to some imaginary

straight man. Then he leaned forward and spoke loud, as if to the hard of hearing. "Poon, Mr. Sherman. Pussy. Did McAdams have a girlfriend?"

"I knew him for less than twenty-four hours," replied Franco. He suddenly realized it had been years since he'd heard locker-room language.

"And during those twenty-four hours?"

"I never saw him with a woman," Franco answered, clinging to a technicality. "What's the point? You think his wife killed him because of a fling?"

"Nope, she was in Florida, where they live part of the year. But there were blond hairs in his bed up on Seventy-second, where we found him. Mrs. McAdams is a brunette. So we have to ask." Jordan stood up stiffly. "Thanks for your time, Mr. Sherman. Here's my card, if you think of anything. This'll blow over, I expect, unless something else turns up. If not, you'll probably never see me again. Bye."

Detective Jordan glanced around the office with an air of regret as he left. Franco sat staring, cold sweat creeping above and below his collar. Were the blond hairs Suki's? Had she come to New York to murder McAdams? To silence his criticism?

Beep. Millie. "Marshall Pierson on one."

And what fresh hell is this? "Yes, Marshall?"

"Uh, Franco, I've done a run on this Bobby Anderson." Oh shit. Franco preferred to forget that anyone had ever made love to Terry before him. "We still can't figure out how he got *The Belacqua Report.*" He lowered his voice. "We may have a mole." Marshall was whispering like a seasoned G-man or a fugitive bootlegger. His sinuses made a noise like a gargle. "Anyway, he doesn't work for us. At the *Enquirer* they think Anderson's a radical. He worked for Nader in '96."

As Franco stared down toward Fifth Avenue, his eyes followed two delivery boys on Rollerblades coming upstream against the traffic, like salmon or sperm. Then he listened to himself with detached interest. "Good work. Listen." His voice lowered to match Marshall's. "If there's any chance we have a mole, we'd better take precautions. Why don't you bring all the copies of the info to my vault here?"

Marshall chuckled. "Good thinking. You always impress me, Franco."

"Thanks. Listen, why don't you bring those up here right now?"

One minute later Marshall dropped a manila envelope on his desk, which Franco picked up appreciatively. "Great. Fine work. Quick, too."

"Why thanks, Franco." Marshall beamed.

Franco stood up and looked counsel right in the eye. "You're a good man, Marshall. I don't want to fire you. The fact is, though, you have a cocaine habit, right?"

Marshall sagged. "I used to," he said.

Franco's voice became much warmer. "You mean, earlier today?"

After a moment Marshall nodded, slow as a junkie.

"Listen, it's going to be okay," said Franco, gentler still, and copied a number from his address book. "This is Dr. Bob Sherin's number—my personal physician. I expect you to call his office within the next ten minutes to make an appointment. He'll arrange for your treatment. When he assures me that you have this under control, you'll be welcome back. If not"— Franco shook his head— "well, good-bye, Marshall."

Marshall stared at the phone number as if it were a prescription for hydrochloric acid. Head hanging, he walked to the door, where he summoned his last sliver of panache. "Thanks, Franco," he said weakly. "I needed that." Then he left the office.

"Millie," said Franco to the speakerphone, "please call Dr. Sherin's office, and ask them to accept Marshall Pierson as a patient."

There was a pause. "Yes, Franco. Of course."

Franco took the notes out of the manila envelope and perused them quickly as he fed them to his deskside shredder. Then he glanced at his watch. It was only nine-thirty.

The first review of *The Belacqua Report* appeared on June 7, 1998, in *The New York Times Book Review*. It was by Henrik Oscarssen, professor of geophysics at MIT, who had authored an exhaustive study of the Larsen Ice Shelf after it broke off from Antarctica in 1995. Oscarssen's review ran four pages, with no art—more space than they'd given Stephen Hawking's latest book, or even Joan Didion's. Berling sent out the following excerpts of the review with the press release.

The Belacqua Report: A Reevaluation of Humanity's Impact upon the Earth's Atmosphere, by Roger Belacqua (Commonweal 289 pp., $26.95). This is possibly the most important book ever written, charting the destiny of life on our planet, which, according to Dr. Belacqua, now waits like a candle under a glass to be snuffed out by its own gases by the middle of the next century. "This gradual but inevitable mass extinction has begun. At this late date, the only policies that could even postpone our eradication are morally and politically unacceptable."

Some experts in this field believe "sustainable growth" can be achieved; others have argued that it is only a euphemism for the destruction of the planet. But Belacqua insists that well before 1998, "the window of opportunity to save the planet had already closed," and illustrates how climate change will progressively impact upon agriculture, marine life, and other biota. The oceans have reached the carbon saturation point; together with atmospheric carbon dioxide, the result is a servomechanism that will raise the temperature of the earth by fully eight degrees Fahrenheit over the next sixty years. As greenhouse gases begin to heat the globe exponentially—the result of further overpopulation—our own offspring face a global holocaust. . . .

According to Belacqua, our social and industrial infrastructure will collapse in disorder well before the year 2040, with few qualified workers left alive to produce and deliver food, and maintain utilities and other critical portions of the public sector. He sketches out several different scenarios as civilization implodes. It will probably be years before the scientific and diplomatic communities arrive at a consensus regarding this work; we can only hope that both will meet Belacqua's implicit challenge and prove him wrong. Until then, alas, his evidence seems uncontestable, along with his argument that, given the architecture of contemporary geopolitics, transgovernmental solutions are beyond reach.

That Sunday, all hell broke loose. This was bigger than the funeral of Princess Diana, or even Fornigate.

Two nights earlier, Belacqua had been interviewed by Ted Koppel on *Nightline,* and the effect had been shattering. Although twenty-two minutes was barely time to summarize the salient features of Belacqua's argument, ABC's graphics department had done a bang-up job for Jeff Greenfield's segment. During the brief interview with Koppel, Roger Belacqua was at his most Cousteau-like. Wrapping up, Koppel's dry editorial implied an unreserved endorsement. "If Belacqua's science pans out, the impact upon all our lives exceeds mortal understanding."

Belacqua's *Nightline* appearance set the stage for the ABC interview that Sunday morning, where, in the free-for-all at the end, Sam Donaldson and George Will collided with unprecedented thud and blunder. Donaldson insisted that at least a *few* people were likely to survive the general annihilation, to reseed the planet. But Will, his sangfroid approaching a rolling boil, expressed his fervent hope that none of them would be Donaldson's offspring.

In his public appearances, Belacqua conveyed a balanced mixture of firm certainty and profound chagrin, with a soupçon of dry wit thrown in at the end. The hint of Machiavelli that Franco detected in Belacqua's observations about society was not in evidence. In his *Time* cover story, Roger insisted again that the measures necessary to postpone extinction could not be achieved; in a best-case scenario, "by the year 2050, there might be enough able-bodied people on the planet to form *one* soccer team."

The next day, *The Belacqua Report* was the biggest news story in America: the front page of the *Times* gave it four columns above the fold, while the *Daily News* ran a three-word headline: THE FINAL CLAMBAKE. The *Post*, with inimitable taste, countered with a photo of cockroaches, captioned "The Meek Shall Inherit the Earth."

Across the spectrum of reactions, in the first rush of commentary, few expressed doubt about Belacqua's conclusions. Generally the press reiterated his evidence in tacit concurrence. But soon knee-jerk opinions flowered like mushrooms, from the front page to the op-ed. This was the Apocalpyse of Revelation; we would be saved by the forces of Gaia; Man deserved his hellbound fate; God could still be trusted to intervene for us; Belacqua was killing off hope; the world could still pull together and save the day; and, it was all a plot by the New World Order to seize control of the U.S. government "like the UN's been trying to do for fifty years."

By Sunday evening, "post-Belacqua" had already entered the intellectuals' patois: at last they had found what followed "postmodern." In no time there was "post-Belacqua neoconservatism," in which social Darwinism provided a rationale for selective pre-extinction programs; "post-Belacqua deconstruction," wherein structuralist axioms negated themselves by abusing nonrenewable reserves of common sense; "post-Belacqua political economy," in which the elite were those with the skills to maintain the infra-structure; and even "post-Belacqua eye shadow" from Mac, which actually absorbed microscopic quantities of carbon from the atmosphere.

When Wall Street opened on Monday, the market reacted like a hippopotamus on a bungee cord. Volume surpassed that of the "crash" the previous October. But at the close of trading, the Dow (which had fallen so fast it tripped the circuit breakers four times) was off only sixteen points, and that was attributed to reports that Japanese HD-TVs outperformed U.S. models.

On Monday night June 15, with the temperature in the eighties, Franco came home to find Juliette struggling for breath in Terry's arms, sucking on her inhaler.

"When did this start?" he whispered to Terry.

"At school," Terry whispered back in tears. This sweet, gasping child took her back to the feeling of helplessness she'd had beside the injured deer on the road. "The nurse called: Juliette heard all about the book."

When Franco reached for her, Juliette turned on him, wild-eyed, pummeling him with her fists, half blinded by tears and gasping for breath. "Daddy," she wheezed, and shook her finger at him angrily.

"Her teacher told the class you published it," Terry explained. Devastated, Franco tried to hug Juliette, who grabbed her inhaler and ran to her room, slamming the door. Max sat aloof from the melodrama, replaying Karpov/Kasparov.

"Max heard about it," said Terry. "All he said was, 'Well, that's the breaks.' "

By dinner Juliette was quiet and sullen, and before bedtime she apologized to her wounded dad, who almost wept with gratitude and described all the wonderful moments waiting ahead in her life as she wheezed herself to sleep. After tucking the kids in, Franco found Terry at her computer checking out the Belacqua chat rooms that had sprung up. She turned and gave him a broad smile. "Look at some of this," she said.

Franco's stomach knotted up and he stopped reading. But then Terry remembered something else she'd run across. "Wait—you've gotta see *this*," and she typed in the address of a website. The next thing he saw was his own name.

<International School, Geneva, Switzerland, class of '69: We're seeking coordinates for the following: Tajit Sucharitikorn, Phil Pfeiffer, Tina Osborne, Franco Sherman . . ."

Those names worked like a time machine: Taj, son of a Thai diplomat, now a major player in the Pacific Rim; Phil Pfeiffer, class drudge, now professor of surgery at Cardiff in Wales; and Tina, the "bad girl" whom he'd fondled during the school production of *Noah*. While he mused upon his privileged youth, Terry typed in his e-mail address. He stopped her. "I'm not sure I want to be online with my high school."

"Oops—too late." She had typed in a rather boastful message about Franco's career, describing him as CEO of Commonweal and publisher of the upcoming best-seller *The Belacqua Report*. She jotted down the online address for the École Internationale (http://www.ecolint.com), in case he wanted to check it out, but Franco—still a newbie—switched off the computer.

They curled up on the bed and chatted for the first time since Friday night: about Juliette and Max, about reactions to *The Belacqua Report*—Terry had been monitoring the TV interviews—and about the Belacqua CD-ROM, which she was now working on full-time while caring for Juliette. She also told Franco about the e-mail from Bobby, apologizing for having sent the backup disk to the *Enquirer* by e-mail.

"Maybe it was for the best," Franco murmured, trying to make her feel better. "Everything's going fine."

Tuesday night the Belacquas met Terry and Franco for dinner at La Côte Basque. After introductions, they made a little polite conversation, skirting the subject of the exploding news event they had detonated together. Meeting for the first time, Terry and Christiane found more to discuss than Franco had expected. Unlike the men, they had both been following the prospects of candidates for the Senate and House races coming up in November. It was already clear to both of them that Congress would undergo a transformation even more startling than in '94: no fewer than twenty-three senators were retiring from public life.

Meanwhile, Roger and Franco admitted for the first time how shell-shocked they were from the tension and exposure of the last weeks. Belacqua was now stuck with the status of genuine celebrity: during their meal a half-dozen rude diners got his autograph on napkins, theater tickets, and even a copy of the book. While port was served, Franco remembered the question he'd meant to press with Belacqua: "Why *did* you choose Commonweal?" The last time he'd asked, he felt that Roger had waffled.

Belacqua smiled. "Christiane had made some inquiries. It seems most publishers had lost money on CD-ROMs. But everyone we talked to suggested Commonweal would know how to market ours in conjunction with the book."

"And why over the transom," Franco pressed, "rather than through an agency?"

"Security, obviously. I knew that if we sent it out to literary agencies, the fuel industries would learn about it in no time. Or the tabloids," he added pointedly. "So General Shreiver sent it to Danvers Creal and followed up with a phone call. But our strategy only worked"—he turned to Terry—"thanks to this young woman's determination."

Terry recalled that morning five months earlier, her reaction to the manuscript, and what she'd done to persuade Danvers. She shuddered, pulling her scarf to her neck.

Belacqua noticed. "The air-conditioning is excessive, isn't it? Try some de la Warre," he advised Terry. "Warms the tummy."

"You really should, darling," Franco urged.

A little tipsy already, she acceded, adding port to the champagne and wine. She was also thoroughly aroused. They hadn't made love in a week, and Franco was showing little inclination this evening. But Terry had a plan.

Belacqua raised his glass. "To the book!" The others followed suit. Terry added, "And the CD-ROM!" Smiling, they drank together, until it struck them all as unseemly, rather like cheering for extinction. For the remainder of dinner they shared an unspoken agreement to forget the book. Then, waiting for the bill, Franco turned again to the older man. "I heard a strange story about you a while back."

Belacqua chuckled. "I've heard some, too. What did you hear? That I installed a pipe outside a chemical plant that directed its noxious waste to its water intake?"

Franco laughed. "I did hear that. But this was about a suntan lotion for babies." Just then the bill was served to Belacqua—the celebrity—diverting him from the question.

As they reached Fifty-fifth Street the hot air almost slammed them back inside. It was more like August than late June: one of those steamy nights that belong to New York alone, with all its incomparable smells. The women were laughing about something as Franco and Belacqua waited for the cars.

"I need your tour schedule," said Franco, "so I can reach you."

Belacqua nodded. "Suki will fax it to you tomorrow. Here's the car, Christiane."

Franco again heard Suki's moans in his ear and felt that familiar cold sweat. "That reminds me"—Franco stopped Belacqua cold with his serious tone—"have you been questioned by the police about William McAdams?"

Belacqua frowned. "No. What do you mean?"

Franco stared, uncertain whether to mention Suki and McAdams. This was, after all, a murder investigation; and if it was a murder, Belacqua might have been involved. And while he couldn't be certain, it seemed to him that Christiane's hair was darker now than when they'd met. "They think McAdams's coronary may have been induced. They suspect he was given a drug at his New York apartment a few days after we returned from Vermont."

"What a peculiar story." Belacqua started to ask him something, but by now Christiane was already in the car, extending her hand to Franco, who abandoned the conversation to kiss her fingers.

"I hope you'll both visit us after this circus ends," Christiane said warmly.

"Me too!" called Belacqua, entering the other side of the car. The old man offered his impish grin. "Unless you'd care to join me on the book tour?"

Laughing, Terry and Franco declined vociferously as they left. Then, in the backseat of Giuseppe's limo, they began their love-making—well, Terry did, in spite of Franco's reluctance, and the boring gray suit she was wearing. By the time they were home she knew what she would do upstairs, and she was just tipsy enough to carry it off.

Rather than follow him to the bedroom, she turned off to the guest room where she kept her clothes and where Max and Juliette were supposed to think she slept. While Franco lay in bed wondering how soon some scientist would step up to repudiate Belacqua, Terry pulled out the costume she'd been saving for the right occasion.

Franco was almost asleep when Terry rejoined him, but his eyes sprang open as he recognized the girl before him. Her purple-tipped hair was twisted into a knot; she had heavy black eye shadow and wore a torn Sex Pistols T-shirt, baggy white boxer shorts over black wool leggings, and high-top sneakers.

"Here," she said, holding out a copy of *Harper's*. "You can have it, mister."

Franco was struck dumb. How did she know about that punkish waif? And where did Terry find her, and why was she delivering her to him? Was this the *ménage à trois* they—well, he—had discussed? Only after she locked the door did he realize that Terry *was* the sexy street urchin.

"That's all right, miss," he said slowly. "I'll buy another magazine."

As she approached the bed he had no idea what was going on: he and Lillian had never explored role-playing. Terry, for her part, recalled the thoughts she'd had about Franco before he'd ever noticed her, based partly on her promiscuous teenage fantasy of picking up married men in the cocktail lounge of the Minneapolis Hilton.

Franco, confronted by this postadolescent urchin, ran his hand up the leg of her oversized boxer shorts, only to find that her black wool leggings were crotchless. His fingers began manipulating her as he watched her with detachment.

"Cheeky of you," she said, as he raised his damp fingers to his lips. "Very cheeky." Then she kissed him. But this was different. It was a kiss full of raw lust but with no history, utterly impersonal—as if he'd just called out her number.

"Whatever you want to do," she hissed, "I'm going to like."

That, apparently, was what he'd been waiting to hear. Now he used her for his pleasure in a variety of different ways, and when she still seemed familiar, he wrapped her scarf loosely over her face, except for her mouth, which he used from time to time.

He shocked her with the ferocity of appetites and urges restrained for a lifetime. This excess was not about love, tenderness, care, or anything shared. This was a craving to use each other's bodies however they pleased. The zipless fuck, Franco thought to himself. Muskrat love, thought Terry.

The more crude their fucking became, the more exciting. When he was done going to and fro between her mouth and her cunt, Terry took over and, riding upon his face as if to smother him, she too succumbed to the rutting stamina unleashed by the notion that they were indifferent strangers chosen for selfish, carnal, anonymous pleasures.

In the first week, sales of *The Belacqua Report* broke all records, and Franco began paying premiums under the table to printers, binders, and truckers around the country for bumping other jobs to rush more copies to the stores. The name Belacqua entered the vocabulary of the culture, joining other unusual names in the lingua franca like Iacocca, Yo-Yo Ma, and Heimlich. *Saturday Night Live* did a skit in which Belacqua was a travel guide for Martian tourists, showing them around the ash heap of the earth: "This is where Joe Montana completed an eighty-five-yard pass. And on this very spot, President George Bush held up the flag and declared, 'I'm proud to be American!' "

The "Belacqua theory" settled in on the op-ed pages, where commentators had their way with it and damn near gang-banged the story to death. Anthony Lewis wrote a scathing piece entitled "The Wages of Sin," declaring that the capitalist commitment to economic expansion had destroyed the earth, while Pat Buchanan reasserted his faith in the invisible hand of commerce to heal the wounds. "Constraints upon free enterprise," he proclaimed, "have choked off the technological solutions."

Translators were grinding out editions in more than 120 countries, including Estonia and Indonesia, but before long somebody scanned the book and put the whole text on the Internet for free: then there were bootleg copies in English everywhere.

In France, *l'affaire Belacqua* instantly permeated every segment of French life, from the weather reports ("... *et, sur notre carte, je ne vois pas la fin du monde cette semaine"*), to the menu Chez Raffatin et Honorine: a forty-course dinner entitled "La Dernière Bouffe." During the weekend of *la grande sortie,* the deconstructionist disciples of Althusser at the École Normale Supérieure held a seminar proving from textual analysis that it was *incontestable:* Belacqua had confused the concept of annihilation with subordinate linguistic structures derived from a decadent *morphologie.* Of course, noted *Le Nouvel Observateur,* they had made the same argument about the meltdown at Metzamor.

The leadership of the People's Republic of China did not address the doomsday report publicly at first, and seized copies from dissident groups to prevent further dissemination. But gradually word spread inland from Hong Kong. Finally the Central Committee promulgated the view that "this propaganda, masquerading as science, reflects the failure of imperialism to control population, or to make the people's communal welfare its priority." China's own noxious wastes were not acknowledged.

In Germany, the outlawed Nationalist Party latched on to Belacqua's argument. In pamphlets and on the Web, these "new Nazis" insisted that "only global totalitarianism could produce a glorious Götterdämmerung." Franco retched when he read their declaration that had the Führer only won, "he would have applied the *Endlösung* to all inferior beings, and this crisis would never have arisen." Chancellor Kohl promptly quashed the group and urged the industrial powers to seek solutions together.

Only one culture absorbed the forecast of mass extinction with aplomb: in India, the Vedas had long prepared the population for the age of Kali, in which the spiraling path of civilization collapses upon itself to start afresh. It was not with indifference that Hindus received Belacqua's universal death sentence, but rather with a profound, shared acceptance, fostered perhaps by faith, humility, and the constant presence of death in daily life.

By the end of the summer *The Belacqua Report* had rolled across the global culture, challenging, like the Holocaust and Hiroshima, the most fundamental assumptions about the nature and destiny of the human race.

When the school year started, a kind of dispassionate despair had reached all the way down to kindergarten. Even popular music, from trip-hop to folk rock, was saturated with references to the end of life. On September 15, *Billboard* listed Travis Folger's "I'll Be Dead Before You Go" as the Number One Country single. Dylan's latest live album included a scathing version of "Idiot Wind" with a new last verse:

> Saints commit atrocities, while monsters play the game by all the rules;
> The prophets dance all through the night, no wonder that we listen to the fools;
> And after all the hope was spent, the high priestess she quickly fled,
> Napoleon, he turned to me, and I just sort of scratched my head:
> Didn't know what to tell him.
>> Idiot wind, blowin' through the dust upon our shelves,
>> We're idiots, babe; it's no wonder that we've poisoned our own selves.

And the Rolling Stones, bless their souls, interrupted their '98 tour in Europe to record an album which featured a thirty-minute jam called "Trash the Earth," including Keith Richards's greatest guitar solo.

Beep. "Franco, Bob Milton's on the line."

Franco picked up the phone, clearing his mind. "Hello, Bob, how are you?"

There was a deathly silence, followed by a low grunt. "Franco, we have to talk."

"Yes, of course. What's the problem?"

"Not on the phone, boy, you know me. Catch the nine-o'clock tonight to Lauderdale and be at the house tomorrow morning. I tee off at nine." Click.

Since Franco had first read the manuscript, the possibility of being fired for publishing *The Belacqua Report* had always been apparent. He had thoroughly imagined Mildred Milton's shame and horror, listening to her Baptist preacher decry the godlessness that had produced this damnable "Belackey book." By now Franco was comfortable with the notion of retiring from publishing and settling down with Terry in a small academic setting—Wellesley, maybe, or Williams—to experience a sense of community. Whatever competitive drive he'd once had in the corporate world had been expunged by his disgust for its politics. He had a little money salted away in blue chips, and if later he chose to return to publishing, his résumé would now boast the biggest title in history. More important to him was that he'd dared to tell the most terrible truth when it had to be told, relying upon Madison's conviction that a free society depended upon a free press, and that—

Beep. "Yes, Millie?"

"Detective Jordan's on the line for you. Do you want to talk to him?"

No, never again. "Sure, Millie, put him on."

"Hello, Mr. Sherman. Sorry to disturb you up there. Would you believe it, my chief still has me futzing around with this damn McAdams case. It seems the coroner has an even bigger problem now: he found microscopic traces of a rare tropical herb in the guy's bloodstream, called ibogaine. It's not even listed in the manuals on toxicology."

"And how can I help, Detective?"

"Well, what's been missing all along has been a motive. But it occurred to me that this Belacqua book might be a damn good reason for knockin' off a belligerent critic—which McAdams was, judging from his preliminary notes. So I was wondering if you could take a minute to drop by Midtown North on West Fifty-third. The chief would love to meet you: he's even *read* your big best-seller. Well, he looked at the pictures. Anyhow, he's developed a personal fascination with the case. He'd like to ask you a couple of questions about McAdams, and whether or not yer book there maybe had something to do with his death. Would you mind? Say, in about fifteen minutes?"

"Of course. My schedule's open this morning. I'd be delighted to meet the chief."

"We'll be waiting."

Franco walked calmly to the door, but in the lobby his hands started to shake.

THE BELACQUA
SYNDROME

The last of the living are in a frenzy: the obedient and
virtuous son kills his father; the chaste man performs
sodomy upon his neighbors. The lecher becomes pure.
The miser throws his gold in handfuls out the window.
The warrior hero sets fire to the city he once risked
his life to save. The dandy decks himself out in his finest
clothes and promenades before the charnel houses. . . .
And how explain the surge of erotic fever among the
recovered victims who, instead of fleeing the city, remain where they are, trying to wrench a criminal pleasure from the dying or even the dead, half crushed
under the pile of corpses.

—ANTONIN ARTAUD, *The Theatre and the Plague* (1938)

Apparently Terry had chosen the hottest day in August to go for a
run down the East River—one of those torpid New York after-
noons when strangers glance at each other in shared disbelief. On
her Walkman, even the Indigo Girls were gasping for breath. Just
past New York Hospital she flopped down on a bench: her shorts
and Franco's blue Lacoste shirt were heavy with sweat. Before
she'd caught her breath, a voice nearby said, "Now *that* is a fashion risk!"

It was Maurice. She hadn't seen him since the Prodigy gig in
January; they hugged and laughed. He was in his splendor in a
glitter-rock outfit. Maurice, who was black, was also gay, proud,
and critical: he clucked at the alligator on her shirt.

"I know, I know," she said. "Otherwise, everything's great. How 'bout you?"

"Great. Listen, I'm on my way to do some girls at the Javits center. Want to come?"

"No thanks, I've got to be home when the housekeeper leaves. I'll give you a call. Let's catch a movie, or maybe a concert."

"Sure," he said. "Beep me later: I've got four tickets to Butthole Surfers at the Garden on the 3rd. Bring your boyfriend. Lose the alligator." As he ran for a cab, she heard him repeat: "Got to be home when the housekeeper leaves." A mocking snapshot of her social life.

She wasn't even sure she still had Maurice's number: her life had undergone such a revolution that she had two address books. In January she had been assistant to Commonweal's executive editor, living alone in a fourth-floor walk-up on $448.32 a week take-home. Six months later she was ensconced in a penthouse on Fifty-fourth and Park, raising two kids, and being interviewed by *Wired* as producer of the eagerly awaited Belacqua CD-ROM; while at night she often dressed in decadent disguises to fuel a carnal passion that had nothing to do with either love or procreation.

While her outer life seemed to be stabilizing, inside it felt like she was melting down. The eeriest part was the unspoken agreement that had evolved with Franco. The rule was, apparently, that neither of them was allowed to discuss the future, beyond next week. This wasn't just about their fear of commitment. It had to do with the message of *The Belacqua Report* and its impact on their own prospects together. There was a lot of chafing between them, too. In hiring the top techno-talent for the CD-ROM, Terry's responsibilities exceeded her authority, which led to haggling with Commonweal's head of R & D, with accounting, and with Franco. At home she often felt like a visitor, even as the responsibilities ate her alive; everything that children expect of a mother the kids expected of her. In just six months she'd gone from Hole-fan to hausfrau. What had happened to her goals? Had she ever had one? Yes. To take a big bite out of life and let the juices run down her chin. . . . Was that still her goal?

All this change was because of the doomsday report. Watching the world discover the book she'd dug out of the slush pile was awesome. So was seeing Belacqua face off with Diane Sawyer, or hearing people talk about the book on the IRT. Moments like that helped her live with what she'd done to get *The Belacqua Report* published.

Once in a while Franco took her to a cocktail party, or to dinner with friends of his, where they were minor celebrities because of the book, even at snooty social functions. That's when their age difference seemed most apparent: culturally, she felt as if she were falling between two stools. Once, when their hostess was describing her country house, Terry actually heard herself say: "Way cool! Uh, I mean, swell!" What a *loser*.

She was still trying to save her much-broken New Year's resolutions. She hardly ever used obscenities, except when they were fucking. But she was still sneaking cigarettes shamefully, four or five a day, and if the truth were told, she and Franco were also drinking a lot. Too often she woke up with monster hangovers that included cold sweat and dry heaves.

On one of those mornings she stumbled into the kitchen looking for Alka-Seltzer. Max was already curved over his chessboard at the kitchen table, in combat with Bobby Fischer. As she fumbled with the wrapper, the eight-year-old rose abruptly and dumped his chess set into the garbage bin. "Fuck it," he said to no one in particular, and walked out of the kitchen.

A turf war had broken out between various organizations offering blight relief. The largest groups—the Red Cross, CARE, Médecins Sans Frontières—were hell-bent on serving accessible areas with high visibility (to attract donations) and low rad counts (since none had adequate protective clothing). The most sought-after areas adjoined government triage camps. Tons of supplies and hundreds of volunteers collected in Italy and the Czech Republic, while little assistance reached the sick and starving in Bulgaria and Romania. As Marcel Hartoch of Blight Relief said to CNN, "The world's generosity is a target for the unscrupulous. Such disregard for the human family speaks to the Belacqua theory that global cooperation is impossible."

At about this time, a charitable website named Ring of Angels appeared. There was an "admission price" to log on, which, like all the money raised by the Ring, went directly to the most critical victims of the nuclear catastrophe. Journalists on-site and online contributed personal reflections about where relief was needed.

The Ring of Angels was a flop, at first. Either Web surfers weren't inclined to charity or philanthropists weren't spending much time on the Web. But after *Wired* ran a flattering article about the Ring, contributions grew, and in a few months several groups recommended the Ring for all blight donations, because its fund-raising costs were significantly lower than other charities'. Next to the hugeness of the need, the amounts were small; still, the Ring of Angels raised intriguing possibilities.

Franco was glad he'd stopped for chewing gum on his way to Midtown North: it gave him something to do with his jaw as he strode into the precinct house. He'd never been in a police station, much less part of a murder investigation. How would all this reflect upon *The Belacqua Report*? McAdams dead was potentially more of a threat to the book's credibility than McAdams alive, but the idea that he'd been murdered still seemed ludicrous; whatever the "evidence" of poisoning, there had to be another explanation. The sergeant directed him to O'Hara's office, where he found Detective Jordan wearing blue serge and half a grin. Together they went in to see the chief.

Chief Garreth O'Hara was a large man with heavy jowls and a high-gloss manicure who had dedicated his life to police work, mostly behind a desk. He greeted Franco with a broad, genuine smile. Unlike Jordan, the chief hadn't copped an attitude about McAdams's death; to him, Franco was a celebrity, and the chief accorded him the consideration that celebrities in New York can expect from police officials. "Mr. Sherman, pleased to meet you. You know, I respect your courage for publishing *Belacqua*. My wife told me about it. You've made us think long and hard about having a fifth child."

Unaccustomed to being cited for the reproductive choices of strangers, Franco mumbled and sat down. Meanwhile, with the detachment of an off-duty undertaker, Detective Jordan propped himself by the door to observe the polite encounter between his boss and the rich guy.

"As Bill Jordan explained, the coroner has problems with the

McAdams autopsy. He is now certain that an exotic herb—iger-baine—"

"Ibogaine," Jordan corrected him.

"—was in his bloodstream. Maybe enough to kill, or it might have been taken recreationally. And in the second autopsy, a tiny needle mark was found in the folds of his right buttock—it's possible the toxic agent was injected there. Currently, the lab is analyzing the hairs found in McAdams's bedroom in New York. But that won't help any until we have a suspect, for comparison. For now, we're guessing McAdams may have been murdered in his bed by a blonde. Jordan here says you hardly knew him?"

"I spent a total of nine hours in his company. Apart from his professional qualifications, I didn't know him at all," Franco replied.

"Maybe you'd tell us about Dr. Belacqua. The Vermont police have been cooperating, but they're a little slow. And we don't have grounds for a search warrant. Tell me, did you see any tropical plants up there? Maybe a hothouse?"

Franco thought hard. "No. Belacqua's research is with specimens of algae and plankton, along with animal studies." Wonderful, he thought. Now the author of the world's most controversial book is a murder suspect. Bob Milton would love that.

The chief walked around his desk, tugging at his lower lip, looking for a delicate way to phrase his next question. "Mr. Sherman, suspicion centers around the most important job McAdams had had in a while, relating to *The Belacqua Report*. His only other jobs this year were as a trial witness. What was he doing for your company?"

"He was one of three scientists we hired to evaluate Dr. Belacqua's research, to determine whether we should publish the book."

The chief's voice softened. "And did McAdams look favorably on the work?"

Franco's pulse accelerated to an uneven tarantella. "He never completed his evaluation. He expressed serious reservations, but he hadn't finished reviewing the work. I wouldn't say he was gung-ho behind the findings."

O'Hara handed him a sheet of paper headlined "Critique of the Frelinghaus Report." There were notes scribbled on the back. "Belacqua's phony use of statistics" was legible; so was "These extrapolations suck."

"Hardly a rousing endorsement, eh? So, after he died, did you hire a replacement?"

Franco dropped the paper onto the desk with a silent thud. "No, we published the book on the basis of the two other evaluations."

The chief nodded, and pushed out his lower lip. "So in fact, you may have published *The Belacqua Report* as a result of McAdams's murder."

A clammy feeling spread across Franco like sweat on a corpse. "I wouldn't put it that way." Still, it was true, the board might have voted the manuscript down if there had been a scorching assessment from McAdams.

"Well, anyway," the chief said, watching him closely, "if you recall anything unusual, let us know. One other thing." The chief opened a drawer. "Would you sign my wife's copy of *The Belacqua Report*?" He handed it to Franco.

Franco took the book reluctantly. "I'm only a corporate executive."

O'Hara shook his head. "I heard this book wouldn't have been published if it hadn't been for you." Franco took out his pen and jotted a greeting.

Jordan's grin widened as he looked Franco right between the eyes. "If we have more questions, we'll call, you can bet yer ass on that, Mr. Sherman. Double or nothing."

Franco found his way to the street, lurching slightly, like a blind man without a cane, feeling rubbed the wrong way by their abrasive suspicions. He went home to pack a bag for Fort Lauderdale. Before leaving, Franco realized this was the first time Terry would spend the night alone with the kids, so while they did their homework, he reminded her about the alarm system, and for the first time told her about the armed intruder with the chesterfield coat, the Borsalino, and the smell of licorice.

"Jeez, Franco," said Terry , duly impressed. "That's pretty weird. Strange you never told me. Or Belacqua. What do you think the guy was after?"

"I figured it was some kind of corporate espionage, but even that sounded far-fetched. I mean, would some other publisher want the manuscript that badly? Then I remembered what General Shreiver said, about people who wanted to make sure it was never published. I assumed he meant people from the petrochemical industries, but I was just guessing. I'd recognize the guy in a heartbeat, but I couldn't describe him. Anyway, he got what he wanted; he won't be back. Just—double-check the alarm."

Two hours later he left La Guardia for Fort Lauderdale.

The first refutation of Belacqua's argument appeared in the September issue of *Nature* magazine. Written by Ivan Benedek, a climatologist with the University of Arizona, the skeptical article focused on the issue of the "eggshell effect." Benedek argued that Belacqua's evidence for this phenomenon was less conclusive than it seemed and that if the eggshell effect did exist, it might produce the opposite effect, diminishing rather than increasing the amount of heat trapped by the water vapor. This hypothesis rested upon doubts raised by Dr. Lindzen at MIT of whether water vapor amplified atmospheric heat or actually diminished it. Benedek insisted, without evidence, that it had a cooling effect. He did not address other issues directly, but his incredulity about the eggshell effect dripped over to the rest of Belacqua's thesis.

For the time being, though, Benedek was the only scientist to even quibble with Belacqua's assertions: the rest of the world bought the whole argument, while the various industries Belacqua had implicated struggled to find suitable ripostes to defend their public image.

Franco stayed at a hotel in Hollywood, Florida, and rose early to swim in the ocean. By 7:00 A.M. his car was waiting, and at 7:55 he pulled up in front of Bob Milton's spacious ranch-style home. Mildred was in the backyard, supervising workmen who were building a brick barbecue the size of Grant's Tomb. As Franco got out of the car he waved to her, and she made a gesture as she turned: he saw her cross herself, mocking the sight of a presumed Catholic entering her home.

Bob Milton, at sixty-four, was in excellent health—except for minor angina and a bad back—and resembled a statue to corporate success: white-haired, with a dark tan, strong as your average ox. He looked to Franco like a Renaissance statue carved in Carrara marble and then painted by Norman Rockwell. But Milton's most memorable and prominent feature was his smile, visible at a thousand feet through heavy fog.

But the moment they shook hands, Franco noticed something unusual about the chairman of Macro Foods and Enterprises: he was not smiling. In fact, his expression was hidden beneath foul-weather gear. He didn't even issue a jovial greeting, although, thought Franco, he couldn't have met his daily quota this early. Bob glanced at his watch, as if to make sure he had time to terminate one more executive career before teeing off.

"Sit down, Franco," Bob growled. "I want to talk to you about your job."

The interior of the house was as plain as a motel room in Missouri, without evidence of wealth or, for that matter, personality. Franco had found that astonishing on his first visit in '95; by now he knew that it was, in fact, true to the Miltons' nature, except, it seemed, when it came to the barbecue.

Settling on the sofa at right angles from the chairman, Franco was reminded of the spanking his father gave him, age eleven, after he'd laughed at Sister Genevieve when a kid sprayed bleach on her habit.

"Franco," Bob began bluntly, "I'm convinced that this whole Belacqua thing is a disaster for Macro, and I'm out to salvage my company. Obviously, that may force me to take some drastic measures. Do you understand?"

Franco shook his head. "No, Bob, I'm sorry—I don't see how the success of Commonweal can harm Macro. Last week the *Financial Times* projected that this may become the biggest-selling book in history—"

"Hold on, boy," said Bob, "aren't you forgetting the Good Book?" Franco was about to add that. Instead he nodded. "How long have you known Belacqua?" asked Bob.

"Since the start of the year," he replied. An ice age.

Bob leaned forward to study Franco. "Do you know how long *I've* known Roger?"

Franco's jaw dropped noticeably. "I didn't know you had ever met."

Bob studied his face carefully, and then leaned back, satisfied that Franco was telling the truth. "That sneaky bastard," he muttered. "It's forty years since I first tangled with him. . . ." his voice trailed off. "He never let on? *That* should tell you something. When you told me about this book, you didn't mention Belacqua's name—believe me, I'd have noticed! Was that deliberate?" Franco shook his head as, again, Bob Milton scrutinized him. "Even then, something didn't seem right. I thought you were talking about a novel! Always a disaster when I ignore my gut. I didn't want to interfere with your autonomy." He chuckled at that quaint notion. "Excuse me," he added as the phone rang, and Bob took the call from his desk.

From what Franco overheard, it sounded as if they were preparing to split Macro's stock, and there was a problem with one board member. Franco paid scant attention. He was wondering if Roger had duped him all along; and if so, what else was he capable of?

After slamming down the phone, Bob glanced at his watch and grunted. "Lousy day. You'll have to come to the club: I tee off with MacElroy in eighteen minutes."

Franco trailed Bob out to the convertible Eldorado, and asked his driver to follow. Then he remembered that Milton was one of the worst drivers he'd ever known.

As they turned into the street, Franco asked, "How did you meet Belacqua?"

Bob grunted, crashing the transmission into low. "When I was twenty-two, I started a synthetics firm called BoMil Enterprises—from my name. Roger was a brilliant young chemist: he'd invented six polymers for us, perfect for electric filaments. He was older than me, and much more savvy. At the signing, he and his hotshot lawyer pulled a fast one. I'd agreed to pay him five percent of net profits from his patents, but one of them must have pulled the old switcheroo, because the contract we signed gave him five points of the *gross*." They were turning into the club's driveway much too fast. Bob swerved, sparing a Cuban parking valet, and slammed on the brakes. "Listen, Franco, you're going to have to come out to the first hole with me."

The whole situation was anathema to Franco. He smiled, and followed Bob into the club, feeling more like a trained spaniel than the president of Commonweal Books.

Bob continued in the locker room while he changed his shoes. "Eventually I cut a deal with Belacqua to buy his five percent—so he wouldn't ruin our public offering. Then a year later my lawyer came to me and admitted that despite the payoff—a million dollars, which actually meant something in the fifties—Belacqua was *still* entitled to one percent of the net until the patent expired." As his eyes focused on some distant lawyer long, long ago, you had to believe him when he added, "I wanted to murder that shyster. I mean, I *really* wanted to kill him."

Franco was dumbstruck. Why had Roger kept this secret? He padded out to the caddy area behind Bob, who found his clubs waiting in his golf cart. But his caddy wasn't there yet, and Mac-Elroy was late: in a few minutes he'd lose his round. So they jumped in the golf cart—but before they reached the first tee, it broke down.

Bob's face was turning blotchy. "Franco, I can't risk throwing my back out again—I've got a tournament next week. Would you grab my bag?" So Franco slung the fancy golf bag over his shoulder—it couldn't have weighed more than a couple hundred pounds—and traipsed to the tee behind Bob; a bad walk spoiled.

"A few years later I sold BoMil to Cavendham. Got out of synthetics altogether, and settled into canned goods. That eventually led to the takeover of Commonweal. I thought by then I was free of Belacqua for good. Cavendham continued a costly suit against him for years, trying to kill him off with legal fees if they couldn't win. For the next dozen years I worked a few other companies: slashing overheads, boosting production. Then in the eighties I took over Gellis Drinnon Gombach, who manufactured cosmetics. I really turned the place around. Thought I could retire early to the Seniors' Circuit."

Still no sign of MacElroy. The next party was approaching from the clubhouse.

"Then R & D came up with a new product and had it tested independently by a panel. This was a crazy idea my predecessor had at GDG: a suntan lotion for babies—can you believe that? Why in hell would babies need suntan lotion?"

Franco's cheeks turned gray.

"Well, I'll be damned if Roger Belacqua didn't get onto that panel, for the sole purpose of sabotaging my new company, I have no doubt. . . . Play through, gentlemen, I'm waiting for my partner. . . . Anyway, in less than a month Belacqua had destroyed GDG's credibility. Fortunately, before the spit hit the fan, Ken

Jameson left Macro and recommended me to replace him. So I bailed."

They watched the party of four tee off as numbness spread through Franco's limbs; it might have been from carrying the clubs. "Next thing I know, this crazy Italian writes the most unholy book in human history, and publishes it with *my* subsidiary."

From the silence Franco guessed he was done. "Why didn't you tell me sooner?"

"You didn't tell me the book was Belacqua's!" Milton flashed his anger. "First I heard was when it hit the best-seller list."

"My memos had his name all over them!"

Obviously Bob never read his memos. "I can't expect you to have guessed all this, Franco. And Roger wasn't about to tell you." He rose and approached the tee. "Out of respect for Mildred's religious convictions I have to take some corrective measure. I've decided to— Look, here he is, in the blue golf cart!"

Suddenly and incongruously, Bob cracked his famous smile: klieg lights seemed to illuminate the first green. "So I'm booting you upstairs. I'm making you president of Macro. MacElroy's moving up to the board. How 'bout them apples?"

Franco couldn't find the right sound to make, much less the words. He stammered, until Bob slapped him a little too hard across the back.

"I'm flattered." What verbal skills Franco possessed were vacationing in Aruba. "You know, I've never really been a corporate animal." *That* came out wrong. "Thanks to you, I stumbled straight from academia into the executive suite. But despite your generous offer, my concern is for Commonweal. If I leave, who'll take my place?"

"Not *if,* Franco. Get it? Not *if.*" Bob unplugged the Smile and the golf course went dark just as MacElroy drove up. "I would have chosen Roy Raymond, but he's a bit old. Anyway, the directors named your successor. They picked Danvers Creal."

Franco gripped the bench. "Have you *met* Danvers?"

"Of course. He was up for the post when I recruited you. He was here yesterday, and he accepted the position. Curious fellow, but the board liked his profile." Which one? thought Franco. "MacElroy, come on, dammit, it's almost nine-fifteen. Still no Manuel, eh? Never mind. Franco, this is Ronald MacElroy, current president of Macro, and soon to move on to greater things." This was news to MacElroy, who stared over his shoulder at Bob with alarm while shaking Franco's hand.

The chairman aimed Franco toward the clubhouse. "Glad you took the time to visit. Let me know soon about the offer: the pay's almost double, you know."

Bob shook his hand, and Franco set off for home. He'd always been lucky in his career, but at that moment he was just grateful he didn't have to caddy eighteen holes.

Roger Belacqua was booked on a whirlwind tour of twenty cities, which was why he returned Franco's calls at odd hours, and failed to reach him. Though the free publicity had been so enormous that Berling had considered canceling the tour, Franco had insisted that it proceed so that Belacqua could correct any misunderstandings sparked by the media. Throughout the month of August, then, Belacqua toured, flying commercially except on the East Coast, where he flew his own Baron. On local news shows, he was often introduced as "the most important guest we've ever had in our studio."

Except for *Politically Incorrect* (which he appeared on with guests Robin Williams, Richard Holbrooke, Steve Tyler, and Kathie Lee Gifford), each appearance lasted about eight minutes, and the first four questions (which usually filled the segment) never varied by more than a word or two: "Why are you certain that life on earth is doomed?" "Is there any ray of hope?" "Won't this gloomy news discourage the search for solutions?" "If the population stopped growing today, how long would we have?"

The print interviews were rarely more probing. The most intriguing questions often came from less experienced journalists. A twenty-three-year-old from the Newhouse School of Communications in Syracuse asked Belacqua if the unforeseen synergies between various emissions might not suggest a synergistic *solution*. And a stand-in for a noted op-ed columnist in Boston asked if the author and publishing house would contribute some of their profits to fund an international panel of scientists to critique *The Belacqua Report* (a proposal Franco had accepted on Commonweal's behalf, but later learned that Belacqua had declined).

By Labor Day, Belacqua had aged visibly. Though he kept his

sense of humor most of the time, the old man paid a price for his equanimity, and somewhere between Cleveland and St. Louis a nervous tic appeared in his left eye. Christiane joined him for the western leg, to share the dazed monotony of TV and radio stations, newspaper offices, and hotel rooms. By the end she was alarmed about his health, and insisted they return to Vermont rather than visit Franco and Terry as planned.

But when Jimmy drove them back to the Last Resort in the early fall, they were met by three Vermont state troopers with a search warrant. The troopers spent three days scouring the grounds and buildings for evidence in the McAdams murder, including ibogaine or the means to grow it. They interviewed everyone, but, finding no tropical plants nor anything else relevant to the New York investigation, they left with terse apologies. For the time being, their investigation was kept out of the press.

Still queasy from his unsought promotion, Franco returned to the apartment by early afternoon. The kids were at school, Emily was in the kitchen watching *Star Trek*, and Terry was nowhere to be found—until he checked the guest bathroom, where she was on her knees, "worshiping at the porcelain altar," as she put it. Above her heaving, she heard him pick up the phone.

"I've already seen the doctor," she said. "It's nothing to worry about."

Relieved, Franco hung up. "Is it food poisoning?"

Terry stood up and gargled with water. Then she watched him closely as she said, "No. I thought maybe I was pregnant, because I fucked up with the pills last month, but I tested negative. Dr. Sherin said it was dyspepsia."

Silent thunder echoed through the room. They'd never even discussed pregnancy. Terry stared at him until another wave of nausea crashed over her. At that point Franco wasn't sure whether to help her or join her, so he did a little of both, holding a warm, moist handcloth to her forehead and retching silently.

In the bedroom, Franco spoon-fed her the chicken broth Emily had heated up. Minutes later, as she started to heave again, she asked to be alone. Franco headed out toward the Central Park Zoo, a familiar refuge since the last turbulent years of his parents' marriage—when he was a kid himself, not the father of two.

He strolled aimlessly in the warm autumn breeze past the ocelot, the panther, and the sorry, soulful tiger, who seemed to be very aware of his imminent extinction. Franco was certain of his love for Terry. But if she became pregnant, would he want a third child? Grateful as he was for his renaissance through Terry, he didn't know if, at forty-eight, he could muster the emotional energy to cope with another child. The idea was more exhausting than exhilarating.

As he entered the primate house, it struck him for the first time just how much Belacqua had altered the notion of having a child. Was it fair to bring children into a dying world? What sort of life was that, when the only prospect was to be among the last? Perhaps now, as Heine said, "the best is never to have been born at all."

Whoa, he thought. I'm reciting Heinrich Heine to a roomful of caged baboons.

But surely the most important thing was to be honest. As he meandered back outside, a less noble thought buzzed through his brain like a bluebottle fly: the difference between having two children and having three children was the difference between zero population growth and overpopulation. It was true, and important: why, then, did he feel like pond scum for thinking it? Because it was utterly reprehensible, that's why. "Sorry, darling, we can't have a child: the world is overpopulated." Now *there* was a way to reduce the population: if he said that to Terry, she'd probably kill him.

What about Terry's wishes? He'd already been blessed with offspring, but she had not, and she loved children, obviously: he'd seen that with his kids, the first night she came to the apartment. And he knew Terry loved him.

His musing continued from the bird house all the way out to the ungulates. By the time he reached the polar bears, he had admitted to himself that she was entitled to have a child.

Terry was lying in the guest room listening to Max quarrel with Juliette as they came back from school. The rising cadences punctuated by shrieks and sobs were more than she could bear. She went into the guest bathroom and, closing the door, lit a butt beside the open window and took a swift drag. Nothing worked better for her nervous stomach. Since she could still hear the kids, she ran a tub; then she decided to have a bath, so she closed the drain and started to undress. To relax, she had only to remember that she wasn't pregnant.

What's wrong with this picture? she thought. This was about "as good as it gets"; and yet, with every likelihood of happiness and financial security, the thought of having a child put her in a panic. Were children no longer an option now? Was that why her relief was so humongous? No. She knew why. Since she had first read *The Belacqua Report* and prevailed upon Danvers to stand up for it, she had come to accept absolutely its scientific conclusions—especially after meeting Roger, whom she thought of as a kind of grandfather. From that moment she had bought into Belacqua's argument and adapted her cosmology accordingly; by now she had a vested interest in its dark truth. Besides, it confirmed the grim epiphany she'd had on the Mass Pike, weeping over roadkill. But she hadn't expected its impact on her life: she simply accepted what Belacqua proved, and readjusted her thinking. It was only when her period came late that she realized how immoral it suddenly seemed to have a child.

But another child was probably what Franco needed most of all, beyond her love, to move past Lillian's death and begin life anew as a husband and a father. He was still unhappy, to gauge from his drinking. And to her just then, it seemed as if her own happiness could only be determined by Franco's. She'd wait to get pregnant, of course, until they'd talked. Meanwhile, she *had* to stop smoking: she doused the butt and absentmindedly flicked it out the window. Oops—pedestrians. Oh well. Fuck 'em.

When Franco got home, Terry was watching Tom Brokaw in the den, groggily, after her bath and a nap. Franco seemed perfectly carefree. "So what's in the news? An outbreak of Ebola? A California earthquake? Any sign of the seventeen-year locusts?" After fixing a martini, Franco joined her in the den and recounted his meeting with Bob Milton. By the time he was done, Terry was wide awake.

"So," she asked as offhandedly as she could, "what'll you do now?"

Franco bowed his head and spoke softly. "Well, I'm going to leave Commonweal. But I won't go to Macro. Maybe I can find a teaching post."

"Oh." She had been hoping to hear that, even while she appeared preoccupied with her cuticle. "Here in the city, you think?"

"Possibly. I'd prefer something smaller, in the country."

"Who's Bob Milton replacing you with?"

Franco managed an ironic smile. "The new president is Danvers Creal."

Terry erupted in an unladylike guffaw. Moments later they were laughing uncontrollably.

After Labor Day the country began revving up for the '98 elections, and from the very overture of the campaigns it was clear that *The Belacqua Report* was going to play an important but ambiguous role in the candidates' positions. The Democrats tried to preempt the issue by blaming the end of the world on the Reagan-Bush administrations, as well as the Republicans' Contract with America, and their "obtuse disregard for environmental issues." In a bit of electoral hyperbole, one Eastern congressman proclaimed that "the extinction of the human race will weigh upon every Republican shoulder until Judgment Day." This was the first clear indication of just how politically divisive the book would become.

Some Republicans hitched their star to constitutional amendments to balance the budget, protect the flag, and affirm a right to life. A few argued that a Constitutional Convention might produce transformations to prolong survival. Democrats balked, warning that Republican money would rig a convention: though they had no evidence, to numerous commentators that seemed obvious.

Franco announced his departure from Commonweal at the next editorial meeting, after he'd told Bob Milton he was returning to academia; he emphasized the need for continuity, especially with skittish authors, and spoke highly of Danvers, who acted like Saint Thomas More but came off more like Uriah Heep.

"Of course, I'll be available to you all, even after I leave. No doubt you'll manage the transition smoothly. Any questions?" The ensuing silence slumped into a palpable dejection. Only Danvers made noises that Franco should stay on.

By day's end a handful of resignations appeared on Franco's desk, including those of Roy Raymond, Jamie Quinn, and both Judy Corliss and Joe Mercer, whose marriage had not survived *The*

Belacqua Report. Most specified that they could not work under Danvers Creal. Roy Raymond went further: "In half a century of publishing," he wrote Milton, "I never saw a more inappropriate CEO than Creal. It insults the staff and the noble tradition of Commonweal. Only a capitalist conglomerate could . . ." Roy followed his letter by a two-week bender that landed him in the hospital with cirrhosis. He died two months later, bitter, miserable, and sober.

A week after Danvers took over as CEO, he commissioned a six-volume series entitled *The World of Bloomsbury.*

Franco repeatedly tried to reach Belacqua after his meeting with Bob Milton, but he and Christiane had gone to Costa Rica for ten days after the book tour. As a result Franco didn't get him on the phone for two weeks.

"Roger," said Franco, after a handful of pleasantries, "you never did explain that story about the suntan oil for babies. What was that all about?"

"Well, it's complicated, and I don't want to bore you—"

"You won't," His voice had an edge he'd never used with Belacqua. "Tell me."

"Well, it was an act of revenge against the chairman of GDG, Bob Milton, who had conned me out of a million dollars years before. Frankly, it was stupid and petty, but after what he'd put me through, I can live with it. You see, I had proof that the suntan oil was carcinogenic. So I documented the facts and gave the sealed evidence to my bank president, to be opened just before the product went on the market. Then I cast the deciding vote in favor of its production. I knew it would end my viability for other peer review panels, but I was prepared for that, I was so damn mad at the fellow."

"What exactly had Bob Milton done to you?" Franco's voice betrayed nothing.

"I told you I'd made money in the fifties with a new polymer? That was with Milton's corporation, BoMil. For years he refused to pay my royalties. Then BoMil was sold to another company that screwed me with legal tactics. This was my revenge."

"And was it sweet?"

There was a long pause. "Like most revenge. Yes and no."

Franco knew it would take a dump truck full of lawyers and accountants to figure out what had really happened. "Listen, Roger, I have some bad news."

"Uh-oh. Did someone prove that *The Belacqua Report* is a hoax?"

Franco laughed. "Not yet. Macro fired me. I'm not at Commonweal anymore."

Belacqua was stunned. "I'm very sorry to hear that, Franco—you know I am. I hope it had nothing to do with my book."

"Well, I suppose it did. Part of the problem was that the chairman's wife took religious exception to your 'blasphemy.' I expect she feels that God alone can decide when the last day will be."

"But this book has made a fortune for Commonweal," Belacqua almost shouted. "Surely Macro's CEO cares more about the bottom line than the ecclesiastical line."

"You don't know this guy." Franco listened hard for some clue in Belacqua's tone.

"I don't need to," replied Belacqua righteously. "His priorities are in his title, whoever he is." His indignation was genuine. "You know what I'll do, Franco? I'm going to pull the paperback rights from Commonweal. *You* were the reason I went with them. This is breach of contract, so I'll take the paperback wherever I want."

"That's arguable," Franco agreed, "but you won't win. This guy enjoys litigation."

"Who the hell is he?"

Now Franco was sure he wasn't bluffing. Roger really didn't know his old foe owned his book; ergo, *The Belacqua Report* was no act of revenge.

"Macro, and Commonweal," said Franco, "are owned by Bob Milton."

Franco heard the sound of Belacqua slapping his forehead. *"Impossibile!* You've got to be joking. Franco, please, tell me you're joking."

"No, no joke. When I first told him about your book, I didn't mention your name. He's furious, too: he can't stand making you rich and famous."

Genuine anguish flooded Belacqua's voice. "I never knew. *I swear upon the souls of my children,* I never knew. He was always in chemicals! After he left GDG, I lost track of him. I never thought he'd own a canned goods company like Macro—much less a publishing house. I'm so sorry."

Franco laughed. "Don't worry about it, Roger. I'll go back to teaching."

Belacqua seemed unconsolable. "But—leaving publishing, after such a career."

"Never mind." Franco couldn't resist adding, "It's not the end of the world."

In October, three weeks before midterm elections, a peculiar and vicious crime took place in Cleveland, the repugnant details of which were recited *ad nauseam* by every media outlet in America and around the world: this was bigger than O.J. At first the coverage was shrill but conventional, with the press harking back to the pantheon of mass murders. Only after the perpetrators were arrested and gave their stories to the *Cleveland Plain Dealer* did the implications begin to outweigh the crimes themselves.

On the night of October 14 a group of sixteen young men and women of varied backgrounds—four came from affluent homes—drove down to the Strand, beside the mighty Cuyahoga River. In a well-planned assault, they approached a chic supper club called the Versailles Room. First they isolated the restaurant, using wire cutters to clip the phone lines. In groups of four and five, the gang members entered the premises and demanded the best tables; since they were not dressed appropriately for the decorous establishment, they were refused service. Then the siege began.

The sixteen assailants, armed with handguns and knives, seized the building. Stripping the uniforms off the staff, the perpetrators posted guards at all exits and emptied the cash registers. Then the staff of twelve front-of-house employees and another ten in the kitchen were led to the walk-in fridge and locked up by two of the assailants, using a long-flanged padlock they had brought along that fitted the bolts of the door (later this was used in court as evidence of premeditation, though the key evidence was the videotape that one of them made of the proceedings).

With the staff removed, the orgy began. As twenty-six customers watched in terror, the group opened bottles of champagne and spirits and began to "party hardy," as they kept repeating. When the perps found the restaurant's CD player, they replaced

Peter Nero Plays Gershwin with the Stones' "Trash the Earth," cranked up to full volume throughout the six-hour siege. As they got drunk and stoned, they began singing the lyrics, and some traumatized patrons, unfamiliar with the Rolling Stones, thought they were being abused by the group who'd recorded the song.

There was a pecking order among the assailants: the alpha punk had unchallenged first choice of the victims. The leaders herded the guests into the bar and occupied the plush velvet banquettes themselves. There they settled down with the women of their choice, showing their "dates" an incongruous degree of courtesy—inviting them to use the ladies' room under the supervision of two of the female perps, who chose men to toy with from among the diners. Before acting out their perversities, they forced the captives to chug liquor and puff the grass they'd brought for the "party." Many swore on the stand that they were delirious throughout much of the siege.

The gentler gang members were determined to elicit sexual co-operation from the terrified, disoriented victims: they courted, wooed, and seduced—at gunpoint. Of course those who failed to get into the swing of things were brutally raped. Otherwise the men made sure that the women were aroused, however involuntarily, coaxing the victims to "join the fun," with assurances that they wouldn't be harmed if they cooperated. Meanwhile the female perps did the same with the male guests, while forcing some to perform oral sex upon each other, to masturbate, and to satisfy the most degenerate fantasies of domination.

This proceeded for several hours, uninterrupted, in shifting groups of victims and assailants. At the end of each playback of "Trash the Earth," the assailants joined in with the Stones:

> Tease my toy and suck my brain,
> I'm at the top of the great food chain!

By two in the morning the perversity had turned to all-out mutilation and mayhem. De Sade and Dahmer, in their most obscene longings, could hardly have devised such bizarre cruelty, such creative abuse of human flesh, such pathological notions of "fun." Numerous kitchen utensils were used to create new orifices; patterns, designs, even corporate logos were carved into the flesh of the screaming victims, nine of whom were murdered outright (seven others died later). Two dinner guests were castrated, while every stage of the victims' destruction—spiritual, sexual, and anatomical—was carefully recorded on a Sony Hi8 Camcorder with 12X zoom. The result was exactly what the group intended: a music video of hell, complete with red velvet, crystal candelabras, and a driving back beat. Against that decor, the torture of the victims was documented in close-up, including the very moment of each death.

At about four in the morning the leader, a tall white male in his late twenties named Nick, told his cohorts he was "all jizzed out." Collecting their money, they left the premises, some with parting kisses for their maimed captives, who were warned that a gunman would be waiting outside for three hours in case they tried to alert the police.

The *Cleveland Plain Dealer* dubbed the crime "Dinner in Hell"; its early account was cited around the world, including statements from a survivor, Mitch Crowe, who was still floundering in hysteria. His eyewitness description was chewed over by the media like rawhide by a wolfhound. A few days later, copies of the gang's videotape were sent to the *Plain Dealer*, the *National Enquirer*, and *Hard Copy*.

The relentless broadcasting of the videotape coated the world like some new form of pollution, searing television viewers everywhere with vivid, torturous images that would last a lifetime. The gang's video pushed innocent viewers right into the scene of the crime, if not as accomplices, then somehow as more than just witnesses. The fact that all the assailants' faces were masked made it much more powerful. Because the night of crime was planned and perpetrated by a group rather than a sick loner, it was generally compared to the Manson murders and "wilding" episodes in New York City; older commentators mentioned *The Clockwork Orange*. One way or another it grabbed the world by the throat. Even a carefully edited copy of the video was more obscene than any precedent: this was the snuff film to end all snuff films. "Watch these images at your peril," warned Rosenthal in the *Times*, "because the experience of their vicious content is easily enough to alter the psyche." "These visions of evil," wrote Andrew Delbanco in *The New Republic*, "could belong to no other era than our own." "How to account for such subhuman perversity?" demanded a Greek chorus of commentators.

Then a young college graduate named Ringo Stervin was arrested, identified by the hardware-store clerk who had sold him the long-flanged padlock. Stervin considered himself an intellectual revolutionary rather than just a street punk, which was how he lived. An intense, short, dark-haired young man whose snaggletoothed smile soon became an icon of depravity more menacing than Manson's, Stervin was a born powder keg. Like his accomplices, most of whom were captured, he'd dropped out of high school to take up high-tech crime: cellular phone theft, Net fraud, etc. In the prosecutor's words, he was "a petty thug with grand ambitions." Doing time in County for raping a nurse, Stervin had earned a GED, and in '96 majored in political science at a community college while working as a tour guide at the Rock and Roll Hall of Fame.

That summer, when *The Belacqua Report* came out, Stervin had digested the book whole, memorizing key passages, from which he fashioned a twisted apocalyptic ideology that he shared with his unsavory friends. The *fin du monde* philosophy he concocted owed mostly to his antisocial psychosis and sexual aberrance; nonetheless, it incorporated passages from Nietzsche and even Dostoevsky: "If there is no God, then there is no evil, and all things are permissible," just as Jonathan Fischer had predicted.

All this was brought out for weeks by the defense counsel during the nine-month trial in '99. In fact, as *Newsweek* reported, "The doomsday report *was* their alibi, cited chapter and verse by defense attorney David Morris, who declared in his opening statement that 'the accused are themselves the victims of a dying world.' " When Stervin began giving interviews, the media focused on the connection between "imminent mass extinction" and "unprecedented lawlessness." Because once this deranged sociopath asserted that his actions were caused by Belacqua's work, their names were linked. Conservatives blamed the media for making the connection.

So did William Buckley who, in the late fall of 1998, chastised the press for crafting a handful of degenerate atrocities into a gladhanders' Götterdämmerung, based upon the spurious scientific speculations of one Roger Belacqua, the latest profiteer to seize the mantle of Nostradamus. In order for such snake-oil salesmen to announce that the End Is Nigh, they must first pay lip service to Destiny, and insist that "the future has already been written." *Then* they must explain why they alone hold the franchise upon the truest tea leaves, the ultimate tarot, the perfect yarrow stalks. Whether they interpret religious apocrypha or scientific "data"—the Book of Revelation or the mating rituals of salps—these doomsayers are, in fact, neither demons nor diviners: in a robust civilization, types like Belacqua are simply part of the scenery. All he has done is to give a bad name to good science; while the Versailles Room Massacre provided a perfect opportunity to those ink-stained wretches who are suspiciously swift to see all human destiny reflected in an aberrant orgy of slaughter.

One op-ed piece asserted that, as in Camus's *The Plague,* the certainty of collective demise was likely to produce an existential liberation of *everything* contained in the human spirit, good and evil alike, but noted that, so far, there was no sign of Mother Teresas multiplying like mayflies. Before long, all that was wrong in the American psyche was attributed to *The Belacqua Report.* In Oakland, the *Chronicle* reported, a man arrested for jaywalking pleaded "not guilty on the grounds of insanity," testifying that he'd been driven to distraction by *The Belacqua Report.*

A new fad swept the chic bars and clubs of New York, Atlanta, Aspen, and L.A.: Brompton's Solution. The demand for narcotics took off like a rocket in '98. Brompton's Solution, a pharmaceutical blend of heroin, cocaine, and Valium prescribed to terminal patients in England, was being mixed up in New Jersey garages. The trendy new drug was in high demand, along with old favorites like roofies, Special K, and Windows 98 (transparent panes of LSD). By Christmas, premixed speedball was available from savvy doormen, pizza deliverers, and bartenders; once again rest rooms were filled with snorting sounds and bent spoons. Black-market quaaludes—"Vitamin Qs"—made a comeback, too. Well-dressed pedestrians weaved the streets of cities as the short-lived "clean and sober culture" faded like a fleeting infatuation.

For teenagers of the late nineties, nihilism blended well with post-adolescent turmoil. Theirs was a self-righteous anarchy, given that their lives were to be cut shorter than the Boomers' and the yuppies'. The logic seemed hard to dispute: why stay sober if the world was dying? Or in the words of Travis Folger's "I Wanna Die Before You Go (That's Why I'm Waiting in Line)":

> Don' wanna go to school an' die a young smartie,
> All I want to do is to party, party!

Roger Belacqua seemed to accept the social consequences of his work with unassailable sangfroid. Franco Sherman did not. His worst nightmares returned with unequaled ferocity and creativity after the massacre at the Versailles Room. Waking and sleeping, Franco replayed every detail of the videotape, overwhelmed by a sense of personal responsibility for each indignity, every brutal rape, and all the deaths that occurred that terrible night. In the worst of his recurring scenarios, Franco dreamed that Juliette was having dinner with her mother at the ill-fated restaurant. Worse, Max was among the assailants. His daughter and his wife were raped and mutilated as Franco watched through his son's eyes. He awoke in Terry's arms, sobbing.

By day he withdrew for long stretches of time, and his drinking, even at lunch, became heavier. Again and again he argued with himself in favor of a free press: its crucial role in democracy, however destructive its results. But the question that really haunted him was, had he made a ghastly mistake?

Terry, for her part, felt she was sinking beneath her burdens, even though sometimes she felt she'd never been happier; in short, she was really really confused. She loved Juliette and Max, but she was just twenty-five, living with a man in his forties so tightly wound that he often seemed to struggle for breath. And still she loved him, and wanted only to be with him. Marcia, her mom, could see that when she visited from Minneapolis, amazed to find her erstwhile punky daughter—at age twelve, the youngest girl on Lake Harriet to have her eyebrow pierced—firmly ensconced in a maternal role. Terry felt especially responsible for Juliette. They'd been through a half-dozen scary respiratory crises alone together, racing to Lenox Hill in panic. Those experiences, more than the playful ones, bound them together.

At night, while Franco thrashed beside her, Terry still fretted over moral issues—like bringing a child into a post-Belacqua world—even as she tiptoed to the living-room window to sneak butts. Sometimes she looked out at the city with admiration for the sheer audacity of mankind. And sometimes she just sat there and cried.

Terry wasn't accustomed to crying. When she was twelve, her Dad had died from a ruptured aneurysm while on a business trip in Sioux City. She must have cried a lifetime's worth of tears then, because ever since she'd had precious few to spare. Now she hardly ever thought about him.

One morning at the end of October, while he was collating his academic transcripts, Franco received a call from Belacqua.

"The strangest thing is going on," said the scientist, after some small talk. "This murder investigation. I had a visit from a New York detective. They still suspect that I'm somehow behind McAdams's death. Has he talked to you?"

"Yes," said Franco, with a taste of bile in his mouth. "His name's Bill Jordan."

"Right. He actually suspects Suki, simply because she's blond."

"What does Detective Jordan want to know?"

"The detective's convinced that Suki went to New York and killed McAdams to 'protect' our work. It's so absurd. But that week, unfortunately, Christiane was visiting her mother in France, and I was down at Woods Hole, so neither of us can confirm Suki's whereabouts. We didn't even speak to her on the phone."

Franco sounded deadly earnest. "You really don't think Suki killed him?"

"It's ludicrous! You only have to know her. Suki doesn't even eat meat."

Franco shot back, "Then why did she go for a cheeseburger with McAdams?"

Belacqua fell silent. "That *was* strange—she clammed up when I asked her about that. She was unusually flirtatious with McAdams. Good-looking fellow, too, in a citified way. I think things were already strained between her and Jimmy; a few weeks later they broke up and he moved to Boston." Roger adopted the tone reserved by men for discussing women. "Suki's a very . . . physical young woman." He paused before illustrating his point. "When she first got here, she actually made a pass at my wife. But she would never be capable of murder. And why?"

"If she thought McAdams could scuttle your book?"

"Even if McAdams had raised objections, you would have published it, isn't that so? Bushnell and Landry—two out of three."

Franco couldn't deny that he'd already wanted to publish the book. In retrospect, he knew damn well that he'd used the scientific assessments to validate a decision he'd already made—and to convince other board members. That was why he felt so responsible. "Possibly," he conceded. "But Suki couldn't have known that." Then he threw caution to the wind. "And there's this: at the Last Resort, Suki spent the night with McAdams."

"What do you mean? You saw 'em going at it?"

"I heard them."

Belacqua whistled. "Jaysus m' beads. Then—I wonder if Suki did visit him in New York? Jimmy was in Boston two of the nights that Christiane and I were away."

As his stress level reached its upper threshold, Franco maintained an offhand tone. "So, she has no alibi at all?"

Belacqua ran out of patience. "No. But it's still ludicrous. I know her: she couldn't sleep with a man and then poison him. She's too . . . flower-child for that. Besides, where would she get ibogaine? I doubt she's ever even heard of it."

Franco sighed. "I don't know. I don't know anything."

Since they first met he had wanted to believe the old man: now he simply had to. The alternative was too painful to consider.

Candidates in the Senate races spent the first weeks after Labor Day avoiding the Belacqua issue, but the tough policy questions kept coming, and after the Versailles Room massacre, the end of the world became a local law-and-order issue that could not be finessed. So most of them issued position papers that were models of firmness and ambiguity, agreeing unanimously that (A) Belacqua's assertions were unconfirmed; (B) if confirmed, they wouldn't justify criminal behavior; (C) all nations shared responsibility for atmospheric pollution; (D) as the leading industrial nation, the

United States should devise a policy for the world to buy additional time; and finally, (E) that faith, not reactionary policy, was the cure for "this gloomy prognosis." Congressional candidates expressed the same narrow range of opinions, from jingoism to fundamentalist outrage. Republican Bertrand Fillmore declared that *The Belacqua Report* was "part of a global conspiracy to crush the American spirit."

Psychologists and sociologists predicted—and then, not surprisingly, they detected—a shift in the values of the age. The post-Belacqua culture, they intoned, would be different from all previous human society. "The most fundamental axioms seem to have turned upside down," wrote Dominick Dunne in *Vanity Fair*. " 'Go forth and multiply,' for example, must now be seen as a sinister appeal to self-destruction."

Lewis Lapham's editorial in *Harper's* in December 1998 expanded on this theme. Lapham decried

> both the revisionists who propose a new ethical framework adapted to the reality of a doomed planet, and the blind traditionalists who insist that, extinction notwithstanding, we must nonetheless cling to the same outdated beliefs which have brought us to the point where, by merely surviving, we are shortening the lives of our neighbors.
>
> So far realists and doctrinaire alike have failed to devise an eschatological escape hatch from this brave new world of inverted morality. Since population growth is what has condemned our planet, we face a hideous new equation: anything that diminishes the population, like the nuclear blight of Metzamor, is good for the earth. With each slaughter, tyrants like Saddam Hussein become benefactors. By this post-Belacqua logic, modern medicines that foil death threaten us, while the monsters of the Versailles Room at least reduced the population. Tobacco companies are prolonging life; flood, drought, and famine help the survival of the species, as does AIDS. And so it seems that Macbeth's witches had it right all along:
>
> > Fair is foul, and foul is fair,
> > Hover through the fog and filthy air.

In a blistering rebuttal, William Bennett responded: "Virtue is not a fad governed by fleeting scientific theories. If Dr. Belacqua had disproved Galileo, that would not alter the Golden Rule. Mr.

Lapham and other ethical relativists may choose this moment to 'out' themselves as admirers of Saddam Hussein, but the rest of us are not compelled to pay them one whit of attention."

The contours of the post-Belacqua culture weren't revealed in a single moment; they became conventional through accretion. As the concept of mass human extinction sank in, a discernible corrosion of traditional values was coupled with the onset of ideological nihilism, generally expressed in the vernacular as "What the fuck."

At Commonweal, the regime of Danvers Creal was in full swing: his vaunted self-regard was all over the office, chiding, needling, and threatening. Thanks to revenues from *The Belacqua Report*, Danvers launched a whole flotilla of moist Bloomsbury books.

Then, in November, Danvers received the first half of a manuscript entitled *Belacqua Refuted*, submitted by literary agent Sterling Lord. Written by one William Kerner, Ph.D., it purported to dismiss scientifically every assertion in *The Belacqua Report*. After studying a summary of the partial manuscript, Danvers offered Kerner a $1.1 million advance to rush the book into hardcover and paperback simultaneously with the paperback of *The Belacqua Report*, in May 1999. Danvers had decided to publish the two paperbacks together, in a boxed edition. To most of the in-house editors, it seemed absurd to publish the refutation of their own best-seller, and soon Commonweal's corridors were filled with the sound of sharpening knives.

Since leaving the publishing house, Franco had had a lot of free time. He spent a few days tending to Historical Perspective and severing its distribution ties with Commonweal. To cancel his existing arrangements, Franco enlisted Marshall Pierson, *former* speedball addict but still chief counsel to the publishing house. Marshall had called one day looking for the notarized copy of the Belacqua book contract.

"Must be in your files," Franco answered, knowing full well it was right there in his desk; he didn't want Milton to have it. After chatting with Marshall awhile, he asked the lawyer if he would please finalize Franco's contractual arrangements "without disturbing Milton." Out of gratitude for his recovery, Marshall took care of business. In a week, Historical Perspective was free and clear of Commonweal.

Franco's little imprint had just a dozen titles in its catalog. Using some of the capital from his modest golden parachute, Franco signed two more academic titles and ordered a large new printing of Professor Wylie's *The Second Republic of the United States,* partly on a hunch, partly as a sentimental gesture; for the fourth printing he wrote a brief new foreword, recapping the scholar's work.

"You've got mail!" One afternoon Franco was stunned to find hundreds of messages for him, from all five continents and Oceania. Some were from alumni of his Swiss high school whom he hadn't heard from in thirty years, though some had been close childhood friends. But most were from readers of *The Belacqua Report.* Franco couldn't understand why they were writing to him, until Terry figured out that "Franco Sherman" was now hyperlinked to "Belacqua" on some website that gave their readers the option of writing to the publisher just by clicking on the blue text. (Much later he learned that one of the International School alumni had inserted the link.) As a result, he got lots of e-mail, some supportive, some very threatening.

On December 2, 1998, Suki Herlihy was arrested and later arraigned in Burlington for the murder of William McAdams. She cooperated with her extradition to New York, since, as she tearily told the crowd of reporters covering "The Belacqua Murder," "the sooner this is cleared up, the better, so the real killer can be caught."

Suki's arrest was widely taken as evidence that Belacqua's book might be a hoax in which she was involved. Though Roger Belacqua wasn't named in the indictment, many were quick to presume his guilt. Only Jordan and O'Hara knew just how weak their case was, but they were counting on the arrest to squeeze cooperation from possible accomplices, and to buy time while they figured out how the young woman had obtained ibogaine.

THE DEVIL'S EYE

Some 30 billion species are estimated to have lived since multicellular creatures first evolved in the Cambrian explosion. . . . According to some estimates, 30 million species populate today's earth. This means that 99.9 percent of all species that have ever lived are extinct. . . . Life's grip on Earth is evidently more precarious than we might like to accept.

—RICHARD LEAKEY AND ROGER LEWIN, *The Sixth Extinction: Patterns of Life and the Future of Humankind* (1995)

One night about a week before Christmas, after Franco had dozed off over a book, Terry sat down at her makeshift office in the living room to sneak a butt—her first in a week. She hadn't been sleeping well: among other things she was just so damn horny, and had been for a month. The same could not be said of Franco.

Checking the website for users of the Belacqua CD-ROM (which was shipped before Thanksgiving in record-breaking numbers), Terry began reading the public's reactions. Amid the spectrum of kudos and kvetches, a cluster of technical problems was showing up in the "Scenarios" section, where variables for population increase, meteorological activity, and emissions were chosen by the user to produce different endings for life on earth. They were based on Belacqua's general circulation model, adapted from the one at NOAA's Geophysical Fluid Dynamics Laboratory.

As producer, Terry had overseen only design and programming, but she was familiar with every aspect of the data, all straight from Roger's book. So, lighting a second cigarette, she examined the problems related to carbon dioxide production—and what she found baffled her. It was as if the program had been built on two different sets of data: that's why, in certain configurations, the whole thing crashed—too often to blame Sparky the Clown. But she couldn't pinpoint the cause.

She was still at her computer the next morning when Juliette came in and, smelling the filthy ashtray on the desk, began gasping for breath and looking for her inhaler. That was when Terry finally quit smoking for good.

The first thing Suki Herlihy did, after submitting to the New York police, was to provide blood and hair samples. The next thing was to call Franco to ask for the name of a criminal attorney. This put Franco in an awkward position; nonetheless, at his request, Marshall referred her to a lawyer, who filed a flurry of motions in Manhattan Superior Court. Two days later, Suki was released on a $500,000 bond and ordered to stay in the city. She promptly asked Franco if she could stay at his place until she was exonerated. This was more than he was prepared to offer. Instead he directed her to a hotel; Belacqua, who had put up her bond, paid for her expenses.

Suki continued to deny having had any romantic tryst with McAdams or visiting him in New York, much less having killed him. And over the next two weeks she was spotted around town by the press, who were more interested in her long legs than her degree in marine biology. She quickly acquired a Kato-like celebrity, visiting the clubs and eating for free at trendy restaurants. If Suki was feigning insouciance, she carried it off like Lady Macbeth.

At Commonweal, petals were dropping off the rose just as the flower blossomed. The huge profits from *The Belacqua Report* were embarrassing, considering its message; but many of the house's most valuable authors and editors jumped ship when they learned about *Belacqua Refuted,* especially after excerpts appeared in *U.S. News & World Report.* The editors who stayed on thought that Danvers would be gone before *Belacqua Refuted* hit the stands, but they hadn't bargained on Bob Milton's enthusiasm for the Kerner book: he was delighted that Commonweal Books was disavowing the blasphemous notion that Armageddon was man-made, not heaven-sent; and he was confident that this move would generate even greater profits, while restoring the company's good name throughout the Bible Belt.

When Franco first learned about *Belacqua Refuted* from Marshall, he couldn't believe it, and for a time he wondered what Marshall was putting up his nose now. But one phone call confirmed the news. So on a Tuesday morning, wearing a business suit for the first time in weeks, Franco was standing in his old office, on the wrong side of his old desk, staring down at Danvers Creal.

"Why did you do this?" asked Franco, in a tone reserved for Max when blueberry syrup was found on the sofa.

Danvers looked up from Lytton Strachey's diary. He'd gained enough weight to make room for a new repertory of mannerisms. "Franco, my boy," he replied *à la* Sidney Greenstreet, with a hint of diphthong. "What seems to be the problem?"

"You're making a mockery of *The Belacqua Report,* Commonweal, and yourself." Franco's voice vividly conveyed his rage. Now that their professional relationship was over, Franco was glad to reveal just how much he loathed Danvers.

"Tsk tsk," Danvers replied, *à la* Rex Harrison. "Under the circumstances I'm compelled to ask, what bloody business is it of yours?"

"I care about the good name of this house," Franco answered incontestably. "You've got to recognize the effect of Commonweal's ambivalence on the world."

Before his eyes, Rex Harrison morphed into John Houseman. "The impact on the *world,* Franco? Isn't that a bit grandiose? We're a publishing firm—an *organ,* as Bob Milton likes to say. We didn't *guarantee* the end of the world with every copy of *The Belacqua Report.* In a scientific controversy like this, it's only sensible to err on the side of caution and offer different interpretations of the data." Suddenly Danvers sounded like Gregory Peck in *To Kill a Mockingbird.* "What matters here is the *freedom of the press.* Why would Commonweal Books suppress the most important scientific report of 1999, just because it disagrees with the most important scientific report of 1998? Why should we adhere blindly to the dogma of the past?"

Franco was amazed at the depth of Danvers's superficiality. "You don't believe in *The Belacqua Report*, do you? Or even in *Belacqua Refuted*."

Danvers shrugged. "What does it matter what I believe, or what you believe? We're *printers*, Franco. Just printers. The grand truths of the universe are not ours to decide."

Franco paused to master an offhand tone. "Have you seen the news lately? Did you hear about the Versailles Room Massacre?"

"Oh, come on, we're not responsible for that. And if we were, then perhaps *Belacqua Refuted* will be just the right antidote. Do you really think we should ignore any critique of your beloved Belacqua?" Danvers was rubbing his hands unctuously. "Surely what's needed is a diversity of views." Now Franco recognized him: Uriah Heep. "I should add that Bob Milton is delighted with *Belacqua Refuted* . . . very happy, indeed."

Franco was restraining himself. "Bob Milton is in the canned goods business. Christ, Danvers, what credibility can Commonweal ever have, trying to prove its own best-seller was wrong?"

"You obviously haven't *read* the Kerner book, Franco?"

"That's not the point."

"Aha. Not the point," Danvers repeated. Uriah Heep was not doing the job, so George Bernard Shaw popped up. "You disappoint me, Franco. First, you should remember that it was *I* who brought the unsolicited manuscript of *The Belacqua Report* to *your* attention."

"Only because of Terry's insistence," Franco retorted. "She was the one who read the manuscript—not you. She told me exactly how it all happened."

"Did she?" Now, at last, Danvers revealed his ancient bitterness toward Franco. "Really?"

"Yes. Terry persuaded you to recommend *The Belacqua Report* to me."

Danvers looked into Franco's eyes. "And did she tell you how she persuaded me?"

"What?" Something in his tone wrenched at Franco's gut.

Danvers strode to the spot by the window where Franco had stood so often, gazing up Fifth Avenue toward Central Park. "I was always skeptical about *The Belacqua Report*, Franco: that's no secret. I didn't want to stick my neck out to publish a scientific paper and cause a big ruckus when, in all modesty, I didn't have the scientific background necessary to evaluate its arguments"—he turned to Franco—"any more than you did. That's exactly what I told Terry." Danvers was still looking out the window. "I told her that I certainly wouldn't go to bat for Belacqua. Not unless . . ."

"Not unless what?"

"Not unless she made it . . . worth my while."

Franco laughed involuntarily. The idea that Terry would have slept with Danvers was as ridiculous as it was offensive. His voice turned soft and hot. "Don't you dare invent crap like that."

Danvers watched Franco's reaction with detached amusement. "Congratulations," he said quietly. "She's *very* good in bed. So animated . . . uninhibited." He leaned forward into Franco's face. "I especially loved the little orange-and-gold butterfly at the top of her thigh. It has such *tiny* green eyes."

Franco stared, speechless, while Danvers braced himself, as if waiting for a right uppercut; when it didn't come, he pushed his luck further. "You know, I feel some pride in your union: you two would never have met if I hadn't hired her. And she was still my assistant when your little romance began." Danvers moved his chin into Franco's range. "But please tell Terry . . . I miss her."

Franco estimated the force required to heave Danvers through the plate-glass window. But he resisted his impulses, even if, for the moment, he couldn't think why.

"You're not worth the hassle, Danvers," he said, his voice coiled like a cobra. "You are a waste of skin."

Turning to leave in disgust, Franco took one last look, then left the door of his old office open as he accelerated down the corridor. Behind him he heard Danvers's new secretary announce a call from Mildred Milton.

At the apartment, Franco went straight into the den, where Terry was on the phone with her mother. He closed the door, waiting impatiently until she had finished.

"Danvers tells me you slept with him to get *The Belacqua Report* published."

She closed her eyes tightly and took a deep breath. "Well, technically, no, that's not true," she answered slowly. "*Technically,* what I did was, I held Danvers Creal's penis in my left hand for thirty long seconds while he rubbed the crotch of my panties with his nose." She shrugged. "He was, um, premature. *Very* premature."

Franco glared. "He knew the color of your butterfly's eyes!"

Terry winced. She was silent for almost a minute. "When I asked him to pitch the manuscript to you, he'd already decided to pass on it. So I went to his apartment that Sunday afternoon to change his mind." She added matter-of-factly, "I did what had to be done."

Franco stared at her as if they'd never met. "Is that why you slept with me, too? To get this damn book published?"

"That's not fair, Franco." A single tear raced down to her lip. "You know that's not true!" She ran out of the room.

As Franco watched her go he remembered how he'd worried about harassing the young assistant. By then she had already done the executive editor. And not just any executive editor, but the multifaceted Danvers Creal. Must have been a gang bang.

That afternoon Franco phoned Marshall, and the next day a courier brought him the galleys of *Belacqua Refuted,* purloined. That did nothing to improve the former publisher's disposition. He was as irritated at Kerner's inconclusive arguments as he was with the more persuasive chapters. To begin with, Kerner had lifted his argument about the "eggshell effect" from Benedek's *Nature* article, adding nothing substantive. With regard to the crucial function of salps as "biological pumps," Kerner was nonchalant about any threat of their overingesting carbon: "What Belacqua's evidence really suggests is that space is being made between existing species for new, more aggressive salps that can dispose of even greater quantities of carbon." Kerner did not address the effect on the aquatic food chain, or the synergistic impact of *billions* of tons of rotting plankton upon global warming. Instead, he nitpicked about Belacqua's water-temperature research, saying the tanks weren't large enough to be conclusive.

That was *Belacqua Refuted.* Each argument was stretched and padded with irrelevant anecdotes, and quotations from Belacqua's book vastly exceeding fair use: almost a third of the book consisted of citations from the very report it was refuting. Permission to use these long passages had been granted, not surprisingly, by Commonweal Books. Altogether absent in Kerner's knockoff refutation was any mention of Belacqua's geopolitical analysis. Apparently

persuaded that he'd demolished all of Belacqua's scientific assertions, Kerner felt no compunction to address the political conun-
drums of population growth, greenhouse gases, or even CFCs.
Instead, he simply asserted in his conclusion that "sustained
growth is the only means we have of perpetuating our kind."

A cheap shot, Franco thought, at the end of the short manuscript. A rip-off. An easy buck. A conscienceless, effortless, throw-
away sample of exploitation lacking even minimal scientific
acumen and patently misusing the threat to human survival for
the sake of money, fame, and Christian respectability. The public,
however, was unlikely to be so critical; most would prefer the conclusions of Belacqua Refuted to those of The Belacqua Report.
Franco knew that. So did Danvers Creal.

The publicity department had begun hyping Belacqua Refuted
as a major news event, challenging Roger Belacqua to debate his
contender on Meet the Press early in 1999. Along with the galleys,
Berling had sent Franco preliminary layouts of the print ads for
the boxed paperback set of The Belacqua Report and Belacqua Refuted. "Decide for yourself the most important question of our
times. Examine both sides of the issue," read the copy, beneath
which there were two images: a grotesque painting of a trashed
and barren world ruled by cockroaches, and a sunny Kodachrome
of happy children playing with a big red ball beside a lush forest.

Juliette's asthma had been better through the winter, so that
evening, after tucking the kids in, Franco took Terry around the
corner for dinner: they hadn't eaten alone together in more than
six months, and besides, they'd be gone less than an hour. Just
before they left, he called Roger to tell him about Belacqua Refuted. From Christiane he learned that Belacqua was in Boston for
a few days, but they were coming to New York the following week,
she said, so that Roger could meet with Danvers to discuss the
paperback. And when Christiane asked if they might be his
houseguests, Franco was quick to invite them. Rather than describe Kerner's travesty on the phone to her, he'd let Belacqua read
the galleys himself. By that time, he thought, Suki would have
been exonerated, surely, and Roger wouldn't be implicated in murder. The Belacqua Report would stand unimpeached. Surely.

After dinner, as they made their way back from the Four Seasons

Grill through the mild January evening, Terry suddenly blurted out what she'd been wrestling with all day.

"I think," she said, "something's screwy with the data in *The Belacqua Report*."

"Screwy?" Franco's tone maintained a skeptical distance.

"Inconsistent. Something in the projected carbon production in coming decades. The numbers come from two different sources. Calculate them one way, it works out. The other way, it doesn't."

A repairman leaving their building bumped headlong into them, distracting Franco with a familiar smell.

Sean, the doorman, stood under the awning. "That's the guy who fixed yer faucet, Mr. Sherman."

"What?" Right then Franco knew the smell. Licorice.

"The plumber guy you called. I let him in with the passkey. He said you had water all over yer floor."

Franco hadn't set the security alarm. "I didn't call. . . ." Then he looked at Terry. "That's the guy who broke in before."

They bounded out the door. Down the street the guy in overalls turned the corner.

"Go check the kids," Franco shouted.

"I'm faster than you!" Terry shouted back, tearing after the man and rounding the corner in time to see him vanish into the service entrance of a parking garage near Lexington. Franco lagged fifty yards behind her as she pulled on the heavy metal door and charged in after the fleeing figure.

Once Franco was inside the dark building, he followed the sounds as Terry scrambled up the metal stairway ahead of him. As he reached the second floor, a gunshot exploded like a cannon through the hollow space. Terry screamed.

"Are you all right?" Franco called, but she didn't answer. After more silence, he heard someone running away, two flights up the stairwell.

Then, from one story up, came Terry's voice. "I'm here," she whispered. "I'm okay." She stood up shakily and came down the stairs. "Wow," she said.

"Are you sure you aren't hurt?"

"No, I'm okay." But her legs were wobbly.

"Come on, let's get back to the kids." Franco took her hand and led her back down to street level. As quickly as they could, they made it back to the apartment.

Juliette was fast asleep, and Max only woke up for a moment when Franco looked in. And they slept through the visit from the police; this time Franco called 911, and two plainclothesmen came and took notes. But Franco didn't bring up the earlier theft of the manuscript, because he didn't want to involve the book.

Once again he could find nothing missing. There were dirt tracks into his office, where the guy had left an empty toolbox behind; that was the only evidence that anyone had been in the apartment.

That night, Terry and Franco slept tightly wrapped in each other's arms.

In February 1999, a second eruption at Metzamor destroyed everything the engineers had accomplished in a single white flash, sending a second huge plume toward the south-southeast in the general direction of Turkey and the Middle East, where it arrived after several weeks over the Black Sea, which was already thoroughly poisoned. The rad values of this second cloud were less elevated than those of the first, and evacuation procedures in advance of its arrival were much more efficient. But the number of displaced persons from this new evacuation, added to the DPs already encamped, created a refugee problem of unprecedented size in fourteen countries. By this time contaminees were estimated to exceed 21 million, but the number of malformed babies in the future could not be estimated. Another victim was the fund-raising effort. No one was sure whether this was because the private sector was tapped out or because the problem now seemed too gargantuan and intransigent to address.

The exception to the donor fatigue appeared on the Web. Although donations to the Ring of Angels had collapsed, some of its twenty creators established a new online charity, called Lifechance International; surprisingly, several of these people were old friends of Franco's. Some of these founders of Lifechance came from the corporate world and the diplomatic community; others were scientists, clerics, or educators. The one thing they had in common was that they were alumni either of the International School in Geneva, Switzerland, or of one of the 768 affiliated International Baccalaureate

Schools around the world. Collectively, the schools had almost a quarter million graduates, almost half of whom were online together, informed by an unusual blend of pluralistic values, and largely indifferent to ideological, ethnic, and nationalist agendas. The online membership had a considerable rural contingent, and most of the participating schools in the United States were public schools. The venture had the feel of a high-tech global barn-raising or Lagrange co-op.

In late '98, Lifechance had held the first international lottery over the Web, offering cybertickets for a dollar, with a prize of $1 million. The deficit, if any, would be made up by the alumni. All the accounting was public. There was a minimal budget for promotion, most of which was provided for free all over the Web. After the prize money had been paid out to the winner—an architect in Denmark—the total raised for blight relief was an unbelievable $42,732,604. This was big news.

The Lifechance Global Lottery, intended as a one-time event, was so successful that a second was held a month later with huge amounts of free publicity, including a two-hour live show on CNN around the world. Like most lotteries, the idea appealed to people's benevolence and greed at the same time. The net profit of the second lottery was an incredible $300 million.

By January 1999, the Lifechance Lottery had become established as a worldwide event that handed out a $1 million prize every day, *five days a week,* and the implications were staggering. In the United States, despite Senate Bill 474, intended to stop all gambling on the Internet, this was the big buzz of the spring. Within three months, close to $10 billion had been raised to assist those in the path of the nuclear blight; of that, less than .01 percent went to administrative costs. How that relief would be allocated was determined by majority e-mail votes among the International School alumni around the world.

For those whose vision of society harked backward instead of forward, Lifechance embodied a terrible threat: a trellis for the development of a global government. Here was the New World Order, a powerful, privileged clique of liberal (i.e., charitable), amoral (i.e., supranationalist) elitists. They were the Militia's worst nightmare, "Satan's Army" to Christian and Muslim fundamentalists alike, and the perfect villains for a Pat Robertson "novel."

In its third month a scandal erupted at Lifechance, casting an ugly cloud over the organization's future. A reporter for the *International Herald Tribune* discovered that the alumni's votes for allocating funds were being manipulated by a French company that warehoused potassium iodide (used to limit thyroid absorption of radioactive isotopes). The company had hacked into the alumni's system and stuffed the ballot box, electronically, so that its product would win out over prefab housing.

The resulting brouhaha almost ended the Lifechance Fund, as commentators suddenly became wary of this unelected global elite with billions of dollars to allocate. But while there were still millions of helpless DPs, Lifechance was financing most of the ongoing aid to devastated regions. What was needed was a thoroughly reliable system of electronic voting. Within weeks, Lifechance adopted a cryptographic system of voter registration for referendums. The general alumni voted on whether, for example, to allocate $350 million to clean up a marginally affected area in the Czech Republic, construct a permanent village for refugees in Romania, or resettle two hundred displaced families on land made available in Eire. In three months Lifechance dwarfed every charitable fund in history, with revenues growing 8 percent a month.

Franco was on his way home from the Vertical Club, where he'd gone to sweat out a ferocious hangover. The cab radio was blaring out news of the latest Global Lottery winner. He was amazed at the whole Lifechance phenomenon, not least because he found himself involved by the accident of his schooling. Now he sat listening limply, feeling his muscles ache from the twenty-minute workout he'd cut short.

The poise he had maintained since leaving Commonweal seemed to be leaching out from beneath his feet like sand in the receding surf. Lost, he thought. In the middle of the forest I dropped my compass, and now I have lost my way. He'd never meant to go into publishing: this was a greatness thrust upon him, when he was drafted into the capitalist fray by a canned goods baron. Then, somewhere down the slippery slope, he'd lost his scholarly ideals, not all at once but gradually, by attrition. The responsibilities that had governed his existence since Lillian's death were beginning to pall, and Terry seemed happy to take them on. By now she was more involved in the care of Juliette's asthma, for example, than he was. Many nights he half woke, alone, and in place of terrible dreams came the short, sharp sound of Juliette's wheeze on the monitor, along with Terry's comforting whispers.

He started to ask the driver to please turn down the fucking radio just as CBS blurted out a news report. "And in the case referred to as 'the Belacqua Murder,' police in New York have released Ms. Suki Herlihy, their prime suspect, from bond because her DNA did not match that found at the apartment of victim William McAdams." Franco exploded with a shout, scaring the bejesus out of the driver from Tobago. "Meanwhile, in Seattle, another suspect has been arrested for his murder: Claire Buday, thirty-one, a member of Green Fist, the radical environmental organization implicated in last year's fatal shooting of Seattle attorney James Schwartzenbach, who has often represented logging interests in the Northwest. The FBI suspects Ms. Buday may have murdered McAdams to prevent him from testifying as an expert witness in an upcoming trial. . . ."

If Suki hadn't murdered McAdams, there was no reason to doubt the book. Suddenly it seemed obvious that *many* people might have wanted McAdams boxed and buried.

". . . Also from the newsroom, Professor Richard Wylie, noted constitutional historian and a presence at Columbia University since 1948, died yesterday. Best known outside academia for his book *The Second Republic of the United States,* Wylie was seventy-seven." They will come no more, the old men with beautiful manners.

At home, Franco found Suki having tea with Terry. They'd never met, but they were clearly enjoying each other's company, especially since the marine biologist was no longer a murder suspect. She was playing a New Age CD she'd picked up, while Max flirted outrageously with this Jungian archetype of the California girl.

After the kids were sent off to do homework, Franco popped a bottle of Cristal, and then another, to celebrate "the triumph of science over injustice." They drank merrily that evening, and by the time the kids went to bed, all three were a little loaded.

Long before coffee, Franco ran out of conversation, while Terry and Suki talked their way from plankton and salps to alternative rock, from Ecstasy war stories to raves they'd mavened. When they moved into the den, Franco settled at his desk with a manuscript,

Jefferson and the Rebellious Spirit, while Suki and Terry sat on the sofa across the room talking about music. Franco struggled to focus on the manuscript, despite the thick fog between him and the page. He used to shower before reading a submission; now he was trying to square his double vision.

When he left to go to the bathroom and look in on the children, Suki was giving Terry a backrub. When he returned a while later, he sat down at his desk before he noticed what was happening on the sofa. The young women were lying in each other's arms, kissing passionately. He watched Terry's hand travel up the inside of Suki's thigh as her dark hair entwined with blondness.

This was . . . well, what was this, then? Shocking? Unexpected? A game to make him jealous? Or horny? Then, as they fumbled like teenagers with each other's clothes, it occurred to Franco that just possibly this had nothing to do with him at all.

But then Suki looked across at him, as Terry's mouth circled her breast, and said, "It's embarrassing, with Franco over there."

Franco glanced at Terry, who paused, her throat flushed crimson; he was just drunk enough to accommodate them any way they pleased. "Should I leave?" he asked.

"No," Suki murmured. "Come here, with us." Terry nodded as her tongue spiraled Suki's left nipple. Franco recognized the ferocity Terry always had in her eyes when he fucked her wantonly like a stranger.

Franco had not felt particularly aroused, but he was when he reached the sofa. A moment later his mouth was beside Terry's, feeding off the soft flesh of Suki's right breast. They shared the adventure of Suki's body between them as their hands explored her, stroked her, and penetrated her together.

Their capacity to resist the opportunity, or gauge the consequences, or even to consider safe sex, had evaporated. Overwhelmed by novelty and a licentious hunger for the experience, Terry pulled down Suki's panties roughly and stretched her mouth around the young woman's cunt as if devouring a ripe peach. She remained glued there a long time, while her tongue danced a knowledgeable ballet, and she drank as if consuming Suki alive. Meanwhile, Franco penetrated Terry in a single stroke.

The den was charged with unfamiliar sights and sounds and smells of debauchery that made their threesome at once lascivious and romantic. So primitive was their driving force it was as if they were forging a path back down the evolutionary ladder. Then Suki began to moan. Franco's thrusts slowed and stopped. He was taken aback: it was different from the moan he'd heard the year before from McAdams's room and in his imagination many times since.

After their guest reached her first climax, Terry and Franco moved around Suki's body until the three were perfectly juxtaposed, as if by feng shui. Settling over Suki, Terry began riding the young woman's mouth toward her own satisfaction, as she guided Franco's throbbing cock between Suki's legs, her eyes gleaming. "Do her, Franco," she said softly. "Go on. Let's fuck her together."

Their arousal was soon more than they could bear, and suddenly, as Terry's finger penetrated Suki beside Franco's fevered shaft, he withdrew and launched his seed across Suki's belly, which Terry lapped up as she turned, and stretched her body over the blonde's, humping her cunt to cunt.

As the two women turned to tongue each other, Suki seemed overwhelmed, and then alarmed, not by what her hosts were doing to her, but how. Their dissolute collaboration gave her the willies, as the atmosphere devolved from New Age sensualism to downright depravity, and she realized that Franco and Terry were losing it completely, making frenzied use of her body for their own satisfaction.

With carnal abandon, Terry tongued Suki for a long time before rolling her over and raising her to her hands and knees. Then, breathless and wild-eyed, she whispered, "Fuck her again, Franco. Do her in the ass."

"No!" Suki turned her eyes back on them with fear and horror. "Jesus, you guys are complete freaks!" Leaping to her feet, she knocked two of the three wooden *objets d'art,* carved in 1689, off the shelf; the brittle boxwood shattered like crystal. Grabbing her clothing and her purse, Suki ran naked into the hall. A minute later they heard the front door slam shut. But by then they were lost together in fevered, erotic delirium, as Franco chanted an obscene mantra. His body slamming against Terry's, flat on the floor, he fucked her till her ears popped.

When the new Congress convened in January, it was apparent that the election of '98 had produced no clear majority in either house.

It did, however, provide something like a referendum on the public credence given to Roger Belacqua: regardless of party, candidates favoring environmental reform whupped their opponents. But while Republicans in the Senate called for further study of the issues, and House Democrats proposed new regulations for industrial sources of pollution, no mandate could be obtained in either house. What had euphemistically been called gridlock in the mid-nineties now appeared to be terminal constipation in the body politic, for which no legislative laxative could be found. Party leaders did not have that problem: looking ahead to the presidential election of 2000, they were already shitting themselves.

In Japan, where pollution had long been a national obsession—especially, of course, radiation and mercury poisoning—Toshi Naoasumi, a former disciple of Yukio Mishima's born-again fascists, had almost six hundred devoted followers, including many former members of Aum Shinrikyo, the fanatical cult that had 50,000 members worldwide when they had attacked Tokyo's subways in '95 with poison gas. This new group surrounded the nuclear reactor at Tokaimura, seventy miles northeast of Tokyo, which had contaminated the region in a fire back in '97. There they began a hunger strike that lasted more than two weeks. At the end of the peaceable siege, Naoasumi read aloud from *The Belacqua Report*: "The gradual but inevitable extinction of human civilization has already begun . . . and the fate of mankind has already been sealed. . . ." Then, saluting the emperor as a god, he led a group of fourteen in the ritual of *seppuku,* driving a sword deep into his gut. After watching him writhe in agony for ten minutes, a comrade stepped forward and lopped off his head. All this was captured on video, of course, and broadcast around the world. From the video, Tokyo police easily identified Naosumi's executioner: his name was "Killer" Yasuo Hayashi—one of the world's most wanted criminals.

Hayashi was one of six former members of Aum Shinrikyo still sought as fugitives, charged with the poison-gas attacks four years earlier, which had left more than four thousand injured and a dozen dead. The larger significance of his presence was truly alarming: Hayashi and the five others were known to have associates around the world with significant quantities of sarin—the gas used in the subways—as well as biological agents (botulism and anthrax) stockpiled in major cities from Asia to the Americas. According to documents seized, they had also been "preparing to weaponize the Ebola virus." Two undercover cops who had infiltrated Aum Shinrikyo shortly before its suicidal spectacle at the nuclear plant reported to Interpol that Hayashi was working with a global network of disaffected nationalists who were preparing attacks on the twenty largest urban areas in the world. They were funded by Osami ben Laden, the wealthy black sheep of Saudi Arabia, with whom they shared one single, blunt goal: to initiate a mass extinction.

Late the next Wednesday evening, Roger arrived at their apartment with Christiane, utterly exhausted and limping slightly. They had left late from Burlington because of fog, and the flight plan assigned to them had taken them all the way to Allentown, Pennsylvania, before veering east to La Guardia. To make up time, Belacqua had requested an altitude higher than was safe or permitted without oxygen, but after twenty minutes above fifteen thousand feet, they had both become giddy; Roger had actually blacked out briefly while the Baron was on autopilot. His age was so much more apparent, Franco thought, than the night when they'd first met at "21."

Roger went to bed before dessert, and Franco went off to finish *Jefferson and the Rebellious Spirit*. But by then Christiane and Terry had each had three espressos, so, "It looks like you and I are going to have to talk," Christiane deadpanned, and they settled on opposite sofas in the living room. Rather than dwell on the future, they talked about the past. After Terry told her about Bobby, Christiane described her own youth, when her father was with the *corps diplomatique* in Tunisia, and she fell for a married businessman named Bashir. Every summer when she finished school near Saint-Jean-de-Luz, she joined her father in Tunis. There she snuck out most nights to be with her lover—who later dropped her when she tearfully told him she was pregnant. Christiane also talked about her mother, now in her eighties, who still lived in the Pays Basque. Christiane was leaving soon to visit her "for the last time, *certainement.*" Which reminded her, could she please use the computer in Franco's office to send some e-mail? That was where Terry left her when she went to bed.

The next morning Roger was feeling much better, at least until Franco handed him the galleys of *Belacqua Refuted*. His first reaction, as he swept through the page proofs, was a blend of contempt and amusement—with a pinch of curiosity about who this Kerner fellow was. His second reaction was anger. So, still wearing their robes, Belacqua and Franco took a bottle of Cristal to the terrace, where they stretched out imprudently in the late-morning heat of early March.

"Commonweal wants you to debate this guy on *Meet the Press,*" Franco told the scientist, who coughed up Roederer bubbles. Franco laughed and refilled their glasses. "When you meet with Danvers tomorrow, he'll tell you you're contractually obliged to promote the paperback. It may be the only true thing he'll say. And what will you do?"

"Well," said Belacqua philosophically, after a long pause, "I'll tell him to stick two fingers up his ass and whistle." Now they both coughed bubbles, almost in unison.

When he recovered, Franco cast about for some way for Belacqua to refute Kerner without personally dignifying his book. "I know! Send General Shreiver in your place."

Roger shook his head. "The general's a valuable ally, but when it comes to the press, he's no help. Anyway, I can handle Creal."

"*Cin-cin!*" saluted Franco, already glassy-eyed as he poured the Cristal down his throat. Then, suddenly, his cheerfulness melted. "Ruggiero, tell me the truth—do you think my children will have a chance to live out their lives?"

"Yes," replied Roger instantly. "Forty years is the worst-case scenario. My guess is that positive reaction to our book will extend the time frame by twenty, maybe even thirty years." Sternly, he added, "You mustn't torture yourself with such thoughts, my friend. You can't take the book so . . . personally."

Franco raised his voice. "How do I ignore my own children? They've already suffered from *our* book. So have millions of other people, dreading the fate you've cast for them. Real people, Roger— they aren't salps. And according to you, they're going to die struggling for breath. You know, every time Juliette has an asthma attack, I think . . ." His thoughts changed tack as Terry joined the two well-oiled men. "So, the world might have an extra decade or two?"

Roger nodded in reply, and then belched politely.

Terry perched on the arm of Franco's chair. "Give or take a hundred years," she added.

"What does that mean?"

"Ask him," she said pointedly, indicating Belacqua, just as she realized how drunk they both were.

"I think it means," said the scientist cautiously, "that Terry has found the devil's eye in *The Belacqua Report*."

"Cumulative carbon production, right? By a factor of ten," said Terry, staring intently at Belacqua, who bowed his head politely.

"Bravo, mademoiselle." He turned to Franco. "This brilliant young woman has discovered a little problem with the numbers."

"I had some help," she said, "from about two thousand disgruntled CD-ROM users. I told them the problem's with our programming, but it's really in the book's data. I found it." She leaned in to his face. "Your secret is safe with me, Doctor."

Franco was going nuts. "What in hell are you talking about?"

With her eyes on Roger, Terry explained, "It was the same problem I had a year ago, copyediting the manuscript. I just figured it out this morning. Your friend here used two different sets of numbers for cumulative global carbon production projections in the future, measured in gigatonnes of carbon—GtCs. One, from the EPA, fits perfectly with his phytoplankton studies—I think that's 14.3^6. The other figure, which he uses in his biomass decay-rate projections, is 14.3^5. Small number—big difference."

"But what does it *mean*?" demanded Franco.

"It means," said Belacqua, "that the biomass will not reach critical carbon saturation until about the year 2080, and possibly as late as 2140, depending upon secondary interactions that haven't been tested yet."

Franco stared at him. "Did you know this all along?"

"No. I found it out six weeks ago." He rose unsteadily and started into the apartment. "Look, Franco, I've been meaning to tell you and . . . But I'm really not up for this conversation right now. Let's talk about it after my nap."

"Why," Terry asked him, "did you just refer to it as 'the devil's eye'?"

"Did I?" he asked. "I have no idea. Just a phrase. But congratulations, Terry. Kerner missed it altogether. Really now, you'll have to excuse me." He left the terrace.

"So," said Franco to no one in particular.

"I've been over it again and again," Terry said earnestly, "and it doesn't mean the book's a phony, at all. It just means there's more time—between forty and a hundred years extra, depending on secondary effects."

"So, do I have to give a press conference? 'Dr. Belacqua is pleased to announce extra innings'? I mean, obviously this has to be made public."

"No," she said firmly, "it does not. And it shouldn't be."

Franco was willing to believe her, he just wasn't able. "How do we keep it a secret? You just said people have figured out something's fishy from the CD-ROM."

"It's taken care of," she replied. "It won't go any further than the website."

Franco was weaving in place. He put his arms around Terry, trying to close the distance between their positions without actually having to verbalize anything.

"Listen," she said, "the report's already out there, and its impact is reverberating around the world. Granted, most of the reaction has been less than positive—"

"Less than positive?" He was shouting now. "The Versailles Room?"

"Listen to me, damn it," she shouted back. "There's been some constructive stuff going on as a result of the book—but it hasn't had a chance yet. What's going to happen if you discredit Belacqua now? Is *that* going to make the world better for our children?" That was the first time she had referred to Juliette and Max that way.

"Besides," she went on, "it was really just an oversight in editing—my oversight. You wanted me to do everything. I knew all along that we should have had experts do a final review of the scientific stuff. Duh! But we were in such a hurry. And anything we say publicly now is just going to help the Kerner book. Then the whole world gets complacent again, without any real change in how people think or governments govern."

Franco tried to reply. Then he said, "This really isn't a level playing field, you know: Roger and I have had a *lot* to drink this morning."

At that Terry turned and walked. Franco shut his eyes and nodded off in a heartbeat. Passing Franco's office, Terry heard his file cabinet roll closed, and when she looked in, she saw Christiane at Franco's desk, staring at the blank monitor—it wasn't even turned on. Terry said good morning, and went off to check the kids.

Advance orders of the hardcover edition of *Belacqua Refuted,* as well as of the boxed pair of paperbacks, were bigger than Godzilla, and as a result, Danvers and Bob Milton were joined at the hip. So when Dr. Roger Belacqua arrived in the president's office the next afternoon, looking rather old for his years, Danvers was holding all the cards; perhaps that was why he affected a poker face, based loosely on Steve McQueen.

"Pleased ta meet ya, Dr. Belacqua," he said. "Won't ya have a seat?"

Roger sat down and turned the full beam of his presence upon the Man of a Thousand Faces.

"I'll get right to the point, Dr. Belacqua," Danvers began, a little like Jimmy Stewart. "We're publishing a book entitled *Belacqua Refuted,* by a brilliant young scientist, William Kerner, Ph.D. The title is—"

"I've read the galleys, Mr. Creal. It's a piece of garbage, of no scientific value. Even the title is a lie."

Danvers was nonplussed, and Roger caught a glimpse of the real man, between masks. It was not a pretty picture.

"Well, I can't imagine how you obtained the galleys," Danvers began, "since—"

"Let me speed this up. I've read the book and seen the ads, and I've heard that you expect me to lend respectability to this impostor. I assure you nothing you can say will persuade me to help you sell his book. Is that clear? Good." Belacqua stood up.

"Sit down, Dr. Belacqua," said Danvers, with a paramilitary clip.

"I think not, Mr. Creal."

Danvers was flummoxed. Speechless, he looked around the office for help. Sure enough, a moment later the door to the private washroom opened, and Roger turned: out stepped the cool, imposing figure of Bob Milton.

The two men stood face to face for the first time in forty years, comparing the toll that time had taken on each. Bob Milton won hands down in that department. He dismissed Danvers with a wave, and the president of Commonweal abandoned his own office.

"Hello, Bob," said Belacqua. "I thought you might show up today, though I didn't expect you to be in the bathroom eavesdropping."

Even as Bob took the seat behind Franco's old desk, the Smile was extinguished. "I wasn't sure I could stomach the sight of you," Milton explained. "But since Danvers here wasn't up to the job. . . . Sit down, Roger. We have some things to discuss."

"I think not," Roger repeated. "I'll hear you out. But I will stand, thank you."

"Well, here's what time it is." Bob Milton was enjoying this. "Commonweal Books is about to demonstrate that your life's work is fraudulent. *Belacqua Refuted* is only the first step: we're only one of several publishers who've started a cottage industry of debunking your work. You should be flattered. Independently of me, Macro's board of directors has decided that everything you stand for deserves to be thoroughly invalidated—that your so-called conclusions are blasphemous tripe."

"So the canned goods boys are running the publishing house now, eh?" Roger leaned forward. "No wonder they've made succotash out of it."

"We will begin releasing one document after another that proves you are a charlatan, personally and professionally. But we're prepared to give you the opportunity to argue your case alongside William Kerner. I'd say we're being generous. Look at this, Roger." Bob extracted a letter from his breast pocket and handed it to the scientist.

Roger unfolded the letter, and blanched perceptibly.

The Smile returned. "This is only a sample of the documentation we'll be releasing. Take it home and reconsider. Maybe you do want to play ball with us—hardball—and defend yourself on *Meet the Press.*"

Belacqua had recovered his composure. "I see. Well, this is lower than I ever expected you to squat. Anyway, Bob, my regards to your Mildred, and say goodbye to Mr. Creal. I'd say you two deserve each other. I sincerely hope the world will end before we meet again, in hell."

He turned on his heels and strode with dignity from the office. But when he was alone in the elevator, his whole frame shrank by an inch.

For some time Terry had worried about Franco's drinking, which began earlier in the day and then remained steady. He was rarely stumbling drunk, even by bedtime, but often his eyes were glassy by the end of lunch, and he remained alternately remote and cynically euphoric the rest of the day. With Roger visiting, his drinking had increased.

When Belacqua returned from Commonweal, Franco had just mailed a batch of applications for teaching posts, so of course he opened a bottle of wine and the two men settled in the living room.

"And how did you like Commonweal's president?"

Belacqua snorted. "Foolish little man. Then Bob Milton showed up."

"*Quelle honneur!* I'll bet he didn't wear his smile."

Belacqua shook his head sadly. "I'm afraid he did—when he promised to destroy my reputation with dirty tricks."

"Like what?"

Roger took the letter from his pocket and handed it to Franco. It was a legal opinion from the National Transportation Safety Board, dated 1987, describing the crash of a Cessna piloted by Roger Belacqua, in which his children were killed. The letter revealed that Belacqua's blood alcohol level was right at the legal limit, and suggested that his drinking was the cause of the accident; it also recommended that his pilot's license be revoked. Franco set it down on the coffee table.

"That's terrible, Roger! Milton's releasing this to the press?"

Roger nodded sadly. "If he hasn't already. Then I expect he'll find some psychotherapist to go on TV and argue that my book is the result of some guilt complex about my children's death. He claims to have more documents with which to destroy my reputation." They sat in silence, sipping quietly, staring at a slim slice of sky through the window. Then Roger's head dropped and he lowed softly.

"I'm too old, Franco. Too old for a pissing contest. Even my prostate is too old." He sighed deeply once again. "Milton will keep me on a treadmill of allegations: he'll pay one expert after another to 'disprove' me. He'll bring up the suntan oil scandal, and attack Christiane for something or other. . . . I don't know how much intestinal fortitude I have left. This afternoon I feel very old."

Franco put his arm around Roger Belacqua and hugged him gently. That's how Terry and Christiane found them when they returned from shopping with the kids.

"They're drunk," noted Terry, glancing at her watch. "It's not even four o'clock."

Christiane shrugged. *"Tous les cons ne sont pas morts,"* she noted, and though Terry didn't understand French, she trusted Christiane's judgment.

The men tried to make jokes, and Roger made naughty suggestions to his wife about a nap, whereupon the men were relegated to the den and warned "to keep their stinking breath away from the children." The women retreated to the kitchen, where Emily was watching a rerun of *Star Trek* with Juliette's resident nurse, Mrs. Freiland. Juliette had been hospitalized twice more with severe asthma attacks, and frequently required oxygen at home. Terry knew she couldn't care for her alone, so she'd hired Mrs. Freiland—handpicked by Juliette from an assortment of applicants.

In the evening the two couples walked to the Oak Room at the Plaza for dinner, the men clinging to each other, singing aloud, *"O venti-quattro mille baci. . . ."* and generally doing all they could to annoy the women. At the restaurant Roger became so amorous with Christiane that Terry and Franco didn't know how to behave. At home, after only two nightcaps on the terrace, they all went to bed.

That night, for the first time in several weeks, Franco dreamed. He imagined that he and Terry were visiting the Belacquas in Vermont, sleeping in that same guest cabin, and in his dream he could hear Roger—not McAdams—making love to Suki in the adjoining room. Franco woke up and dozed off again, still dreaming, and still he heard the sound of Suki's moaning as Belacqua, well, rogered her.

Then Franco woke up dehydrated and stumbled to the bathroom for water. But even when he turned the light on over the sink, he could still hear Suki's voice, exactly as it had sounded in Vermont. He rubbed his eyes and walked to the hallway. Sure enough, he could hear the sound of Suki's pleasure coming from the guest bedroom.

But of course it wasn't Suki that Roger was pleasing. And neither was it Suki's voice that Franco had heard that night a year earlier, coming from William McAdams's room.

8

THE NATIONAL DEBATE

According to the U.S. Environmental Protection Agency, to stabilize atmospheric concentrations of CO_2 at the present level, carbon emissions must be reduced to 50 to 80 percent, back to the level of the 1950s. Otherwise there is little prospect of avoiding global warming, no matter what happens in China and Brazil.

—PAUL KENNEDY, *Preparing for the Twenty-first Century* (1993)

After the Belacquas left, Terry could no longer ignore Franco's drinking, which had reached a pernicious plateau. For some time he'd had a regular crop of nicks and scratches on his neck that he couldn't explain, until one morning she pointed out how his hand shook while he shaved. And more than once, in midmorning, when she set out on errands and kissed him goodbye, she distinctly smelled white wine on his breath, mixed with mint. Confronted, Franco observed that a traditional feature of the European working-class day was a *balon* at the local café on the way to work. Terry did not bother to reply that Franco was an out-of-work white-collar American. Instead she asked Dr. Sherin to call and remind Franco that his annual checkup was four years overdue.

Franco complied reluctantly, and Dr. Sherin could find nothing wrong with him, apart from a welcome loss of six pounds. But he'd also known Franco long enough—almost thirty years—to see that his cheerfulness was feigned. The puffiness of his face said more about him than his wan smile. Franco explained that he'd always been devoted to his work, and that until he resumed his teaching career, he was feeling a tad . . . useless. That made sense to Dr. Sherin, who gave him a clean bill of health. So Franco proceeded to the dark, empty Café Carlyle for the rest of the afternoon to get loaded.

Sitting beside the silent piano, Franco ordered a double single-malt whiskey. Then, like so many lushes before him, he stared at the pretzels and contemplated the fate of the world, from a perspective that was even more self-involved than your average drunk's. He could not get a grip on his unraveling life: out of work, spending down his investments, living with a woman half his age, as his daughter grew more pale and angelic by the week, fading into the wallpaper despite Ventolin and Vanceril and the four industrial air purifiers. At the same time he was halfheartedly applying for posts he wasn't sure he could fill, convinced he wasn't going to get hired anyway.

Because at that very moment Franco's reputation was being trashed globally by the appearance of *Belacqua Refuted*. He knew damn well that in the wake of his removal from Commonweal, the publication of the Kerner book would appear to reasonable minds inside the industry as a personal repudiation. With newfound diffidence, he was learning just how tightly his career and his personal life were wound up with *The Belacqua Report*; and for now, all three were hanging fire. Three labs had announced that they were duplicating Roger's work, but their preliminary results would not be available until mid-2006. Until then, the jury would be out.

And what if Belacqua *was* a fraud? Or perhaps merely mistaken—more mistaken than he'd admitted to? What did he mean by "the devil's eye," anyway? Franco had seen that phrase somewhere before. And what if all the anguish and mayhem caused by the decision to publish was unnecessary? What would this mean to his hope of a job? And to his relationship with Terry, so entwined with this book from the beginning? And to his stock portfolio, for chrissakes, which had lost *20 percent* of its value since *Belacqua* was published? With that, he ordered a triple single-malt.

To survive, he would have to be reborn again. And if anyone could help him do that it would be Terry. But it had begun to seem as if their mutual trust was eroding, just when they needed it most. He still couldn't come to grips with the fact that she'd been intimate with Danvers. From the start, everything had happened so quickly. It had only been a year since she first seduced Franco—that was how he saw it—and so much had happened. Their sexual ferocity frightened as much as it aroused him. Once they began exploring the darker caverns of the libido, the search had taken on a life of its own. And just when they'd exhausted their imaginative games, the encounter with Suki had increased their deliberate wantonness. Where was this going? Where would it stop? The fact that they did not discuss their sexual excesses produced a dark and eerie silence: friction that made heat, not light. Neither wanted to bring it up, each, perhaps, dreading what the other might say. Besides, it might interfere with the fucking.

How had this happened? His head, like the stratosphere, was filled with high cirrus clouds. But it was all his own doing, brought to this point by the hasty, harebrained decisions he'd made: publishing Belacqua, crashing the first edition, and falling for an assistant editor.

But in all honesty, he wondered, could he and Terry blame their personal problems on Belacqua? They certainly could. Hell, everyone else did. After all, their relationship began with the doomsday report, maybe even because of it. Looking back, Franco knew that a big part of why he'd decided to publish the manuscript had been to spend time with Terry.

After Lillian's death he had become, for lack of a better word, toxic. Psychic decay had set in above his neck like gangrene, while his soul rotted like a putrid melon. Long before he'd heard the name Belacqua, his personal Furies were plaguing him with nightmares that shot him out of bed with a jolt, forcing him to check his own pulse.

With Terry, he had selfishly hoped to be reconstituted and renewed, made innocent again, down to his essence. Instead, here he was a year later, quietly decomposing, and corrupting this innocent young woman with degenerate fantasies. Not that he'd had to twist her arm, exactly. In fact, when it came to their extremes, she was leading him around by the cock, even when she pressed it into Suki.

A searing flash traveled down his spine. HIV. Christ, he hadn't even thought of that till now. Could Suki have . . . ? But no, she wasn't loose, Suki was just—Californian. A salp expert couldn't have AIDS, for God's sake. Admittedly, she was amazingly eager the other night, at first. But that wasn't his doing, no sir. Obviously, it was Terry's fault that he had fucked Suki. Yeah, that's the ticket.

To save his sanity, he put that ugly thought away; to save his soul, he knew he'd have to find some trace of *hope*. The same way, perhaps, that a salamander grows a new tail—appropriate image, since at that moment he was feeling small and reptilian. Without hope he could not help himself, his family, or the world. But hope for what? That Belacqua was wrong? That Belacqua was right? Franco didn't even know what to hope for. So instead he sat in a dark bar on a sunny afternoon and drank Laphroaig Scotch until he could no longer operate heavy equipment. Like his fingers.

At Metzamor, the underground nuclear reaction was fully terminated in April by the suicidal courage of more than two hundred military personnel and scientific experts from four countries, who drove under the damaged building in lead suits to encase the radioactive mass. The scientists who'd volunteered, as well as the French Légionnaires, were celebrated as "Heroes of the World" even before they began dying.

Meanwhile the second radioactive cloud had been largely dissipated by an unusual spring cyclone, diminishing the immediate threat to life but prolonging the agricultural impact. So there was enormous anxiety about food supplies for coming years throughout the European Community, where double-digit unemployment had been entrenched for a decade. Now any financial resources earmarked for economic expansion shriveled up. In the Middle East, political accommodation grew, partly because of the dense nuclear blight on the Golan Heights. Since Israel, Syria, and Jordan relied upon international aid, they had the moral compunction (and global scrutiny) to offer as much goodwill as they needed to receive. So each country offered medical and other vital relief to DPs without regard to nationality. Hospitals in Haifa treated Syrians and Lebanese, and Israelis in the Negev were often flown to Amman for treatment when Israeli hospitals were overcrowded. This was not accomplished without shrill eruptions and cantankerous fisticuffs in the Knesset, and an attempt on the life of King Hussein. But for the first time, historical hostilities were dwarfed by the magnitude of a catastrophe, and the immediate issue of survival became a higher priority than complex questions of ancestral addresses.

On Thursday, March 4, 1999, the New York Stock Exchange went splat, along with every other market around the world. At ten-fifteen the Dow Jones fell below 5000 for the first time since early 1996. By the Friday bell it sat just above 3000. To investors, what followed was forever after known as "the longest weekend."

Saturday all eyes were on the Tokyo Exchange, to see if the implosion was universal. There the market gyrated skittishly for an hour and then settled into a waiting mode. The "conspiracy theory" was that Asian investors had yanked their American portfolios in unison, intending to trigger program selling across the board. Sunday's talking heads speculated that this "conspiracy" heralded Japan's vast scheme to provide solar power globally. The gigantic project, more than a decade in development, envisioned solar-collecting "farms" placed around the world within twenty degrees latitude of the equator, creating a continuous grid to supply electricity to every country in the world. For a price. And no one was sure what that price would be. At the same time the Japanese government had lobbied aggressively with other countries, bilaterally and through the Security Council, to reduce pollution. Although some thought these were gestures intended as a public response to the suicides of the former Aum Doomsday Cult members, cynics were convinced that this too was part of the country's economic nationalism, aimed at applying diplomatic coercion on Third World equatorial countries to provide favorable land deals for the solar farms.

Inside the Beltway, the crash was blamed on the '98 elections that had thrust environmental issues to the forefront, so that political professionals at every level were scrambling to invent an agenda of emergency environmental rehabilitation without, of course, increasing taxes.

But another possible reason for the crash came from a more modest place: the Delaware state senate. There, on the Tuesday preceding the Thursday sell-off, a resolution was passed asking Congress to call "a Convention for proposing Amendments" to the Constitution as provided for in Article Five. With that vote, Delaware became the thirty-third state legislature to call for a convention. If one more state government petitioned, Congress would be obliged to organize a national convention that could entirely rewrite the U.S. Constitution. And that possibility had the market quivering like a spastic colon.

How such a consequential movement had grown so quickly across so many state governments was no mystery. In the year since *The Belacqua Report* was published, an earnest dialogue had begun at dinner tables and coffee shops, and on the op-ed pages, the talk shows, and of course the Net, upon the weighty possibility of a Second Constitutional Convention. There was only one blueprint for such a gathering: a short, bold book that suddenly rose to fourth place on the nonfiction list, behind *Belacqua Refuted*, *The Belacqua Report*, and *Chained to the Wheel: The Vanna White Memoirs*. It was *The Second Republic of the United States*, by Professor Richard Wylie (Franco Sherman, ed., New York: Historical Perspective, 1997, $24.95).

The new appendix to Wylie's *Second Republic* envisioned plausible scenarios for the convention, analyzing how factions across the political spectrum might play their roles, from the left fringe beyond Jesse Jackson to Pat Buchanan's far right, way out there where the buses don't run. Wylie walked the reader through possible judicial challenges from Congress (to a convention that could throw them all out on their ears) and the threat of a "poison pill" inserted in the revised Constitution to prevent its ratification—the reestablishment of slavery, for example. The safeguard was that any amendments produced at such a convention had to be ratified by three-quarters of the state legislatures or by state conventions. Finally, Wylie described two different kinds of "Second Republics" that might emerge from a deep edit of the Constitution: one leaning toward authoritarianism, the other toward populism.

The whole thing terrified Wall Street. By Monday noon, the average share had lost 17 percent of its value one week earlier; after four more trading days, 21 percent. By then five men and one woman—suckers for tradition—had leaped to their deaths in the busy streets of the financial district, incidentally killing a dope dealer below.

Terry sensed something was wrong as soon as she stepped out of the elevator: she smelled smoke. She walked anxiously to Franco's den, where she found him on the sofa with a flute of Cristal in one hand and a cigarette burning in the other. He had nodded off.

She smiled and said softly, "What are you doing, you goof? You don't smoke."

He awoke with a jerk, and proffered a stupid grin. "What? Oh. I've just started."

"Why?" asked Terry. "What are you doing?" As she wrapped her arms around his shoulders, he burned his fingers and shot to his feet with a howl.

"Ratfuck!" he explained, dropping the butt into his glass. Terry laughed at the whole scene, and after a moment, sucking his blistered fingers, Franco laughed too. It was the first honest laughter they'd shared in weeks. Then she said with simple earnestness, "Okay, what's going on?"

"I'm sick," he grunted. "Sick at the thought that *The Belacqua Report* is wrong. That Roger lied to me all along. Maybe he thinks he's saving the world, but *I'm* the dumb fuck who announced the whole damn thing and made the world crazy with fear."

All this caught Terry off balance. "What suddenly makes you think it's wrong?"

"Because even Roger admits his carbon data were skewed. Because it was Christiane who went to bed with William McAdams, and then he was murdered. Because for millions of years the earth has repaired damage from meteors, glaciers, and volcanoes. Surely it can repair the damage done by man."

"Extinct species can't be revived."

He squinted unevenly at her. "What is it about you that makes this your *cause célèbre*? From the beginning you were ready to do anything—and I do mean *any fucking thing*—to announce that the earth is doomed." Cocking his head, he said softly, "Are you some kind of ghoul?"

"Ratfuck," seconded Terry.

"What? No lemonade?" he sneered. "No suggestions on how to paint a happy face over the worst disaster in publishing history?"

"First you morph into a lush, and now you turn into a *mean* drunk. You know what, Franco?" she said, leaning forward. "I miss you."

Franco nodded slowly. "So do I. I'm sorry."

Terry pushed Franco back on the sofa and planted her knees on both sides of his chest. "Look, what's there to question? Do you doubt that overpopulation is ravaging the planet? So Roger tinkered with the numbers a little—is that so terrible, if his report raised the alarm, and bought time to save the world?"

"Just a dollop of hyperbole, eh? 'Oops, I said the world was doomed, when I meant everything's okay.' A lacuna."

"Belacqua or no Belacqua, we know everything's *not* okay. But if the window of opportunity is still open, and the book actually jars governments into action, we might go down in the history books as the people who saved the world."

"If Roger's right, there won't be any history books, and if he's wrong, *we* won't be in them. Maybe the *Guinness Book of Records*, for liability suits. What's for dinner?"

Terry shook her head as she rose from his chest and rearranged her skirt. "I don't know. Probably spaghetti—I left it up to Emily. I have to go out till about ten."

"Oh? An assignation?"

"No, not tonight, dear. I have a meeting."

"Mm-hmm. Is it the copy editors' convention?"

"That was uncalled for. No, I'm going to a meeting of Al-Anon."

This struck Franco hard enough to whip his head around. He started to stammer. "But—but you don't think . . . Are you accusing me. . . . ?"

Terry kissed him on the forehead. "Don't think about it, my love. Just keep telling yourself it's an assignation."

That night, while she was at her first meeting of Al-Anon, Franco, in a fit of drunken depression, called AA and scribbled down the address of a noon meeting the next day. The next morning he was still shaken up enough to make it there. A little fear is a powerful thing. At his first meeting, in the basement of St. Bartholomew's Church, Franco recognized that by now, one drink was too many for him, and all the drink in the world wasn't enough. He had never been a heavy drinker before: he was not prepared to become an alcoholic. So, while it seemed like a betrayal of his beloved white wine, his single-malt mate, and his Cristal whore, he decided to resist drink altogether, by himself, for six months. If he couldn't, then he'd return to these rooms. Soon after, he felt a huge burden being hoisted from his shoulders.

A week after Belacqua returned home with his wife, he e-mailed a message to Berling. "Upon reflection, I would enjoy confronting

Kerner," he wrote, and agreed to appear on *Meet the Press* on March 21. Then he called Franco. "This is probably my last chance to make the case in a national forum," he explained, "before Bob Milton empties his dump truck all over me."

"He hasn't released the NTSB letter?" Franco asked the old man warily.

"Not that I know of."

"You think a serious discussion is possible with this fellow Kerner?"

"I don't know, Franco. All I can do is hold up my end. I expect Kerner will drag the debate down to some rudimentary level of name-calling."

Franco tried to sound offhand. "You don't suppose he found some fundamental flaw in your theory?"

Belacqua laughed. "What's the matter, a crisis of confidence?"

"No, but it'll still take ten years to confirm your findings."

"Oh, I'm *well* aware of that," said Belacqua, and then took pity. "Do yourself a favor, Franco: go pick up the latest *Scientific American*. It may relieve some of your distress. And it'll make Kerner roll over a few times. *Ciao*, Franco."

"*Ciao*, Ruggiero."

Franco was so eager to believe the world was doomed that he raced down to the newsstand across the street. It didn't sell *Scientific American*, but he bought the March *Harper's* when he saw the cover: SO THE WORLD IS COMING TO AN END . . . GET USED TO IT! The next newsstand didn't have it, or the next. He was gasping for breath.

Finally he found a copy on Fifty-second, at the newsstand where he first saw Terry in her waif-wench attire. He ran up to Central Park South and found a park bench opposite the Plaza Hotel, in the shadow of his old office. The article, by Lou Blackledge, Ph.D., of Cornell, was entitled "Belacqua Reconfirmed: Further evidence that the 'window of opportunity' has already closed." Franco started giggling a little feverishly. He did not absorb the scientific fine points made by the atmospheric chemist. As a matter of fact, the only phrases his frantic eyes found in the piece were "Belacqua left no shadow of a doubt," "Kerner's numerous failings," and "the facts established by Dr. Belacqua's impeccable science."

Franco rushed home breathlessly to show the article to Terry.

Once she'd read the piece carefully, they laughed and kissed and hugged while Juliette watched them adoringly and Max frowned upon "all that mushy stuff."

On Sunday morning, March 21, 1999, *Meet the Press* almost canceled "The Belacqua Debate" because of continuing turmoil in the financial markets. But at the last minute NBC went ahead as planned; there'd been so much publicity about the debate, and moderator Tim Russert had done considerable research to prepare for "the event."

Belacqua flew down to Washington on his own the night before. The next morning, in the green room of the NBC studio, he met William Kerner, Ph.D. Kerner was only about thirty, rather short, with a full head of curly blond hair. Kerner had studied at the University of Michigan and completed his graduate work in climatology at Georgia Tech. Belacqua noticed that the earnest young man carried a small Bible in his sports bag. Despite Roger's friendly efforts to set him at ease, Kerner was clearly not comfortable in his presence.

The debate had been hyped blue by everyone from the White House chief of staff, who confirmed that the President would be watching, to *TV Guide,* which provided a scorecard so that viewers could rate the "contestants," which further distorted the discussion. Generally, the meeting was touted as a sports event rather than a scientific debate—more like "Gladiators of Science" than *Jeopardy*.

At home, Terry and Franco were in the living room watching, while Juliette was curled up on the floor with her inhaler. Even Emily was watching in the kitchen, while making the kids' lunch.

The debate was held around a circular table, upon which sat hardcover copies of *The Belacqua Report* and *Belacqua Refuted*. Tim Russert began by outlining the history and the social impact of Roger's book, and the possible significance of Kerner's. Then he asked Belacqua to summarize the conclusions of his work.

"Through no fault of our own, except the spectacular success of our species," began Roger, in a tone that would have made Cousteau proud, "mankind's scientific and industrial ingenuity have produced an atmospheric catastrophe we can no longer control, much less prevent, triggering a chain of events that will end in our extinction in forty years."

Watching intently, Franco was amazed at the aplomb with which the old man reiterated the time frame that he'd admitted privately was wrong. It made Franco feel like an accomplice.

Russert turned to his second guest. "Dr. Kerner, perhaps you'd like to begin your refutation. Dr. Belacqua can respond as you go along."

Kerner cleared his throat. Even Belacqua seemed sympathetic as he noticed the shaky voice with which he began. "In *Belacqua Refuted,* I pointed out numerous flaws in Dr. Belacqua's research and his arguments, demonstrating that his doomsday conclusions are mistaken. But after my book was rushed into print, I found other troubling problems with his work. I have no personal animosity toward Dr. Belacqua. Like most environmentalists, I applaud his success in bringing urgent issues to the public's attention. I suspect that's why he hasn't been taken to task by the entire scientific community. Two colleagues of mine have refrained from criticizing *The Belacqua Report,* as if the effect of the book outweighed the truth itself. I don't share that opinion. This week I've discovered that virtually *all* of Dr. Belacqua's projections are based upon a single piece of misinformation, which appears to be deliberate."

"Uh-oh." That was all Terry said.

Kerner picked up *The Belacqua Report* from the table in front of him and flipped to the start of the book. "In Chapter One, the carbon production projections for the coming decades are from the EPA, while figures for other nations come from the World Health Organization. I have no quarrel with their numbers. But look at Dr. Belacqua's projections in Chapters Three through Seven: you'll see that that number has increased, from the power of five to the power of six." He showed this to Tim Russert on the page, as Belacqua watched, mildly amused.

Russert hadn't expected Kerner to pick his fight so quickly. "Dr. Belacqua?"

Roger smiled. "I applaud Professor Kerner, just as he applauded me. The error he has found certainly is critical to my calculations." He seemed regally unconcerned.

Franco closed his eyes and groaned.

"And what is the effect," Russert asked, "upon prospects for human survival?"

"What it means," Kerner said, jumping in, "is that even if you accept the rest of his conclusions, he has to allow that the 'window of opportunity' for reversing our situation will be open for at least twenty more years or even double that *by his own calculations.*" He turned to Roger with a fierce sincerity. "Isn't that right, Doctor?"

"Yes, according to the data published by the EPA." Roger bided his time for a beat or two. "If only they had got it right."

"I beg your pardon?" asked the moderator.

"The mistake," said Belacqua, "was the EPA's—not mine. There was a simple printing error in the tables they published, which I copied. But the number I used in my calculations, 14.3^6 giga-tonnes of carbon, is correct. In fact . . ." From his breast pocket, Belacqua handed Russert and Kerner copies of a document. "Here's a letter from the EPA's director of archives, Grace Feder-man, acknowledging that the EPA's table included the wrong value. And that the correct figure for carbon production is indeed the figure I used."

Kerner scanned the letter. "Impossible."

"Hard to imagine? That a government agency made a mistake?" His eyes twinkled.

Kerner spoke straight into the camera. "Still, the idea that we are threatened with extinction is, frankly, claptrap."

Juliette looked up at her father. "He's the one who's right, Daddy," she said, with a passion in her eyes he'd never seen. "Not that old man."

Franco stamped a kiss on the top of her head and whispered, "Shh."

Just then Russert went to a break, and Terry sat forward. "If that was a misprint," she mused, "why did Roger call it 'the devil's eye'?"

Something clicked in Franco's brain. He ran off to the den and returned with Lillian's oversized *Encyclopedia of Design.* "Here!" he said, and read the entry aloud.

> **devil's eye.** A feature of native American designs (tapestries, mosa-ics, etc.): a carefully planned "error" in an otherwise flawless pat-tern, token of the belief that only nature is capable of perfection.

Terry looked at Franco. "Why did Roger include a carefully planned error?"

Just then Russert reappeared with his guests, turning to Roger.

"Dr. Belacqua, in his book, Kerner writes that your work 'fails to credit Nature's empirically proven power for healing the wounds inflicted upon her.' How do you respond to that?"

Belacqua smiled. "That, of course, harks back to the Gaia theory of Lovelocke *et al.* I bow to no man in my admiration for Madame Nature. But even she has her limits, and regrettably we have exceeded them. Nature created *Tyrannosaurus rex*; but once extinct, she cannot reanimate them. Only Steven Spielberg can do that. Nature can heal the scars of asteroids and the ravages of epidemics, but she cannot bring the dead back to life. And what we are talking about is a dying earth."

At this Juliette jumped up and threw her inhaler at the image of Belacqua. "Daddy, I *hate* that man," she shouted. "He's wrong. And he's bad. He's the reason I got sick!" With that she ran out of the room.

"Professor Kerner, surely you agree with most environmentalists that the earth cannot support the ongoing growth of the human species without a profound negative impact upon the biosphere?"

"No, Tim, I don't agree." Berling must have told Kerner to use the interviewer's first name. "Sustained growth, if monitored responsibly, is the only solution. Dr. Belacqua is digging up Malthus out of the eighteenth century, where he deserves to remain. We must trust that God did not create mankind only to destroy us. And if we just look around us, we *see* that things are all right for the time being."

Roger sat forward and spoke softly to Kerner. "For *whom*, Professor Kerner? For the thirty thousand irreplaceable species that are swept from the face of the earth *every year*? And why, then, did God create the forty thousand people who die of malnutrition *every day*? I assure you, things in the world are not 'all right' for them." He leaned back in his chair. "As for faith, no matter how devout we are, we are still responsible for our mistakes. If, on the highway, we suddenly veer into the oncoming traffic, we should not expect divine intervention. Unwittingly, we have created a situation we cannot get out of. God is not to blame, nor is Nature. As stewards of the earth, we can't escape the consequences of our own thoughtlessness. Professor Kerner, just how many species do *you* think can vanish before the food chains that sustain life collapse?"

"Well," replied Kerner, "that's really not my field of expertise."

Russert waited for Kerner to continue, but the young man had nothing to add. "Dr. Kerner," he proceeded, "a new study in *Scientific American* accuses you of numerous oversights, especially in your purported refutation of the 'eggshell effect.' Would you care to address that article?"

Even on TV you could see Kerner's hands trembling; at the best of times he was short on self-confidence. "I'm sorry, I haven't had a chance to see it. I've been on a book tour, and . . ." His voice drifted off like a loose dinghy in a strong current.

"I've read it," Belacqua volunteered amicably. "It's the current issue of *Scientific American,* available across the country: I recommend it. I couldn't do a better job of demolishing Professor Kerner's arguments." There was a pause as this sank in.

Tim Russert turned to the camera. "We're going to take another break, and when we come back, Dr. Belacqua and Dr. Kerner will discuss the issues directly with each other, here on *Meet the Press.*"

Terry ran to the kitchen for fresh coffee, and Franco went to the bathroom. They both returned as the program resumed.

"Dr. Kerner, why don't you pose your first question to Dr. Belacqua?"

Kerner had recomposed himself. He glanced down at the notes he'd prepared. "Dr. Belacqua, leaving issues of Christian faith aside for the moment, it's apparent you don't believe that mankind is truly a part of Nature, but rather some separate, destructive force put here to annihilate all life. Could you explain why you think nature is so powerless? After all, God is *not* a malicious shyster."

That gave some pause to Roger. "Nature," he finally began, "is not an infallible mechanism. We've all lived with the knowledge that our species could destroy life on earth with nuclear weapons; now we know that we've had much the same effect simply by *thriving*. It's the same when fish multiply beyond the capacities of their pond."

After a polite pause, Russert invited Kerner to pose another question to Belacqua, though his tone suggested the show was all over.

Kerner was obviously a man in a classic physiological dilemma: fight or flight. But all he had left to fight with was the weapon Bob Milton had supplied. With a self-loathing you could almost smell on TV, Kerner reached for his breast pocket. Franco knew what was coming next. "Dr. Belacqua, I think you are an irresponsible man, and always have been. I have a letter from the National Transportation Safety Board confirming that, as a pilot, you killed your own children by being, and I quote, 'near intoxication while in command of an aircraft.' Would you comment on these charges?"

Sitting at home in Florida, this may have seemed like a good ploy to Bob Milton, but on a Sunday-morning talk show, the gambit was mostly remarkable for its irrelevance.

The old man appeared stunned; then he gazed at Kerner with compassion. "Oh, Bill," Belacqua intoned with a sad smile, like Lloyd Bentsen, "what shall it profit a professor, if he shall gain tenure and lose his immortal soul?" Then he pressed on with chilly dismissiveness. He reached into his own pocket and handed Kerner a small gray card. "You are foolish to think you can discredit me with a personal tragedy from 1979. Look, here is my pilot's license, which is current: I flew my own plane down from Vermont yesterday. In thirty years I've never done anything to deserve its revocation, not even in that accident." By the end of his reply, tears had appeared in Belacqua's eyes, yet he never lost his compassionate tone toward his accuser.

The camera cut to a close-up of Kerner: in utter disgrace, knowing he'd made a ghastly mistake, he hunched over Belacqua's license like a suspicious cop on a Saturday night.

"Thank you, Dr. Belacqua and Professor Kerner, for joining us here today. And to you at home, please join us again next Sunday for another edition of *Meet the Press,* when our guests will be three leading contenders for next year's Republican presidential nomination, Newt Gingrich, Dan Quayle, and Trent Lott."

A few minutes later, while Franco started in the general direction of the muted television, Terry went to look for Juliette. When the phone rang, Franco answered reluctantly. It was Christiane.

"I'm so sorry," Franco said immediately. "Kerner's callous disregard for your feelings was so—"

"Thank you, but that's quite unnecessary. We were expecting that." Christiane was impatient with the topic. "Roger would have won a debate with the burning bush. Franco, would you do us a favor? Do you still have our book contract there at home?"

"Yes, yes I do," he answered slowly. Had he told her that?

"Would you please send it to Commonweal's comptroller? The first royalty check is due soon, and I want to make sure they make the disbursements correctly."

"I certainly will," he replied, wondering what that was about. Then he remembered something he'd meant to ask her. "Pardon my asking a personal question, Christiane, but I've been wondering about something you said to me up in Vermont."

"Yes?"

"Well, before you and Roger had children, you had another child, is that right?"

There was a long silence. "Yes," she answered coldly, "but we do not talk about him. Now, if you'll just send the contract."

"Right away," he promised. "Good-bye, Christiane." But she had already hung up.

As he set the phone down, Terry ran back down the hall. "Franco, Juliette's gone! Emily says she went down to the basement storage locker more than an hour ago."

"She'll be all right."

Terry picked up Juliette's inhaler. "Not without this."

"Oh, God." Franco jammed his feet into his shoes and ran to the kitchen, where they kept the basement key—which, of course, Juliette had taken. He searched frantically for the super's number, missing from the kitchen bulletin board. Finally, he ran down to the lobby, but it was Sunday and Sean was off duty.

He shouted to Terry to call 911 for EMS, and began ringing every apartment on the house phone in the lobby. Finally 7B answered: the lady didn't know where her basement key was, but Franco was welcome to come to her apartment to look for it.

It was fifteen minutes before Franco made it to the lobby with the key; by then, four ambulance personnel were poised outside the basement fire door. Hands shaking badly, he turned the key, opened the heavy door, and raced down the dark stairwell to the morbid, dusty hallway, with Terry and the medical team following close behind.

There he found Juliette, sitting on the cement with one of her old dolls.

"Hi, Daddy," she said. "Look, I found Missy!"

By this time Franco was so pale that the ambulance crew looked at *him* like a possible customer. Catching his breath, he put Juliette's inhaler to her lips.

"No, Daddy, that's okay. I don't think I need that anymore." She picked up her doll and led the adults back up to the lobby.

In fact, Juliette did not need her inhaler again that day, or the next. It was the first time in a year that she'd gone more than a few hours without using it.

On the steps of the capitol in Sacramento, California, Brandon Stableford, state senator from Alameda County, took a deep breath before he continued his speech. As he stood sweating in front of a few cameramen and a handful of capital stringers, he flourished a sheaf of papers dramatically in the air. ". . . and now the bill we introduced last month has just passed both legislative houses of the state of California." Stableford wiped his brow as the wind delivered the day's baking from the San Joaquin Valley.

"So today, March 28th, 1999, the great state of California becomes the thirty-fourth in the Union to demand that Congress call a second constitutional convention, as required by Article Five. The opportunity for fundamental reform is now a reality: a chance for a new beginning, reflecting the dreams and realities, not of 1787, but of the twenty-first century. Hallelujah, folks! They can't stop us now!"

Like much of America, Terry and Franco lay in bed watching Stableford's speech rebroadcast on *Nightline*. The huge unknown that lay ahead exceeded anything the nation had faced since the Civil War. By comparison, the near impeachment of the President in 1974 was small fry as a constitutional crisis. This realization was coupled with the grim certainty that a deluge of rhetoric had just been loosed that would surely rival the melting of the polar ice caps. Terry's hand went to Franco's chest, as if checking for a heartbeat.

Franco grunted and slipped out from under her arm; on the way to the bathroom he grabbed his Sulka robe. They hadn't made love since the night with Suki. By this time Terry was damn near ready to pour him a cognac and do the can-can, if that would do the trick.

But the truth was they'd both been shaken by their close encounter with the Californian. Terry was really glad that Franco had been there and had partaken; he certainly would have been weirded out if they'd excluded him. But now they were going to have to reacquaint themselves with each other sexually.

When Franco returned and removed his robe, Terry was on top of the covers wearing only her panties and a come-hither smile. Franco ignored both and grabbed his book in one hand—a new biography of John Hancock—and the remote control in the other, flicking it to ABC. Koppel was reporting on the verdict in the Jon-Benet Ramsey trial. He clicked to CBS.

TOP TEN REASONS FOR BELIEVING
THE BELACQUA REPORT

NO. 10. THINK OF WHAT YOU'LL SAVE ON YOUR KIDS' COLLEGE TUITION!

[polite laugh from the studio audience]

NO. 9. SHARES IN ORKIN ROACH CONTROL WILL GO UP AS WE GO UNDER.

[big laugh]

NO. 8. YOU CAN FORGET ABOUT ALL THOSE NASTY SPEEDING TICKETS.

[bigger laugh]

NO. 7. MAYBE YOUR LOONY AUNT WILL SUCCUMB TO SUICIDAL IMPULSES.

[huge laugh]

NO. 6. GOOD-BYE, ED MCMAHON! HEY, WHO NEEDS LIFE INSURANCE?

[polite laugh]

NO. 5. NO ONE'LL LIVE TO REMEMBER THAT PESKY AIDS EPIDEMIC.

[big laugh]

NO. 4. DAVE PROMISED NOT TO HOST OSCARS AGAIN "TILL HELL FROZE OVER"; THANKS TO GLOBAL WARMING, THERE'S NO DANGER OF THAT.

[big groan]

NO. 3. MURDER YOUR SPOUSE: "LIFE WITHOUT PAROLE" MEANS FORTY YEARS.

[huge laugh]

NO. 2. WE CAN USE THE SOCIAL SECURITY FUND FOR A BIG PARTY.

[raucous cheers, and applause]

". . . and the Number One reason for believing *The Belacqua Report* is . . ."

THE CHILDREN YOU MOLEST MAY NOT LIVE TO RECOVER THE MEMORY.

[riotous laughter, followed by applause]

Franco clicked again. "Tonight on Ricki: 'The End of the World? Get Over It, Girl!'" Click. Charlie Rose was interviewing Kerner. Click: MTV was showing the Stones' video of "Trash the Earth."

"Would you like a massage?" Terry asked, slipping up behind him in bed and rubbing the tips of her nipples lightly against his shoulder blades.

"I'm fine, thank you," he answered, stirring a little despite himself. He clicked the remote again: *Star Trek*. Brain death. Relief.

Suddenly Franco heard a familiar male voice, and a moment later Terry noticed it too. It wasn't someone he knew well, and from the voice alone he couldn't have placed the man. Franco fixed his eyes on the screen: the fellow was standing beside an adolescent-looking William Shatner. Franco didn't recognize him right away because he had an extraterrestrial accent and Vulcan ears; he also looked much younger, and he didn't have a mustache. So it took several minutes of disbelief to be certain who the man was. Then Franco and Terry turned to one another and their jaws dropped open.

Beyond any doubt, the actor in the Vulcan uniform was the man who had introduced himself as General Shreiver.

PART THREE

THE CEREMONY OF INNOCENCE

The force that through the green fuse drives the flower
Drives my green age; that blasts the roots of trees
Is my destroyer.
And I am dumb to tell the crooked rose
My youth is bent by the same wintry fever.

The force that drives the water through the rocks
Drives my red blood; that dries the mouthing streams
Turns mine to wax.
And I am dumb to mouth unto my veins
How at the mountain spring the same mouth sucks.

The hand that whirls the water in the pool
Stirs the quicksand; that ropes the blowing wind
Hauls my shroud sail.
And I am dumb to tell the hanging man
How of my clay is made the hangman's lime. . . .

—DYLAN THOMAS,
"The Force That Through the Green Fuse Drives the Flower" (1933)

FREE FALL

Some say the world will end in fire,
Some say in ice.
From what I've tasted of desire,
I hold with those who favor fire.
But if it had to perish twice,
I think I know enough of hate
To say that for destruction ice
Is also great
And would suffice.

—ROBERT FROST, "Fire and Ice" (1923)

Despite huge advance orders, the boxed paperback set of *The Be-lacqua Report* and *Belacqua Refuted* hadn't sold half the copies that were anticipated, and the number of early returns was gargan-tuan; and in hardcover, Kerner was remaindered after three months. According to most polls the televised debate had been a TKO by Belacqua; his hardcover continued to sell worldwide, with relentless free publicity from commentators, some of whom of-fered an impassioned defense of one scientist or the other, while a few carried water on both shoulders.

At Commonweal Books there was the smell of blood in the air: Danvers Creal might not be indestructible after all. This could have been wishful thinking, but the number of books commis-sioned about Bloomsbury authors and their world seemed like a deliberate attempt to pre-spend the profits of both *Belacqua* books. There were new biographies of E. M. Forster, both Woolfs, Lytton Strachey, Vita Sackville-West, and all three Sitwells (*even* Sachev-erell!). Only Marlene knew the true total; she had reluctantly moved out of her editorial post to become Danvers's new assistant as well as vice president in charge of Lost Weekends—that was the new imprint for "classic paraliterature." She kept a thermograph of Bob Milton's voice every time he called in from the golf course, and by now the buzz from her was that Danvers Creal was goin' down, bio by bio by bio.

The chairman of Macro wasn't even sure what Bloomsbury *was*: naturally, he'd assumed it had to do with gardening, and would therefore please Mildred. But as his handpicked president continued spending hundreds of thousands of dollars on manuscripts on the subject from obscure academics, Bob grew concerned, then leery. He'd begun asking Marlene new questions about Danvers each time he called, and soon enough he lost the Smile. Then it was rumored that at their last meeting, despite huge profits, the directors had moved to cut off further acquisitions by Danvers.

Time had not been kind to Danvers Creal. Despite what appeared to be a huge initial success, after almost a year as CEO he looked like a flash in the pan who'd benefited from Franco's savvy decisions; he knew that. And where he had expected his colleagues to demonstrate more respect to the president of the house—Danvers really *enjoyed* the bowing and scraping of subordinates—in fact they showed him less. Worst of all, he still couldn't get laid.

On the last night of Carnaval, when every public inch of Rio de Janeiro was carpeted with people, a helicopter approached the city from São Cristóvão to the north at an altitude of just four hundred feet, discharging a fine aerosol spray as it trolled slowly above the crowds. Six days later, an estimated 44,360 people had died terrible, protracted deaths, poisoned by sarin, the same toxic gas that poisoned thousands in the subways of Tokyo in 1995. Before long it became clear that this was a "mission" carried out by the Anjos de João, Brazilian allies of Japan's Aum Shinrikyo, the Japanese terrorist group now commanded by fugitive Yasuo "Killer" Hayashi. He had not been seen publicly since the mass suicides at the nuclear plant five months earlier. Hayashi was said to have virtually limitless funding from the fanatical Osama ben Laden, the renegade revolutionary of Saudi Arabia who, with petro-assets exceeding $300 million, had underwritten the bombing of numerous Al Hayat offices in early 1997.

According to three members of Anjos de João captured by authorities, Hayashi had networked on the Web with dozens of revolutionary sects, some as small as the Viper Militia or the New Symbionese Liberation Army, whose "ideologies" had nothing remotely in common, apart from incoherent allusions to *The Belacqua Report*. Interpol corroborated the fact that Hayashi had transferred sealed canisters—of anthrax and botulism bacteria as well as sarin—to the autonomous control of these local groups, along with detailed instructions on how they were to be sprayed by fogging machines from helicopters to maximize their effect.

So the poison gas attack was no surprise to those at Interpol, though they'd had no idea what city would be hit first. They had also been somewhat complacent. Japanese undercover police mistakenly believed that all the canisters had been safely defused before they left Osaka: agents had infiltrated Aum Shinrikyo and surreptitiously siphoned off the deadly gases, replacing them with inert mist. The intention was to track down the whole global network of terrorists. But after Rio, it was obvious that while some of the canisters distributed around the world might be harmless, others were still lethal.

The FBI had uncovered cells of the Aum Doomsday cult in the United States, as NBC had reported back in 1997, at about the time ABC had revealed that the Japanese cult intended to "weaponize Ebola." By the spring of 1999, there was evidence that some of the canisters from Osaka had been stockpiled in the northeastern United States by a thirty-year-old French businessman, Théo Lapine.

By the time the name Roddenberry filled the screen, Franco knew that "General Shreiver" was really an actor named Peter Roth. What embarrassed him most was that wrong zip code on "the General's" business card; it would have told him everything he needed to know about *The Belacqua Report* if he hadn't been so distracted. A few minutes later he left word at Midtown North for Chief O'Hara to call. Then he left a similar message on Danvers's machine; Commonweal, after all, had been the first target of Belacqua's fraud. Roger *must* have known all along it was Milton's company he was bamboozling—McAdams had been right when he called Belacqua "Oscar material." In fact, it was time to admit that McAdams had been right about a lot of things.

At the same time—shortly after midnight—Terry started writing a short narrative of Roger's deceit, including the false General Shreiver and the devil's eye (a virtual admission, she thought, that the error was deliberate). She also noted "nagging doubts" surrounding the death of William McAdams, without mentioning what Franco had told her about the sound of Christiane in the throes of passion.

Franco was now governed by his towering anger at the mayhem that Roger had caused, so vividly epitomized on videotape at the Versailles Room. His rage was also fueled by a pungent sense of betrayal. Belacqua, his phony friend, had hired a phony character actor, for chrissakes, got him a phony uniform, and sent him to Commonweal with the phony manuscript: all this just to dupe him, personally, along with the world. Strange the shrewd scientist had risked his elaborate hoax with a cheap stunt like Shreiver, given his bona fide connections with NASA and even the White House. Then again, were *they* bona fide? Or was the photo from the Oval Office computer-generated? It must have been key to Belacqua's scheme that the manuscript pass scrutiny from the first house approached, lest other publishers learn of its shortcomings.

But if *The Belacqua Report* was a sham, why hadn't it been uncovered by peer review? Why hadn't leading scientists, better equipped than Kerner, busted Belacqua yet? Was this a vast conspiracy of silence among hundreds of ecologists? Absurd. Yet why would *Scientific American* have published the Blackledge article if it was phony? Well, of course, it wasn't *all* made up; clearly Roger's data were close to the truth.

But as he tossed his way through the night, Franco became even angrier. Maybe Belacqua had done it for the money. But he was approaching extinction himself, with no children to provide for. Why did he need a fortune? Right about now Commonweal would be cutting Roger the first of many fat royalty checks. There was Christiane, of course. Which reminded him, he'd promised her he'd send their contract to Commonweal. More awake than not, he rose quietly and went into his office.

The contract was in his file cabinet where he had put it, but when he glanced at the last page to make sure it was the notarized copy, he noticed something strange: Roger Belacqua hadn't even signed the document. There were two names indicated as payees, just above the notary's seal: Christiane Belacqua and Théo Lapine. Familiar. Must be their lawyer. And Christiane, of course, handled all their money. He thought about keeping the contract as some kind of leverage—but for what? This was between the Belacquas and Commonweal. Still, he made a copy of the twelve-page document on his fax and then slipped it into a Priority Mail envelope and went back to bed.

The next morning Franco intended to call Roger and weasel out some answers, but he wasn't up to it yet; he didn't have a plan. Instead he tried Midtown North again. It was afternoon before he finally got through—not to O'Hara, but to Detective Jordan.

Franco began diplomatically. "We now know that Roger Belacqua committed fraud. I also think he may have instigated the murder of William McAdams."

"Izzat a fact? What happened? You two have a tiff after you got fired? And now you're supporting the Kerner book to try an' get your old job back?"

"I beg your pardon? I'm giving you information in a murder investigation."

"Thanks, but we're flying in the killer tomorrow night, from Seattle."

"The woman from Green Fist? Claire Buday? I think she's a decoy somehow."

"You goin' into police work now, Mr. Sherman? If so, ya oughta know the hair sample we have puts Claire Buday at McAdams's apartment. She also had the opportunity and a damn good motive, and so far her only alibi is one of her eco-terrorist buddies. So, ya see, we don't *need* another killer."

"You really think she—? Tell me: did you get hair samples from Mrs. Belacqua?"

"Yup. So thanks for the tip, Mr. Sherman, but no thanks." The phone went dead.

He dialed Danvers's home number again and left a second message. He hated—*hated*—admitting to Danvers that Kerner was right.

He called Connors, his FBI contact. They hadn't spoken since the background check on Belacqua more than a year earlier. Connors's name had appeared in news reports about government agencies that infringed upon citizens' rights by secretly downloading data from their computers. In February, for example, AP reported that the IRS had experimented with downloading data from taxpayers who filed electronically; that triggered a congressional hearing. The next month, in an article entitled "bigbrother@hacker.com," *Rolling Stone* exposed cases in which the FBI had lured specific suspects—accused pedophiles, so there wasn't much outcry—with offers of free software online, and then downloaded their personal files. Finally, Connors himself was interviewed for a scorching piece in *The New Republic* and acknowledged that in his efforts to track down Tiny Messingkauf, he had searched the personal files of those employees of Commonweal Books who had worked on the serial killer's diaries. That's when Franco realized his own computer had probably been rifled. Terry's, too.

Connors got back to him from Rio, where he was investigating U.S. connections with the sarin gas attack. Franco reported what he knew about Belacqua's deceit, and Connors listened dutifully, if distractedly, on a terrace overlooking Avenida Presidente Vargas. Though preoccupied with the terrorist network, he jotted it all down. Then Franco returned to his applications for lecturing posts.

In mid-May, Franco landed a job interview at Vassar, so he and Terry picked up a blue Ford Escort from Hertz and meandered through the spring swelter to Poughkeepsie, getting a feel for the area. He didn't trouble her with his financial woes, but he'd taken a big hit when Wall Street went splat, and neither of them had had an income for a year; by now, he needed the job. Of course, after his executive pay at Commonweal, an academic salary would be a joke, but he was hoping to land an administrative job as well, based on his corporate experience, and take home two paychecks. Anyway, he still had equity in the Park Avenue apartment.

While Franco met with the search committee, Terry watched the rehearsal for commencement; that's where she was when Franco returned ten minutes later, noticeably shorter. Someone on the committee had identified him as the man responsible for publishing both *The Belacqua Report* and *Belacqua Refuted*. "Certain members of the staff find this particular *aventure* incompatible with a post here, Dr. Sherman. We're only sorry we didn't realize early on who you are."

"That is *who I am*," Franco told Terry on the way back down the Taconic Parkway. "That's my identity. I'm the leper who published the doomsday report. 'Now I am become death, destroyer of worlds.'"

"Oh, Franco!" That really made her angry. "Where do you get off saying crap like that? You published a damn book, you didn't invent the atomic bomb."

"The only history department that'll ever hire me is one that doesn't know *who I am*." Her attempt to deflate his self-pity came much too late; he was on a roll. "Of course, if I just lie a little, I can probably get a job somewhere. Maybe Guam. Ever thought how beautiful it would be to live in the middle of the Pacific Ocean?"

Terry wanted to grab him, like a catcher on a trapeze, as he plummeted toward despair. She was strong, stronger and clearer now that she knew *The Belacqua Report* was a sham. But the man beside her was AWOL inside his own skin.

"Hey." She nudged him. "What did the Dalai Lama say to the hot-dog vendor?"

He shook his head glumly.

"Make me One with Everything."

Franco nodded condescendingly, but a moment later he chuckled softly, and soon they were laughing aloud together, most of the way home.

The impact of *The Belacqua Report* was being felt in Congress almost daily now, as policy was reexamined in terms of post-Belacqua assumptions. Senate Resolution No. 729 was an appropriations bill setting aside $200 billion over the next ten years for the "safe disposal" of thousands of nuclear warheads, to be sealed in huge cubes and then buried among the Arizona mesas of Four Corners. Proponents insisted this would offer full protection for the half-life of enriched plutonium—250,000 years, give or take. Skeptics and critics abounded. Senator Wallace Burke, leading the opposition, demanded to know if the White House expected mankind's imminent extinction, and if so, "Why, sir, should the voters have their pockets turned out and shaken down jus' ta protect the damn cockroaches that'll be takin' over our jobs?" Proponents shelved the bill pending "clarifications." Meanwhile, reporters continued pressing the White House to issue a policy statement on the environmental crisis, but the President actually canceled a scheduled press conference, to avoid questions about "the doomsday book," it was rumored.

Similar issues exposed the rifts between those who were sure humanity was doomed and those who thought *The Belacqua Report* was a fraud. Like most polarizing issues, it left no middle ground, and everybody was shouting, "Which side are you on?" Nowhere more so than on the talk shows. From early in the morning with Don and Howard till late at night with Ricki and Sally, there was an endless stream of talkers whose lives had been altered by Belacqua's book—or so they told the shows' producers. Some had found religion, others turned to crime, and many, it seemed, were now devoted to endless rutting. A handful claimed their lives had been enhanced by the contemplation of our collective mortality, and a few felt "empowered." But for a growing number, the biggest impact of the book upon their lives came from the latest national craze. It was called bomping.

Bomping was played either competitively or as a solitaire, and the rules of the game were simple: players drove their cars onto the *exit* ramp of an interstate highway and, horns blaring, raced against each other *into* the flow of cars and trucks. To score three points, the players crossed from the outer lane to the inside and back, through the rush of oncoming traffic, in time to exit by the next entrance ramp: that was a "ringer."

Bomping began as a gang-related game of chicken, but the copycats ranged from daredevils to genuine suicides. Like other folkways, it had spread around the country, with some regional variations, and quickly became an established fad among thrillseekers in their teens and twenties. Young men and women who went out on a bomp were looking for a high from "extreme driving," and if a few innocent drivers happened to die as a result, or lived out the rest of their maimed lives in a hospital somewhere, well, like they say, man, life's a bitch and then you die.

Of course, it was way more cool if you mounted a video camera on the dashboard first, to record the incredible thrill of station wagons, sports cars, and tractor trailers coming at you at closing speeds of 130 to 150 miles an hour, especially in case you didn't live to describe it. 'Cause then your own death was sure to be on TV. By the time the first amateur bomping video appeared on network television, some two hundred people around the country had died from the game, and hundreds more had been gravely injured. Gravely injured bompers weren't cool.

From numerous interviews it appeared that the only common denominator among these sociopathic drivers was the conviction that they'd already been condemned to an early grave by "the selfishness of our parents' generation," explained one kid from his hospital bed in Greenwich, Connecticut. Facing lives cut short by an environmental holocaust caused by the negligence of their parents, the most alienated youth were "acting out." Psychologists were the first to have their way with this social epidemic, followed by sociologists, family counselors, and columnists-without-portfolio; theologians were last and possibly least. The experts diagnosed the problems variously as an acute form of "Belacqua Syndrome."

Meanwhile beleaguered commuters, for whom daily life was suddenly as fearsome as minesweepers' in Bosnia, broadcast alarm in every possible way. As a result of their demonstrations in cities with the highest rates of bomping, police threw up patrols on the highway exit ramps during drive time with orders to shoot to kill any driver who tried to enter there. They were known as "firing squads" (Howard Stern called them "spoilsports"). But that wasn't enough: obviously, people who were seeking thrills this way—if that's what bomping was really about—were highly motivated. So especially in competition, bompers began entering the highway on the usual entrance ramps, then waiting on the shoulder till they could make a U-turn.

Commonweal Books promptly reissued *Football and Freud*.

Bomping, like many other social ills at the end of the second millennium, was the fault of Franco Sherman. If you asked him, that's what he'd tell you, because that's how he felt. Terry tried to catch him as he slipped into sober despair, until she realized that instead of rising up, he was trying to drag her down into the hole he was in.

Instead of sinking, Terry began building the wall, as Franco called it, brick by brick: he saw it in her eyes the day her psychic ramparts went up. This defensive perimeter was designed to shield herself and the children from the deep funk in which Franco now dwelled. Juliette's startling recovery was too precious to risk; and Max built his own wall right after Terry showed him how, without a word of explanation. So Franco dug his hole, and Terry built her wall, and once in a while they made love in such a perfunctory way that even their more exotic sexual rituals became dull.

But at night Franco's mind caught fire: with all the pyrotechnics of Hieronymous Bosch, Franco's rupturing psyche spilled out his fiercest visions yet, fusing images of nuclear blight victims, diners at the Versailles Room, bodies bloating beside highways, all in the vivid, grainy colors of a Surgical Studies film he'd seen once when he was dating a premed. Asleep, Franco was the Eisenstein, the Murnau, the Roger Corman of his nightmares, where *Hiroshima, Mon Amour* met *Night of the Living Dead*. And so, once again, that great wall of human flesh appeared before him longer than Fifth Avenue, taller than the Empire State Building, and carved in bas-relief.

From atop her wall, Terry could see Franco's soul plunging toward the canyon floor, bouncing off ledges of short-lived hope and enthusiasm. She knew he was almost broke; Wall Street had recovered somewhat from its five-thousand-point "correction," but Franco had lost a big chunk of capital. Most of the balance was tied up as collateral to cover the latest printing of Wylie's book, and now the bills were coming due well ahead of the earnings. And try as he might, Franco had little hope of finding another job in academia. He put out a few halfhearted feelers in the publishing world, but his fundamental lack of interest in that option showed through all too clearly. Especially to Terry, who certainly wanted to help. To begin with, she suggested, they could rent something "cheap and cheerful" and sell the Park Avenue apartment.

"In this market?" Franco snarled. "I'd rather swim in acid than take that kind of bath." He could still apply to other publishing houses, she insisted. "I don't like the publishing world, and the publishing world doesn't like me," he explained patiently. "When *The Belacqua Report* has been publicly discredited, I will be, too. Besides, just as some chairman offers me a job, Mildred Milton will report to his wife that I do strange things with gerbils."

There was nothing Terry could say that didn't irritate him. While she knew he'd been right to publish Belacqua—especially given her own role—she was coming to see how the book that had brought them together could also tear them apart. With everything negative in his mind, including his dreams, Franco's greatest problem was still the knot of moral dilemmas surrounding *The Belacqua Report*. Should he attack its veracity publicly with the story of "General Shreiver," and risk returning the world to destructive ecological complacency?

Terry had her own dreams. Most nights she was living on the outskirts of Taos, married to the man who'd saved the world, with three grown children who, as if by miracle, had all survived punk adolescence, drugs, and unsafe sex in one long, horrendous afternoon. But sometimes she could be alone in her dreams, without feeling sad, as if all the man she needed was right inside her own bones. She was self-sufficiency itself, O'Keeffe after Stieglitz. That was Terry's saddest dream, and one morning it made her shudder to realize how happy it could make her. That was when she decided to spend the day alone in the park.

After circling Wollman Rink, she settled on a bench that faced the Sherry-Netherlands and the climbing sun. By the Central Park Carousel she sat down and prayed. She actually closed her eyes, joined her hands, moved her lips, and begged for moral clarity. None came, and fifteen minutes later she needed to pee, so she wended her way back to the zoo and found a ladies' room. When she came out, she stared at the gnu and wondered why, after all, she had felt it was her responsibility to get *The Belacqua Report* published. Because even if Franco thought he was responsible for it, Terry knew better. *She* had read the phony manuscript, *she* had distributed copies to all the editors; above all, *she* had pitched it to him. And yes, *she* had held Danvers Creal's penis in her left hand while he ejaculated. If that didn't make her responsible . . .

She found another park bench near the chess tables, and after just a few minutes there she knew exactly what she should do. Which felt like moral clarity to her.

A week later Franco received an invitation to speak at Smith College's Summer Seminar on Writers and Writing, on the topic "Between Author and Reader—the Publisher." Of course, money wasn't mentioned, though Terry assured him that guest speakers received about $150, which would cover a hotel room in Northampton.

Franco was as enthusiastic as a dyslexic at a Bible reading. "I have," he told her solemnly, "nothing to say."

"C'mon, it's my alma mater! I mean, the coincidence is incredible! Please, Franco, it would be so great if we could visit my old school together. You've heard me talk about Professor Phillips— look at the letter, she heads this committee. It's not like you're too *busy*."

That was when he knew he had no damn choice. He grunted, and his head dropped to his chest in a half-nod to the inevitable.

So right after Memorial Day they picked up another blue Ford Escort from Hertz on a cool late-spring afternoon and, heading north through Westchester, began to shed their thick city skins. Terry was eager to drive. Unlike their unhappy visit to Vassar, this trip was to rejuvenate Franco, who was content just being a passenger. As soon as they left the city, he stared out at the farms and meadows, when he really should have been preparing a speech, which he had thus far neglected to do.

Somewhere in Fairfield County it occurred to Franco that for all his concern about nature, he'd seen precious little of it in the last . . . oh, twenty-five years. In fact, apart from the Vassar debacle, the only time he'd left Manhattan in the last two years was on his visit to the Belacquas' place in Vermont. He had been city-bound since childhood; even his few vacations with Lillian and the kids had been to London, Paris, and Rome—not the Grand Canyon, or Pago Pago, wherever the hell that was. He was far more familiar with the world that humans had made than with the world God had made, even in southwestern Connecticut, where admittedly Nature was kept on a short leash. How irretrievably precious it was, how just plain natural. As coils of citification unwound from their shoulders, they bathed in the surroundings near the Massachusetts state line. Franco felt his burden—having mucked up civilization—evaporate, among rising tendrils of hope.

For her part, Terry was glad they didn't talk during the drive: she was a little worried about what was going to happen when they got there. Okay, maybe this wasn't going to turn it all around for Franco, but it might snap him out of his torpor.

After they crossed the Mass Pike at Springfield, heading north, Nature's dominion was more convincing. These forests and fields didn't look boxed into man-made grids. Arriving in her college town, Terry reverted to squeaks and giggles of recollection; it had been four years since she'd graduated. Meanwhile Franco turned dour. He was about to address a roomful of intellectual women without a prepared speech. Ratfuck.

They parked in front of the Forbes Library just in time for the obligatory tea party and strolled over to Professor Phillips's residence. Terry was delighted to bring the man she loved to the campus where she had grown up—even knowing that Franco hadn't written a word.

Franco survived the tea party, and even produced a handful of *bons mots*. As they walked toward Dewey Hall, where thirty or forty young women had already gathered, he tried to *guess* what he was going to say—but could not; he had no idea whatsoever.

"Good afternoon. Our speaker today, Dr. Franco Sherman, is no stranger to academia, having earned his Ph.D. at Columbia University and lectured at two of the country's finest institutions, after Smith. But today, Dr. Sherman isn't here to speak as an author, or professor, or historian. Until recently, Dr. Sherman was president of Commonweal Books. He has come to discuss the publisher's role in bringing authors to the public. Please welcome Dr. Franco Sherman."

Listening to the sedate applause, Franco noted that Professor Phillips had not mentioned *The Belacqua Report*. He was still wondering about that as he reached the podium with nothing to say. Nothing at all.

"Thank you, Professor Phillips, for the honor of inviting me here today to speak."

After standing a full sixty seconds in silence, Franco suddenly smiled, incongruously, like a boxer who's taken a right uppercut. He looked around at the anticipation on the faces, which slowly turned to mild alarm. He saw Terry near the back: she seemed like the only one in the room who wasn't worried. Finally, as Professor Phillips rose, he thrust his throttle forward, putting his brain on auto-lecture.

Turning to the well-stuffed bookshelves behind him, he picked out a book arbitrarily and held it up for all to see. In a light-hearted tone, he asked, "Tell me, someone, please—is this a *good* book, or a *bad* book?"

Now the audience fell silent. Finally one young woman spoke up. "You can't tell a book by its cover," she said, to murmurs of approval.

Franco made his way to her and handed her the book (*North-ampton Genealogy, 1909*). "Well, Ms., perhaps you could just glance through it quickly and tell me."

"No," said the young woman conscientiously. "I'd have to read it."

He pursued his point amicably. "Ah. But if you read it, you'd know if this is a good book—if this genealogical study has value?" She nodded. "But if it is inaccurate, it would be a *bad* book, right?" She nodded. "So you'd have to do more than just read it, wouldn't you?"

"Well," she objected, "if it were a novel, I could tell if it was good or bad." Franco didn't mean to persecute her, so he moved around his small audience.

"Because different criteria apply to fiction, true enough. But for the moment let's confine our discussion to what is called 'nonfic-tion.' By the way, isn't it curious that the publishing industry desig-nates books which claim to be factual as '*non*fiction'? It's like defining the truth as a 'non-lie.' "

His listeners were beginning to relax. Sighing, he showed the room his open palms. "Alas, I come to you empty-handed today. I have no answers for you, or for anyone—only questions. You see, just a year ago I published a book entitled *The Belacqua Report*"—that produced a buzz—"which, in case you haven't heard, predicts that mankind is condemned to extinction within forty to fifty years."

"And womankind," someone called out.

"But to this day, the sad truth is, I don't know how much of *The Belacqua Report* is true—whether it is a good book or a bad book. Frightening, since it's already had such an impact. This is the first time I've really admitted it. There was no way I could be certain if Dr. Belacqua's work was accurate; all I could do was to rely upon the judgment of some experts." Something in his vertebrae popped, loosening a cramp he'd had for about a year. He could see Terry beaming at him from the back row. "I had a duty to verify Belacqua's earth-shattering predictions—up to a point. I don't subscribe to the view that publishers are merely printers, without responsibility for what they issue. But neither can they always guarantee a book's accuracy, though it is only through the lasting value of their books that they enhance their imprimatur."

"Why did you leave Commonweal, Dr. Sherman? Do you regret having published *The Belacqua Report*?" This from a punky young woman in the second row.

"Fact is, I was fired by the chairman of the conglomerate that owns Commonweal, because *The Belacqua Report* offended his Christian sensibilities. Now, do I regret having published it? What I do regret is publishing the book without sufficient peer review, given its momentous message."

"But whether or not *The Belacqua Report* was entirely right," said a thoughtful young woman in the first row, "it has raised awareness. So, like, what's to regret?"

"Because so many have suffered as a result," Franco snapped back. "Before shouting 'Fire!' in a crowded theater, you'd better make damn sure the fire is real, and it isn't just smoke and mirrors."

"But overpopulation is real, right?" said the same young woman. "So the fire is real. And you're not to blame if people get hurt leaving the theater!"

Franco paused to consider that. "Well, the metaphor is deceptive—"

"But the fact remains," she pressed on, "that you're not responsible for the actions of others. And now, maybe, the world won't take the future for granted."

Bingo! That was the moment of his epiphany. Given the condition of the planet, this was no false alarm. The earth was in genuine peril, and even if *The Belacqua Report* overstated the case, Franco could not hold himself responsible for the actions of others.

He felt immediate relief. Professor Phillips led the audience in a slightly confused applause, and Terry came to the podium smiling. She kissed him on the mouth and, holding his hand high, led him through the audience and out the door. It seemed like a conspiracy to make him feel better; but since it was working, he didn't care. All he wanted was to get home and begin to put his life back in order.

Franco's "speech" had been so short that there were still several hours of daylight left, so they canceled their hotel reservations and Terry aimed the little car back toward the muggy city through the humid mist that already filled the valleys. For the next hour, as they wended their way south, everything that he'd bottled up came pouring out at Terry: his nightmares since Lillian's death; his hastening *The Belacqua Report* into print, partly, he admitted, to spend more time with her. He spoke of his initial ambivalence and then his delight in her love, and he poured out the anxiety that had accumulated about their financial situation. All before they reached Springfield.

Then she explained how she'd gone crazy when she read the manuscript, thinking it was the most important thing in the world. And how that was because she had once been driving along this same highway they were on now and hit a deer, and had held the falling doe in her arms—and then abandoned it to die alone beside the road.

In the early-evening fog, she turned on the headlights, and then slowed down when she saw that something looked wrong up ahead. It was as if a car was coming straight at them, in her lane of the highway. Oh God. There were two cars speeding toward them, horns blaring, and there was nowhere to go.

"Terry!" He grabbed the steering wheel and pulled. The little car spun clockwise and rolled four times before settling on its crushed roof.

THE WORLD TURNED
UPSIDE DOWN

History is neither to be considered as a formless structure, due exclusively to the achievements of individual
agents, nor as possessing a reality apart from and independent of them, accomplished behind their backs in
spite of them, the work of some superior force variously known as Fate, Chance, Fortune, God. Both
these views, the materialistic and the transcendental,
must be rejected in favour of the rational. Individuality
is the concretion of university, and every individual action is at the same time superindividual.

—SAMUEL BECKETT, *"Dante . . . Bruno . . . Vico . . . Joyce"* (1929)

On August 12, 1999, the Lifechance Global Lottery announced
that its charitable fund for victims of Metzamor had reached the
preliminary target of $50 billion. Since it began operating daily,
more than $250 million had been paid out to prizewinners from
twenty-one countries. In the meantime, the founding Members
had become a force to be reckoned with. Lauded as philanthropists, courted by governments, and imitated by con artists, the
Members (there were 102,418, from all 916 associated International Schools) took a series of online votes. In a process that
would literally have taken years by international mail, alumni
around the world debated options, proposed alternatives, and
voted on initiatives; their extensive dialogue leading to each vote

was open to public scrutiny. By September they had settled upon an agenda ratified by 90 percent of the Members.

That agenda was presented in a declaration known as the September Plan, announcing that the lottery would continue indefinitely, but that hereafter half its projected receipts—$80 to $100 billion annually—would be used to assist projects for environmental reform in other regions around the world. Short-term projects would be considered on a nation-by-nation basis: one example was the complete elimination of chlorofluorocarbons worldwide within a decade, making good on the sometimes hollow promises of the Montreal Protocol. The cost was enormous but not incalculable; proceeds from the Global Lottery were easily equal to it.

Lifechance also allotted funds "to commission an assessment of the overall condition of the biosphere." From the caliber and range of specialists already enlisted, as well as the funds available, it was clear that this collaboration would build upon and supersede the UN's IPCC studies. Because of its accomplishments as a charity, Lifechance received encouragement from many governments, including tentative signals from the People's Republic of China, which was seeking aid in converting from coal—the Yangtze Dam was still many years from completion. Four national space agencies offered satellite data from the ocean floors to the rim of space for this global assessment. Among the alumni, one of the early sponsors for this plan was Franco Sherman.

Then the September Plan outlined its most controversial resolve. Lifechance announced that it would allocate $10 million to a feasibility study aimed at extending its voting procedure.

> The Members acknowledge that many of these consequential decisions exceed our qualifications, and the responsibility for such enormous allocations that can effect so many lives is onerous. Therefore we have voted "to explore methods of opening the Lifechance voting process *to the broadest possible population worldwide.*" Assuming that the Lottery continues to generate an enormous charitable fund, communications technology might make it possible within a decade for every citizen of the world over a certain age to register and vote upon specific issues of global concern, either at urban "hubs" or mobile centers through rural regions, or from individual modems. After consultations with Intel and Microsoft, and a variety of Internet service providers, an inter-

national consortium of corporations have agreed to contribute their expertise in creating voter rolls.

This is a daunting prospect. But given the emerging technologies for telecommunication, it is not inherently less feasible than, for example, the human genome project. And we believe there is a powerful intrinsic value in the establishment of an enduring "town meeting for the global village," and seeking the opinions of the greatest possible number of individuals on earth. Experts suggest that, with the cooperation of governments, we might involve 30 to 60 percent of the human race—a great chorus of voices. This global plebiscite will address subjects as local and specific as clean drinking water and as global and far-reaching as the population explosion. Ultimately these referendums may determine exactly how much we are prepared to sacrifice for the benefit of future generations. While Lifechance offers no opinion regarding the much-publicized threat to human survival, it seems at least prudent to provide this scaffolding for future global projects. Naturally, to achieve the largest possible participation, the cooperation of governments is a prerequisite. But we believe that even wary nations will recognize the benefits of participating, and encouraging their citizens to vote freely. As well, it should be noted that the Membership may choose to withhold funding from nations that prevent their citizens from voting freely.

Education is a requirement for any real change, and that truth raises the most difficult issues of conflicting value systems. It is not clear how meaningful a referendum can be among the least educated populations. Nonetheless, we believe that this project represents an important goal.

The September Plan was soon the center of enormous debate all around the world.

From thousands of feet beneath the ocean's surface, where salps devour the phytoplankton that feed upon carbon, Franco rose toward consciousness. He was in pain—fuzzy, indistinguishable pain, from his head to his knees. And his eyes were covered with white gauze. No . . . fog. Thick morning fog hid the trucks roaring by the spot where he lay on the wet grass. There was no sign of Terry or the car.

He had been there overnight. He could not move his arms. As he struggled to his feet, the lacerations that had congealed on his forehead opened, drip-feeding blood into the eye that was open. He still heard screaming, but that may have been from his nightmare about Lillian.

Limping, he followed a corridor through the tall grass strewn with pieces of Ford, until he heard a soft moan. He turned awkwardly to the left, toward the sound, and saw Terry, propped up against a tree, her head lolling on her shoulder.

Bob Milton was so serenely comfortable with the job at hand that he wasn't even smiling when he arrived on the twelfth floor of Commonweal. He strode past Marlene's desk with a wink and wandered into Danvers's office as if he owned the place, which, in a manner of speaking, he did. Danvers shot to his feet like an adolescent with a dirty magazine on his lap.

"Why, Bob, what a great surprise! I was just going to call you. . . ."

"Hello, Danvers." Milton was in a good mood, doing what he loved best, second only to golf. Instead of the Smile he wore the Glower as he checked his wristwatch. "Any parting gestures?"

"Parting . . . gestures?" said Danvers.

"That's right, boy," responded Milton, amiable as your average flamethrower. "Your contract is terminated as of now. Choose five items from your desk to take with you—Marlene will return the rest of your property. Good-bye, Danvers."

"But what did I do wrong?" begged Danvers, grabbing his address book, three pens, and a roll of Certs.

It was a relief to them both when Bob, angina notwithstanding, finally ignited his rage. "You idiot," he exploded. "why the hell didn't you tell me that Bloomsbury was a club of English perverts flitting around London seventy years ago? Accounts told me that in twelve months you've shelled out more than five million bucks to a bunch of academic poofters to write about this little clique of queers. Then you lied about it, and tried to hide half the money! You *knew* these books wouldn't sell, but you went ahead and committed fraud to publish them. So, goodbye, Danvers. See you in court."

In shock, Danvers searched for an appropriate personality until, by conditioned reflex, he chose the Trusty Bootlicker. It was what he did best. "Uh, well, I'm sorry you see it that way. So, I guess this is good-bye, Bob. If you don't mind my asking, who's taking my place?"

Milton glowered at him. "I am, until I find a guy who won't steal me blind!" That's when Bob hit the button on his stopwatch: fifty-two seconds—a new record for the Wall of Fame in Macro's executive washroom. As Danvers stepped out the door, Bob's voice stopped him in his tracks. "Danvers, why *did* you piss away all that money on those British weirdos?"

Something in Danvers snapped. Bob could attack his professionalism, his manners, and even his manhood, but nobody could speak that way about Bloomsbury. He drew himself up to his most formidable stature, which was unimpressive, and for the first time since he entered the publishing world, he spoke from his heart. "Bloomsbury, you ignorant mogul, was the most refined coterie of creative artists in the twentieth century. I would be a fool to try to explain it to *you* any further!" He turned and marched out.

"Stupid bastard," Bob Milton chuckled to himself. "There went his pension." He beeped Marlene. "Hey, get me that hotshot down in legal, would you?"

"Yes, Mr. Milton. Would that be Marshall Pierson?"

"Right, that's his name. Ask him to come up. Oh, and honey, tell him to run down to the lobby on the way and pick me up a Clark Bar."

Franco struggled to revive Terry. She was dehydrated and barely conscious, but she whispered his name. Pressing his cheek against hers, he ordered her not to die. Then he struggled to his feet and stumbled to the side of the road.

It took him an hour to stop a car, and it was midmorning before an ambulance delivered Terry and him to the ER in Springfield. The next day she was moved to Hartford Hospital, with lacerations, broken ribs, and a fractured left arm. Franco had a concussion with severe lacerations to the head and scalp and a broken shoulder blade. And there was damage to his left eye, the extent of which wasn't known.

A week later Franco's former driver, Giuseppe, drove up to Springfield and took him to Hartford, where he spent half a day at Terry's bedside. The afternoon was a blur—they were both still in shock. The next day, when her mother arrived from Minneapolis, Terry didn't remember his visit.

Leaving Hartford, Franco had the presence of mind to stop for a hat—a silly-looking beret—to hide the bandages on his scalp so as not to frighten the children. By the time the car reached Manhattan, Franco was too weak to make it up to his apartment without Sean to lean on. The kids greeted him with shock. He was still limping, his arm was strapped to his torso, his face was every shade of purple, green, and yellow, and his eyepatch had a bloodstain. He tried to make light of it. "See!" he said. "Now I look just like Long John Silver!" But Max ran off to his room, while Juliette wept and promised to take care of him like Terry would. Emily was there making spaghetti.

For the first few days, until the shock faded, everything seemed unfamiliar without Terry. Nor would she be back soon: her mother was taking her back to Minneapolis for the time being, to care for her. "I just feel she needs to be home awhile," Marcia explained, and Terry apparently felt the same.

This was a relief to Franco, once he got used to the idea. He knew he'd miss her, as the kids would, but he was in no shape to care for her, nor she to care for him. So, with Emily, he packed up most of her things and gave them to Giuseppe to take to Hartford, along with a brand-new Gateway laptop with Pentium IV, 500 Mhz, and all the bells and whistles as a gift. He bought the same for himself, and as they recuperated they communicated mostly by videophone on the Net.

One of Franco's first preoccupations was prodding the Springfield police to pursue the two drivers who'd caused their "accident." The cop he talked to wasn't reassuring. "They're bompers, Mr. Sherman," he said, as if that explained everything. "If they don't get hit, they don't get caught. Anyway, why put 'em in jail? They'll only live longer there." Franco didn't bother to make the obvious reply. Instead he turned to the mass of work that had accumulated thanks to the phenomenal sales of Wylie's *Second Republic*, now in its third week at the top of the nonfiction list.

A few weeks later, when his eye was almost fully recovered and most of the rainbow had leached out of his bruises, something else absorbed his attention. It began with a flood of e-mail: Lifechance had chosen him to be general editor of "the comprehensive assessment of the biosphere" outlined in the September Plan. The fact that he had been editor for *The Belacqua Report* apparently was to his credit.

This undertaking was far beyond his capacity even to contemplate while he was recuperating, and he promptly declined. But a week later he regretted that, and before Lifechance had endorsed a replacement, he accepted the project enthusiastically, while warning that he now believed *The Belacqua Report* was the product of bad science. This was the chance he'd dreamed of—a second chance—to get it right. Lifechance awaited a preliminary budget estimate from Franco, and he was assured that they had allocated millions of dollars for this multivolume evaluation—whatever it cost to produce a study that was comprehensive, unbiased, and compelled by a sense of urgency. Participating scientists would be chosen by a large international committee, but Franco would select an even-handed editorial board from among the consortium of international publishers (some of whom owned houses in the United States) that had agreed to publish the results of the two-year project.

As work got under way, with multilateral meetings online almost daily between Lifechance and legions of environmental scientists around the world, Franco became utterly absorbed in the project, which, because of its open-minded spirit of inquiry, was so fundamentally different from Roger's book. He hired Millie away from Commonweal, even though she had to give up her benefits. He also reorganized his den as a full-time working office with businesslike furniture; he removed the damn sofa and put his mother's possessions into storage. And he took down his last remaining wooden sphere carved in the seventeenth century, his father's legacy, and packed it carefully away. Later he had it photographed, perhaps for a book jacket. Then he began writing a lengthy outline of the Lifechance study based upon wide-ranging conferences online.

At night the horror movies in his head were replaced by a recall of the accident in slo-mo that lasted a month of Sundays. There was strange comfort in the recollection: it brought him closer to Lillian for one last, liberating moment. Now he'd shared her final experience of the Chevy pickup coming at her, a moment he'd imagined so often that it had perhaps saved his life and Terry's: he was primed to grab the steering wheel in what would have been a suicidal maneuver in less critical circumstances.

The news that the editor of *The Belacqua Report* had almost died in a bomping incident had produced a lot of media attention, rich in cheap irony, thanks to which Franco heard from many friends and associates. But not a word from Roger Belacqua.

> *If I ventured in the shipstream,*
> *Between the viaducts of your dreams . . .*

Terry lay on the thick pink carpet listening to *Astral Weeks,* surrounded by adolescent icons—tickets to the Steel Wheels tour, a sketch she had done of Vonnegut when she was twelve, and posters ("Girls Just Wanna Have Fun")—that were comforting, like the Pepperidge Farm cookies her mom brought upstairs on a plate with a doily.

Terry knew this had been one of those "lucky" accidents: it was a complete miracle they hadn't been killed. Still, she had been in bad shape at first, when they weren't sure about internal bleeding. The doctor said she shouldn't get up till her ribs stopped aching, but the cast on her arm was itchy 'n' scratchy and made her restless, so she lay on the floor. From there she could see Lake Harriet and the stark skeletons of the trees— Oh, get off it. The trees are always bare in mid-October. Duh.

Terry was grateful for this retreat, and she was taking her sweet time to scroll through all her options. There on her pink carpet, where even the stains were familiar, everything she'd experienced in New York seemed like a remote island of time, separate from her real life. And even though she was jonesing for Franco and the kids, she wasn't sure New York was the place for her. Maybe. Maybe. But things in Minneapolis seemed simple and good, while everything back there seemed difficult and bad. At the Park Avenue apartment she had had too many responsibilities and not enough authority; and that was just with Franco. Right now he was all jazzed up about this Lifechance study; and his election as its general editor did seem like a vindication, if it wasn't just the old-school-tie thing. But would he still be Lifechance's choice after Belacqua was exposed? And could he really handle a public pillorying without sinking back into his hole?

So much was right between them, but . . . there was the age difference, of course—twenty-three years!—which had a whole lot of downsides: the Lacoste shirts, for example, not to mention early widowhood. And then there was the sex thing: it seemed like they'd gone completely *crazy*. All right, all right, she'd started it. But she always knew it was a bad thing, even when it was really really good. And yet at the same time the sex was so deliberately impersonal that they were like strangers on a train. No, like ships in the night: *Strangers on a Train* was the Hitchcock movie where two guys exchange murders so they can't be connected to their victims. She always mixed those up.

But was it really an accident, or some nasty instant karma? She couldn't help feeling that she had it coming somehow. She had finagled that damn manuscript into print, which had driven the human race crazy and started the bomping craze that had almost killed them. Sounded like karma to her. Spooky action at a distance. *The Belacqua Report* was a bad thing, she knew that now, which was maybe a sign that her moral clarity was returning, there at her mom's. The doomsday report was a sham, and now they had to tell the world. Like Robert Frost said, the only way out is through.

> . . . *would you kiss my eyes?* . . .
> *Lay me down . . . in silence easy . . . to be born again* . . .

Washington officeholders were finally acknowledging that the citizenry's corrosive disgust had eaten away the foundation of republican governance. For twenty years the public had simmered with anger and perplexity at Congress, knowing full well the country was governed by a venal political culture that legitimized wholesale violations of the Constitution. Policy was determined by bribes for legislators, federal agencies were corrupt, and there were liars in public places. With a turnout under 35 percent in the '98 midterm elections, scorched-earth negative ads had reached the point where the electorate could only agree with them: *all* the candidates were unworthy.

After Labor Day, Congress reluctantly began debating a formal call for the Second Constitutional Convention to begin on May 25, 2000, in Philadelphia, where the Framers had begun drafting "the old Constitution" on that same date 213 years earlier. Delegates elected by each state would take their oaths in Independence Hall, where General Washington himself had once presided. In a public appeal, Quentin Reese, senator-elect from Minnesota, offered a measured, thoughtful argument in favor of the convention. "I do subscribe to the notion that, if it ain't broke, don't fix it—and our Constitution is not broken. However, at the grass roots of our system—in the state legislatures—Americans have told us that our fundamental law has been outstripped by the social, political, and technological transformations of two centuries. And while the Constitution is not broken, it has in some respects become outworn. How could the Framers have imagined the impact of telecommunications, multinational conglomerates, and political action committees—not to mention a level of civility beneath anything they experienced? From its inception, our Constitution was a flawed treasure: let us not forget how it championed the right of some humans to own others, asserting legal distinctions between 'free persons' and 'other persons.' The original Constitution didn't even have a Bill of Rights until it was improved. And if *we* fail to make the improvements we believe are crucial, then we are truly captives of history, servants to an old piece of sheepskin. If it should prove true that the earth itself is in peril, it is not as captives and servants that we shall meet the challenge." Later that night the Senate voted 76 to 24 in favor of the convention; a week later the House followed suit. The presidential campaign, now gearing up for primaries, was undercut by preparations for Convention 2000, which had the power, as William Safire put it, "to make the Oval Office round." To all of this agitation was added Millennial Fever, with its fundamentalist overtones and misapprehensions about the start of the thousand years of Christ's reign. The whole year was certain to be charged with drama.

With the Constitutional Convention approaching, Wylie's *Second Republic* owned the top nonfiction spot, beating out *The Belacqua Report, Belacqua Refuted,* and related titles (*Belacqua: The Trilling Symposium,* and *Belacqua for Dummies*), along with *Chained to the Wheel: The Vanna White Memoirs, Vol. 2.* The book's astonishing success was owed to the Appendix, which Franco had coaxed Professor Wylie to write for the '96 edition, to justify giving him a handsome premium. This addendum, according to *The New York Review of Books,* "serves as the only primer of its kind for a new Constitutional Convention. . . . [The book] provides a blueprint for lawful revolution." "Wylie addresses key issues in the formation of a contemporary convention," wrote *U.S. News & World Report,* "such as how the president of the convention is chosen; procedural options and their consequences; the pros and cons of an open (i.e., televised) or closed convention." Americans were suddenly fascinated with constitutional history, of all things, and *Publishers Weekly* was predicting that *Second Republic* would top the list through the end of the convention.

From Kansas to California, the summer of '99 was worse than the drought of '96; the topsoil was blowin' in the wind, and the effect was approaching another dustbowl. The price of wheat and feed grain started to soar, and cattle futures went through the roof, along with poultry and pork bellies, triggering an inflationary spiral like an Oklahoma twister. This was on top of increased prices of fruit and vegetables owing to infestations—mainly the dreaded medfly throughout the Southwest—and bacterial contamination, especially cyclospora, which first appeared in '96. As a result of rising food prices, the Cost of Living Allowance for Social Security pushed projected deficit totals back up, making it impossible to balance the budget by 2002, as planned in the '97 budget, and again scaring the market. When questioned by Louis Rukeyser, one broker threw up his hands. "My advice?" he said. "Invest in handcuff futures."

The San Joaquin Valley, the country's breadbasket, had suffered unprecedented flooding for the second time in three years, and 19 percent of privately owned farms went belly up, devoured by agrobusiness at county auctions for a dime on the dollar. Families were displaced and smaller communities crumbled.

Whether caused by global warming or not, outbreaks of cryptosporidium—the bacteria that shut off water to Milwaukee in '93—bloomed in sixteen cities over the long, hot summer of '99. The impact on public health wasn't enormous, because of warnings from the municipalities, but all tap water had to be boiled, and was shut off periodically in a half-dozen cities at a time, which was both unsettling and expensive.

Toward the end of October, Roger Belacqua called Franco to ask if they could meet in the city later that week. It was a brief, awkward conversation, full of guarded exchanges. Belacqua didn't know about the bomping incident, which Franco mentioned in an off-hand way. After expressing regrets, Roger proposed lunch on the 31st, once again at the "21" Club. Franco suggested they meet at twelve; he had to take the kids trick-or-treating that afternoon.

Franco was by now immersed in *The State of the Earth, 2000*, the Lifechance project. He no longer anguished about having rushed *The Belacqua Report* to print, but he was determined to wrench the truth out of Roger, and to see justice done. He considered notifying Chief O'Hara about their lunch date, or Marshall, in case Commonweal wanted to serve Belacqua with papers. He even thought of hiring a private investigator, but that was patently absurd. Instead, he purchased a mini-recorder with a microphone that pinned to his lapel. A frank confession from Roger Belacqua could set the record straight.

When Roger arrived late at "21," he was ailing visibly. He was dramatically thinner and walked painfully with a cane in one hand and an attaché case in the other. When they first met, Belacqua had looked a decade younger than his seventy-some years; now he seemed that many years older. He sat with difficulty and offered an apologetic smile, but waited until he had mastered his discomfort to say hello.

"What's wrong, Roger?" Franco asked with real concern.

"Nothing that a cold glass of water won't improve. I see you're teetotaling, too," he added, pouring himself a glass from Franco's bottle, before he replied directly. "Aging," he said with a weak smile, "is filled with indignities. Bits and pieces fall away. A few weeks ago I left my prostate in Boston." Franco didn't know what to say, as Roger studied the pale scars around his eye. "Has your vision recovered?"

"Mostly. By evening it's a little blurred." With that they ordered their lunch.

Roger was breathing normally. He wiped the sweat from his brow. "Sure is hot."

"Ah yes, the weather," sighed Franco. "Everybody talks, but no one does anything about it." He didn't even smile. "Still, it's an ill wind that blows no man *some* good. By the way, have you received your first royalty check?"

"Yes," he smiled, "Christiane has it. I leave the accounting to her. Bob Milton tried to block payment, but your friend in legal already had the check cut. We're buying a property in Costa Rica: after twenty Vermont winters, we've had it. So—" he emptied his glass—"this afternoon, we're leaving. Christiane's meeting me here, and then we're off, by way of Florida and Yucatán, to begin our new life." He checked his watch. "She ought to be here. She came in on the Boston shuttle."

Franco knew then that he would not see Roger again. The Belacquas were fleeing, leaving him holding the bag for the hoax and its pernicious consequences. "Costa Rica, eh?" he said, sounding both jolly and bitter at once. "Better wear plenty of suntan oil, it gets hot there. But, say—aren't you the fella who was predicting hotter weather?"

Roger's face was beaded with sweat despite the air-conditioning. "Okay, I lied."

Franco nodded sadly. "I already figured that out."

"It *isn't* for the weather that we're moving there. The book's earnings are in a foundation in the Caymans. By the time the IRS adds it up, I'll be a handful of dust."

Franco thought about that, then he shook his head. "No, I don't buy it, Roger. I'm not sure what drives you, but it isn't greed. What's really going on?"

"Well, how shall I put this? I'm dying," Belacqua answered simply. "It seems I got to Boston a little too late."

Franco's detachment was running out. He loved this strange old man whom he did not trust. "Okay—now, is *this* true?"

Roger nodded. "That's why I wanted to see you today, before we left: to apologize. I had anticipated most of what's happened since we met here two years ago, but I never guessed the book would bring you so much grief. Or that it would be so hard to admit to you"—he took a breath—"that *The Belacqua Report* is a hoax. The end of the world will not come about in your children's lifetime, or even your grandchildren's." He paused. "Next week several papers will be published that prove *The Belacqua Report* was a sham. But I suspect you already know that."

Franco nodded as he poked at his meal. "I'm trying not to take it personally. You had a lot invested in this long before we met.

So . . . what was all this really about, Roger? I'd like to know. But don't expect me to keep any secrets for you." With that, Franco clicked the switch on his tape recorder.

Belacqua wiped a rivulet from his brow and began. "After the children died, Christiane and I weren't much interested in life anymore—not our own, at least. As a memorial to Jean-Loup and Cybèle, we settled upon a series of research projects, the ones you saw. About a year later, when they were up and running, I noticed Christiane had made a mistake entering the week's data." His hands came to life and began to flutter. "When she argued that she was just one decimal point off, I lost my temper. 'What if we made that mistake every week?' I scolded. 'Ten years from now, our results would show the earth was melting!' "

Belacqua smiled. "That's how it began. Soon after, we decided to 'prove' the biosphere was collapsing and, like crooked accountants, we started keeping two sets of books. We weren't sure what we'd do with the false data, but we knew that ten years' worth would be very persuasive, and it would take time to disprove, during which the planet's perilous situation would sink in. Of course, we also kept the actual results on disk"—he patted his attaché case—" and what *they* indicate will keep the debate alive for years. During this time I did all I could to enhance my reputation: networking among scientists, playing the NASA card, and meeting with President Clinton. Oh, yes, that *really* happened—shortly after I made a sizable contribution to the Democratic National Committee."

"Amazing you had time for writing."

"Actually, I didn't write the book."

"Oh," said Franco nonchalantly. "Who did, then, Elvis?"

Belacqua smiled. "No, Christiane."

"Christiane?" This was unexpected.

"Yes, of course! She was the driving force from the start. We really should have called it *The Christiane Belacqua Report*." This was said with some embarrassment, as he turned wistful. "She's a remarkable woman. I wish you had known her better. Anyway, I wrote the science and Christiane wrote the fiction. Sometimes, when she was brooding about our kids, her vision of humanity became unbearably grim—humanity as metastasis and the like. She really never recovered from their deaths, you know. She couldn't bear to blame me, so she blamed the rest of the world. She took a certain . . . pleasure in condemning the earth. And she loved doing the graphics."

Franco frowned. "And what *exactly* did you accomplish with all this lying and phony data?" He wanted every detail on tape.

" 'Phony' sounds so judgmental; let's just say—premature." Belacqua paused to cough painfully, before summoning a wan smile. "Maybe in the nineties our scheme sounds subversive, but when we began, the United States had a President who thought trees caused pollution and a secretary of the interior who was auctioning off the store. It was as if the inmates had taken over the asylum. We wanted to remind the world, vividly, that life is precious and perishable." Belacqua's eyes sought forgiveness, but found none.

What a smooth old grifter, marveled Franco. How effortlessly this failing poseur had presented himself as a paradigm of integrity: Cousteau with an edge.

Belacqua continued his defense. "Why do you think other ecologists haven't blown the whistle yet? Because they know that the threats we dramatized are real and urgent. The two fellas you brought to Vermont with McAdams—Landry and Bushnell? During your visit, I spoke to both of them, alone. I only gave them the drift, and assured them that I would take all the blame for misleading them. They didn't mind going along, as long as their endorsements weren't public. With McAdams, we didn't try to change his mind. And no, we had nothing to do with his death: I was at Woods Hole, and Christiane was in Seattle. That was an unfortunate coincidence."

Franco cast a sidelong glance. "You told me she was in France."

"Uh, no, she had just been to France. But right after your visit she went to Seattle to see a friend. I think that's right. It doesn't matter anymore. Believe me."

"*Why* doesn't it matter?"

Robert pushed the attaché case to Franco nonchalantly. "This contains thirty disks of our genuine research results: use it as you see fit. But please don't let Christiane see you've got this case, or she'll give me hell from here to Costa Rica. It also contains a statement I had notarized this morning, explaining how I tweaked the data every day for a decade, just to give the world . . ."

"A wake-up call?"

"A whack on the side of the head. Possibly even an inoculation. We knew that our gambit might result in some social upheaval, but if it brought the world to its senses, we were prepared to live with that. And didn't we shake things up! Can't you take pride in that?" Franco shook his head. Belacqua fixed his eyes on the younger man. "Look, half the book is geopolitics, and nothing's contrived there: the world has political and diplomatic mechanisms for increasing growth, but none for restraining it, and so the growth rate will only continue to accelerate, until it's too late. The truth is that with better medical care and food distribution, the population could triple to almost twenty billion in the next forty years—ten times what it was when I was born in 1927. I swear, Franco, the biosphere cannot withstand such punishment. Still, I almost didn't go through with it, you know. In '97 I refused to go public with this fraud. Christiane left me—returned to France. But then I saw that some of the finest scientists and writers were already publishing dire warnings: Edward O. Wilson, Stephen Jay Gould, Richard Leakey, Niles Eldredge, Paul Kennedy, Ross Gelbspan, among others. And they were being completely ignored, by policymakers and the public alike! Their warnings never once broke into the headlines. I realized then that the schlock scientists who are paid by the fuel industries had succeeded in confusing the public by muddying the waters. Well, Christiane came home, and finally, after the Kyoto debacle, she was able to persuade me that the public needed a powerful shock to the system, as a last resort. That's right, like the name of our place; I finally agreed to go ahead with the scheme. And it worked. I must tell you, though, that I still don't have much hope for the biosphere beyond the next century or so. Maybe, if nations begin cooperating today, the worst can be avoided. I think this Lifechance Fund for victims of Metzamor is the most promising development yet. How ironic if mankind was saved, indirectly, by a massive radiation leak! Pure serendipity."

"Serendipity? Roger, millions of people have died of contamination!"

Belacqua shrugged. "But billions more are at stake, just in the next few years. And not only human lives." He spoke from the heart, and watched Franco's reaction closely. "I'm sorry I had to lie to *you*. It's really my only regret."

But Franco was still collecting the details on tape. "Was Suki in on the hoax?"

"No. No one was. Christiane insisted we keep everyone out of the loop: they were all so honest, they might have done something foolish. No, the blame is all ours."

Franco sighed. His brain was tired of it all. Ends and means. What is expendable to save the planet? The truth? The flag? Democracy? "Remind me again, Roger: what was it that made all this righteous? What *exactly* did we do?"

Belacqua looked at the younger man he'd grown so fond of and said, without remorse, "We forced the world to think big. It takes imagination to grasp the magnitude of our problems and their urgency, given the huge time lag, in the atmosphere and the oceans, between actions and reactions. *That's* what's hard for people to understand. The sheer scale of the problems defied the popular imagination, and our problem-solving skills were not addressing the biggest problem of all. Only a handful of people seemed even aware of the approaching tidal wave. How many scientific reports would it take to change Jesse Helms's mind about global warming and the Kyoto Protocol? Or Robert Byrd's? Face it, Franco: representative government will never be representative as long as money decides elections."

"And the victims of your book?" Franco's voice betrayed his distance from Roger's position; it trembled as he spoke. "The ones who died in suicides, massacres, bompings? What are they, corollary damage? Acceptable losses?"

Belacqua responded impatiently. "Do you really think those events were *caused* by our book? That *we* are responsible for the fanatical fringes of a self-destructive civilization? No wonder you've been troubled. Well, I certainly am not. So, a handful of sociopaths acted out. Anything at all might have sent them over the edge."

Franco shook his head; hell, by now everything else was shaking. "The difference is, you did what believed you had to do. I can't say the same myself."

The warmth in Roger's eyes was no hoax. "That's why I just gave you the accurate data, Franco. Now—*do whatever you feel you have to do.*"

Just then Christiane appeared beside the table in a white silk Pucci dress with a subtle but elaborate pattern. She also wore a frown.

Belacqua looked at her admiringly. *"Bella!* That's a lovely new dress!" He glanced at his watch. "We take off from La Guardia in about an hour."

"I'm late," she said to her husband as she kissed Franco on the cheek, and added briskly, "Roger, have you filed our flight plan to Florida?" Her eyes flashed when Roger shook his head sheepishly.

Christiane was all business; now, for the first time, Franco saw that clearly. She was the impresario of the show in which Roger had merely played out his role. Christiane called the shots. Even now Roger might have offered the world an apology, but not Christiane: for her it was clear that what's done is done, and cannot be undone. Franco wondered if that was true from the beginning, in 1968, when Christiane met him in the back of a paddy wagon, eight months pregnant.

Snap. With the sound of a whip cracking, Christiane shut her cellular phone. "It doesn't work in here. All right, Roger, I'll go phone Butler Aviation, but then you *have* to call the tower." She left abruptly.

"Roger . . ." Franco paused before proceeding. "Tell me about Théo Lapine."

This was the first time he ever saw the old man completely flummoxed, unable to pretend. "How," he asked, "did you find out about him?"

Franco continued with his bluff. "That was thirty-one years ago."

"Has Théo been trying to extort money from you, too?" Franco assumed an indifferent expression. "We didn't hear from Christiane's son for years—he was raised by his grandmother after she followed me to the States. Then two years ago he turned up here in New York. When he learned that this huge project was coming to fruition, he demanded half the proceeds of *The Belacqua Report* as some kind of punitive legacy. He wanted to choose the publisher himself and control the royalty payments. Théo was very unstable. He played on Christiane's heartstrings, but toward me he was simply a menacing drunk. He tried to intimidate me when he came to Vermont, even threatened to tamper with my airplane. He was drinking a bottle of pastis a day."

The smell of licorice. Bingo. Franco said, "What kind of hat did he wear?"

Belacqua pursed his lips. "Black. A sort of Borsalino."

"With a dark chesterfield overcoat?"

Roger nodded. "Ah! So he did approach you! He was *furious* that we'd taken the manuscript to Commonweal; he wanted to get it back so that he could negotiate the worldwide rights with Bertelsmann or Rupert Murdoch. But we never even gave Théo a copy of the manuscript. Did he threaten you, too?"

"After a fashion. He broke into our apartment twice. He even shot at us."

"Once again, I'm sorry. Christiane finally got fed up and exploded at him; he ran off, tail between his legs. We haven't heard a word since."

As Christiane returned to the table and Roger left to make his call, Franco quickly nudged the pieces of the puzzle together, trying to make them fit. When he was finally alone with the mastermind of this global con job, he had to wonder if she'd *ever* had the same agenda as the old man.

"So," she began. "Now you know everything, *n'est-ce pas?*"

"Perhaps," Franco answered slowly. "But how much does Roger know?"

Her eyes flashed again. "What do you mean?"

Franco folded his napkin. "Does he know you seduced McAdams?"

She looked at him with incredulity. "How *dare* you? Have you gone mad?"

Franco proceeded methodically. "For the purpose, I presume, of learning enough about him to have him murdered? Does he know that you went to Seattle to commit another murder, in exchange for which the young woman from Green Fist killed McAdams?" Now Christiane wasn't answering. She didn't have to. For just long enough her face betrayed everything: her calculating complexity, bitterness, pain—everything Franco needed to know he was on the right track. "Does Roger know," he pressed on, "that your son Théo was working for *you*? That he brought you the ibogaine from Europe?"

The accusations registered on her face like slaps; Franco couldn't be sure which ones hit their mark, but their cumulative impact was obvious. Proving any of this would be another matter; and from Christiane's obduracy it was clear that though her perimeters had been breached, she was clinging to plausible deniability.

"I don't know what you are talking about." Christiane rose slowly from her chair. "These are delusions, Franco. *Des conneries*." She leaned over the table and added, with an intensity he'd never heard from her before, "But if you try to prevent us from leaving today because of your misguided theory, I promise you the consequences will last the rest of your short life."

With that she turned and walked out toward the telephones and the front door. Franco immediately checked his mini-recorder: it had run out of tape some time earlier.

And when, after ten minutes, Roger still had not returned to the table, Franco knew there would be no farewell. He picked up the attaché case and left the restaurant.

Oprah Winfrey's guest that afternoon was one of the Hollywood's hottest superstars, a man whose silhouette was known around the world. His action-adventure films had grossed over $1 billion, and his personal fortune was estimated at well over $100 million. Since he hadn't given an interview in seven years, it came as a surprise when his people asked Oprah's people if she would do an hour-long prime-time one-on-one with him. They said yes, naturally, and right away the network boys started inflating the occasion into a Big Deal.

Oprah began the interview with a brief sketch of his early life, before he'd received the calling to star in action epics. In the second segment they discussed his career, with film clips, and talked about his wife and daughters, while showing cute home videos. They quickly glossed over his recent problems with the IRS. Then, without warning, he cut to the chase.

"Personally, I'm shocked by these terrible stories about the environment an' human extinction. But ya know, I'm positive a *few* people are gonna survive, and the way I see it, they're the champions. Obviously, it's gonna be a dog-eat-dog world. But you know me, Oprah, I've always been competitive: I want *my* genes to be among the winners. And the surest way to do that is by havin' lots of kids, right? Only thing is, my wife—God bless her—I don't want her ta get no more stretch marks."

Oprah jumped in with a gentle smile. "Where are you going with all this?"

'Well, here's why I called to do your show, see. I'm making my sperm available to every woman who calls our 800 number and pays for the *in vitro* fertilization herself." That's when he opened his suede jacket to reveal, embroidered on his collar, 1–800–ILL-DOYA. Oprah almost slid off her chair. But there was more.

"We've got enough on ice to impregnate over two thousand women. So all ya gotta do, you lonesome ladies out there, is call, and an operator will explain how it works, which is: the lady sends us her latest medical checkup and a onetime thousand-dollar administrative fee. Then we tell her which fertility clinic in her area ta go to, and we FedEx my little guys, on the rocks, direct to that clinic. Naturally, the woman has ta pay her own medical costs, an' fer raisin' the kid, an' whatnot. Oh, an' there's a fourteen-page legal affy-david she has to have notarized, to make sure none of these broads expects me ta pay for nothin'. Anyway, by the end of next year we'll have enough samples ta service about twenty thousand of you babes out there—from my loins straight to yours. An' I still go down to the bank twice a week, ta store more samples, with my wife's help. Ya know, some of my children won't be born for twenny years, or maybe not till after I'm dead! But I'll be lookin' down, rootin' for my kids. 'Cause, Oprah, I believe life's really sacred, ya know what I'm sayin'?"

Struggling for words, Oprah blurted out, "Your wife *helps*?"

He smiled his famous smile. "Well, it's her job to procure the samples—right there at the sperm bank, in a nice sterile setting, of course. At first I was doin' that part myself. Ya know: 'Comes in hand-y.' But I felt like a damn teenager, so I said, 'Honey, ya gotta come help me put it to the bank,' ya know what I'm sayin'? So she comes with me, and she does her thing, and I do my thing, and the next thing ya know, I got twenny thousand kids runnin' around in Peoria an' Palermo, Athens, Australia, an' maybe Timbuktu. And I picked *your* show to make the announcement, 'cause you're the greatest, gal! Hell, after this airs, we could maybe end up with fifty thousand little versions of me."

Oprah was still gasping. "Don't you worry about . . . overpopulation?"

"Hey, I just work here, ya know what I'm sayin'? So forty years from now, if I'm aroun', I'll be the father of a small nation. Ain't that somethin'? My lawyer calls me a one-man die-ass-pora! Take that, Dr. Belacqua! Wham! And when the crunch comes, I'll bet-cha dollars ta doughnuts the last person alive on this earth is gonna be wearin' *my* genes. That's why I'm so pumped up 'bout this project, ya know what I'm sayin'? 'Cause when it comes to the human *race,* well, I'm out ta win it!"

The agricultural shortages impacted the nation's entire food chain, bottom to top: from grains, fresh fruits, and vegetables to beef, chicken, and pork, and finally to prepared foods, including pack-aged goods. The impact was greatest on the canned goods industry, and hardest hit was the industry leader—Macro Enterprises.

In a matter of months, Macro lost 31 percent of its market share to lower-priced competition. As sales plummeted, shares in the preferred stock dropped below their '95 level, and Macro's board of directors panicked. Then they learned they were the target of a hostile takeover from a high-tech publishing business called LMS, Inc.—some upstart on the NASDAQ, for chrissakes!—that had made an overnight fortune by selectively publishing CD-ROMs. By early 1999 they owned Broderbund, and now they had their sights on Macro. Imagine, a publishing company taking over a canned goods business! Now, this was truly the world turned up-side down.

The directors thrashed about frantically for a scapegoat. With-out warning, and in record-breaking time, they unseated Bob Mil-ton from his chairmanship and locked him out of his office. They also cut the strings on his golden parachute and withdrew corpo-rate sponsorship of the Power of Deliverance Church retreat. They even went so far as to cancel his stock options, which represented the bulk of his wealth on paper, leaving Bob Milton without his woods, as it were.

TREMBLING ON THE
BRINK

Do not despair, one of the thieves was saved;
Do not presume, one of the thieves was damned.

—Saint Augustine, *The City of God* (411)

After three months in Minneapolis, Terry suited up one sunny morning for her first run since the accident. Just before going downstairs, she logged on to check her e-mail, and then went to her news site.

THE END OF THE WORLD? NOT!!!
NEW YORK, Nov. 3, 1999 (AP) Franco Sherman, former president of Commonweal Books and editor of *The Belacqua Report*, announced today that Dr. Roger Belacqua had fabricated evidence to substantiate his doomsday report. "Dr. Belacqua admitted he had altered some findings," said Mr. Sherman at a press conference here, "to alert the world to real and imminent threats to the biosphere and to human survival." He had only learned of the deception three days ago, Mr. Sherman explained, when the scientist admitted that some of the data in the best-seller had been manipulated. But he bristled when one reporter compared Dr. Belacqua's hoax to Orson Welles's *War of the Worlds* radio broadcast of 1938. "Martians are fiction," he said, "but some 30,000 species become extinct each year."

Dr. Belacqua himself could not be reached. Federal Marshal John Doyle, attempting to serve papers to Dr. Belacqua on behalf of Versailles Room Massacre victim Jim Sander, said the scientist may have fled the country.

Mr. Sherman was recently appointed general editor of the upcoming *The State of the Earth, 2000,* a project of the Lifechance Fund. "We have all been victims of a deliberate fraud," he said. "Now, with this new study, we have the financial resources to supersede all previous research."

So that was that. The chain of events that had begun one rainy January morning two years before had played itself out. All that remained was a little scar tissue and a daisy chain of lawsuits. She put on her coat and went out for a run.

By now she had fully recuperated—was in the best shape, actually, since she left college. Most of all, her mind was clear and sharp. This had been a one-foot-in-front-of-the-other, back-to-basics kind of time, and as of this morning she felt . . . wonderful. Her breathing was steady as she circled Lake Harriet, and she felt as if she could run for a hundred miles without stopping for breath. The autumn air was beautiful, the colors were crisp and fresh, and the lake was already partly frozen. The world was well again.

She missed Franco, though not as much as she'd expected. Their e-mail had tapered off in the last ten days. Maybe there just wasn't much shakin'. Or perhaps they were drifting apart. Her counselor at University Hospital, Ms. Rubinger, had explained that after a serious accident, couples often couldn't overcome the blah blah blah. And though she loved him with all her being, she couldn't deny that they had . . . issues.

Franco came with so much history. To begin with, he had been in love with Lillian all along: that was their real *ménage á trois.* As a result, there was a remoteness about him: the emotional unavailability you read about in Karen Horney, Jonathan Fischer, and *Cosmo.* It was still really Lillian's apartment, where Terry had perched precariously between the guest room and the master bedroom; that was what she'd always felt, along with pangs of resentment for being cast prematurely in the role of mother and wife. (Here she flopped down on a bench near the lake to catch her breath.)

She hadn't lost sight of the blessings they'd shared together, and make no mistake about it, Franco Sherman was the love of her life. Even this moment she missed him like hell. Yet, from the beginning, their relationship had been centered around the Belacqua fraud. How much had the book's grim message colored their life together? It had actually been so liberating to believe that it was just too late. She remembered lighting that cigarette the day after she'd read the report, thinking, Hell, if we're going to be extinct . . . (With that she resumed her course around the lake.)

She was going to have to make some decisions very soon now: she couldn't go on spending down her mom's savings and putting the checks Franco sent her in a manila envelope. She'd learned more about publishing in two years than most editors ever do, and she wanted to put that experience to work in her next job. But most of the publishing houses were in New York, of course. She could probably get a good job back there, and that way she could still see Franco. But no matter what he said, she wasn't moving back into that apartment. It could never be her home, and she was convinced its atmosphere fed Franco's dour tendencies. Though come to think of it, maybe he'd always been that way.

As she turned up toward her mom's, she saw a man at the front door, and with a pang she wished it were Franco. Of course, he'd never be that impulsive, to hop a plane and come surprise her, just when she really really wanted to see him the most—

It was him. With a fistful of flowers and a broad smile, Franco was waiting at the bottom of the stoop. Terry rushed at him. He wrapped around her and they clung to each other as they hadn't done since long before the accident.

"Yesterday," he said softly, "I found a buyer for the apartment. That was Juliette's idea: she said that if I wanted you back, we had to build a new nest together."

"Did she also tell you how happy it would make me if you surprised me like this?" She squeezed him really hard.

"No." He shook his head. "Max did. Last night he sat me down and said: 'Ya know, Dad, now that Terry's had time to think things over, she needs to know how important she is to you. And what you have to say to her is, how can the world be saved if you two can't save your love?' "

"That's, like . . . really corny," she said. "Max didn't really say that, did he?"

He shook his head again. "No. I made it up. He thought it

sounded pretty good, though. And he said I should wait six months before I ask you to marry me."

"Smart kid. You know, there's a lot of stuff we need to straighten out."

"I know," he said. "But I'm hoping that if we can get it right—"

Terry smiled. "Well, if we do, then of course I'll marry you, you goof."

And with that much understood—or that little—they went into the house, and Terry began packing her things, with eyes wide shot.

Three developments were announced in the week before Thanksgiving 1999. First, SolElec S.A., a Swiss company headquartered in Berne, announced a breakthrough: a power-storage system that increased the reserve capacities of solar energy a thousandfold, allowing sunlight to power large urban areas with only a few square miles of solar farms. SolElec also had a prototype for an inexpensive electric engine that would fit any midsize car; heavier engines were in design.

Two days later, planktologists in South Africa announced that by selective breeding, they had developed two hardy new subspecies of aquatic life: a phytoplankton capable of removing twice as much carbon from the ocean, and an equally gluttonous form of salp that could digest three times more carbon-loaded phytoplanktons. The addition of these hardy species to the oceans would deposit huge quantities of carbon, inert, on the ocean floors. Skeptics warned that it was dangerous to manipulate nature, but they were outnumbered by pragmatists. And in a wide-ranging discussion with Bill Moyers on *Beginning to End: The Belacqua Dialogues,* the Dalai Lama, with wisdom and humor brimming from his eyes, suggested that Nature might be using human ingenuity for her own ends. "Such purposes," he added, "are not ours to know."

Last, the Lifechance Scientific Panel reported that the authentic data on the disks Franco Sherman had passed to it "suggest a rapid, progressive threat to the biosphere." They also released excerpts from a letter notarized by Belacqua on October 31, taking responsibility for the hoax.

These genuine data confirm the substance of the report. Only the time frame for the collapse of the biosphere was altered to make our point; the threat itself remains real. We must recognize the scale and the urgency of the crisis, because this much is certain: *By the time there is irrefutable proof that the collapse of life has begun, it will be far too advanced to reverse.*

Our most crucial problems have both local and global dimensions. So do our solutions. The peoples of the world are already interwoven by economics, telecommunications, travel, epidemics, and multicultural exchange—and by a shared responsibility for the damage we are doing. . . .

The nations of the world, like its species, have evolved together, and by now they are as mutually dependent upon one another as the organs of a body. All of humanity is as intertwined over the Earth as the Internet is, like the neurons of a single, global mind. Similarly, our biosphere is a single organism, in which intelligence spread throughout all species. That is clearly the direction in which we too are proceeding. If humanity can learn to function with the resolve of a single spirit, then it may yet be possible to escape the consequences of our "success" as a species. But until we adapt, the human race remains very much in peril. And if the nationalistic concerns of each ship of state outweigh those of our planetary ark, then truly we are doomed.

This was what Franco had read, the day he took the attaché case back to the apartment after their lunch. This could only have been written by Dr. Roger Belacqua; it was certainly not the product of Christiane's dark specter. And in the following weeks, as he pondered the letter's import, Franco felt he had finally begun to understand the old man's driving vision.

Belacqua's letter went on to explain that profits from *The Belacqua Report* (and, upon his death, his entire estate) had been committed to a Cayman Islands trust fund aimed at developing scientific and political solutions to environmental problems.

As a result of Belacqua's signed confession, federal agents were seeking him and his wife in the Caribbean and Central America on a variety of charges ranging from public fraud to larceny. They also obtained the Belacqua Foundation's bank records from the Caymans, only to learn that, apart from an initial deposit of $1,000, there had never been any activity in the account.

On the Saturday after Thanksgiving, when Orlando, Florida, was filled to bursting, a Sikorsky helicopter flew low over the city, from Disney World to Universal Studios Park, dispensing a fine aerosol mist. Before officials realized what was happening, the helicopter had vanished, and by the time they had quarantined the theme parks, an unknown number of people had left, returning to their cars and to their homes, possibly contaminating many others with the anthrax, botulism, or even Ebola virus that might have been discharged in the attack.

It seemed like a miracle when, six days later, health officials determined there was not a single case of contamination among the tens of thousands exposed to the spray. Authorities speculated that either this was a hoax or, more likely, the assailants had unwittingly used one of the deactivated canisters from Japan.

These high-tech, wannabe terrorists in Orlando were never caught, and their identity remained a mystery, though their affiliations were obvious. Brian Jenkins, ABC's expert on terrorism, pointed out to Charlie Gibson that it must have taken both local organization and a lot of cash to hide a Sikorsky before and after the attack. Back in the summer of '97, NBC had reported that Aum Shinrikyo had cells in the United States; this suggested that a home-grown, fanatical splinter group, like the Anjos de João in Brazil, had been given financial support, along with the canisters—some of which might still be lethal. And since no arrests had been made, the threat of future attacks remained very real. Now, around the world, helicopters—including traffic reporters—were forbidden over metropolitan areas.

With some apprehension, Terry began apartment-hunting as soon as they got back to New York, and in a few days she found a large loft off Gramercy Park with a one-year lease and option to buy. Franco liked the view of the square from his office, and the kids were just happy to leave Park Avenue behind. Franco felt no regrets about the old apartment: he was finally at peace with himself, with the memory of Lillian, and with the future he hoped Terry would share with him and the children.

She was already helping to assemble an editorial team for the Lifechance project, while Franco worked on its budget and continued to cope with fallout from *The Belacqua Report*. But most of his free time now was devoted to the kids. Max, who was nine, was coming into his own as an aggressive young competitor, possibly even headed for grandmaster, his trainer said. Juliette, eleven, never left the dean's list despite all the distractions downtown and her new interest in boys.

Slowly, when Terry and Franco were alone together, something new began to emerge, too fragile to name, too essential to describe. It held promise, but whether or not it could outgrow their unwholesome beginning as a couple wasn't a question that would be answered all at once.

Nor were the questions that remained about Christiane Belacqua. Franco's mini-recorder had picked up only part of Roger's confession, without reference to Christiane, whose final threat was the only thing she'd said implicating herself. Franco spoke to Chief O'Hara and repeated what he'd said to Christiane: that she had gone to McAdams's room that night in Vermont and initiated a liaison, in order to plan his death; that she had gone to Seattle soon after, perhaps to shoot James Schwartzenbach in exchange for the murder of McAdams by Claire Buday, rather like the plot of *Strangers on a Train*. But O'Hara had never seen the Hitchcock movie, and besides, the DNA evidence they had from the blond hairs placed Buday at the crime scene. He was brusque, almost hostile with Franco: they had the right suspect in custody, he insisted, and the unsolved murder of Schwartzenbach in Seattle wasn't his business.

But a week later Franco read in the *Times* that Claire Buday had been released. Her name had been cleared in the McAdams murder after more than two dozen witnesses confirmed that she had been in Seattle during the three-day period in which McAdams must have been poisoned; these included two police officers who had ticketed her for speeding. There was no explanation for the presence of her hairs in McAdams's apartment, and some suspected that they had been planted. But now police in New York announced that they were working with Interpol to locate Mrs. Roger Belacqua.

That was the last report Franco ever saw about the McAdams murder. His own guess was that Christiane had killed both McAdams and Schwartzenbach, and left Claire Buday's hairs in the bed just to buy enough time for them to flee to Costa Rica. But that was only a guess, and he expected that the truth would never be known.

One last piece of the puzzle came the evening Franco switched on Peter Jennings and learned that a French national named Théophile Lapine had been arrested when he arrived at JFK on a flight from Nice carrying several vials of a substance later identified as ibogaine. During his arrest, Lapine had ingested a cyanide capsule he was carrying in his pocket, and had died almost instantly. His suitcase contained ample evidence of his involvement with former members of Aum Shinrikyo, along with bank records proving that he, in fact, had controlled every penny earned by *The Belacqua Report,* from the initial advance to the last royalty payment. Eventually a forensic accountant showed that on the same day Roger Belacqua had signed the deal memo for the book, Christiane Belacqua had notarized a document which gave to her son, Théo Lapine, power of attorney for the Belacqua Foundation, as well as for her personal estate and Roger's.

At 4:17 A.M. on December 12, 1999, an earthquake measuring 7.3 on the Richter scale struck Southern California. It lasted just fifteen seconds and caused only a handful of deaths and injuries. But the Santa Monica and Hollywood freeways, the 405, the Ventura Freeway from Tarzana to Sherman Oaks, and the Pacific Coast Highway at Sunset were all chopped into pieces like worms under a lawn mower. It would take years to reopen them; until then, the drive from Malibu to Morton's would be a six-hour nightmare.

While this was not "the Big One" that scientists had been forecasting for twenty years, seismologists noted that it had the characteristics of a "harbinger temblor," indicating bigger temblors to come: even as the rebuilding began, scientists warned of unprecedented strain along the San Andreas Fault. Soon after that announcement, a whole generation of West Coast TV execs opted for early retirement *en masse,* either from fear of the next quake or just dread of the traffic. This was widely hailed as the most promising event in network television since the advent of cable.

By the end of 1999 *The Belacqua Report* had become an enduring feature of global civilization, and while many took the affair as a clarion call for action, others remembered only that there had been a threat that was later lifted. But in some respects it was impossible to return to pre-Belacqua innocence. False instruction is as difficult to unlearn as the truth, and now at least the possibility of mass extinction from overpopulation and global warming was part of the popular culture. That, Franco believed, was exactly the impact the Belacquas had intended.

The book had rubbed off on many of the major events that evolved during its eighteen months in print, not least of which was the upcoming Constitutional Convention. As the ship of state entered heavy weather, the country realized that any changes proposed—whether an amendment or two or a broad restructuring of the American government—still had to be ratified by three-quarters of the state legislatures to change the law. "Euclid's *Geometry*," wrote Russell Baker, "could not pass thirty-eight state legislatures."

Attempts were made to prearrange the convention's procedures, but those who'd championed it from the start jealously defended the delegates' right to determine their procedures for themselves. Many people, for example, took it for granted that the complete convention would be televised gavel-to-gavel on C-Span, perhaps even on the networks. But that choice was the delegates' alone to make, and they might well prefer to mandate absolute secrecy until their deliberations were over, exactly as the delegates to the Constitutional Convention of 1787 had done.

The event was poised to either bring forth the best that democratic government could yield and reanimate the federal covenant, or shame itself as history's most spectacular failure of self-government. Terrifying as the whole thing was, the oft-repeated argument by its supporters was hard to ignore: if a majority of voters are unhappy with the infrastructure of their government yet unable to change it, is that still a government of, by, and for the people?

The number of victims of Metzamor would multiply for decades to come. So too would those who were assisted by Lifechance, which announced that within twelve months it would undertake the first global referendum, acknowledging that results would not be meaningful until a comprehensive database of "registered voters" had evolved: theoretically, a list of every adult who chose to participate. Some governments, like the rump regime of North Korea, were certain to prevent the participation of its citizens. As for the People's Republic of China—one-fifth of humanity—Lifechance still waited to learn if its government would permit its citizens to participate. It seemed wildly unlikely, but the amount of aid available from Lifechance for critical environmental projects was hard even for the repressive government to disregard. Still, it wasn't expected that citizens of totalitarian regimes would participate anytime soon.

Simultaneous movements toward constitutional reform within the United States and international organization by Lifechance might have suggested a possible linkage between the two, but cooler thinking prevailed. No one imagined for a moment that nationalism was about to vanish: across America there were thousands of men ready to kill, die, and bomb federal buildings just to prevent such a phenomenon, and the same was true in many other countries. Nationalism was hardly about to fade away conveniently, however vestigial it seemed in the harsh light of the looming global problems.

On New Year's Eve 1999, Juliette made dinner—macaroni and cheese—in the nearly empty apartment; the next day the last of their possessions were being moved down to the loft. While they ate, they watched the celebrations broadcast live from all across Asia and Europe. A most remarkable thing was happening: for over a year, with every lottery ticket sold over the Internet, Lifechance had e-mailed the suggestion that at the stroke of midnight in every time zone, the people of the world should share in a moment of silent prayer. Grassroots organizations to promote the idea had sprung up on every continent, with the help of local religious leaders, who unanimously supported the idea. Now, from Tokyo to Bombay, Calcutta to Tehran, Rome to Dublin, people were participating in prayer together in unprecedented numbers. Around the Taj Mahal in Agra, in the Potsdamer Platz in Berlin, and at the Millennium Dome in London, millions and millions of people stood in respectful silence and prayer as 1999 came to an end. Rabble-rousers and troublemakers at the fringe of each crowd were hushed by the sheer power of the silent gathering.

Franco and Terry had decided to stay in for the night, but the extraordinary sights from all around the world won the argument Juliette and Max had been making all week: that they should experience this historic moment and join the throngs amassing throughout the city center and moving toward Times Square.

So at about ten they left the apartment and followed the streams of people merging in midtown. While there was some drunkenness and revelry, the predominant atmosphere was one of civility, shared wonder, and cautious solidarity. It was just above freezing, a little warm for the end of December, but beautifully dry and so clear you could almost see the stars. From Grand Central Station west, it was pedestrians only—millions of people milling along toward Times Square—so they turned crosstown at Fiftieth Street. Forty-sixth was as far south as they could get down Broadway before the crowd became too thick too move, but from their spot they could see the lighted ball. And there, as he looked around him, Franco experienced a powerful *déjà vu*: a wall of human flesh, carved in bas-relief, out of which stared the eyes of ninety billion human souls. . . . Soon Terry, Franco, Juliette, and Max were wholly subsumed within the mass of humanity.

For the entire hour before midnight the quiet atmosphere prevailed in the streets, as the imposing silence of millions suppressed the riotous impulses of a few. The New York crowd seemed inspired by what they too had seen on television from around the world, and as the year 2000 approached, by sheer force of prayer, the growing crowd transformed Times Square temporarily into an improbable cathedral.

In the last minute before the New Year, as the lighted sphere began descending, instead of a noisy countdown, the silence thickened, as people throughout central Manhattan directed all their attention to the forces that transcended them as individuals. And in the last seconds even their whispered prayers were hushed, until all that could be heard among the millions in the streets was their collective heartbeat growing louder and louder, like the sound of an approaching helicopter.

EPILOGUE

There was things which he stretched, but mainly he
told the truth.

—MARK TWAIN, *The Adventures of Huckleberry Finn* (1884)

After the Belacquas left Franco at the "21" Club, they took a cab
to La Guardia. Christiane asked the driver to take his time: they
were not really in a hurry. It was unusually warm for the last day
of October, and they were enjoying the sights and sounds of the
city. They even asked the driver to pull over for a moment at the
corner of Second Avenue and Fifty-third so they could watch a
swarm of fairy princesses and mutant tortoises trick-or-treating
their way home from school.

"So, did you confess to Franco?" Christiane asked as they
headed up the FDR Drive.

"He already knew. I expect Terry had figured it out." He erupted
with laughter. "Or maybe they saw Peter on some old episode of
Star Trek." Christiane had to laugh at that idea. Then Roger
turned serious.

"Are you certain," he asked earnestly, "that you want to do this?
Now? Today?"

Christiane replied emphatically, "Of course! Oh, Roger, we've
planned this for so long. There's nothing left here for us except
lawsuits and aggravation. No, this is what I've been waiting for
all along."

At Butler Aviation they walked slowly to the Baron, where the
gangly linesman asked Roger to sign for the fuel and then helped

him up onto the wing, barely believing that this frail old man with the cane was going to fly a twin-engine to Wilmington, Miami, and on to Costa Rica.

"Tower, this is Baron three seven six eight Sierra, ready to go on runway one three for a straight-out VFR departure."

"Baron three seven six eight Sierra, cleared for straight-out take-off, climb to eight thousand."

"Copy."

The tower came back: "Baron three seven six eight Sierra, squawk nine niner four five."

"Roger, air traffic control: squawking niner niner four five." But instead, Belacqua dialed 5321 into his transponder and chuckled. "That should confuse their radar while we're still within range." He pushed the throttles forward, and in a moment they were airborne, headed northeast.

"Will they track us?" Christiane had learned the rudiments of aviation in the eighties, and even practiced landing in case of an emergency, but she had never studied for the license.

"No," said Belacqua, smiling.

When the altimeter settled at eight thousand feet, he set the small plane on a southeasterly course out over the Atlantic, and engaged the three-axis autopilot. They loosened their seat belts, and Christiane reached behind the seat for a bottle of Cristal in their cooler. "Shall we open this now?" A moment later Roger popped the cork and Christiane held out chilled flutes.

"Long live the earth!" toasted Roger, above the engines' roar. Twisting in their seats, they looked into each other's eyes and clinked their glasses.

"*Bravo, amore*," he said.

"*Bravo, Dottore*," she replied. They kissed, and put their glasses to their lips. When air traffic control repeated their call sign disagreeably, Belacqua switched off the radio. They tapped their glasses again, and said in unison, "Long live the earth!"

An hour later and two hundred miles east of La Guardia, climbing slowly, Belacqua popped the second bottle of Cristal and refilled their glasses. Christiane extracted two capsules from her bag, which they swallowed at the same time. By now they were both pretty loaded, and at only nine thousand feet the oxygen was thin enough to add to their giddiness. Christiane had set a silver-framed photograph of Cybèle and Jean-Loup beside the compass, which continued to indicate a southeasterly course. While gazing at their children's faces, they recalled aloud the stories of their short lives.

Then Roger noticed that the fuel gauges had passed the halfway mark. He nodded to his wife, and put a tape of the *St. Matthew Passion* on the sound system. Once again they toasted, "To the earth!" They stared for a time at the cloudless sky knitted seamlessly into the endless horizon of ocean around them.

"From up here," said Christiane, "it all looks so . . . clean."

He didn't hear her at first, distracted by memories. Then he craned his head to look up at the sky above them. "Yes, you're right, darling," he replied, pausing dramatically. "Not much sign of any 'eggshell effect,' is there?" They laughed long and hard over that. Then Roger looked her straight in the eye and said, "You know, my love, it's even more beautiful higher up. Are you ready to see what that's like?"

"I've been ready for a very long time," she replied, staring right back at him.

The altimeter read ten thousand feet as he eased the throttles forward to 60 percent power. The Baron began rising, and Roger locked in a 3 percent climb on the autopilot. Then he helped Christiane climb tipsily into the rear seat and followed her a moment later. There they settled back, put up their feet, and poured themselves each a last glass of champagne.

"To the children," Christiane said, her lip trembling.

They drank, and hugged tightly for several minutes, until their last stores of energy were exhausted, and Christiane's head started to loll. Belacqua looked out the window long enough to see the ocean glittering beneath them, and the sky so bright it seared his eyes with crystalline radiance.

"Look, my angel," he said, but Christiane could no longer focus. With an enormous effort, he leaned toward his wife and took her head between his hands.

"My darling, I love you."

"Je t'aime," replied Christiane, and they kissed.

Then, as the oxygen grew thinner and thinner, they began to

laugh. At first they just giggled, but soon they were rolling about the seat with hilarity. A few moments later, just before they fell unconscious, Belacqua laid Christiane down beside him and wrapped his arms around her.

The Baron continued to climb higher and higher, into the jet stream, where turbulence shook the little plane. But it no longer disturbed the occupants. As a lasting stillness settled upon their souls, the world below them seemed as pristine as the day the human animal first stood on two feet.

APPENDIX

The panorama of human history spans more than a million years, from the first flickering campfire to the pulsing light that delivers your e-mail by ISDN. In that time some ninety billion lives have been lived, the vast majority of which have indeed been nasty, brutish, and short.

The Industrial Revolution that began less than two hundred years ago signaled the flowering of our species's unmatched intelligence. While it dramatically improved the lives of millions of people, the Industrial Revolution also started a revolution against the natural world that has profoundly altered the relationship between *Homo sapiens* and every other species. The technological and economic successes of the twentieth century have produced a population explosion of alarming significance that has been ignored by all but the specialists in demographics and earth sciences. At the same time, life expectancy (in the United States, by way of example) has risen from forty-nine years in 1900 to seventy-six years. As a result of these unprecedented trends, the human population has tripled in three generations.

In the waning days of the 1990s, it is already apparent that the contours of the next century will be shaped by the critical issues that have arisen in just thirty years: global warming, overpopulation, the needless suffering of the most wretched on earth, and the progressive elimination of tens of thousands of irreplaceable species *every year*. Each of these critical issues underlines the urgent need for international cooperation on an unprecedented scale, as allies in a war that no nation can afford to lose.

It is not by abandoning our most sacred traditions, or our compassion, that we will save the planet from ourselves. Only by finding a way to reconcile *what we believe in* with *what we know* can we diminish a calamity that has already begun. As Dr. Belacqua observes, to avert global disaster, we must grasp the simplest of nautical truths: you cannot sink just one side of a ship.

"Is humanity suicidal?" asks Edward O. Wilson, our preeminent naturalist. "Is the drive to environmental conquest and self-propagation embedded so deeply in our genes as to be unstoppable?" And if so, can we survive the next millennium? Or was the human race always destined to extinguish itself on its own exhausts? The answers will be determined by what we do and do not do—and by how soon we begin.

—ROCK BRYNNER
January 4, 1998

BIBLIOGRAPHY

The selections below include valuable studies of global warming, population trends, mass extinctions, and the future of humankind. For further reading, as well as specific scientific references in *The Doomsday Report,* visit the website at: http://www.netcom.com/~rbelacq

BOOKS

Eldredge, Niles. *Dominion* (Berkeley: University of California Press, 1997).

Gelbspan, Ross. *The Heat Is On: The High Stakes Battle over the Earth's Threatened Climate* (Reading, Mass.: AddisonWesley, 1997).

Heilbroner, Robert L. *An Enquiry into the Human Prospect* (New York: Norton, rev. ed., 1991).

Huntington, Samuel P. *The Clash of Civilizations and the Remaking of World Order* (New York: Simon & Schuster, 1996).

The Intergovernmental Panel on Climate Change, *Climate Change 1995* (New York: Cambridge University Press, 1996).

Kaplan, David E., and Andrew Marshall. *The Cult at the End of the World: The Aum Doomsday Cult* (New York: Crown, 1996).

Kennedy, Paul. *Preparing for the Twenty-first Century* (New York: Random House, 1993).

Leakey, Richard, and Roger Lewin. *The Sixth Extinction: Patterns of Life and the Future of Humankind* (New York: Doubleday, 1995).

Mathews, Jessica T. *Preserving the Global Environment: The Challenge of Shared Leadership* (New York: Norton, 1991).

Wilson, Edward O. *In Search of Nature* (including the essay, "Is Humanity Suicidal?") (Washington, D.C.: Island Press, 1996).

Yergin, Daniel. *The Commanding Heights: The Battle Between Government and the Marketplace* (New York: Simon & Schuster, 1998).

ARTICLES
(also available from the magazines' online archives)

Gibbs, W. Wayt. "Thriving Tunicates . . ." Scientific *American,* December, 1995 (on salps).

Karl, Thomas R., Neville Nicholls, and Jonathan Gregory. "The Coming Climate" (Parts I & II) *Scientific American,* May/June 1997.

"Human-Dominated Ecosystems," a special issue of *Science,* July 25, 1997 (several important articles).

Myers, Norman. "Mass Extinction and Evolution," *Science,* October 24, 1997.

Slaughter, Anne-Marie. "The Real New World Order," *Foreign Affairs,* September/October 1997.

WEBSITES

Institute of Ocean Sciences:
www.ios.bc.ca/ios/plankton/welcome.htm
United Nations Population Information Network:
www.undp.org/popin/popin.htm
Union of Concerned Scientists:
www.ucsusa.org/global/gwscience.html
World Scientists' Warning to Humanity:
ddi.digital.net/~wisdom/environment/science.html
Visions of Governance for the Twenty-first Century Project—Harvard University
ksgwww.harvard.edu/~ksgpress/visions2.htm